Welcome to the
Legend of the Five Rings!

You are about to enter Rokugan, a land of honorable samurai, mighty dragons, powerful magics, arcane monks, cunning ninja, and twisted demons from the Shadowlands. Based on the mythic tales of Japan, China, and Korea, Rokugan is a vast empire, a unique world of fantastic adventure.

Enjoy your stay in Rokugan, a place where heroes walk with gods, where a daimyo's mighty army can be thwarted by a simple word whispered into the right ear, and where honor truly is more powerful than steel.

Legend of the Five Rings

Legend of the
Five Rings

THE DRAGON

REE
SOESBEE

CLAN WAR
Sixth Scroll

THE DRAGON

LEGEND OF THE FIVE RINGS™ Books

©2001 Wizards of the Coast, Inc.

Distributed in the United States by Holtzbrinck Publishing. Distributed in Canada by Fenn Ltd.

Distributed to the hobby, toy, and comic trade in the United States and Canada by regional distributors.

Distributed worldwide by Wizards of the Coast, Inc., and regional distributors.

Cover art by rk post
First Printing: September 2001
Library of Congress Catalog Card Number: 00-191033

9 8 7 6 5 4 3 2 1

UK ISBN: 0-7869-2670-8
US ISBN: 0-7869-1883-7
620-T21883

U.S., CANADA,
ASIA, PACIFIC, & LATIN AMERICA
Wizards of the Coast, Inc.
P.O. Box 707
Renton, WA 98057-0707
+1-800-324-6496

EUROPEAN HEADQUARTERS
Wizards of the Coast, Belgium
P.B. 2031
2600 Berchem
Belgium
+32-70-23-32-77

Visit our web site at **www.wizards.com/fiverings**

For all the samurai of the Emerald Empire, who cheered at its victories and wept at the deaths of its heroes. To those who fought at the Day of Thunder, the Battle of Oblivion's Gate, and who served the empire with their hearts and deeds.

You will never be forgotten.

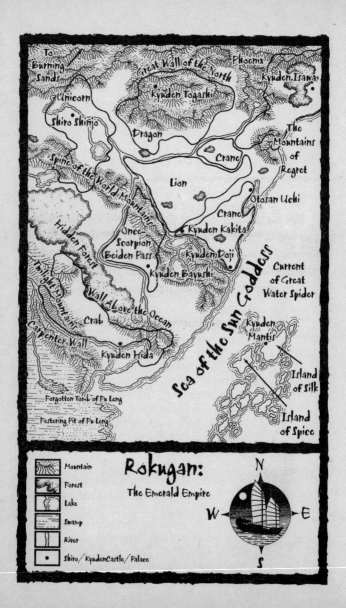

EPILOGUE

We *have reached the end together, you and I.*
The final days have come.

The hallway is dark and cold. Sounds of battle outside the palace echo only faintly through the thick stone. Dust covers the paneled floor. Dirt and blood stain my sandals. For once, though, I am not alone. Seven Thunders, one prophet, and I walk down the shadowed corridor, and only the light of a single torch reflects from stained armor. Battered helms and unsheathed steel shine in burnished hues.

I can sense their caution.

I know their fear. It is the same fear I felt, deep within my heart, when I realized what I must do to prevent this day. The moment had passed nine hundred years ago. An eternity.

I look at the white-lipped Unicorn maiden, the cold eyes of the Lion general, and I remember their faces from times long past.

"Yokuni," the Crab whispers my name. "Can we defeat him? Can he be destroyed?"

I look toward him and see that his shattered arm has been sheathed in jade. I remember his ancestor, my brother. Hida was first among the Crab, and he raised them to fight the darkness. Mountain-tall brother, you taught them to strive and never give up.

How they have failed you, Hida. How they have fallen.

I shake my head, unwilling to answer, and the man looks away.

The wooden gates at the end of the corridor lie closed before us. For a thousand years, they have waited for our entry. I stood here, then, when the first Hantei commanded that they be placed in their brackets. Iron hinges, now rusted, cling to ancient stone. The Scorpion woman opens them with the touch of enameled fingers, a bruise staining her cheek, half-covered by shadow. One by one, they enter— the Unicorn first, as tempestuous as my sister who bore them. Behind her strides the Crab, then Crane and Lion together. With a glance, the wounded Isawa steps forward, his broken leg trembling beneath his weight. At his side, the prophet walks.

Before she can enter, I step before her. It is time for the Dragon to speak alone.

Her name is Hitomi. Coal black eyes, barely more than slits of anger in her sharp-featured face, glare up at me. I tower over her silent form, but she does not look away. A thousand years and more I have watched the world, and for a thousand years, I have feared nothing; no sword or spell. I have watched these mortals, and I have cared for them. I have never been afraid.

Until today.

A word appears in my mind, but I still it before it becomes speech. I pause to look at her once more.

Hitomi's hair has been shaved away, clean-shaven for war and out of remorse. She has borne much, and the scars on her heart-shaped face haunt her future. Her shoulders bear the caustic marks of war, and her soul still bleeds from the torment she has endured. At her side, her hand glistens in the faint light, stone over flesh. It is black, obsidian and cold, as black as the moon.

"Yokuni," she hisses, weary of the silence. I do not reply.

She begins to turn toward the open doorway. I grip her chin, forcing her eyes to meet mine. There. I see my death hovering in her soul. Where is the riddle? Where is the answer for which I have sought a thousand years?

You must not fight Fu Leng. I whisper, hearing the words echo a moment before I speak them.

Her face changes, and confusion ripples over her harsh features. "But you brought me—all of us—here to kill him. To save the empire."

I shake my head. The weariness rests on my bones like a cloak covered in mold and dust. The world is ending, and so am I.

"I have come so far, sacrificed so much," her voice is a curse. "Already, you have forced me to give up too much. I will not do it anymore, Yokuni. Not for you, not for the empire. Not for anyone." Hitomi drew up her right hand and clenched her fingers. Her fist of black glass shone in the flickering torchlight. Her fingers, veins of steel through obsidian flesh, clenched with titanic fury. "I have given my flesh, my honor, and my brother's soul. There is nothing left of me for you to take, old man. I am not the child I once was."

She is right . . . but she was not always like this. A faint image of her, laughing in the sunlight, echoes in the recesses of my ancient mind. Once, she was beautiful. She was the child of a powerful lord, trained in steel and meant for gentle places. Peaceful times. She was once a soul who could give birth to the dreams of men; a woman whose honor would stand true against the passing of time. Once her name meant hope. She cast aside that name long ago, when she cast aside her future. She threw it away with her honor. With her duty.

Now, she is only Hitomi.

You must not fight Fu Leng, I repeat, and the words are stone.

"You've told me what to do for too long, old man," she snarls at me. "Who to kill—who not to kill. I am weary of it, Yokuni, tired of all your games and riddles. What is my purpose, old man?" She is bitter. "To destroy myself? Slaughter the Sun? Bring the Moon down from the sky?"

Your purpose is not to kill him, but to kill me.

Hitomi pauses, her cold stone hand matching the blackness of her empty eyes. I see the indecision in her stance—to move forward and obey her champion, or to stay and question my judgment. Perhaps it has been too long. After a cold and silent span of time, she nods.

I tell her. *The moment will seize you.*

"Why do you trust me?"

Because it is my karma to die at your hand.

She lingers a moment longer. "No questions for me to answer, Yokuni? No talk of paths and enigmas, and no more vanishing into the night? No more riddles?" I shake my head, and she believes me.

The answer is my death, Hitomi. The riddle is yours to ask. I see my reflection in her black eyes, and beyond, I see starlight. She has no reply except to turn away. As she vanishes into the darkness of the room beyond the archway, I hear the whisper of my brother's voice.

Fu Leng . . . Fu Leng, youngest child of the Sun and Moon. Favored son of the darkness. Once, he was my brother, and Onnotangu's cherished son. Thrown from heaven to his death, cut free from the Celestial Heavens by the lash of Hantei's sword, he has fallen to madness and destruction. Now he has attacked the empire.

He calls to me, and I must go. I step into the room, behind her.

The Celestial Heavens open around us, swelling to fill the room. As they do, I feel each mortal heartbeat within the room, within the palace, the fields, the empire. I feel the pulse of the world, and we are wrapped around it, our claws and fangs tearing at each other with the fury of two gods sworn to kill. I have the advantage—his weakness lies in his hatred. He has the advantage—I know that I must fail.

Two dragons battle, their bodies twisted and scattered amid the heavens. I feel each cut of his claw against my body, and I hear his bone snap beneath my massive jaw. An eternity is passing in an instant, and each claw-strike releases a shower of stars into the heavens. Where our blood falls, trees wither and mountains rise. Our weight shatters the sky, and the clouds of the Celestial Heavens flee from our fury.

I know him so well . . . my brother, my friend, youngest of my companions, Fu Leng. You must die, and your madness must die with you, or all of Rokugan will be destroyed. Your vengeance, Fu Leng—I must stop it, even if it will mean my life.

As I have always known it would.

Fu Leng cries out, and the throne room shakes. The samurai beneath us stay back, watching as a battle that has waited an aeon is played out before them. Strike, counterstrike, great coils far larger than the room spread into infinity. The Celestial Heavens draw close. Teeth snap on bone and muscle, tearing the flesh of two gods.

At last, I falter. I cannot continue the charade any longer.

I withdraw my strike and feel the steel of his coils crush my torso into pulp.

Massive iron claws shred skin, tearing through scale and spilling the blood of the heavens. A scream echoes through the cosmos, and I know the voice to be my own. My brother's breath is hot against my bone, his iron teeth ripping through my body. I feel his power grow, and mine begins to weaken. He releases me with a terrible roar of victory, and the Heavens withdraw their face from me.

From the roof of the world, I fall, and I hear Fu Leng's voice following after me. *Die, brother. Die, as you once left me to die, in anguish and in fear. And when you do, know that you will forever be, as I was . . . alone.*

His cackling madness chases me as my body collapses to the floor. My dragon self dies, leaving me in blood and agony. He stands above me for only a moment, and then moves to join the battle with the Thunders. Calling each of them by name, the Dark God opens his arms. I cannot raise my head to see, but I hear the sounds of battle join around me. I hear the sounds of death.

And then, I see Hitomi.

She stands apart, unwilling to end my torment, watching each labored breath pause within my collapsed chest. For a moment, I believe she will kill me, but she falls to her knees at my side. Even after all I have put her through, all the pain and anguish, she still holds within her soul a glimmer of bushido. "I . . . cannot. . . ." she whispers. "You are my champion."

It is the only time I have ever known her to hesitate.

You are Dragon. I hear my own command, but my voice is as weak and empty as the fading heavens that surround me. The fight seems far distant now, the sounds of steel and sorcery echoing in two worlds at once. I remember hearing someone speak these words even as I say them, long before this day, and I remember her brother. But that was another time. Another death. I whisper, and my voice is faint. *You must become the riddle.*

Her eyes close, and I see furrows on her naked brow. Then, they open, and I see the fire of conviction.

I see my death approach, in the strike of an obsidian hand. Cold fingers close, crushing my immortal heart, stealing the rhythm of my life. Pain . . . Pain . . . and glory.

I look up at her cold features, feeling her fingers close about the secret that I have held within my soul. She seems startled to find it there. She is uncertain. But I look once more into her chiseled face, her shorn hair, and I feel the world shift around us.

Betrayer. Savior. Fool. Destroyer. Enigma.

She is all of these things.

She is Hitomi.

The world spins, and my flesh begins to crumble beneath the touch of her cold stone hand. The fingers close, wrapping tightly about my heart, and my form falls limp beneath her. My swords lie on the ground, a twisted tangle of iron and steel. My spirit rises, no longer at home in the decaying flesh that once housed it. The room changes in my vision, becoming at once the star-filled void of the Celestial Heavens and the earthbound throne room of the Hantei. The festering palace of my brother, Fu Leng.

I, an immortal kami, child of the Seven Heavens, look down at my own flesh and watch it die.

Hitomi's back arches, her mortal hand clutching at the ceiling as if to ward off some terrible blow. Her black eyes close, and then open. When they do, they are filled with starlight and the shadow of the moon. Her mouth twists in agony, and her bones shake within their fragile flesh, afraid of what they might become. She screams, but it is swallowed by the darkness between the stars. She is cold and alone. With a spasm, her black hand jerks out of my ruptured chest, dragging my blood-covered heart in its stone fist.

I feel her mind open beneath me, and I am washed in images of past and the present. A young man's face. A woman's laughter. The bright summer sun of a day I never knew. I see all these things and more. Her soul spreads before me like a tapestry of color and sensation, and I am drawn within it as certainly as a thread is spun within the weave. This is the prophecy of my death—the riddle destined to be answered.

I die, and she is born. It is done. My soul forever trapped within her, my heart crushed within her grasp. I feel her body shake, her obsidian hand slowly lower to the floor, and I see the reflection of Hitomi's face within the mirror of my forgotten swords. My eyes open, and I see the path that has led us both to this place. I feel her heart pound as her story becomes mine, our souls merging into one. Her past lies before me, and I watch it unfold once more.

Her eyes have become my own.

1 RISE OF FIRE

S trike!"

The two swords clashed. Steel rang on steel, and the mountain cliffs echoed their call. As one blade slid down the other, the gathered samurai began to cheer.

Sword leveled at his opponent's throat, the young samurai allowed himself a victorious grin. The entire fight had lasted a mere heartbeat.

The loser, a rough-looking young man with a curious grin, bowed. "Domo, Dainisan," he murmured to his opponent. "Well fought."

"And you, Taki-san," the other replied, smoothing his elegant mustache as he placed the saya of his sword firmly in the folds of his elaborate obi. "You very nearly defeated me." His flippant tone held no sincerity.

Taki flushed with annoyance. Still, the crowd that chanted around them left no room for a rebuke—and the brother of the

Mirumoto daimyo had already begun to walk across the tournament field to claim his prize. Taki simply stood silently in the center of the field, slowly sliding his blade back into its sheath.

"Well done," one of the watching samurai cried to the victor. "Well done, Daini. Don't you think so, Sukune-sama?"

By the empty ivory seat at the edge of the tournament field, Mirumoto Sukune smiled down at his foster son. He had raised Daini from the time the boy could walk, and though Daini had been born to Sukune's brother, it felt as through the young man was his own flesh and blood. The bright summer sun shone down on Sukune's bald pate where his topknot did not cover his forehead. His light brown eyes sparked with pride.

Around him, fields spread out where the mountain had been tamed. Rich green grass rustled in the cold wind of an approaching autumn. Banners fluttered, and orange leaves spun from still-green boughs. The tournament ground was filled with brightly garbed courtiers and bushi, for this was a day of festival. The Dragon Clan had every right to celebrate. The harvests had been good, and the clan was prosperous. Beyond the fields, jagged mountain peaks rose to break the crisp blue of the sky. Small white clouds clustered around the palace in the distance—Mirumoto Palace, the Iron Mountain.

It was Sukune's home, and Daini's as well. Since the death of their parents, Sukune had raised both Daini and his elder sister. Sukune's duty to his deceased brother was finished, but his pride remained. As Daini approached, Sukune's smile faded into solemnity, as befit the general of the Mirumoto armies.

Daini knelt at the edge of the daimyo's dais, placing his sword before him in a gesture of obedience.

"Well done, indeed, son of my heart." Sukune peered at the boy he had fostered for more than ten years.

The sixteen-year-old had pale skin, and hair drawn back in an oiled topknot. Each strand was carefully smoothed, and his elegant new mustache—one the youth had grown for more than six months in anticipation of this day—was carefully combed.

"You have taken the last test required of a Mirumoto samurai and proven your mastery of niten, the Strike of Two Swords. I wish that your sister had been here to see your victory, but other duties have kept Hitomi from the field."

At the mention of his sister's name, Daini's face clouded. "Hitomi has the duties of a daimyo," he said politely, each clipped word sharp and rote. "She cannot be expected to attend to each small thing in her provinces. Even such a celebration." His voice held sarcasm, though faintly, and Sukune was glad the youth kept his voice low. Despite the reasons for Hitomi's absence, Sukune knew it had nothing to do with her duties as daimyo. Hitomi had not performed them since she had taken the position.

Still, Sukune thought, it is bushido that a samurai did not speak poorly of his lord—even when that lord was his sister. "There are wars, Daini-san, and she must learn of them. The messengers that came this morning speak of dark tidings. Hitomi has a duty to fulfill."

"They say she is afraid of Yukihera," Daini's voice dropped to a low, bitter whisper. "He performs her duties and gives orders as the daimyo should, and she does nothing. The samurai say—"

"I do not care what they say, Daini-san. For as long as Hitomi is daimyo of the Mirumoto, it is your duty to obey her."

"And I will, Sukune-sama, for as long as she leads us. My life belongs to the Dragon Clan. One day, I'll be general of the Mirumoto, in your place. And when that day comes, I will show the empire that the Dragon are strong." Daini's face shone with pride and confidence. "You'll see, Father. That day will come."

Sukune tried not to chuckle at the raw arrogance in the youth's cultured voice. It was good for a boy to have dreams—better, still, when those dreams gave the clan strength.

A sudden shout came from the field. "Hitomi comes!" A messenger child jogged swiftly to Sukune's side, pausing only for the swiftest of bows. "She's on her way. She's almost here. . . ." The young boy's exuberance overstepped the bounds of protocol, and he nearly hopped up and down in impatience.

Sukune grunted. Damn her that she had not come a scant ten minutes ago. Her absence from the final rounds of the tournament was an embarrassment, and her arrival now would make it seem she deliberately slighted her brother. Most of the guests had assumed Hitomi would not arrive—she rarely attended public gatherings, even in her own lands—and the courtiers had already begun speaking to Mirumoto Yukihera, Sukune's son, about trade negotiations. In Hitomi's absence, her cousin took charge of such things. Her appearance now could only disrupt the negotiations.

Sukune sighed. "Tell Hitomi—"

"Too late." Daini muttered softly, looking across the field toward the stone gates of Mirumoto Palace. "The daimyo has already arrived."

Few of the courtiers in the crowd even recognized the often-absent daimyo of the Mirumoto. She marched across the turned earth of the tournament ground. Tattooed monks scattered before her. The swords at her belt hung loosely, and her face was dark with thought. It seemed Hitomi barely noticed the gracefully fluttering robes of the courtiers, or the shouts of brave samurai near her, but she did see Sukune. Mirumoto Hitomi did not waver even to step around a kneeling servant. Rather, she lifted her foot over the heimin and walked directly until she reached her foster father.

Once the clan had thought Hitomi would grow to be a great beauty, but no more. Where her long, straight hair had once fallen, a thick crop of torn shag hung around her face. It was untamed, hanging in thick scattered locks above her shoulders, barely long enough to make a topknot. Her almond-shaped black eyes shone in the bright sunlight. The faint lines around them had come from squinting, not laughing.

Sukune hoped she would emerge from her chrysalis. One day, perhaps, when she could set down the pain of all the deaths she had endured. . . . One day.

"Sukune-sama." Barely more than eighteen summers, Hitomi nevertheless spoke with the unmistakable ring of authority and command. "We must speak."

"Speak, Hitomi-sama? Now? There is much left to do, and your brother has claimed victory in the niten fights. This year, our family has much to celebrate." A crowd began to gather on the far side of the dais. "Come, Hitomi, and speak for your brother when I announce his victory. I'm certain he would consider it a great honor—"

"Iie."

Sukune felt his face grow warm.

"I have no time to speak for him. Enough celebration. We must prepare for war."

"Hitomi," Sukune continued. "It is not proper that we disrupt such a day's festival. There will be time to speak, tonight—tomorrow. The Dragon does not strike on impatience and impulse. We do not move without stone beneath our feet. Yokuni would not approve. And there are . . . other matters to attend to, Daimyo-sama. Matters of importance."

Hitomi's black eyes clouded at the sound of her champion's name, and her teeth clenched onto her lower lip.

A childish habit, thought Sukune, one she had best forget if she is to lead. "Come, now, Hitomi-sama. Let us finish the day's events, and there will be much to discuss tomorrow." This was not the time to leap to battle. Doing so would only make the empire believe the Dragon was afraid, or Hitomi was afraid. All the same.

Slowly, but resolutely, Hitomi nodded. "The festival will continue, Sukune-san. But we will not be swayed by politics. Let them believe what they wish; words do not change the mountain." Ignoring Daini's kneeling form, Hitomi stepped lightly to the ivory seat at the edge of the tournament field. She rested her antlered helm by her feet.

Sukune bowed once to his lady, showing his thanks and respect. Then, he raised his voice and called for the attention of the crowd. Slowly, the other contestants answered the general's call, their faces cheerful and proud. Sukune raised his hand, and the noise faded to pleasant whispers. The young samurai sank to their knees.

"Family, honored guests, citizens of the empire—for the third time, I welcome you to the lands of the Mirumoto, to witness a sacred day—the day when we celebrate what it is to be samurai." Mirumoto Sukune stood proudly, shifting within his ornamental armor. The plates fastened intricately into a pattern of scales that shone golden in the sunlight. "The Dragon is a clan of ancient tradition, of study and the search for enlightenment. Rarely do we invite visitors to our palaces. Today, you have witnessed one of our most sacred rites—the test of niten, the two-sword style. The First Mirumoto, our founder, created niten. He taught it to his children, as we taught it to ours. Now, we pass the niten style to a new generation. Today, our sons and daughters join the traditions of our clan and become part of our history. Today, they become truly Mirumoto."

A respectful murmur rose in the crowd at Sukune's stirring words. The faces of the young samurai lit with pride. Sukune looked down at the kneeling Daini and lifted the youth's sword from the ground. "Mirumoto Daini, you have won the day. Step forward."

"This is not your sword, Daini," he said. "It is the sword of your brothers—the sword of each samurai who will stand beside you. From now on, you will also wield another weapon; the honor of the Mirumoto house. Never forget your duty to it—or to your family line. Never let it be forgotten. Who speaks for you here, Mirumoto Daini?"

"I do, Sukune-sama." The voice came from the pavilions to the left of the field, near the back of the gathered throng.

Samurai turned, craning their heads to see who had spoken.

One man stood at the rear of the gathering, his five guardsmen kneeling with pikestaffs raised at their sides. "Daini is worthy of this honor. He has been my brother for ten years, and now I call him samurai of the Mirumoto. I am Mirumoto Yukihera, son of Mirumoto Sukune, general of the Dragon and born of the lineage of the first Mirumoto. I have traveled through the Phoenix lands, to the Shrine of the Ki-Rin and south to Carpenter Wall. I speak for my brother."

A surprised murmur went through the crowd near the dais. It had been Hitomi's place—as daimyo and Daini's closest relative—to speak for him. Eyes turned toward the raised platform and courtiers began to recognize the woman seated there.

Without looking at the wooden dais, Yukihera strode forward through the throng, He wore his finest robes, as golden as the sun and covered with fine dragon scales. His topknot of light brown hair gleamed, and his pale eyes caught the attention of many maidens, who sighed behind their fans. Yukihera held a sheathed sword out before him. "Hear my words, samurai, and remember. For ten years, my father was daimyo to the Mirumoto, sovereign lord of the Dragon Clan, obeying the dictates of our champion, Togashi Yokuni. Our family was strong. Prosperous. Now, the son of Shosan has won a place within the honored ranks of the Mirumoto Guard. As it is my place to honor you, I offer you this sword. It was borne by your own father in the battle of Gosan Gennai. It was his second blade, the blade he had saved for you, when you came of age. Now, it is yours. I know he would be proud of you."

"Proud?" Hitomi's voice was low and cutting. "I suppose my father would be . . . *proud* to have you speak his words for him, Yukihera, while his daughter sits by silently."

Yukihera spun around in shock, his face whitening. Samurai tensed in anticipation, but courtiers snickered behind their fans. Yukihera looked at Hitomi for a long moment, and then sank to his knees. "I am sorry, my daimyo . . . I did not know you were . . . I did not . . ."

"You would presume to speak in my place, Yukihera? That is forbidden."

"I presume only to serve the clan, Hitomi-sama," he said quietly.

From among the chuckling courtiers rose a stage whisper: "Is the Dragon Champion here?"

Kakita Yugoro—a portly Crane with an oily mustache and a smile twice as slippery—replied, "No, Ushiheri. Only the Mirumoto daimyo."

"Then who is chastising the Mirumoto daimyo, that he sinks to his knees?" Ushiheri asked with the appropriate amount of innocence.

Yugoro smiled, enjoying the farce. "The Mirumoto daimyo chastises the Mirumoto daimyo."

Hitomi reddened. "*I* am the Mirumoto daimyo."

Yugoro nodded, but a third voice interrupted him before the stout Crane could respond.

An old, wrinkled man covered in spider tattoos knelt by the tournament field. Rolling his eyes and clutching his bald head, he crowed, "What is, must be! Where the daimyo walks, swords follow, and where the leader falls, there lies the taint. . . ."

"Be silent, ise zumi!" Hitomi cut him off, her voice sharp. "We have no time for your riddles."

Ushiheri broke in. "No time for riddles? Dragons are riddles, so they say. Yugoro, look again for me; my eyes are poor. Are you certain she is a Dragon and not a Crab?"

The courtiers laughed, a mocking murmur.

Hitomi rose furiously from her seat, throwing aside the cushion.

"Perhaps that is part of the riddle, Yugoro-sama!" Another bystander said above her fan. "A Dragon who does not riddle is like a Scorpion who does not sting. Perhaps she is seeking a riddle that will sting."

Hitomi rashly reached for her katana's hilt.

"Perhaps she doesn't have one." Yugoro clicked his fan together and made a tsk-tsk sound of disapproval. "Yukihera-sama, shall we still meet this afternoon to ensure the treaty between our clans? I will offer you a copy of Akodo's Sword. The Lion certainly have no use for it; perhaps it can help a daimyo of the Dragon, instead."

Scattered applause greeted Yugoro's twin-edged remark.

The tournament of blades had become a test of wits, and Hitomi was losing. To be compared to the fallen daimyo of the Akodo family stung enough, but to be publicly snubbed in favor of the man who routinely handled the duties of daimyo—! This banter had become dangerous.

Sukune scanned the assembled guardsmen. They looked to Yukihera for guidance. None came. Leaning toward his ward and daimyo, Sukune whispered, "You will have to act, my lady, and now, before this grows to be a political disaster."

"And I will." Hitomi stepped down from the edge of the dais, striding into the center of the tournament ground as the applause died.

To the side of the field, the spider-tattooed monk whimpered, hissing at the Crane in anger. "Bone and fallen flesh, rot inside, rot outside. I will be silent, I will be still—but the silent river knows what lies beneath it. Do not forget."

Yugoro smiled, speaking over the monk. "Let me explain this to you, Ushiheri. Yukihera's father kept the throne for ten years and ruled well. But he had three children to raise: Hitomi, Yukihera, and Daini. The first was given the throne, the second the duties, and the third the sword. A sad story, indeed. They were given to the wrong children, you see."

"Enough, Crane!" Hitomi snarled.

"Do you deny it, Mirumoto-sama?" the Crane asked smoothly.

"I do."

"Then there is to be a duel? Splendid." Kakita Yugoro raised his fan once more, calling to the tournament master.

"I will gladly duel you, Crane." Hitomi's eyes narrowed as she stared at the portly ambassador. The courtier carried no sword, no weapons at all.

"Then, as hostess of this gathering, you must accept my request for a champion. As you have no doubt noticed, I am not prepared to defend myself against a duel of niten." Slickly, the fat courtier pointed at Yukihera, still kneeling on the field. "I choose him, in hopes this contest will solve the riddle before us and prove who is truly the daimyo of the Mirumoto."

Damn them, Mirumoto Sukune thought in the split second after the Crane's plan became clear. Damn the Crane, and damn Hitomi for showing up unprepared for the dangers of court. No matter who won, the Dragon were in danger.

The rules of such a duel were simple. Whatever befell the Crane's champion also befell the Crane. Even if Hitomi bested Yukihera, she would have to kill him in order to kill the Crane. If she did that, she would be killing the only man who could ensure a treaty with the wealthy families of the south—and fulfill the duties she loathed. However, if she lost, Yukihera became daimyo in name as well as duty, even if he left Hitomi alive.

Yukihera was a model samurai, a scholar, and a weapons master who trained in the beautiful dance of blades. He was dashing, bold and clever—but he lacked discipline. Once, long ago, he had tried to master the tests of the Dragon monks but had not been not accepted into the mystic order of the ise zumi. He had returned to the Mirumoto and become Sukune's chancellor, the same position he held beneath Hitomi. He would have made a good daimyo—but that title belonged to Hitomi. Now, the Crane had forced the two Dragon to duel . . . and the Mirumoto would lose one or the other. Either way, the Dragon became weak.

Sukune watched Hitomi desperately, hoping she would see some escape.

Unmoving and unmoved, Hitomi did not flinch or turn away from the Crane. Rather, she watched him as a snake watches the fluttering of a bird too weak to take flight. Though Yukihera was a true master of niten, Hitomi was not afraid. Faint whispers in the crowd broke the stillness of the autumn day.

With fire in her eyes, Hitomi turned to face the kneeling Yukihera and snarled, "So be it."

Sukune's son respectfully touched his head to the ground, and then stood to face his daimyo. "I do not wish to kill you, Hitomi-sama." The golden samurai said. "Please, reconsider this duel."

Hitomi shook her head. "I will not. Only one of us can be daimyo, Yukihera, and for too long, you have stood in that role. It is time, as the Crane has said, that I restore the title of Mirumoto daimyo to the true heir of the line. It belongs to me."

"You do not have the skills to rule, Hitomi," Yukihera said respectfully, bowing to reduce the insult of his words. "If you kill me, the Mirumoto will fall. I beg you once more. Relent. Release us from this duel."

"And give you the throne of the Mirumoto? Do not be a fool. We will fight, and I will win." Her words were bitter, angry, and many of the Mirumoto guardsmen tensed. Their hands clenched the shafts of their pikes as if ready to strike. Yukihera bowed again. The guards grew even more angry.

What kind of daimyo can she be, Sukune wondered, if her own clan does not wish her to lead?

As the two combatants prepared themselves, tying back their kimono sleeves and testing the draw of their swords, Sukune's quick eyes caught a glimpse of movement.

Across the field, the Crane nodded, flickering his fan behind his sleeve as though signaling. Yukihera nodded faintly, his eyes shifting to one of the Mirumoto guardsmen. A bag of koku slid from the guardsman's palm into the hand of the second Crane, Ushiheri. Yugoro seemed pleased, and both men looked away.

Sukune stopped, stunned. Was the duel . . . planned? He had no time to consider such riddles. The duelists were ready.

Stepping away from the center of the tournament field, Hitomi signaled to Sukune to come forward.

Chosen to arbitrate the duel, the old general walked as though stone held back his steps. His own son—his own daughter. Formally, Sukune stepped between the two samurai as they reached the central ground.

The duelists lowered into their stances.

The crowd flocked to the edges of the field, breathless in anticipation. This was more than a simple festival duel. This bout would determine the future of the Dragon Clan.

"By tradition, a challenge of this nature is to the death, but I ask that you consider your actions carefully. Choose to grant mercy. The clan cannot afford the loss of either of you. The empire falls into war beneath us, and our personal disputes must not be allowed to weaken the clan. Do you understand?" Sukune looked back and forth between the two Mirumoto, praying that they would heed his words.

Yukihera nodded.

Hitomi said nothing, moved nothing, but stood as still as a statue in the green grass.

Sukune raised his left hand above his head, slowly backing away from the two participants.

Hitomi leaned forward into the duel, eager to face her opponent. Yukihera remained more passive, holding his blade's hilt in a relaxed hand.

The Crane would have ended this duel in a single swift flurry of iaijutsu—the unerring practice of single-strike defeat—but that was not the Dragon way. Niten would decide the day, a full duel of kenjutsu where timing, rhythm, and the extended blows of twin swords would make the difference between victor and defeated. The Dragon dueled not just to win, but to prove complete superiority. Rarely did any defeated opponent survive. Those who did were never allowed to make such a challenge again.

It was their way.

Staring coldly at the Crane, who stood to one side of the tournament ground, Sukune held his hand high. "Begin." Sukune dropped his hand with a clear stroke, and the two competitors burst into movement.

Every motion was a feint. Each shift of footwork and ringing clash of blade drew the eye away from the real battle. It was a contest of wills, brought across in the massive sword strokes of Hitomi's blade and the swift strikes of Yukihera's katana. A charge and a sidestep collided with a staunch blow and kick. Both opponents twisted to gain the advantage.

Hitomi shouted, charging past Yukihera and falling victim to his feint. His return blow rang innocently on her lowered sword. She was too fast for him, despite his finesse. He stepped to the side, and his second weapon flew into his hand. Hitomi turned back. Her first strike twisted into motion as katana and wakizashi spun in her hands.

Yukihera cut in front of her with a swordsman's grace, double slashing toward her throat. She leaped back before he could complete the stroke, and his weapons fell far short. The two samurai passed each other again, their weapons thrusting and sliding. Yukihera slipped beneath her guard and feinted to gain room.

Sukune watched every motion. Instead of the cool, collected face of a cultured opponent, Sukune saw something in

Hitomi's eyes that he had never seen before. Open fury painted her strikes, tearing at her skill like a beast ripping at the cage that bound it. Were that beast released, Hitomi would likely kill them all.

Hitomi's twin swords shifted beneath the pressure of Yukihera's blades, circling for the kill like a pair of hawks in flight. She shouted, a tremendous kiop scream that shuddered through the crowd.

Yukihera flinched once more. He froze for an instant, his strikes paused, and in that fleeting second, she had already won.

Her sudden downward chop caught his leg. With an expert flip, Hitomi turned her strike into a blow, using the flat edge of the sword to land stingingly upon his calf.

He staggered back, surprised.

Hitomi lunged for his throat with both weapons, catching his open neck just a hair's breath short of her katana's edge. With a swift motion, she passed the short blade of her wakizashi over his own, pushing his sword to the ground. In a second, he was trapped—dead.

Sukune watched in anguish as his son fell to his knees before the Mirumoto daimyo. "Kill me," Yukihera hissed, "I cannot watch the clan die beneath your rule." For a moment, Sukune thought she would do it. Then Hitomi eased the pressure on her blades, and her steel moved away from Yukihera's neck.

Time began to move again, and Sukune drew a long, shuddering breath. The voices of the crowd overwhelmed him, and he wondered when they had begun to shout. During the duel, he had not heard them. Nothing had existed except the sight of his son and his daughter—killing each other.

Sukune approached Hitomi as she coldly sheathed her wakizashi. He knelt before her. "Thank you, Hitomi-sama," Sukune whispered. "Thank you for sparing my son."

"Crane," the Mirumoto daimyo snarled, sheathing her katana with a violent thrust. "By the time the sun falls, you will be gone."

Yugoro and his brother bowed smoothly, their sky-blue robes fluttering with each movement.

"Finish your treaty, and leave. You are no longer welcome here," Hitomi hissed.

"Hai, Daimyo," the Crane said quietly, bested.

Hitomi turned to the crowd, raising her head and speaking with authority. "I am daimyo of the Mirumoto family, as my father was before me, and I owe no man. I will no longer be questioned. Is that clear?" Looking down at the Mirumoto samurai once more, Hitomi's stared blackly into Yukihera's eyes until he was forced to bow his head.

"Hai, Hitomi-sama," Sukune whispered. "Hai, domo. Thank you."

Kneeling at her feet, Yukihera said nothing.

The war had only just begun.

2

WINDS OF WAR

The interior of the Mirumoto mountain twisted through barren rock and thick granite, passages that pulsed with samurai and their families. Protected from the bitter air of the mountain autumn by thick walls of rock, the Dragon Clan lived in solitude and peace. No force had ever conquered Mirumoto Palace; it was said none ever would.

Deep within the palace, where only high windows opened to faint sunlight or the cold glow of stars, the central chamber of the Dragon Champion nestled within thick stone walls and iron buttresses. Only three items decorated the cold antechamber: an ornate ivory throne as old as the mountain itself; twin swords that rested on a low mahogany table beside the throne; and an elaborate circle, carved deep into the rock at the center of the room. The circle's borders were formed by deep cuts into the granite, filled with glistening silver and gold. Each twisting line consisted of thousands of tiny dragons, flying in serpentine patterns and forming a single golden curve. At each of four edges, the serpent circle broke into wide wings, framing a low cushion of gold thread and green silk. On these cushions rested three of the most powerful members of the Dragon Clan, summoned by their ultimate ruler: Togashi Yokuni, champion of the Dragon.

But his ivory throne was empty, and the three daimyo argued for the future of their clan. One was a young girl no older than eighteen summers, her hair shorn close to the skull and her black eyes filled with fire. She was Mirumoto Hitomi, Lady of the Mirumoto family.

A second rested on his cushion, sipping tea from a simple cup as though at peace with the world. His name was Tamori, lord of the Dragon lowlands and the finest shugenja in the clan. His robes reflected his place as daimyo to his house, and the elaborate serpent tattoos that wove their paths across the bare skin of his face and hands proved his rank as Master of the Agasha, the sorcerers of the Dragon.

Another samurai with youthful features occupied the third place, kneeling as if uncomfortable even on the magnificent cushion. His gi was travel-stained, his elegant haori vest wrinkled as though he had slept in it, and his movements were quick and unrestrained from lack of rest. A fan rested on the ground in front of him, signifying that he had been the one to ask the champion to arrange the gathering. His name was Yasu, master of the Kitsuki family—another young Dragon daimyo, only three summers older than Hitomi.

Hitomi did not completely trust Yasu, but he was an ally. Two years ago, he had asked Hitomi for her hand in marriage, vowing he would give up his own title and take the position of husband when she became daimyo. She refused him, and nearly challenged him to a duel for his presumption. Since then, they had hardly spoken—but he had never opposed her. Not like Tamori had.

Only two hundred years since their inception, the Kitsuki had already gained a reputation in the empire—one that did not speak well of their nature. The Kitsuki were investigators, ignoring the ways of bushido and studying "evidence" rather than proving testimony. They were discoverers, explorers, students of the world, too willing to ignore a samurai's honor in favor of some small token of "proof." Whatever he had found, it had better be enough. Within the guarded heart of Mirumoto Palace, the samurai of each family gathered, ready to face the future under the command of their daimyo.

A daimyo who even now cursed the name of the emperor they were sworn to serve.

"Damn it, Yasu," Hitomi interrupted him with a snarl. She leaned forward. "The emperor turns his back on the empire, allowing the Crane and the Lion to make war. The Unicorn attack the Crab—the Crab abandon their ancient duty and march north, through the empty Scorpion lands. There is chaos and disruption, death and plague, and you want us to join them? Better that we come down from the mountains with the strength of steel and crush every one of them to the ground. That is the only way they will understand 'peace.' Tell me that this is our purpose, and the Mirumoto will gladly join you. But for a fool's errand? Never."

Kitsuki Yasu blanched at such open disrespect, but stammered, "The empire n-needs the Dragon. Our clan is the only one left untouched by the devastation that has swept the lands below our mountains. We must . . ."

"No, no, Yasu-san." Agasha Tamori smiled pleasantly, sipping the green tea that cooled in his porcelain glass. "Hitomi-san is correct. For centuries, the clan of the Dragon has remained outside the petty conflicts of the empire. We must remain apart; that is our duty."

Shivering slightly at the sound of the man's snakelike hiss, Hitomi leaned back on her cushion and tried to control her impulse to reach for the hilt of her sword. Asahina Tamori could slide smoothly into any conversation, as if he were the most talented Crane diplomat, but his words held the cutting edge of fangs and poison. His golden robes rustled against the cold stone around her cushion, making waves against the black surface of the floor. The man was weak, a coward, thought Hitomi. It galled her to agree with Tamori, but she realized the wisdom of his words. For hundreds of years, the Dragon had watched one conflict after another tear at the empire, and had remained apart. Each battle subsided, each conflict died, and still the Dragon watched.

It is the Dragon's way, Hitomi thought. It is our place to do nothing at all. Damn the Dragon for being cowards, and damn them for giving me birth.

"Yes, the Lion attack the Crane. What of it?" Tamori was as smooth as obsidian. Ripples of amusement tinged his cultured voice. "We have enough to do, feeding our peasants when the snows come."

"Now is the time to move, knowing we will be safe. . . ."

"We are safe already, Yasu-san." Tamori smiled. "Safe enough, behind our walls."

"Safe, perhaps, but for how long?" The voice belonged to Togashi Mitsu, one of the secretive tattooed ise zumi that were the personal servants of the champion. Each ise zumi dedicated his life to discovering the secrets of the Dragons' Heart, the ancient riddle that leant the clan strength. They made the torturous climb through the wilderness and sharp cliffs to desolate Kyuden Togashi, arriving with bloodied hands and a singular purpose: to serve the champion of the Dragon Clan. It was said that those who were unworthy would wander into the lost mountains forever, dying because they could not prove themselves.

Part monk, part samurai, the ise zumi are an enigma to the empire, Hitomi thought. They ask riddles that hide truth, and they know more than they are allowed to tell. It is their nature, and their enigmas keep the clan strong. They are our heart, but they are not our steel.

The steel, Hitomi reminded herself, is the Mirumoto. Untempered, perhaps, but still steel.

The thick-bodied ise zumi knelt at the edge of the ivory throne's dais, looking out at the circle of kneeling daimyo with respect and a touch of mischief. But it was not Mitsu's half-grin that caught the attention of the three daimyo. It was the tall man, standing in the shadows behind him.

No one had seen the champion enter the room, but the whisper of his presence sent chills up Hitomi's spine. The doors of the chamber, thick oak between an arch of stone, had not seemed to move; yet he was there, bringing Mitsu to be his voice. The champion of the Dragon did not speak in conventional ways, even to his most faithful servants. It was said that no creature in the empire had ever heard his true voice. Yokuni towered above his three daimyo, his steel and gold armor glinting in the torchlight and the faint starlight that streamed from a high window.

"Hail, Yokuni-sama," all three daimyo chimed, and they pressed their foreheads to the floor in respect.

Turning his eyes upon each of them, Yokuni surveyed the room silently. As he moved toward his throne, his steel-masked helm showed no sign of emotion. There was neither anger nor joy in his precise steps. Within the darkness of his shadowed mempo, nothing betrayed the champion's thoughts.

"The lord champion bids you all to be comfortable." Mitsu began to speak as if spurred by some silent cue. The tattooed ise zumi grinned faintly, seeming to forget his place for a moment, and then went on. "You have been called here at his bidding, to witness the future of the Dragon Clan."

As Mitsu spoke, Yokuni stepped through the stone chamber. Pausing briefly in the center of the ring formed by his three daimyo, he looked up at the filtered starlight of the high window.

"Yokuni-sama has heard your news of the empire, Yasu-san," Mitsu said as Yokuni remained still for many long moments. "He is pleased that your diligence has returned such useful information. Honor to your house, Daimyo of the Kitsuki."

The champion's robes rustled in the breeze, a wind that had not existed before he entered the room. Mitsu turned to gaze upon Yokuni's silent mask as if listening to unspoken words. After a moment, the monk turned hard eyes on Hitomi.

"Our champion is pleased that you could join us, Daimyo of the Mirumoto," Mitsu said with forced casualness. "He is sorry that your business did not allow you to attend the command council. The discussion with the Unicorn was most enlightening. I am certain you can be informed as to the events of that council, should you speak to your second-in-command, Yukihera-san. He was there in your place, and his advice and wisdom were most appreciated by the other clans, and by our champion."

Hitomi's face darkened at the rebuke. "I will speak with him. I was . . . to the south, seeking information on the Crab. . . ."

"On a particular Crab, Mirumoto Hitomi. Hida Yakamo. Yes, Yokuni knows how you spend your days. You will speak with Yukihera. When you do," Mitsu said, tilting his head enigmatically. "You should also ask Yukihera of his dealings with Toturi. Yukihera spent a great deal of time with the ronin general and can give you insight into the man's mind."

Again, the sting. Yukihera had done all her work for her. And where had she been? Seeking a lost vengeance. They did not understand.

Hitomi swallowed her pride and her excuses. "Hai, Yokuni-sama," she said quietly, seething with anger.

The wind furled Yokuni's thick cloak as if caressing the skin beneath the steel, turning the light into half-heard whispers. It was rare that the champion came among them; rarer still that he allowed Mitsu to speak his mind so clearly.

Yokuni turned back to the three daimyo. He stared into each leader's eyes for a long moment.

Unlike the others, Hitomi did not avert her gaze. The action was too bold, too rude even for an accomplished senior daimyo, much less the stripling chieftain of a scattered family. Yet somehow, she knew that Yokuni had expected her to stare. She looked into his eyes for the briefest of moments, and as she did a cold wind swept through the chamber. For an instant, Hitomi felt an unreasoning, desperate fear touch her heart with cold fingers. Something was terribly wrong.

Before she could speak, Mitsu continued. "In times of trouble, history will be written by the victors. The empire has been threatened. This is not unusual. We have always remained apart, Tamori-san, you are correct. But the Dragon has remained apart from the empire for a reason."

Yokuni moved to rest upon the ivory throne. The serpent-like arms of the chair seemed to come alive and twist about his wrists in welcome.

Above the throne, carved on the wall of the antechamber were three kanji—words placed there by the first Togashi, ancient kami of myth. His final act was to carve these words above the throne of his successors, that his spirit would inspire their actions for future generations. Now, the words haunted Hitomi as if the enigma had been posed to the depths of her soul.

Become the Riddle.

When it became his time to take the throne, every Dragon Champion spent a hundred days alone in this room. Chosen from the ranks of the ise zumi, the Dragon Champion became solitary, taking a position of silence and emptiness. Never again would the ise zumi's face be seen by anyone— but only the mempo of the first champion. Once a man had taken the name "Yokuni," he ceased to be a member of the ise zumi and had become the incarnation of the first Togashi. His former identity was lost beneath a metal mask and a shell of armor.

"Now it is time to leave our mountains. The Dragon are needed, and Yokuni commands that we will go. Hitomi," Mitsu turned to each of the daimyo one by one, pointing from his seat at the base of the ivory throne, "will lead the Mirumoto armies south, toward Lion lands. Beneath the mountains, you will meet with our allies, and you will assist them as needed. Tamori, you are commanded to assemble a guard of twenty-five of your best shugenja. They will go with the Mirumoto legions and aid them in every way. Yasu, you will travel with Hitomi. She will need you." Mitsu cocked his head curiously, a half-smile appearing on his lips.

"Need . . . ?" Hitomi whispered, but her protest was ignored.

Yokuni gestured toward the open sky with one gauntleted hand.

Mitsu continued without pause. "Hitomi, you will take the Mirumoto legions to the Kitsuki palaces and visit the Gardens of Shinsei. There you will meet your guide, and he will lead you the rest of the way. You leave in three days."

"Three?" Hitomi said. "Forgive me, Champion-sama," she began, trying to remain respectful of his position and her own duty. "It will take weeks to prepare the caravans of supplies, to arm the troops, to make ready the guard who will remain behind. . . ."

"Perhaps you do not understand, Hitomi-sama," Mitsu turned to her, a touch of sorrow on his face. For once, he spoke no riddles, nor did he quote the eternal Tao of the prophet, Shinsei. "None of your troops will remain behind. All the forces of the Mirumoto must join our allies at the base of the Dragon Mountains and continue south from there. As it is, the Crab will beat us to Beiden Pass—and once there, the fighting will begin. We will not have time to prepare a reserve, and there is no reason. If the Crab seize the pass, the empire may fall. But the Dragon will not remain unguarded."

Mitsu turned toward Yasu and continued. "A smaller force of Kitsuki will remain here to guard the passes, though Yasu will travel with you as aide and advisor. Your supplies, and an apt guide, await you at the Kitsuki palaces."

"All . . . ?" Hitomi's face darkened, but she knew better than to defy the champion of the Dragon when he had given a direct order. Beside her, Yasu bowed gratefully.

"My men will be pleased to serve, Yokuni-sama." Of all the daimyo, only Yasu seemed excited about their orders. His open face shone with honest respect and admiration, and he eagerly clutched the hilt of his sword. "The Kitsuki scouts will come with me, to find the best way out of the mountains before the snows seal the passes. The others will remain behind. Although my family is small, with the thick blanket of snow and the treacherous passes, the palaces of the Dragon will be safe for many months. Even if an enemy chose to attack, they would have to wait until spring, and by spring, my men will have the resources they need to stop any enemy advance."

Though Tamori seemed no more pleased than Hitomi, he too nodded in assent. "I will do as my champion asks. Gennai, twenty-three others, and myself will assemble to follow the . . . armies," he said with barely covered distaste. "Our magic is at Hitomi-san's disposal."

After a moment, Mitsu rose from his place at Yokuni's feet. "Your orders are clear, Daimyo-sama, and I have served my duty. You should hasten to prepare your men for their journey. There is much to do and little time to begin." Mitsu looked at Yokuni as if loath to speak, but the champion's stone demeanor revealed nothing. Turning back to the daimyo, Mitsu concluded, "Go."

As one, the three daimyo bowed from their cushions once more and rose fluidly. Yasu beamed his emotions like a man with no sense of the fool he makes of himself. Beside him, Tamori's face twitched with rapid calculations. They crossed the wide room like snakes retreating toward their burrows, seeking out safe havens within the mountain's rocky heart. Both of the other daimyo had much to do tonight, Hitomi knew. She doubted if any of the three of them would sleep.

What rest could there be in a world gone mad?

As the other daimyo exited through wide oak doors in the stone corridors of the palace, Hitomi heard Mitsu's rapid footsteps behind her. The ise zumi neatly scampered to her side, his warm eyes troubled and his hands in protective fists.

He knows something he does not want to tell me, Hitomi thought, noting the concern that masked the monk's movements.

"Hitomi-san?" Mitsu began, stepping closer to her and bowing briefly. "I have one further message for you. One that I was not allowed to say in the presence of the other daimyo." He paused, and Hitomi nodded. "The champion wished you to know your enemy." Now that he was no longer speaking for Yokuni, Mitsu once more spoke in riddles and enigmas.

"I see." Choking back her anger, Hitomi said icily, "Against whom do I bring war?"

"The enemy of our enemy is our friend. Your orders, Hitomi-sama, are to make war against the Crab."

A sharp intake of breath, and Hitomi's demeanor changed from ice to fire. "Crab . . ."

"Iie, Hitomi-san!" Mitsu spoke quickly. "This battle is for the clan, not for your own personal vengeance. You must seek out the answer without carrying the future of the clan on your shoulders."

"Will the Crab Champion's son be there?" Hitomi asked.

"Hitomi-san, I . . ."

"Will he be there?" her tone changed from that of a petulant girl to the strong crack of a soldier's command.

Unwillingly, the ise zumi felt his spine bend, and he fell to the ground on his knees before the daimyo of the Mirumoto family. "I do not know," he said quietly. "Perhaps. We are content to speak, and we suppose, but only the secret truly knows."

"Hida Yakamo." Hitomi's face contorted in rage and hatred. "I would give my life to take his from this world. He murdered my brother, and I have not forgotten. Before I die, the life of Hida Yakamo will end on my blade."

"No one has forgotten, Hitomi," Mitsu said frankly, looking up at her with sorrow. "Your brother's spirit does not rest—not so long as you keep it here with your anger."

"Rest," Hitomi said, looking down at Mitsu and thumbing her sword's saya. "Does my brother rest in Jigoku? Does he have peace, knowing that the man who butchered him still lives? For more than ten years, Mitsu, I have heard Satsu's voice in the night. I still remember his face when the Crab slew him. The Crab's blow was false. Honorless. Yakamo is a dog, and he deserves to die like one."

"The Crab's blow was true, Hitomi."

Her mouth twisted in rage, and Hitomi nearly drew her sword. After a moment of barely contained fury, she pressed the blade back into its sheath with a click. "Never," whispered the Mirumoto daimyo, "repeat that lie to me again. A man who did not respect the rules of an honorable duel murdered my brother. Yakamo knew he would fail, and so he struck without warning. My brother did not even draw his sword." Her voice held a lethal threat. "Remember that, the next time you are asked to tell the tale." With that, she turned and walked angrily toward the oak doors of the council chamber. She paused once to look back at the monk who still knelt on the floor in the circle's center. "When I find the Crab, I will make him pay for his treachery with his life. I swear it on my brother's sword."

Raising her eyes from Mitsu, Hitomi glanced at the dais and the high ivory seat of state, hoping to gain insight about Yokuni's silent thoughts. It served no purpose.

The throne was already empty.

3

THE DAIMYO'S COMMAND

he Mirumoto must march to the base of the Iron Mountain and meet with our allies in Lion territory." Hitomi's generals did not reply; they had not been invited to. Still, as she scanned the weathered faces around her, Hitomi could guess their thoughts.

Unicorn? Allied with the Unicorn Clan ... preposterous. . . .

We'll see fighting even beyond what we saw ten years ago with the Phoenix. Shugenja won't be enough. . . .

She's too young. Too young, and too obsessed. . . .

She believes that she has the answers ... but does not even know what questions to ask.

The daimyo of the Mirumoto shook her head wearily, refusing their concerned eyes.

Beside her, servant heimin brought forth sake and rice cakes. The discussions had been going on all night, and Hitomi was bone-weary. The cramped war chamber of the Iron

Mountain was cold, the stone covered with shadows of early morning. A long wooden table stretched between the generals, covered with papers and small ceramic figurines. Padded cushions rested on the granite floor, soft against the mountain's heart. Dawn had brightened the horizon some three hours past, but Hitomi continued to address her generals.

At last, she said, "You are dismissed. Now is the time to sleep. Tomorrow we continue the preparations. Tomorrow, we leave for the border."

The men stood slowly, uncramping their weary legs. Beside Sukune, Mirumoto Yukihera rose to his feet, looking away from the preparations with a stoic face. His silence hung like a cloud at the end of the table, but Hitomi ignored him. He left with the others. Only Sukune and Daini remained.

"I wish to speak with you." Sukune bowed, and raised his head to stare into the Mirumoto daimyo's black eyes.

"You speak too freely." Hitomi glared at him impotently. "Daini, you may go—"

"Your brother should stay. I wish to speak to my daughter."

"Your niece, Sukune-san." The formal title snapped from her tongue like a strike, but the old man did not retreat.

"To the child I raised, and whom I know better than any in this world."

"Of what would you speak?" Hitomi asked, knowing the answer.

Daini did not shift on his cushion, but his ill-concealed look of nervousness revealed everything.

The boy is still young, Hitomi thought. *He does not even remember the brother I fight to redeem.*

"Yakamo."

An image of the Crab warrior rose unbidden to Hitomi's mental eye. He was tall, dark skinned and laughing, and his thick black hair hung down over his shoulders like wet rain. His tetsubo was covered in blood, and his eyes narrowed with pleasure. The joy of the kill. Hitomi shook her bleary head, willing her thoughts to obey her commands. "He is mine by right, Sukune."

"Hai," he nodded. "But not if it threatens the Dragon. At Otosan Uchi you abandoned your troops to engage him in single combat, a combat that by right of honor, should never have happened. You were nearly killed."

"But I was not. And I took his hand. A small price for my brother's life, don't you think, Sukune?" Hitomi unfurled from the cushion like a battle cat. "I think he has not paid enough."

"Hitomi," Sukune growled, forgetting protocol, "you led twenty men on the field and then abandoned them with some insane order, 'Guard the wall,' I believe you said. Then, you charged into Crab lines—allied lines, I remind you— and you assaulted the son of the Crab Champion. You're lucky you weren't considered a casualty of war." Sukune's face turned red, and beads of sweat formed on his brow from the effort of keeping his temper. "The Dragon have never gone to war as much as they have in your lifetime, and I believe you are a product of your time. But you must know your duty comes before your honor, Hitomi. You must."

"Have you forgotten, too, Daini?" Hitomi turned suddenly on her brother, who sank slightly into the cushions at her icy tone. "Have you put aside our brother's death as a 'casualty'? Is it so easy for you to forget?"

"Hitomi-sama," Daini began unhappily. "I was only five, and you were eight. I hardly remember. . . ."

"I remember, even if you do not. At least I have some sense of family honor."

"Hitomi," Sukune interjected. "It is no use to berate Daini so deeply. His place is not yours, and you cannot—"

"He is my brother," she said simply. "He must live up to his blood."

"Live up to . . . ?" Daini's eyes flickered with anger, the first since the discussion had begun. "I am a man. If you had attended the niten tournament, you might understand that." The words were a bold man's threat, but on Daini's lips they sounded almost ashamed.

Hitomi's short hair fell into her eyes like a lion's tangled mane. "You are still young, Brother, and you have much to learn."

"And I will learn, Hitomi-san. But not from you. I will learn from the memory of a daimyo who cared for more than vengeance. Our father wanted what was best for this family, and for the empire. He had higher goals—goals of honor." The sentences spilled from Daini's head, uncontrolled by the strict training of a samurai. It was considered a death sentence to speak out of turn to one's daimyo, but it was also a samurai's duty to speak, even when the consequences were dire. Daini knew that, but he apparently ignored the fact that pride, more than honor, prompted him to speak. "You hardly speak of our father, Hitomi-sama. Do you remember him as well? The man who raised you after our mother died in childbirth? The man who committed seppuku out of loss for our brother? You constantly harp about Satsu's honor, Satsu's death, and yet not a word for the man who gave you life. Or is your memory only useful for what you wish to believe?"

Hitomi's eyes narrowed. "I remember, better than you will ever know. Every night I dream of it. Every day, I pray for the release of my soul, but that release will not come, not until Satsu is avenged, yes, and our father, too. But I remember more than that, little brother. I remember a spoiled child standing at the edge of the tournament field and crying while his older brother was butchered. I remember, Daini, because that is all you are and all you will ever be. A terrified boy, falling apart at the mention of combat and failing to understand the nature of honor."

"Hitomi!" Sukune bellowed, but it was too late. "That is enough!"

Silence fell upon the stone chamber with a lingering dread. For a long moment, Hitomi and Daini stared at one another, their eyes locked in ferocious contest. Hitomi slowly turned away.

Daini hissed, "You're not a woman; you're a monster. You only want revenge because you don't know anything else. Satsu would be ashamed of you."

She spun fist lashing out to catch her brother squarely on his pale chin. As his jawbone cracked beneath the impact, her other hand reached for the katana in her obi.

"Hitomi-sama!" Sukune's shout went unheard.

Hitomi's sword flew faster than thought, tearing into Daini's haori and ripping away the seams that held the elaborately woven vest to his chest. It fluttered to the ground as Daini staggered back and fumbled for his own weapon.

Watching him coldly, Hitomi lowered her sword toward his throat with the elegance of a trained killer. As the vest crumpled at Daini's feet, the golden mon of the Dragon shone mutely in the morning light, cut in half by Hitomi's blow.

"You do not deserve to wear the mon of our father, Daini, or the swords of this family. My family is everything to me, but you have cast our honor aside. You have forgotten that we have been insulted, our brother murdered, our father forced to an early grave. When your family is truly in your heart, then you will deserve to wear our father's mon."

Sukune pressed himself between the two siblings, raising his arms and falling to his knees before his daimyo. "Daimyo-sama," he began, his voice shaking. "It is early. We have been awake too long, and Daini-san is yet young." Sukune looked up at Hitomi's black eyes. "He is your brother," he whispered. "My son, as you are my daughter. Daimyo . . ."

"Yes," Hitomi interrupted, uncaring. "I am daimyo of this clan, and that means my word is unchallenged. I have already spared one son for you, Sukune. If I am to spare two, then this one comes with a price."

"Hai, Hitomi-sama," Sukune said, cutting off Daini's insulted exclamation. "The boy is proud—as he should be. He comes from a proud family, one with honor and courage, whose history is brave and true. Your family. He is your brother. Forgive him, and I will give you anything."

"You are my oath-sworn samurai, Sukune-san, and that means you have nothing that is not already mine," Hitomi's demanding hiss reminded him. "But there is one thing. I will not be questioned again. I grow tired of it. I am daimyo, and you, as well as the rest of our little family, will remember that. If I am questioned again by my brother or your son, you will commit seppuku to support my words. Is that understood?"

Sukune's eyes were haunted. "Hai, Hitomi-sama."

"I do not want to be daimyo, Sukune, but my blood demands it. And if I am to be the master of these provinces, the samurai under my command will serve me as I demand. Without question. I have little desire for the position, the title, or your respect. I only want vengeance for my brother's soul, and if I can best achieve that as daimyo of the Mirumoto family, then I will be daimyo. And you will obey me."

She turned toward Daini and sheathed the family's ancestral sword. "Never wear the symbol of our family again, Mirumoto Daini. Not until you have earned it." Hitomi headed for the doors, knowing she was once more in control.

There was much to do. Deep in thought, she stalked from the room, her anger restrained with thoughts of a bloody future. She would accept nothing less.

Daini and Sukune stared after their daimyo as she marched down the stone corridor outside the council chamber.

Nursing his cracked jaw, Daini caught his father's sleeve. "Your own daughter would ask for your death, Sukune-san!" He said with passion, "This has gone too far!"

"My daughter?" Sukune whispered sorrowfully, shaking his head. "No, Daini-san. She is my daimyo. It is her right to kill me if I give offense. That is bushido." Sukune turned suddenly toward the boy, and for a moment Daini thought the old man would raise his hand to strike him. "You will not question her again."

"Hai, Sukune-sama!" The once-proud boy stood cowed by his father's anger. He followed in silence as the old man walked slowly from the room.

4 DESCENT

The Dragon Mountains spanned most of the northern provinces of the empire of Rokugan, a wide wall of rock pointing toward the clouds and the sky. The armies of the Mirumoto moved slowly down twisted paths, passing beyond tall box canyons and into the hills beneath the mountain peaks. The trails slid slowly into less frigid lands, rolling over sharp passages and thin bridges of stone. If the armies had been advancing into these passages, they would surely have been lost to ice and assault from the guarded watchtowers of the Kitsuki. These were armies of the Dragon, though, traveling out of their homeland and into the empire. Once past the gates of the mountains, the way proved easier, and the days were marked with relief rather than concern.

At the root of the highest mountains, the Kitsuki palaces awaited them, opening their homes to the weary legions and restoring their food and supplies. Hitomi had often seen the Kitsuki palaces, but never felt truly welcome within them. Hitomi walked down the cliff side slowly, keeping her distance from the sharp edge of the mountain. She had been commanded by Yokuni to visit the gardens—commanded through Mitsu, which meant more puzzles to solve.

"In the gardens, you will meet your guide." Mitsu had grinned. "A guide fit for a celestial quest, a journey from darkness to light, from mountains to cities, from wilderness to war." It did not help when Mitsu spoke in riddles, but the Mirumoto daimyo had no choice except to comply.

At dawn, she left the encampment at the bottom of the mountain and headed for the gardens of the Kitsuki. She would not return without their guide. The others—her troops, advisors, and the still-forming supply train—would wait below until their daimyo returned.

She followed paths carved by a hundred years of labor. Her destination was a temple, the Kitsuki's most sacred site. It was called the Light of Shinsei, a fitting name for a structure made of glass and quartz. The clear stone shone with refracted light, glistening between the bosom of two majestic mountains. Built with soaring towers and high cliff gardens, it seemed to have formed from the stone by themselves.

Hitomi had visited the site once before, as a child, and the memory pulled at her heart. For a moment, she remembered Satsu carrying her to the center of the gardens so that she would not be afraid of the fall. Hitomi steeled herself against the image, and it faded with the early morning mist.

As she ascended the mountain path, Hitomi stared at the brilliance of the reflected light above her. The lowest edges of the temple melded into the stone, shining quartz blending into natural earth. At the front of the temple hung a mighty bell made of reddened bronze, surrounded by a maze of gardens and high walls. The bell was ten times the size of a man—three men high and as wide, hung from a carved stone torii arch that could be seen from outside the garden. The bell had no hook, no line of casting to mar its perfect surface, no sign of having been formed by the hands of man. Hitomi stared over the great hedge at the bell, marveling at its size and depth. Even through an adult's eyes, it seemed unreal—a monstrous work of iron and bronze that hung in silence at the center of a tremendous maze. When she reached the edge of the tall hedges, she could no longer see the torii or the marvel it supported. High walls of green and brown shrubs rose around her, a massive puzzle that must be solved. When she reached the center, she would see the bell once more.

Hitomi smiled as she entered the maze, remembering the tale Satsu had told her when they had walked the garden long ago. The first Mirumoto, challenged to prove his righteousness before Shinsei the prophet, had been told to navigate the gardens and return within an hour—an impossible task. The garden maze was limitless, formed by Agasha shugenja, conceived by those gifted with the sight of the Celestial Heavens. It was mystic, enigmatic, and fathomless. Many men had tried to make it through the elaborate gardens. Most had failed, turned back by the mysterious paths.

Mirumoto had simply smiled, bowed to Shinsei, and cut a way through with his sword.

It took Hitomi seven hours to navigate the maze. By the time she reached the bell at its center, it was past noon. She was pleased with her speed; Togashi Mitsu may have been able to walk through it faster, but it was no mean feat to find the center in the first place. Approaching the huge bronze bell, Hitomi smiled in victory.

The bell was considered a magical marvel, a site that holy pilgrims and those seeking enlightenment journeyed to visit. As she approached it, Hitomi could see that the frost-covered ground was strewn with prayer beads, written blessing strips on pure white paper, flowers, and incense. The bell's rich red bronze gleamed beneath the direct gaze of Lady Sun. It was a simple construct of metal and rope, but serenity and power emanated from it. It was as if Shinsei himself still stood beside the bell, giving his prayers voice through its sound and deepening the awe of the magnificent gardens.

Reverently, the Mirumoto daimyo touched the great bell, feeling warmth where the sun caressed the bronze. All was silent except for the wind that whispered inside the cupola. Hitomi noticed that the bell had no clapper, only a long wooden pole on its side, suspended from the edge of the torii arch. It was rung when a new Dragon Champion ascended the throne, and when an emperor was coronated— and some say it sounded by itself when Shinsei himself passed nearby.

Myths and legends, thought Hitomi.

Still, when the bell mysteriously sounded in the dead of night, all too often the guards of the maze could find no cause—no one who had been close enough or had strength enough to sound its call. That happened rarely, once in a generation or so, but often enough to keep the hearth-legend of Shinsei's immortality whispered through the Dragon lands.

Stretching her muscles and unwrapping the day's lunch, Hitomi rested within the central grove and waited for Mitsu's guide. The grounds around the bell were brown with autumn, and early snows lurked beneath the branches of each tree and shrub, hiding from Amaterasu's fiery gaze.

As she waited beside the huge bell, Hitomi scooped up a handful of snow and let it fall between her fingers. Winter was deepening across the Dragon Mountains, yet the Dragon were marching to war. She scowled with annoyance, unable to puzzle out her champion's orders. Dropping the snow, Hitomi looked for signs of others in the maze, but found none.

Hours passed. The sun sank in the heavens, full and warm on Hitomi's cheek. To amuse herself, Hitomi created a maze of sticks on the ground. Ants crawled between the makeshift walls of her labyrinth.

Are we only ants to Shinsei, she wondered?

Wind shook the trees, but when she looked up at the maze, it became as still as glass. It had been too long. No one was coming; the guide was no more than another riddle of the ise zumi, designed to make her puzzle out some elaborate truth. Hitomi kicked over the maze of sticks, watching as the ants scurried and fled in panic. Their little world had been destroyed, and they did not even know why it had existed in the first place.

Hitomi stood, brushing the dust from her clothing.

Satsu, Satsu. Where was your maze, at the end? What course would have left you alive beside me? My brother, Hitomi thought, kicking the sticks and watching the ants scurry about at her feet, what greater purpose took your life? Shaking her head and turning to leave, the daimyo of the Mirumoto sighed in exasperation. No matter what Mitsu had said, there was nothing here.

"Good afternoon, Daimyo-sama." The voice startled her. Only a moment ago, he had not been there.

The guide was tall and dark, but not handsome. His features were too bland, eyes too gray to be purely brown, hair the color of the muddy spring earth. He bore a rude staff, its tip whittled into a flute. Hardly a samurai at all, Hitomi thought, despite the aristocratic tilt of his slanted eyes and the courteous bow he performed for her. He was clean-shaven, his short hair covered by a brown hood that clung to the sides of his face, shadowing the hollows of his eyes. The man—a ronin, Hitomi presumed by his lack of a proper mon—wore a thin brown gi and hakima, hardly enough to shelter him from the morning frost and the cold wind of the Dragon Mountains. "You may call me Hyoji."

"Hyoji?" Hitomi said, not returning the ronin's greeting. "The word simply means 'guide'. You have no name?"

"No, my lady. I never needed one."

She looked curiously at him, noting his calm demeanor and completely assured stance. This was no ordinary ronin. Perhaps he had become dishonored through deeds that were not his own, or through the death of his lord. This could well have been a man with some sense of duty hidden beneath his drab clothing. Behind his false name, perhaps he hid a noble lineage—or perhaps some greater shame. It would pay to be cautious, but Togashi Yokuni himself had chosen this guide. It would only be correct to treat him with a modicum of honor.

"You are the man of whom Yokuni spoke?" The ronin nodded. "And how can you prove your purpose?" Hitomi stared frankly at the man, taking in his dusty and unkempt appearance.

"The Tao of Shinsei says one should never question a falling star, only follow where it leads." The ronin smiled easily.

Hitomi sniffed. "Quoting the Tao only tells me that you are educated, guide. Not that you can be trusted."

"True. But having come this far, how can you afford not to trust me?" His eyes twinkled in the shadow of his hood, and his hands fluttered expressively.

"Hmmph." Hitomi bowed slightly, accepting the man's purpose. "Come with me, and I will show you the armies of the Mirumoto. I hope you are more convincing when you meet them."

"My thanks, Lady Daimyo," he smiled gently. "I assure you, I will be." In the next few minutes, the mysterious guide proved very convincing, navigating the maze with unerring ease.

As they walked down the mountain toward the encampment, Hitomi lifted the cloth from her shoulders and wrapped her face in its folds. The valley where the Mirumoto camped was cold and it still had snow. The winds in it blew bitter and sharp.

"So, you are to lead us to the Unicorn legions?" Hitomi began, feeling out the man's thoughts and loyalties.

The ronin chuckled politely beneath his hood. "Oh, no, my lady."

"But Yokuni said that you would take us to Beiden Pass? That is in the Lion lands. Lions, then?"

"Lion lands, yes, Hitomi-sama," he smiled as he said her name, "But not Lion armies."

"Whose armies do we go to meet, then?"

"Toturi's."

Toturi. The very name was anathema. The man was a ronin, cast out of the emperor's presence and his own clan, a traitor to the Emerald Throne, allowed to live only as an example. Toturi's name was synonymous with shame. If he had armies to command, they were armies of ronin, warriors with no honor and little sense of duty. These were not men that could be trusted.

Though Hitomi had never met Toturi, she knew his description from numerous letters of the court, and from Yukihera's discussions. He was broad and handsome, with shoulders that could carry the world. His sword was plain, and his armor was laced with gold. Decorated once with the mon of the Akodo, it had been stripped with the destruction of his house. The Akodo had been destroyed by the emperor for failing in their duty to his father. In the madness of the Scorpion Clan Coup and Shoju's betrayal, Toturi had performed the greatest dishonor a samurai could: he had defied the emperor.

Seeing the distaste evident on Hitomi's face, poorly hidden even by the veils of bushido, the hooded ronin smiled. "Toturi's army rivals even your own, Hitomi-sama. I think you'll find that Togashi Yokuni-sama was wise to choose such an ally." Casually invoking the Dragon Champion's name, the ronin continued, "Yokuni knows how these battles will end. It is his way. We must trust him to choose the path that will best suit the Dragon—and the empire."

"Hai," Hitomi replied discouragingly, walking with even strides down the mountain path. If the ronin wished to prove his point, let him do it with speed, at a samurai's pace. With this new revelation, there was no time to argue. The Dragon Champion's orders had to be obeyed. Hitomi had no choice but to believe that this Hyoji had been sent by Yokuni to lead the Mirumoto to the ronin encampment.

An army of ronin, cursed Hitomi silently. And Sukune thinks to berate me about honor. When he hears this, he will truly have something to condemn.

"Hyoji, we must tell my generals that this is our champion's plan. I am certain they will like it no more than I do."

"Agreed, Hitomi-sama," the ronin said cheekily. "And I will go with you to explain Yokuni-sama's point of view."

"Yokuni-sama does not ask for explanation." Hitomi glared at the ronin, who trotted along beside her.

"Perhaps not, but today, he will need my voice."

"We shall see, guide. We shall see."

▲▲▲▲▲▲▲▲

The tent where the Mirumoto commanders met was sparse and bare, with only faint reminders of the prestige gathered within it. Kitsuki Yasu rested by the arched ceiling pole that held aloft the tent's silk roof. To one side, Mirumoto Sukune chewed a rice ball impatiently. His son knelt behind him on the plush cushions. Other samurai clustered on pillows and futon cushions around the small space, each commander wearing the badge of his or her legion on haori vests of shining gold and green. As one, they stared in confusion at their daimyo, unsure where this new path would lead them.

"Toturi," Hitomi repeated again, "is our ally. He will meet us in the Kanpun Vale, where his armies are located."

"This is by Yokuni's orders?" Yasu piped, his forehead furrowed in thought.

"So says the guide," Hitomi countered.

"Are we certain he was sent by the champion, Daimyo-sama?" Yukihera said quietly, without moving.

Eyes flickered toward the stranger, who walked quietly through the command tent, ignoring the others around him. As if unaware that he was being discussed, the ronin casually glanced at the Mirumoto swords, the gilded armor that Hitomi and her brother would wear into battle, and the tremendous golden banner of the Mirumoto guard. As he passed a corner table with loaded with food, the ronin lifted a bottle of water to his lips and seemed to savor the sweet purity of the far-off mountain stream.

Sukune coughed once sharply to gain the ronin's attention. "What say you, guide?"

"Yes, I was sent by Yokuni, General Sukune-sama. I ask you to trust me. You will follow me to the encampment of

Toturi the Black, and there, you will place yourselves under his command."

This casual statement raised disbelieving stares from the Mirumoto generals. Hitomi smiled in amusement at their distress. Some samurai muttered in anger, but before the mob could lose it temper entirely, one of the older and more revered commanders spoke.

Mirumoto Yendaku, a woman twice Hitomi's age, challenged, "Tell us who you are, ronin, that you would speak so frankly."

Many more challenges and arguments died out as the ronin stepped before the assembly. "No, lady," the ronin said bluntly. "Rather, let me tell you about yourselves." Amid the outraged cries of the generals and their aides, the guide lifted his hands and began to speak. "The Dragon sleep within their mountains, content to dream of puzzles and riddles while the world around them changes. You believe that in a single answer, you will find unalienable truth." The ronin grinned wickedly. "You are lying to yourselves. With no outside enemies, you find enemies among yourselves. You tear at the clan with claws and teeth, ripping open bellies to make a feast of your brother's flesh. And yet, the sleeping Dragon does not awaken—not for war, not for peace . . . not even for honor."

Several of the generals leapt to their feet at this blatant insult. Many gripped their weapon hilts with anger.

Hitomi watched the ronin smile behind his hood, his back to her generals as if uncaring. When she spoke, however, her voice was somber and stern. "Speak, guide. What do you have to say before we kill you?"

"Only that Yokuni has commanded me to take you to Beiden Pass, and I will do so with all speed. It is my place to show you the way." Hyoji shrugged casually. "Once there, the Dragon will do as Toturi commands. Block the Crab's passage. Drive them out of Beiden Pass. If you kill me, I cannot lead you. Do Dragons always disobey their champion so quickly?"

Mitsu smiled at the ronin's words, seeing some amusement hidden there. The ise zumi were unpredictable, and with a few words could change everyone's perspective. "I have heard the Master say we shall follow," Mitsu said, speaking of Yokuni, "and I know the guide to be true. Not all clams have pearls, says the Tao. Not all riddles have answers."

Tamori seethed. "It will take more than pretty words to convince me to ignore my honor. I will not serve a ronin."

"You will serve," Hitomi said slowly, "Because Yokuni has ordered that we serve, and because I order that you perform your duty. In the champion's name, I command it. I do not know Yokuni's mind, but I understand his orders and will obey them. Will you do any differently?"

Tamori said nothing, but Hitomi knew he was not convinced.

Sukune turned and sharply bowed to his lady. "Hitomi-sama, I beg permission to tell the Mirumoto troops. They will wish to know our plans and to make ready for the journey."

Slowly, Hitomi spoke. "Hai, Sukune-sama. I suggest the rest of you do the same for your men."

Yukihera and Tamori left together, disapproval written on their features. The two samurai were staunchly in the isolationist camp, though direct orders from Togashi Yokuni should have been enough to change even their stubborn minds.

There will be trouble there, Hitomi thought, but it is too late to change the past. The future must be seized with an iron fist, or it will be lost forever.

Hitomi caught murder in Yukihera's backward glance.

The ronin approached. "Will the Mirumoto believe?" He passed close to her shoulder and spoke softly as the generals bowed and filed out of the room. "Will they do their duty, or will they join the Agasha in rebellion?"

Hitomi gritted her teeth. "They will obey."

"Shall we go and see?"

"What?" Hitomi stared straight into his strange gray-brown eyes. "Go and see?"

"Yes, Hitomi-sama. You have shown me that you are a leader of generals, but not that you can lead simple men.

Do you think your Dragon samurai will so simply accept your command, based on the word of a ronin? Do your men trust you?"

"They do," she growled.

"I'd bet a zeni that they do not."

Impudence and arrogance again. Hitomi stifled the urge to strike the ronin down. "How dare you . . . ?"

He simply grinned. "Prove me wrong. Show me that they will listen."

Hitomi's face reddened in anger. With a fierce yank, she removed her ornate haori vest. Placing the embroidered mon of her rank and title aside, the daimyo of the Mirumoto gathered a plain brown cloak from the nearby clothing chest. "Very well, guide." She spun on one heel toward the silk door. "Come with me."

▲▲▲▲▲▲▲▲

As the herald of the Dragon passed through the encampment, shouting news of their new orders, a wave of anger and denial swept among the samurai.

Hitomi pulled her clothing close around her face, listening to the arguments at each cluster of tents. At last, she stopped at one of the farther groupings and listened as the herald finished his call. The messenger boy went on into the night, but Hitomi and the ronin remained to hear the samurai gathering for their meal.

The men talked around a large bonfire, ignoring the darkness and chill. One man, a Mirumoto with a scruffy beard and long hair pulled into a ponytail, cursed softly as he warmed his hands by the blaze. "Not our fault, really. Follow a ronin. We'll all die."

Others nodded, muttering in agreement.

The first man spoke again. "Pass me the rice, Gofumin-san, and help me forget my troubles. I've a girl waiting for me on the slopes of the Sekui mountain village, and it'll be many a long, cold night before I see her again." Laughter from the troops encouraged him, and he took a long swig from his draught.

"Puzzle this, Dragon," the first one said. "You'll never see her again. Forget her, Kuike-san."

A third and lower voice, somber and as bitter as the wind, said, "We're cursed, Gofumin. Cursed by bad blood, bad luck and a bad daimyo. Follow a ronin! Bah! Her father never would have allowed such a dishonor. We are all less because of Hitomi. Have you seen them? Kitsuki Yasu is no more than her ignorant puppy. Damn us all."

Hitomi shivered.

Mutters answered, and the man called Kuike stood up, tossing back his blanket angrily. "Remember bushido!" he cried, half-drunk.

"Bushido says your lord should be worthy of respect," Kitsuki Gofumin replied, holding out his rice wine. "Now, let's all drink to your lady at home, for the Fortunes know we cannot drink to our own. We should listen to the Agasha," he said to muttered agreement around the fire. "Even if they all commit seppuku before the battle, they'll at least die with honor and not in the command of dogs."

The others murmured agreement.

Hitomi faded back into the shadow of a larger tent and clutched her hood close about her face. So, the samurai did not trust her. Well, that did not matter. Only obedience and duty mattered. They would be enough.

The voices of the men at the bonfire grew loud once more, and Hitomi could not force herself to edge away.

"Ronin army?" one shouted, before the others could yell him down. "I am Mirumoto Shindo. I ask you, what honor lies in obeying the commands of an honorless dog?"

"Be quiet, you!" Kuike cuffed the speaker, shoving him back to his seat by the fire. "We serve. We do not ask questions or pass judgments. No, Gofumin, I'll speak now, and you'll be silent." The second man glowered grimly, but closed his mouth.

"We fight because we are Mirumoto. Because we are Kitsuki. Because we are Dragon. That is our riddle: to follow someone who is not worthy to lead; we must put aside our honor for honor. Like it or not, we serve Mirumoto Hitomi-sama. We are samurai, and we will fight for our clan, the same as any other samurai in the empire."

"If we fight under a ronin, we are dishonored." Shindo scowled.

Kuike guffawed. "No! If we fight at our daimyo's command, we are honorable! It is she who must bear the dishonor—or Yokuni, who commands her." At the mention of Yokuni's name, the men grew silent, drawing their blankets closer to their skins. "There is no dishonor for us."

"I am afraid, Kuike-san," Gofumin suddenly murmured, his voice drawn and his face pale in the flickering firelight. The others looked at him, shocked by his frank admission.

"A samurai is never afraid," Kuike said, kneeling beside his companion and pushing a warm cup of sake into the other man's hands.

"This is madness, to follow a daimyo we do not trust."

"We do not trust Hitomi, you are right," another Mirumoto samurai said, lifting his sake to his lips. "But honor will prove a substitute for loyalty, Kuike. Remember that, and you will see your Sekui mountain girl once more. I promise you."

A voice close by Hitomi's ear caused her to startle. "Hitomi-sama?" She jumped, reaching for her katana, but the speaker was only Yokuni's guide. The man stood hidden in the darkness by her side, his hood pulled close around his features. "Have you heard enough?" he whispered. Beneath the shadow and darkness, Hitomi could have sworn he was hiding an eagerness she had not felt in him before.

"Enough, damn you," she cursed. "More than enough to know that they will do their duty. And that is all I need to hear."

"Perhaps," the ronin nodded. "But you will be alone in this battle. Your samurai do not trust you."

"They do not have to." Her reply held a bitter finality. "Their duty is enough for me. These men are chattel, to be thrown before the wolves. When they die, their names will be forgotten because they were never even known."

He turned away. "And that is enough for me." Disapproval whispered through his voice.

Hitomi felt a strange sense of sorrow and loss.

"Come, Hitomi-sama. The sun has set, and it is time for rest. Though you choose a solitary path, even the single sword must know its saya and be sheathed." Bowing faintly, the ronin stepped away from the light of the bonfire and walked beside her into the darkness.

5 A WOLF IN THE FOLD

Hitomi spent the next several days riding alongside the massive armies, listening to her commanders plot their journey and hearing the endless messages sent by Kitsuki scouts. One pass was too small, another had snow, a third held a village that could not survive an army marching across its fields. By the time they reached the foothills of the Dragon lands, Hitomi was exhausted. The men did not fare much better.

On travel-weary legs, they made a lagging march across the plains of the Lion. Ahead, the Spine of the World Mountains rose with agonizing slowness.

"So much for fortitude," Sukune said mournfully when they finally neared the mountains. "The Dragon are not prepared for war. We have been too long in our mountains—too long. . . ."

"Enough, old man," Hitomi said without malice. She pointed across the dry plains.

"Look there."

Ahead, in the foothills of the Spine of the World Mountains, lay Toturi's encampment. Unicorn banners and the banners of several smaller clans fluttered from the tents. Above them, a wolf mon—unknown to Hitomi—stood out against the breeze.

"The ronin encampment." Hitomi said thoughtfully. Lifting her gaze above the banners, she made out Beiden Pass—a narrow cleft in the wall of mountains. "So, the guide did know what he was talking about."

"Toturi's personal banner is not among the tents. That means he has already left for battle," the ronin called back as if aware of Hitomi's scrutiny. "There . . . there he is." The ronin pointed toward a hillock where several riders raced over the crest of the hill. "Those are reserves. There is a battle. I'd recommend you send a messenger to the encampment Hitomi-sama. When they send word of Toturi's position, we can join in the fight."

As the messenger raced toward the encampment, Hitomi turned the rest of the army toward the distant hill. With luck, they would arrive in an hour, perhaps less. Soon enough to make a difference, if the Fortunes favored them.

Hitomi paused to look at the stream of Dragon legions as they marched past. Her commanders saluted, each one showing respect to the mon she bore. Few showed any more than was necessary, and no salute was accompanied by even a glance of favor to Hitomi herself.

In the ranks of the Agasha, Tamori rode a gentle bay steed beside Mirumoto Yukihera's large palomino.

Yukihera and Tamori, Hitomi thought critically. What plans are they making now?

Though Tamori had not made good on his threat of seppuku, Hitomi could feel the rising tensions in the troops as they approached their destination. Conflict was inevitable—and treachery . . . more so.

They rode with their heads bowed together, Yukihera smiling pleasantly as the older man laughed at some amusing quip.

Hitomi set heels to her mount and rode onward. She leaned into the gentle rocking of her horse's gait and tried to still her mind. The Mirumoto had taught her to meditate, to hush her inner voice, but Hitomi had never been very successful. Even now, it whispered past her mental barriers, shattering the silence with a word . . . Satsu.

How she missed him, his wisdom, his laughter. It felt as if her brother were only inches from her, as if her soul could reach out and take his hand. He was so close to her, yet his soul had never spoken. Not in the years that she had searched for him, searched for the answer to the riddle of his death. Satsu, why did you leave me? Where have you gone?

"Hitomi-sama." The sudden voice startled her out of the meditation. "Yasu has sent word. A messenger from the ronin encampment has arrived and is waiting to take you to Toturi's tent. The stonecutter awaits." Togashi Mitsu strode at Hitomi's side, his callused hand stroking her horse's fine mane. He smiled a wide, toothy grin at her.

"Stonecutter? Hmmph. And when did you get here? I thought you were marching with the Agasha."

"I have been with you all along, Hitomi-sama. You simply have not been looking."

"More riddles," she said. "Riddles tire me, Mitsu. Can you not speak plainly?"

"I am speaking plainly, daughter of Shosan. Listen closely, and you will hear the wind in my words."

She sighed, kicking her horse into a swift walk. "Come on then, Mitsu. If you intend to play this game with me, at least let me do my duty as daimyo between your enigmas."

"Better that you speak as a samurai than as daimyo. It will get you farther."

Hitomi laughed. "Speak, Mitsu? I don't speak. I only shout. Haven't you heard that from the men?"

"I'll teach you a speech, Hitomi-sama."

"Do."

"Have all, be all, see all, Daimyo." He chortled. "Know all, take all, break all, and let the thunder come. Forget."

"That's meaningless, Mitsu, and you know it. If you must teach, can you not find something more interesting . . . maybe some lessons from Shinsei's Tao?"

The big man grinned, and his muscled rippled under the coiling dragons tattooed across his bare chest. "You are not ready for the Tao. Shinsei speaks, and you do not hear him. Nothing comes from nothing, daimyo of the Mirumoto; your empty heart should know that, better than most."

Hitomi growled. "You strike too close, monk."

"I strike too high, and so do you."

Ignoring him, Hitomi stood up in her stirrups to see above the front line of her legions. Ahead, the banners of the ronin messengers flapped in a strong breeze, and Hitomi paused to consider their makeshift mon. "A wolf for mon. The blazon of a dishonored man, aloft on banners and tents. Toturi's gone mad."

"Mad wolves fight better." Mitsu countered. "They do not know death."

"Come on, riddler," Hitomi said, kicking her horse again. "Let go see what the ronin has in store."

▲ ▲ ▲ ▲ ▲ ▲ ▲ ▲

The lands of Beiden Pass were sharp and rugged, much like the mountains of Hitomi's home, except with sharper peaks. They reached toward the sky not as if to embrace it, but as if to tear the stars from their cradle. As the Dragon legions charged over the first hillock, Hitomi could hear the sounds of battle below. She looked down on a wave of Crab samurai within the pass, set against the scattered legions of Unicorn and ronin troops.

There, in the center of the conflict, Toturi's ronin banner waved.

"They fight without us," Daini snorted arrogantly. "Let us show them the difference between a battle and a war."

For once, Hitomi agreed with her brother. Turning in her saddle, she flashed him a sharp smile. "Very well, Daini. If you think so bravely, prove your courage. Take the first legion there," she pointed, "and destroy the archers that are ruining the game."

It was an honor to take the field first, and Daini straightened in his pony's saddle.

"Hai, Daimyo-sama!" He said sharply, signaling a unit of Dragon bushi to his side. They stormed down the hill toward the right, scattering Crab samurai before them like bark before a woodcutter's blade.

Hitomi swiftly put on her helmet, commanding each of her generals forward. A unit of bushi followed her down the hill, their faces serious with expectation. They met with the Crab at the edge of the clearing, their swords shining bright sunlight into the scattered scrub brush. Small groves of trees clung to the rocky the ground, their twisted branches recoiling before the mountain winds. Beneath the trees, ronin and Unicorn samurai littered the ground. The battle had been hard.

"There!" Hitomi's scout called. "Toturi!"

He fought on foot, garbed in armor painted black over gold laces.

Hitomi commanded her men to enter the combat, ignoring their weary faces. Fifteen days of hard marching, and then directly into combat; her father would disapprove. Hitomi grinned ferally. He would no longer disapprove when he saw the field littered with Crab.

The Dragon smashed ferociously into the Crab lines, taking out their commander with the first savage assault. Charging near Toturi, Hitomi and her elite guard cut down three Crab, sending their blood-spattered tetsubo flying in the air. The Dragon struck cruel cuts. There would be no mercy.

Toturi glanced toward Hitomi and her men, parrying another Crab and dancing out of the way of an arrow. His light-brown eyes brightened, and a smile showed beneath the ronin's mempo mask. A mane of thick black hair spilled from beneath his helmet and out over his do. The ends of his hair were still golden, a remnant of his days as champion of the Lion. Some things took time to heal; others never healed at all.

Which is Toturi, she wondered? The past, or the future?

Two Crab surrounded Hitomi, but she fought them both. Her katana twisted the first tetsubo blow aside, and her wakizashi cut through the laces of the second Crab's obi. He was not injured, but his armor fell open where the belt had been cut. With a savage stroke, Hitomi opened his belly.

Toturi stood his ground beside a gully, but his forces retreated ever farther from his position as the Crab pressed their line back.

"To the general!" Hitomi commanded, driving her mount forward. Her troops swiftly moved to follow her will.

They engaged the Crab almost immediately. To reach Toturi, the Dragon Clan would have to fight their way through the Hida line. A Crab screamed, and Hitomi turned to look.

Toturi cut the Crab's wooden club in two. "Fight with your grandfather's sword, Hida," Toturi said angrily, "and your honor will not fail you. Fight with a stick," the ronin sliced the Crab's head from his shoulders, "and you will fall."

Nearing Toturi, Hitomi caught another Crab's blow on her sword. She pushing the steel tip of his tetsubo away from Toturi's back. The Crab outnumbered them, and their long polearms reached through their guard.

One swing knocked Toturi's legs out from beneath him. The ronin was not injured, but as he rolled to find his feet again, another Crab charged.

Three of Hitomi's men leapt forward, cutting down the Crab warrior and fighting their way through to Hitomi and the ronin guard. Now she could see why Toturi had not been able to move away from the gully. Two of his ronin huddled there wounded, and the general had been protecting them with his own life.

What kind of commander risks himself for so small a price? Hitomi wondered. She stood above the wounded ronin, trading blows with a tremendous Hida.

The Crab smiled down at her, fetid breath wafting through the holes in his teeth. "Little Dragon," he said. "Die fast."

Cutting into his leg, Hitomi brought her wakizashi up to knock aside the Hida's massive axe. "Good suggestion," Hitomi countered, her black eyes shining with bloodlust. Slicing first through the Crab's arm and then his torso, she watched as the Hida fell.

Toturi pushed himself to his feet, lifting his sword into a ready stance. If Hitomi and her men had not arrived . . .

"Mirumoto Hitomi-sama?" Toturi said.

The Mirumoto daimyo nodded in return. "Do the Crab have reinforcements?" Hitomi called over the press of battle.

"Yes, in the west." Toturi pointed with his katana at a shattered cliff wall. "They will have to dig their way out. We have until nightfall before they can reach the battle, but by then, it will be finished. Thanks to you."

"Iie." She said curtly. "Thanks to my champion, who sends his regards."

He nodded. Toturi had a serious face, as if he rarely smiled. These days, Hitomi thought, what would he have to smile about? His family was dead, cast out, his name ruined. Though he had once been the greatest Akodo general in the empire, perhaps in history, now he was nothing but chaff before the wind. As were his men.

A cluster of Unicorn samurai charged past, their horses stirring the dust and grass. They drove back one Crab contingent, easing the pressure on the ronin and the daimyo. Another Crab unit swelled toward the field to meet them, outnumbering the Unicorn two to one. The odds were fair, Hitomi realized, because the horses fought for their masters. A Unicorn samurai fell from an arrow, but his steed continued to fight, tearing into the Crab with hooves and teeth. The stallion was brought down by a polearm with sharp teeth, but not before it had killed three men.

"The Unicorn samurai fight for you?"

"Hai. The Unicorn Clan has leant me some aid, now and again. I find their cavalry indispensable. Hanari in particular," Toturi gestured to a standard that bore the Shinjo mon, "is quite dedicated to defeating the Crab. He's remarkable."

"How many Crab are there?" Hitomi asked.

"Tens of thousand, and more, Mirumoto-sama. They have taken the pass and camped within it. We have skirmished with them a few times as our forces gathered, but never before have they fielded such a force as today. It is as though they plan to advance, not simply defend. They would have entirely overrun us except for your arrival. Now with your legions, we may be able to root them out of the mountains and back toward the Bayushi lands." Toturi smiled.

"The Dragon will crush them. Even now, they scatter." Hitomi glanced out at the battlefield.

Crab units sounded the retreat. The Dragon legions shouted victory, and raised their banners into the air. Their ronin and Unicorn allies cheered with them.

"With our aid, this war will end in days."

"The Crab have allies." Toturi said grimly. "Do not think peace will be so easy."

"Allies? Who? The Crane hate them, and the Phoenix are pacifists."

"There, Hitomi-sama," Toturi pointed, and his face turned grave. "There are the allies of the Crab, and pray to Shinsei that you never have to face them."

The Mirumoto daimyo looked at the retreating line of Crabs, beaten back by the Dragon troops. Sorcerers stood at the rear of the armies, chanting and lifting blood-stained knives. Where the Crab had passed, bodies began to move— the fallen, returning to life through dark powers of magic. Maho coursed through the air, raising bloodied corpses and returning their shattered bodies to a form of blasphemous life.

"By Togashi," Hitomi whispered, and the words caught in her throat. Some of the bodies lifting themselves to follow the Crab retreat were Dragon—her own men, fallen in combat. "Undead?"

"And more, Mirumoto. And more. They have summoned the beasts of the Dark God. Oni. Goblins." Toturi sheathed his sword as the tide of Crab warriors left the field. "Enough,

Hitomi-sama. Do not think on it now." Toturi's voice was commanding, and Hitomi fell back into stride beside him. "The Hida will send ambassadors. They were not aware that the Dragon were coming to our aid. We must shake them from the pass, and if we are careful, convince them that it is too big a risk for them to continue their war."

The two ronin in the gully stood, one supporting the other, and began to make their way back toward the encampment. As Hitomi watched the Crab and their undead hordes stagger back into the twisting corridors of Beiden Pass, she heard her own forces sound the retreat. The day was won.

Summoning her guard, Hitomi followed Toturi and pondered the implications of the ronin's words. The Shadowlands were a place of vile beasts and foul magic, where swamps of blood and brine swelled over wasted lands. If the Crab truly had allied with these creatures . . . Hitomi's thoughts grew angry. For nearly a thousand years, the Crab had protected Rokugan against such beasts, and now they fought beside them. It was obscene.

Tears stung Hitomi's eyes as she thought of the souls of her own men that had now been enslaved to the Shadowlands . . . by the Crab.

The Hida had fallen, and they deserved to be destroyed—utterly.

▲▲▲▲▲▲▲▲

That night, after the sun had fallen, the Crab ambassadors arrived. The Hida wished to speak with the Dragon Clan representative as soon as possible.

Hitomi followed Toturi toward the command tent where the Hida waited. She considered the Crab's options. They would try to force her to take her troops back to the Dragon Mountains, Hitomi surmised, and cut Toturi's reinforcements away before they could change the outcome of the war. She smiled to herself, but her eyes were as black as coals.

The Crab were in for a terrible surprise.

"They are waiting for you, my lord," said a guard at the command tent, and Hitomi recognized the Akodo accent. So this was where Toturi found his men. They were his brothers, members of the family that had been cast out with him. Sensible.

Toturi nodded. "Very well. Let us not make them wait any longer."

Inside Toturi's tent, samurai gathered beneath a flag of truce. Maps on rice paper were spread across a low table, depicting the pass and the lands surrounding it. On one side of the table sat Hida Tsuru, and two men in Crab armor. To the other side, space had been left for Hitomi and her men, and a seat in the center for Toturi. The Unicorn sent no ambassador—no doubt their legions were not large enough to warrant one, or else they did not wish to make their 'official' presence known. Most likely the latter, Hitomi thought quickly as she bowed and took her seat. Better that the Crab did not know the true strength of their enemy.

After polite greetings and small talk between Toturi and the Crab, Toturi sat at one side of the table. He was well aware that his position as a ronin gave him no authority here. The Mirumoto and the Hida glared across the table at each other, their weapons hanging tensely at their sides

Toturi began, "This is Mirumoto Hitomi-sama, daimyo of the Mirumoto family of the Dragon Clan. These are her men, Daini and Yukihera." Toturi began cautiously, "I assure you, we have the authority and the ability to drive your armies from Beiden Pass. Still, we do not wish to war with you, Hida-san. We all wish nothing more than peace."

"I have a greater wish than peace," Hitomi said suddenly, and all eyes turned to the female samurai in golden armor. "I wish to see the son of the Crab Champion strung on pikes from one end of the pass to the other. I desire his head skewered like a ripe tomato, looking down on his broken armies, and I wish his final moments to have been spent discovering the greatest pain that the empire has ever known." As Hitomi spoke, the Crab general turned to look at her, his eyes growing narrow. She continued, "And I wish, Tsuru-san, that you would

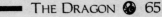

leave this tent, cut out the heart of Hida Yakamo, and place it at my feet."

"By the Fortunes," Daini whispered behind her, stunned at the hatred in his sister's voice.

Astoundingly, the Crab did not reach for the tetsubo at his belt. "Now, I remember you," he said, tugging on his beard. "You're that little girl who attacked Yakamo-sama on the fields of Otosan Uchi. So, you're daimyo now?" He snorted. "The Dragon are not men. Their books and riddles have softened their heads as well as their bodies. If you are their finest samurai, they should leap from their mountains like lemmings in a storm. The empire has no use for your clan, Mirumoto. Give yourself in penance to some Lion; perhaps they will break your stubborn spirit when they break your vow of chastity. In any case, you will get nothing from the Crab."

Hitomi leapt forward, her cushion sliding beneath her feet as she rose. Shaking with anger, she pointed a thin finger at the Hida and snarled, "You will be destroyed, along with your Shadowlands allies. It is a blasphemy to the emperor's name that you bring such creatures so far north. Have the Crab forgotten their duty?"

Tsuru's face turned gray and hard. The Crab stared coldly at Hitomi. "We will be keep Beiden Pass, and there is nothing you can do to dissuade us. You do not have the strength to carry on a large-scale war for long. Our troops are unending. You only feed them with your deaths. Can you afford the cost of such a war?"

"The cost?" she shouted. "It will cost us our souls if we do not fight you and your filthy hordes. Be warned, Hida. We will drag you screaming back to your wall and feed you to the beasts on the other side. If the Crab have forgotten their duty so easily, perhaps someone else can serve in your place."

"Hitomi-sama," Mitsu began warningly, but she ignored him.

"The Crab have butchered too many samurai to be forgiven, Tsuru," she said. "Too many have fallen to your pride. We will no longer sit quietly for your crude insults and your threats of war. Those threats are not currency any more. Take it back, and we'll pay your men instead with red blood and Dragon steel."

Toturi's amended, "The Dragon are correct in one thing, Tsuru. You will not continue to hold the pass with this army. We will not allow it."

"Allow? You?" Hida Tsuru barked sharp laughter, and his men grinned broken smiles. "As if we care what you allow. This is pathetic. A broken man, and a girl barely old enough to have curves on her chest think to bar my way? You'll die when the sun rises, mark my words." Tsuru spit upon the ground at Toturi's feet. "Take your pathetic legions away, Dragon. You are not suited for command. You should be home bearing children and bowing to your husband's desires. Your failure I can understand. But this?" he pointed rudely at Toturi. "A ronin who still thinks he is a general?" Loud laughter accompanied Tsuru's speech. "I will not bow to your idiocy. Death first."

"Then death you will have, Crab." Hitomi's blade was swift and sure. Before Tsuru could raise his own weapon, she was upon him.

Ronin guards jumped forward from the edges of the tent to stop her strike but were too late.

Tsuru recoiled in shock and reached for the tetsubo at his belt, but he could not stop her sudden motion.

At the last second, one of the Hida guards at Tsuru's side moved between the arc of the strike and his master's neck. Hitomi's katana fell short, cutting into the guard's throat instead of harming the Hida lord.

The guard's head fell to the ground. A scarlet pattern sprayed across the wall of the tent. The treaty papers were covered in blood.

Tsuru drew his weapon. His other guard stepped forward to defend him from another Dragon assault.

Hitomi fell into a battle stance, her katana ready to strike.

Behind her, Daini drew his own weapon, following his daimyo's lead. Beads of sweat stood out on his pale forehead.

Yukihera did not move, but stood as silent as the stone beneath their feet.

Toturi's bass voice rumbled through the tent. "Stop this carnage!" Ronin guards poured in through the tent opening, surrounding them all.

The Crab and Dragon samurai froze as the guards formed a barrier of human bodies between them.

"So, this is your 'hospitality' Toturi," Tsuru spat. "How quickly a man without honor becomes no more than an animal."

"Go, Tsuru. Return to your encampment. There will be no treaty," Toturi said coldly.

"No, Toturi. No treaty, and no peace." The Hida stared menacingly at Hitomi. "And there will be war. So much that Beiden Pass will run a river of blood for years to come."

Without putting away their weapons, the Crab left the tent, feet stomping on the hard-packed ground.

Once they had left, Toturi whirled on the Mirumoto daimyo. Losing his façade, Toturi's true anger showed past his solemn face of command. Now there was nothing but contempt and bitterness in his eyes. "Are you mad?"

"No more than you," she retorted angrily. "To think that Crab would ever honor a treaty, no matter how well planned. Now there will be honest war."

"Honest . . . ?" Toturi's hands shook in rage, and he clenched them into fists. "Damn you, you've condemned my men—and your own—to death."

"My men know their duty. Bushido . . ."

"To die foolishly?" He barked, "No, Daimyo, that's no one's duty."

Hitomi stepped forward until she stood only inches from the mighty general. Her black eyes were barely at shoulder-height, but she showed no fear. With fire in her voice, Hitomi said, "Bushido demands that they serve me, and I say they war upon the Crab. Toturi, I am sworn to lend you my troops, but I am not sworn to respect you." Her scorn colored each word. "You are a ronin, Toturi. You lost your right to tell me what to do when your honor was stripped away. My troops fight beside you because they know it is their duty to obey me, and I must obey Yokuni-sama. They fight for no other reason.

"Remember that."

Toturi's eyes narrowed. "Hai, Daimyo-sama," he said slowly, biting back angry words.

▲▲▲▲▲▲▲▲

Outside the command tent, Daini and Yukihera waited during Hitomi's argument with Toturi. They listened to each word, hoping the fiery accusations would die down. They watched the retreating backs of the Crab ambassadors. Blood stained the silk of their gi. The ronin guards whispered of Hitomi's rash actions.

Hitomi emerged, her face red and clenched. She strode past them as if they weren't there.

"She is mad," murmured Daini.

When Hitomi was out of earshot, Yukihera responded. "She may be, Daini. I do not know her reasons, but I know they are not ours. For ten years, Hitomi has done nothing for the Dragon except seek to further her own goals. Since Satsu died, she has been consumed by this . . . revenge that she seeks against the Crab Clan. She stood before the Shrine of Shinsei and swore that, before she died, the life of Hida Yakamo would end on her blade. These are not the commands of a daimyo; they are the bitter words of a child.

"Daini." Yukihera's words were calm. "Something is wrong with Hitomi. Her soul is broken, and it always has been. Ten years ago, my father invited you and your sister into our home after your father's death. I have spent ten years watching Hitomi squander your heritage, Daini. Where was she, when you won the contest of niten? Where was she when you proved your worth and honored your family name? She has refused the lessons of Shinsei and the prophets, and turned her every thought to battle. She does the same today. Soon, Dragon samurai will die for her obsession." The Dragon general stood beside the youth, hand balanced on the hilt of his sword. "She is too eager, Daini. Yokuni was wrong to send her. He was wrong to send us all here. The Dragon have no place in this war."

"He is our champion. . . ." Daini began hesitatingly.

"Hai, he is, and I will serve him to my death. But even Yokuni is a mortal man. He could not have known this would happen." Yukihera stared after the retreating figure of the Mirumoto daimyo. He placed his hand on Daini's shoulder in a gesture of brotherhood. Daini flinched from the touch, but Yukihera did not seem to notice. "Thank the Fortunes, Yokuni also sent you."

"Me?"

"Yes, Brother." Yukihera shook his head. "I only hope you have the courage to take command when Hitomi falls."

"Falls? Hitomi will not fall."

"You have heard the tale of how she took Yakamo's hand? She will charge the Crab lines, seeking Yakamo, and when she does, they will kill her. The Mirumoto family will turn to you for courage, for strength. It is your duty. Your sister may be consumed, but you are a beacon of honor that will drive away her madness. You must be strong, Daini." The samurai's voice was impassioned. "Only you, son of Shosan, can save the clan. You will be a hero—the savior of the Dragon Clan."

"Rightful path . . . Yukihera, you speak treason."

He smiled. "No, Daini. To save the clan from destruction is not treason. It is bushido—to serve the clan more than yourself. You know as well as I do that these lands are not the place for us. When you lead us home, Yokuni will certainly know that you are the wise and noble samurai your father once was. All you must do is claim the title of daimyo after Hitomi has destroyed herself through her madness. Then you and Tamori can vote to bring us home again. The clan will know that you are right."

"Like my father," said Daini only half-listening. "Yes, Shosan was a good man who knew the price of duty. I would do well to be like him."

"And you are like him. It is your destiny, Daini. Only you, the true son of Shosan, can save us."

Daini's voice was filled with wonder and arrogance. He asked hopefully, "My destiny?"

"Yes, Daini-sama." Yukihera afforded the youth the title typically restricted to the daimyo, and Daini's face lit with pride. "And if you do not fulfill it, we are all doomed."

"Hitomi's path could destroy the clan," Daini nodded, nearly convinced. "But I will save it."

"You will be daimyo, and you will command the loyalty of thousands of men. Your time is soon, if you choose to step forward and grasp it. Your time will begin, when Hitomi falls."

"If she falls, Yukihera," Daini said, already lost in visions of banners and parades.

"Of course, my daimyo." Yukihera bowed politely. "Of course."

6 THE TIES OF BLOOD

The dawn brought with it winds of battle, blowing through Beiden Pass and howling across stone precipices. Thick fog rolled down from the high mountains, covering the valleys in clouds and mist. The morning sun was too weak to pierce it, and it clung to the ground like a snake, twisting slowly through the pass.

Within that fog advanced a huge army of Crab and Shadowlands monsters. They were shrouded from sight, but their feet made a low thunder against the stones. They marched out of the pass, as if they sought battle elsewhere.

Ronin and Dragon alike were ready for them. They rushed down the foothills like an avalanche to catch the Crab near a hollow gorge. Thin columns of stone loomed across the misty hills and cut the battlefield with their dark shadows.

It is not the pretty battlefield of Crane

stories, thought Hitomi as she ran full out toward battle, but more the nightmare terrain of Jigoku itself.

Hida Yakamo, commander of the Crab, had arrayed his forces with the undead in front, sacrificing mobility to provide a fearless line against the ferocious Dragons. Shadowlands mujina, winged scouts no longer than a man's arm, swirled in the mist that eddied before the Dragon lines, shouting out the Dragons' position and movements. Archers shot arrows at the small creatures, but they dexterously avoided them, screaming wildly and looping in the air above the legion lines.

"I have the small ones," Togashi Mitsu smiled, tightening his hands into fists even as he ran. He stared at the mujina scouts, his tattoos beginning to glow and his eyes brightening in anticipation. For a moment, he closed his eyes as if in prayer. When he opened them, the tattoos on his body writhed like dragons come to life. Smoke bellowed from the thick man's mouth. With a kiop scream, he roared fire from his lungs toward the darting creatures.

A long, arching gout of flame burned away the fog and struck squarely. Mujina twisted within its heat. Togashi Mitsu continued the incendiary stream, burning the spies down from the sky.

Other tattooed ise zumi ran to his aid, leaping among the scattered boulders with the surefootedness of mountain goats. As they reached each mujina, the ise zumi stepped on the creatures' necks to silence their screams. Sharp snaps echoed from beneath ise zumi feet, and the small creatures flapped limply on the ground. Soon, no more came near the Dragon armies—none dared.

Mitsu headed off through the fog, wanting to guard the Kitsuki lines from similar spies.

Another ise zumi sprang into the air near the Mirumoto lines. He reached the first rank of undead well before his fellows. With a chant to Shinsei, he gripped the arms of two of the undead and stomped upon the ground. From beneath his feet came a dangerous rumble.

Trying to pull away from the ise zumi, the two undead swordsmen turned empty eyes on the tattooed monk. Before they could swing, the ground where they stood shattered, sending stone splinters up through the two undead. They exploded into pieces, torn apart by the massive stalagmites.

At the ise zumi's silent call, more shards of stone, as high as a tall man, burst up from beneath the ground. The monk continued his dance, and the summoned stalagmites cracked, rolling down the steep hillside toward the rest of the undead. Boulders and shafts of stone formed a rockslide that swept the legion's brittle legs out from under them and crushed their armored skeletons. Soon, half the undead legion had been crushed, buried by tons of stone.

Weary from his magic, the Dragon ise zumi bounded away. His mountain tattoo gleamed brightly on his muscular back.

Arrows launched from the Hida lines, parting the Kitsuki and Mirumoto into two units. The Crab archers poured shafts into the center of the charging Dragon, trying to force them to retreat and regroup. It did not work; the Mirumoto continued their charge, driving through the ranks of zombies. With a thundering clash, the two armies met at last.

Hitomi's men leapt into the fray, following their commander with a speed born of duty. They met the Hida guards, piercing the left flank of their army and driving the Crab farther down the incline. More Crab flooded the flat ground at the bottom of the hill. They lowered their pikes to deflect the rush of Dragon steel. Three men died, screaming, on the tips of those iron spears before Hitomi's unit could stop their rush. Four more fell to Crab swords as they tried to avoid the fence of iron before them.

While her troops fought to break up the pikemen, Hitomi scanned the battlefield for Yakamo's guard. She found them easily, fighting beneath bright red banners. Yakamo led the human vanguard, and his troops slaughtered the Kitsuki that had pierced the zombie guard. Yakamo's men cut down the Dragon with glee, their shouts clear over the sounds of closer combat.

"Damn you, Yakamo. Fight me!" Hitomi said, driving her katana through a Crab samurai's chest.

"My lady, we should retreat," one of her men told her. "The fighting on the east has grown worse. The Kitsuki are outmanned and overwhelmed by archers. They won't last long without us."

"Damn them!" Hitomi cursed. "You see that tall guard to the south?" Hitomi pointed through the thick mist, outlining the huge forms of ogres. "Those beasts guard the rearward flank of the army, between the lines and the archer reserves. If we can destroy that unit, we can assault their reserves," Hitomi said. "Their archers won't stand for long after that strike."

"My lady, wouldn't it be better to head for the Kitsuki troops and guard them? The assault would be slower but preferable to the losses we will take from charging the Crab lines—"

"Do not question me!" Hitomi screamed in rage. "Charge that line! NOW!" Sword raised, she led her men. A company of sixty formed up around her and charged.

The ogres hunched in a clearing at the bottom of a ridge, beneath the line of pikemen. Hitomi's men ran full out toward them. The ogres were slow to rouse, but then delightedly lifted their tremendous tree trunk clubs.

Hitomi sliced into an ogre's leg with all her might, stunned that her blade did not reach all the way through the creature's massive calf. Dark blood gushed forth, but Hitomi leapt away. A club smashed to ground just behind her, and then the ogre that wielded it.

Another ogre dropped his tree trunk, grasped a Mirumoto samurai by his torso, and hurled him toward the Crab lines.

The man screamed, his body landing on the sharpened iron spikes. Pierced by their blades, he twitched in agony for a few seconds, and then lay still.

The ogre laughed at the sport, reaching to hurl more of Hitomi's men after the first. By the fistful, the Mirumoto were borne high into the air. They arched wildly as they landed on the dark and bloody pikes. The Crab cheered the ogre's game.

Hitomi's eyes narrowed. Hatred filled her soul, and she charged two of the ogres. She leapt to plant her sword in a great, gelatinous eye.

The wounded ogre shrieked, swinging his club to strike the samurai, but she was already gone.

Hitomi dropped to the ground and flung herself away from the ogres, keeping the Mirumoto sword close to her chest as she rolled. She had dodged the club, but the ogre had also misjudged its strike. Hitomi saw the wounded ogre's massive club fly past her and crush his companion's head. Screams broke out among the ogre guards, and fighting soon followed.

"Now!" she shouted. "Bring them down!"

The last of her men charged once more, assaulting the tendons of the ogres' ankles and cutting the backs of their giant knees. When the last of the ogres fell, clutching at now-useless legs, the Mirumoto backed away.

Hitomi rose, her family's sword clasped in a steel fist. Thirty more of her men were dead, and at least fifteen lay on the ground, clutching their bleeding wounds. Hitomi nodded to the survivors, noting that the ogres had fallen well inside Crab battle lines. They had penetrated deeply through the line of defense and were close to the Crab reserve.

Fourteen men and the Mirumoto daimyo against as many as a hundred Hida samurai—their chances were not good. Looking back through heavy arrow fire, Hitomi saw the Shadowlands troops close behind them. Only the confusing mists kept Hitomi and her band from being swarmed. It would be impossible to take the men back through the lines to safety.

The only way to go, then, Hitomi reasoned with a feral smile, was toward the Crab generals, and attempt to remove the head of the serpent before the body had died.

Yakamo's unit was near the archers. It was a common tactic to allow archer fire to weaken an enemy, and then send a small but elite force to mop up any resistance. Yakamo and the Crab had used it two years ago, against the Scorpion at Otosan

Uchi; they would be using it now. The mist would hide the Dragon from Crab eyes . . . until it was too late for the Hida to stop them.

"Form a wedge behind me, and we will carve our way there," Hitomi pointed across a unit of undead toward the main Crab command group. "The Hida have lost our position, and that will be our advantage. They will not know where we are going to strike. We will crush their archer line, and keep them from murdering our reserves."

"But, Hitomi-sama," said a shocked Mirumoto, "that will take us directly into their elite squads. We'll be destroyed. Please, is it not better to circle the lines and travel east, through the brush and slopes, and form back at the ronin camp? Toturi will be waiting for us there, and he would not approve—"

Before the man could finish speaking, her sword was pointed at his throat. Hitomi had murder in her eyes. "Any man who believes I need Toturi's approval may slice open his own belly now. I have no time for traitors."

Shocked, the men stared numbly at their general. "Hai," one whispered, unwilling to call her bluff.

"For the Mirumoto, and the Iron Mountain," Hitomi hissed. She turned as she pulled her second sword free of its scabbard and began a silent charge. The others followed.

Shrouded in mist, the Crab archers had not anticipated an aggressive strike. Blades leapt at them out of the fog. The bows in their hands snapped, sliced in two. Dragon swords continued on to chop heads from shoulders and cut men through the middle. In moments, the Crab archers were decimated.

Hitomi and her small band stood in the midst of slain foes. Battle sounds rang and echoed through the mist, and Hitomi glimpsed the forms of Crab samurai as they advanced.

"He is here," Hitomi snarled, pushing a Hida from her blade with a shove of her boot. "Yakamo!" She howled into the sorcerous wind. "Show yourself, son of Kisada!"

Then she spotted him, bathed in the sickly green light of the fog. Hearing his name, Yakamo turned toward Hitomi, and he peered through the flickering light.

He was as she remembered; tall, broad, ruggedly handsome, his mustache sweeping down past the line of his stone jaw. Black hair that had once been tied tightly back beneath his helmet now sprang free, clinging to the sweat on his face and neck. He wore no mempo mask—the son of the Crab Champion needed none—and he stood nearly a head above the men he commanded. Dark eyes flashed as he lifted his tetsubo from the broken remains of one of the Kitsuki. One hand was covered by a steel gauntlet, but the other . . . where his left hand had once been, there was now a hideous claw, fashioned of some strange carapace or steel. It moved as if with the power of Yakamo's thoughts. All around him, nearly forty Hida battled staunch Kitsuki troops.

The Dragon samurai were losing, and Hitomi could hear Yakamo's laughter as he shattered their line.

It could not be. She had taken his hand at Otosan Uchi. He should have been a cripple—a broken man, one-handed and weak. Hitomi's brow furrowed as she fought to understand.

The claw snapped through a corpse that stood in Yakamo's way, cutting through the man's spine with little effort. The Crab smiled, a wide, mocking smile, and he stepped over the bodies of the dead to approach her. She had expected a one-handed samurai, capable only of tactics and small defense, but now she faced a monster.

Hitomi stared toward him, her hand frozen on the hilt of her katana. "You," she screamed. "You will fight me!"

Yakamo shouted from across the short distance. "I know you, girl," he yelled. "You took my hand."

"You killed my brother!" Hitomi cried, tears stinging her eyes as she faced this demon of her nightmares. He was larger than she had imagined, with rippling muscles tensing across his bare shoulders.

"Your brother, the fool. I remember Satsu well, I do. He died too quickly. But you . . ." Yakamo smiled broadly, snapping the tremendous claw together with a thunderous sound. "For taking my hand, girl, you will die slowly."

Hitomi's men streamed past her, engaging the Crab squadron and holding back their lines. A few of the Kitsuki joined Hitomi's guard, renewing their strength against the Hida. The Mirumoto daimyo did not move, but stood still and waited for Hida Yakamo to come.

Time . . . the time had come . . . finally. . . .

Hitomi struggled to calm her inner voice, but her thoughts were as short as her own breath, whistling out in ragged lines. Far off, she saw Mirumoto Daini and his small guard, standing atop a prominence and staring down at the fight. Daini's eyes were fixed upon her.

Yakamo was hers. Hitomi gritted her teeth. "Watch all you wish, little brother," she whispered. "Now you will see how a true samurai claims vengeance for the dead."

As soon as Yakamo was within range of her katana, she struck. The swift song of her first strike screamed into the Crab's claw, ringing as if it had struck pure stone.

Hida Yakamo laughed as her sword continued in a fierce flurry of blows. He blocked each of them unerringly with his massive arm.

Niten taught nothing within its ancient scrolls that had prepared Hitomi for this moment. Yakamo continued laughing, watching as she parried his tetsubo and struck again.

Again, the claw bashed her blade away. It did not matter how swift she was, how cunning—the claw stood ever in her way. His return tetsubo blows rained down like lightning strikes. The steel-spiked club tore into the earth beneath her feet as she leapt and spun. Timing and rhythm, timing and . . . a perfect strike, but Yakamo's claw parried easily. Hitomi screamed in frustration.

His tetsubo crashed into her leg, bruising the bone and nearly knocking her from her feet. His claw snapped toward her thigh. Her leg twisted from the pressure of claw and iron. Another ruthless blow, and her helm was crushed, tilting crazily across her eyes. Yanking it from her head and throwing the useless piece of metal to the ground, she turned to face him. Blood trailed from the wound on her scalp, but she did not care.

"An exceptional weapon, is it not?" Yakamo taunted. "Kuni Yori granted it to me, when you took my hand at Otosan Uchi. I am so glad you came to test it. I have been waiting to see exactly what it can do. I'm told that it burns with fire when it cuts you," he laughed. "I think we shall soon see, little girl."

Hitomi limped forward, raising her swords once more for another series of strikes. Her leg had almost certainly fractured beneath Yakamo's blow, but it still held. Each feint, each movement was an agony as her twisted leg burned from pain. Quickly, as they circled, Hitomi assessed the wound. Suddenly, she realized her danger. Wounded, she would not survive long behind the Crab lines. At any moment the troops could break free of her guardsmen and come to the aid of their commander. If she was going to do something, it had had to be now.

"You won't be running away this time, child," he laughed. "Nor will your Dragon clan mates save you. In a moment, they are going to watch you die."

As he spoke, Hitomi took advantage of the terrain. She leapt onto a large rock that was sunken into the ground. Moving with agile steps up the face of the boulder, she twisted her body through the air, above his guard, her sword ringing against his helm as she leapt upside down toward his throat.

The sounds of battle stopped. She felt her sword sink bloodily into his flesh.

Landing heavily, Hitomi staggered forward from her acrobatics, her leg giving way. The fractured bone buckled, and she fell to the ground. Hitomi looked up, sweat stinging her eyes, desperate to see if Yakamo still stood.

He stood, though the left side of his armor was stained with his own blood. His tetsubo lay upon the ground at his feet, but he did not seem to notice. His human hand reached up to touch the mark that shone redly across his left shoulder.

"You don't understand, girl," he snarled, looking down first at the slash, and then at the claw. As he did, the maw of the pincers started to close. The claw began to move. The wound seemed to knit together before her eyes.

"No . . ." Hitomi whispered in shock.

Yakamo grinned, catching her left hand in his human one before she could recover. "It gives me strength greater than any man has known. I am no longer a man. I am something more." He flexed his massive muscles, and the claw snapped together, echoing the ringing sound of steel.

With a precise motion, he lifted the massive claw to her right hand, catching her katana, handle, and fist within its mighty embrace. She screamed as it touched her, feeling the taint within the monstrous hand. Slowly, like a vice and a lever, Yakamo closed the twin jaws of the claw, piercing her skin and shattering her bone. Fire burst from her wound where the claw tore her flesh. Greenish and foul, the flames burned within her wound, charring her enameled do and scorching her skin. Hitomi screamed in anguish.

"I should have killed you when you were a child," Yakamo snarled viciously, watching the fire burn. He twisted her limb beneath the terrible strength of his steel and armored claw, ripping part bone and sinew.

Hitomi cried out twice more before he finished with her—once when her own hand was severed, and once when she heard the unmistakable sound of the ancestral Dragon sword, the Mirumoto sword of her forefathers, breaking in two.

The Dragon reserves suddenly crashed through the Crab lines, scattering their samurai like chaff.

Yakamo looked up and saw his Hida guard being torn apart by the renewed Kitsuki legions. He threw Hitomi to the ground. The Dragon were coming, and soon he would have no place to hide. Faking bravado, Yakamo spat, "Enough of this game. There is a war to be won. A victory that you will never see, girl," he said to the fallen samurai. Backing away from the advancing Mirumoto, Yakamo summoned his Hida guards. "Now that you are broken, your death does not interest me. I will leave you, as you once left me. Your death will come, soon enough." Turning, Yakamo strode toward his men to continue the fight.

Behind him lay the ruined form of the Mirumoto daimyo, twisted like a paper door in a sudden storm. She had lost too much blood. Hitomi's body lay on the field, blood streaming from her nose and eyes, limbs bent in a mockery of the human form. One hand—the right—was severed completely, lying beside the remnants of a broken katana. Blearily, Hitomi looked across the field.

Mirumoto bodies littered the ground like wooden dolls, covered in the blood of their wounds. The Crab drove the Kitsuki back once more. With Yakamo at their side, the Hida were unstoppable.

With the last of her strength, Hitomi looked at the silhouette on the cliff. "Daini," she whispered through her agony, trying to rise. "Daini, help me. . . ."

▲▲▲▲▲▲▲▲

From high ground, Daini looked down at Hitomi's fight with the son of the Crab Champion, his eyes haunted and afraid. He stood above the main battlefield, watching.

Daini's legion had been one of the first to charge; badly injured, they had been called back soon after their battle had been won. From then on, Daini had stood above the massive combat, watching the battle unfold. He had seen Hitomi charge into the Crab lines, had seen her throw away her men's lives against ogres and Hida guards, had seen Yakamo find her, seen them exchange blows. . . .

Even now, Yakamo struck her savagely. Daini watched in silence. His sister fell. The Crab bent over her, clasped her wrist in that horrid claw, and pinched. There was blood, lots of blood. When at last the Hida dropped her to the ground and marched away, Daini turned from the battle.

"Sir," one of his men called, pointing down at the fallen daimyo. "Hitomi might still be alive . . . There is a chance. . . . She is still moving."

"We cannot move that far through the Crab lines. It is too dangerous." Daini tried to believe his own words, fighting to sound confident. "Where is your command?" he asked the Kitsuki soldier.

The man's face paled in shame and anger. "Dead, my lord. All dead, to a man."

Daini nodded arrogantly. "Yakamo has reinforced their northern perimeter and is using the high wall of that canyon to block any further Dragon advance. We must strike on the south side, as Toturi-san advised. If we try to save Hitomi, we will lose the battle." Forcing sorrow into his words, he said carefully. "There is nothing that can be done. My sister is already lost," Daini said to the soldier. "Let us give her death honor through our valor."

The soldier bowed understandingly. "Hai, my daimyo. As you command."

As the man strode to relay his orders, Mirumoto Daini looked down at the faintly struggling form in the ravine below.

Is she still fighting to live, he asked himself?

Instead of the elation that he had expected, Daini felt dread creep through his bones.

I can still help her. The thought came unbidden to his mind. Hitomi is still alive.

"No. She is dead," he said firmly, willing it to be true. Then without looking again, Mirumoto Daini turned his back on the field.

▲▲▲▲▲▲▲▲

Sukune rested inside the command tent, allowing one of the Agasha healers to tend a minor wrist injury he had suffered that day. Nearby, Togashi Mitsu ate like a hungry wolf from a lacquered bowl, humming to himself softly between scoops of thick noodles.

Toturi looked over the day's maps. The fighting had not gone well for the allied armies. Grim reports were still coming in. The Crab had struck several mighty blows against their position. More ominously, Yakamo had led a huge contingent of Crab and Shadowlands forces southeast along the foothills of the Spine of the World. Toturi hadn't enough troops to chase them down and simultaneously take back the pass, but he sent mounted Unicorn scouts to dog their heels. It would not do to let Yakamo circle around behind them. The battle had quickly turned grim.

The tent flap opened. Mirumoto Daini stood there.

Sukune looked up and motioned for the Agasha healer to move away.

Daini stepped inside the tent, removing his gilded helmet and bowing politely to the men before him. He approached his surrogate father, general of the Dragon armies.

With a low nod, Sukune acknowledged his son's respect. Noticing that Daini was alone, he asked, "Where is Hitomi-sama?"

Daini spoke carefully, as if he had rehearsed the words. "She is dead, my lord, on the field of battle." His voice was weary, laden with grief, and his hand reached unconsciously to stroke his thin mustache.

Sukune gasped, his face tightening with the sudden news. "Dead? My daughter is dead? You have seen this, Daini? You are certain?"

"I am, Father," Daini replied. "I witnessed it with my own eyes."

Sorrowfully, Toturi said, "You have my condolences, Sukune-sama. May her soul find with ease the peace of Jigoku."

"Oh, Fortunes." Sukune's voice broke with sudden grief. "I feared this day would come. My daughter, why did you not listen to our warnings?" The old man seemed to shrink, and his head lowered with sorrow. "We must have a ceremony for her soul. Her ashes must be sent to the Iron Mountain of the Mirumoto, to be kept with those of her father and brother."

"No," Togashi Mitsu said suddenly, looking up from his bowl. "She is not dead."

Daini countered, "She is dead, Togashi-san. Fallen to the Crab, as I had feared. Our warnings were not enough. . . ."

"She is not dead," Mitsu insisted stubbornly. "You did not see her fall. She could be a prisoner, captive, something."

"No, Mitsu-san," Daini interjected. "I did see. I watched her being cut down by Hida Yakamo. She did not live through his attack."

"No. You must be wrong."

Toturi raised his hand to the tattooed man. "Mitsu-san, Daini has given testimony."

"But Yokuni-sama would have known—she can't be dead."

"She is lost to us," Daini said. "There are many who saw her fall against Yakamo, and she has not returned. I know that Hitomi was companion to you, and perhaps friend. Many here will miss her," Daini lied easily. "But I say with honor that she is dead. I saw more than the others did. I watched from the lines of command as she was struck down, and I saw her die at Yakamo's hand. You have my word."

Togashi Mitsu paused, obviously dumbfounded. To question a samurai's given word was tantamount to personal insult; Daini would demand the right to a duel. The Dragon could not afford another death. "But, my lord Daini-san," Mitsu struggled, "the Tao teaches us that a stone unturned is enlightenment ignored. Should we not send scouts to recover the body?"

"Not necessary," Daini said. "No doubt the creatures of the Shadowlands have taken the body away." His voice was uncomfortable, and he shifted his weight between his feet.

"I'm certain, Mitsu-san," Toturi's diplomatic voice came from across the tent, "that Daini's word is unquestioned. This is a time of sorrow and grief. Come, let us leave the family to their memories." The general motioned for his men to move outside. He stared openly at the tattooed ise zumi until Mitsu moved reluctantly to the tent flap.

"Hitomi has a destiny to fulfill, Daini-san. I pray, when next you meet—in this life or beyond—that she will forgive you." With that, Mitsu turned and left the tent.

Toturi followed behind him, brow furrowed in thought.

Sukune motioned to the Agasha. With a polite bow, the healer gathered her herbs and departed. Soon the news would be spread across the armies.

"You saw her die," Sukune demanded after they had gone. His eyes were guarded. Mitsu's outburst had offended him, yes, but more telling was Daini's obvious discomfort.

The youth looked down, his eyes darkening and his hands clenching into fists. "I saw her die."

"Look at me, Daini," Sukune said, rising from his seat. He moved dangerously, anger rising in his belly. "Look at me!"

Daini looked up, then, and Sukune was amazed at the rage and hatred in the young samurai's eyes. "Yes, I saw her, Father," Daini said. "I saw her charge the Crab lines, murdering her men and butchering the Kitsuki with her arrogance. I saw Hitomi call out Yakamo, daring him to fight her. And I watched her die at his hand."

"You are certain she was dead? How far distant were you—one mile? Two? From the hilltop where you were stationed, you must have had a clear view.

"I did," Daini said, eyes flashing a challenge. "Do you wish to dispute my word? I am certain that Toturi-sama would arbitrate our duel."

Sukune's fist clenched.

Daini reached for his sword-hilt before the old man could move. "Hitomi tried that on me once, Father. I learned my 'lessons' from her, and there will be no more."

"Hitomi is not dead," Sukune whispered. "I see deceit in your face, I see the lie in your eyes. I am your father. You will tell me the truth!" Sukune's fist pounded the table, making the maps and figures dance from the blow.

"She may as well be dead, Father, and if she is not, she certainly will be before dawn. The creatures of the Shadowlands feast during the night."

"By Shinsei's Tao, Daini. She is your sister!"

"You know as well as I do, Father, that she would have seen us both dead. She threatened your life, because I had the audacity to ask a simple question. The Mirumoto were falling apart. Her vengeance and hatred of the Crab nearly destroyed our clan, and would certainly have destroyed us. Can you say that I have done wrong to save their lives?" Daini stepped closer to his father, his face within inches of Sukune. "Can you say I have acted with dishonor, to save my father's life? If you do, Sukune, then by all means question my word. Ask Toturi to arbitrate a duel, and kill me. I won't take back my words, but you may take my life for trying to give you back yours."

"You have lied to the clan, and brought dishonor on our house. Your word means nothing."

"You have already lost a daughter, with or without my lies. Even if I had saved her life on the battlegrounds today, she would have only charged the Crab again tomorrow. And the next dawn, and the next, until the entire Dragon Clan was slaughtered to please her mad quest. I will do what is necessary to save the clan, to save my family, and to save my father from her insanity." The young samurai stepped away, headed toward the tent flap with petty, angry strides. "I am daimyo now, Sukune-san. You are no longer my advisor." Daini made a slashing motion with his hand, cutting off the old man's protest. "Yukihera knows all the wisdom that you once held, and he will be a more fitting advisor for my new reign. The Dragon Clan is mine. Let the world mourn Hitomi as an honorable woman who died for her cause. Better that than to allow the Dragon to die for her revenge."

As the tent flap closed, Sukune sank to his knees. The weight of his burden settled on his shoulders. Hitomi would die on the bloody soil at Beiden Pass, her flesh eaten by the beasts of the Dark God, and he would forever bear part of the blame for allowing the lie to be believed. They were all lost—Hitomi, Daini, and himself. Cursed for their dishonor, and for their weakness.

"Daini, my son," he whispered brokenly, "What have you done to us all?"

▲▲▲▲▲▲▲▲

The woman's body was cold, but not yet dead. Scavengers scuttled about the battlefield, their howls and eerie cries lifting the hair on the samurai's neck. Men were still dying, and their moans drifted on the evening's last light within a cold, uncaring wind. Occasionally, one would scream—and the cry would be cut off, killed by creatures that feasted on the dying and dead. Necromancers lingered like smoke in the hills of Beiden Pass, working their foul magic on the bodies left behind. Others walked there as well, but their steps were silent, hushed by the shadow of the growing night.

The man who walked through the shadows did not envy those who would fight on the morrow and see the dead faces of their own men. He knew the sorcery of the necromancers . . . and he did not approve.

Kneeling beside the woman, he looked for life within the twisted limbs. Her chest rose and fell faintly. Good. The bandage he had applied to her severed arm was red and hard with blood. Signs of death hung close around her, hovering like a crow's wings in flight. Even if she survived, she would be a cripple, broken and cut to pieces like so much rotten flesh. The world had no further use for her.

Therefore, she would not be missed.

He lifted her shattered form from the cold ground and cradled it in his arms, chanting the mantra of light and darkness. Where one could not go, the other thrived—and all shadow was alike, to him. His deep voice whispered beneath his mask, and his eyes closed. The air thickened, and darkness clustered about him in blankets of heat and the faint smell of decay. One word, another, and a step into the shadow. . . .

When the moon rose into a jealous sky, they were gone.

7 OMENS

Yukihera sat in the daimyo's tent, his noble brow furrowed in thought. Outside, the battle with the Crab had hardly begun; Hitomi had been slain in the opening salvo, the Mirumoto line had broken, and the Crab had become completely entrenched. From the outside, Beiden Pass was a losing battle, one that no samurai would have wished to join. To Yukihera, it was already the site of his greatest triumph . . . and his destiny.

From inside the Dragon commander's tent on the hillocks above the battlefield, Yukihera studied the maps of the battle. So many dead . . . so many Dragon lost to this foolish war. Now the Mirumoto samurai were even less confident in their ability to find victory. Hitomi had been insane, but she had been a known quantity. Already, the troops of the Dragon guard whispered that his cousin, Daini, was not fit for the throne. He was only a boy, ten years younger than Yukihera, and already he was to lead them into war? Preposterous. The troops were nervous, facing a war with no general save a stripling who had barely traded his childhood toys for a sword.

It was exactly as Mirumoto Yukihera had known they would respond.

Outwardly, he appeared somber, thoughtful, even concerned. The flush on his thin features could be attributed to his eagerness, even excitement, at being taken into his lord's confidence. After all, the Mirumoto youth before him would need all the assistance he could find, if Daini were to keep his father's throne.

With swift strides, Mirumoto Daini paced through the tent, turning this way and that as the silk walls barred his movements. Sweat beaded on the young boy's brow, and with an impatient hand, he fingered the enameled hilt of his elaborate katana. "He should have returned."

"No, he is on time, and will be a bit longer. Meetings with the commanders go well," Yukihera lied smoothly. "You have the trust of the men."

"Good." Daini looked no further than his cousin's words.

"Do not worry, Daini-sama," Yukihera said smoothly. "Such unrest is common when a daimyo dies. It is even more common in times of war. This is both, and we must expect the men to be unsettled."

"They admire you, Yukihera. You should talk to them. Tell them I am worthy."

"I will, and I do, my daimyo. I spend a great deal of time with the men, I assure you."

Daini paused in his pacing, considering Yukihera's words.

For a moment the golden samurai thought that he had underestimated his cousin. Then, Daini seemed to shrug away the discontent, and Yukihera nodded in approval.

Poor Daini, thought Yukihera. If you cannot trust your own cousin, then your battle is already lost.

Daini's nervous eyes flitted toward the tent opening once more, and he counted the seconds. His hand clenched on the hilt of his weapon, and his light brown eyes flared as the boy sought peace. After a moment, Daini opened his mouth to speak, but his words were lost in the sudden rustle of the tent flap.

Kitsuki Yasu stepped into the tent cautiously, his eyes adjusting to the gloom from the bright sun of the summer day outside. "My lord called for me?"

"Hai," Daini said swiftly—too swiftly. The Mirumoto daimyo nearly jumped toward his cushion, sitting down on it in a rustle of expensive silk. He wore the hakima made for his sister, tied back to fit his more slender form. "Sit down, Yasu-sam—san. Sit down."

Yasu cautiously settled on the pillows, a look of concern in his eyes. "My lord, should you not be readying for the battle?"

"Yes, of course, but there is something more important right now."

"More . . . ?"

"I need you to perform a task for me, Yasu."

"Me? Perform a task for a Mirumoto? You think too highly of yourself, Daini. Such pride is not worthy of your new position."

"Bah," Daini waved his thin hands in the air as if to ward off an invisible spirit. "I do not ask you as my servant, but as my compatriot beneath the banner of our clan." Seeing that Yasu was skeptical, Daini rushed on. "My sister is dead, we all know that."

"Your testimony—"

Daini cut him off. "She is dead, but she died bearing my father's sword. I cannot leave the men in this condition. To see me vanish from them would cause them to lose confidence in me. I must remain here and give them a leader." Daini did not even seem to realize he was using Yukihera's words, so easily did they follow his thoughts. "I cannot go into the battlefield to retrieve it. Even if the men could afford to be without me for the hours it would take, to risk my own life would be dangerous. If I die, the Mirumoto have no daimyo, and they will not fight. Your own men are not here."

"Not a large contingent, no, but I have my guard."

Waving this aside, Daini plunged forward. "Yukihera believes . . . I believe," he said with more confidence, "that you should be the one to retrieve my father's sword. It would be in the best interest of the clan. I will stay with the men and raise their spirits and their trust. If the sword is found, then they will know the Fortunes are still with us."

Yasu's eyes flicked first to the silent Mirumoto Yukihera, and then back to the rambling boy, whose elaborate hat slid slightly down over his too-thin face. Yukihera could almost hear the Kitsuki daimyo's obvious thoughts: Daini was only sixteen, and already making critical errors. Send a Kitsuki to retrieve his father's sword? Ludicrous.

Then Yasu looked back at Yukihera, and the young Mirumoto general whispered four words that he knew Daini would not overhear. "Agree. There is more."

Obviously uncertain whom to trust, Yasu nodded.

"Excellent!" Daini flushed, believing he had won the point. Proud, he began elaborating on Hitomi's position, where her troops were when she fell. "You must check that entire rise," Daini said. "The sword could be anywhere."

"Are you certain it was not taken by the Crab?"

"Oh, no," Daini countered. "It can be touched only by Dragon hands. Its magic prevents anyone who is not loyal to our champion from touching the blade. They say it knows our blood."

"Interesting magic," Yasu muttered.

"You will go?"

"I have not said that, Mirumoto-san."

"You must. You must!" Daini's impatience colored his voice, and he leaned forward to place one fist on the low table between them. "The sword is everything. I cannot go. What else do you need to hear?"

Yasu's scorn was apparent. "I need to hear some good reason why my life and the lives of my men should be wasted for your pride."

Daini reared back as if struck, and his mouth hung open. Twisting it into a snarl, he shouted. "You will go, Kitsuki! I command it!" Pounding on the table, Daini bawled again, "I command it!"

"You command nothing here, Daini. I am a Kitsuki, not a Mirumoto. Send your own men, if you wish, but I have no duty to you." Standing abruptly, Yasu managed a curt bow before throwing open the flap of the Mirumoto tent. "Think better on your words in the future, Daimyo," he said sharply. "And find your own damned sword." Yasu stormed out of the tent, insulted and furious.

"He thinks I am nothing more than a boy who wishes his toy returned to him!" Daini fumed.

"He does not understand, my daimyo," Yukihera said swiftly, standing to follow Yasu. "Allow me to speak with him." Daini nodded, and Yukihera stepped out of the tent, jogging to catch up to Yasu.

"Let him find it himself," Yasu muttered angrily as Yukihera approached. "The Kitsuki are lapdogs to no one; not the Agasha, not this arrogant ronin general, and certainly not the Mirumoto." His feet pounding the ground beneath him, Kitsuki Yasu marched toward his family's golden banners.

"Yasu, wait," Yukihera called. "I wish a word with you."

"Tell me quickly, Mirumoto," Yasu snapped angrily. "For I have little patience with your family today."

"Very well. Then I shall tell you without on—without the face that covers our actions. You are a Kitsuki. You can speak freely. Listen as freely, and understand." Yukihera fell into step with the Kitsuki daimyo, keeping his voice lowered as they headed for the outskirts of the encampment. "You know that I have asked Daini to allow you to do this, but you do not know why."

"The boy is a fool to listen to you. This is madness."

"Not madness. Pride." Yukihera stopped short, blocking Yasu's path. "The boy is too young, Yasu-sama. We both know that. He watched his sister fall, and his father's hatred prevents him from honoring her spirit."

"What?"

"You asked for Hitomi's hand. I believe you loved her." Watching the other samurai's face flush, he continued. "I am correct. You did. Then you understand why Daini—and I—

cannot leave her body on that field for the crows and the necromancers. Sukune has forbidden any Mirumoto from looking for her body on the field. He does not wish her to be buried, does not wish her soul to find the peace of Jigoku and the afterlife."

Shocked, Yasu stared frankly into the Mirumoto's eyes. "Why?"

"For the same reason he forbade your marriage. Oh, yes, Yasu, I know this. And you would do well to believe me. Hitomi would have married you, but her father forbade it. You were not suited, he said, to rule at her side."

Yasu's face turned dark, his brows clenching under a wave of anger. "You do not tell the truth."

"I am a samurai, Yasu. I tell only the truth. What reason would I have to lie? She is dead now. The past is gone. There is nothing to be gained from making you angry at my family. By your own logic, I must be telling you the truth, for a lie would be useless.

"Hmmph. Then you send me to find Hitomi?"

Yukihera stepped closer, his voice low. "I send you to break a lie, Kitsuki, as your family is renowned for doing. We do not know. . . ." He paused as another group of samurai passed the Kitsuki daimyo, bowing as they walked by. "Only Daini has given testimony that she is dead. Another samurai— one of the men in the honored daimyo's command—tells a different tale."

"You accuse Daini of lying?"

"I accuse no one. I wish to find the truth. If Hitomi is alive, then every second counts. The search for the sword is nothing. You are right. I have persuaded the boy to allow it, out of his own pride and arrogance, but I have asked that you perform this task not to find the sword, but to find her. The Kitsuki are not bound by the traditions of law. Where other samurai must listen to sworn testimony and not question, only your family in all the empire has the right to seek fact and evidence."

Despite his distaste for the Kitsuki methods, even Yukihera had to admit that they were effective. The Rokugani system of law was clear: A samurai's word was his bond, and if questioned, a duel had to occur in view of a temple of Shinsei the prophet. The victor, obviously blessed by the Fortunes, was deemed correct. This law was inviolate and revered by every family in the empire. Except for the Kitsuki.

"Yasu-sama, please. Listen to me. Your family is the only one allowed to question the word of a samurai. Your own ancestors tracked down a poisoner and brought him before the court—despite all testimony to the contrary. Your house was founded on asking questions when no one else in the empire would ask them. How is this different? Daini believes one thing, and he will swear to what he believes. But he does not know. None of us know the truth, and without it, we cannot let her spirit rest. Daini will do nothing. If he questions this, he questions himself, and he cannot allow that to be seen. Only the Kitsuki can honorably question the sworn testimony of a samurai without calling for a duel."

"You believe she is alive?" Yasu asked, hope lighting his features.

"I cannot say. It is not my place, as a Mirumoto. But where you find her father's katana, I am certain you will also find Hitomi." Yukihera's face was the very model of hope and frustration. "I believe that you loved her, Kitsuki Yasu. Find her."

In an instant, Yasu made his choice. "Tell your daimyo that I will seek his sword."

"Go with Shinsei, Yasu."

"I will, my friend. And thank you," Yasu bowed to the Mirumoto, his swords clicking in his obi, "for all you have done."

As Yasu hurried to find his horse and travel to the battlefield, Yukihera allowed himself the faintest of smiles.

▲▲▲▲▲▲▲▲

The battlefield was littered with corpses—some moving, some still. Zombies marched toward Crab lines, led by foul necromancers with power over their decaying flesh. Yasu crept silently, leaving his horse behind the first knoll.

She had to be alive. She had to be.

From his first days at Mirumoto Academy, he had loved her. Remembering now, he blessed the long fall of he hair. When they had been children, they had held hands and giggled behind shoji screens, playing a game of daimyo and samurai that held some hint of courting. Then came that fateful duel, and Hitomi had cut her glorious hair. They grew older, Hitomi grew harder, and Yasu desired her all the more. He wanted to marry her, but her brother Satsu stood in the way. Not as some men do, with protective eyes and a frown, but from the otherworld, Jigoku, where the spirits go.

Sighing, Yasu moved from rock to rock, using the light of the full moon to navigate his path. No lanterns were needed, and it was easy to recognize the frozen looks of horror and pain on the faces of the dead men he passed.

Some of were his own men.

Yasu closed his eyes to death and remembered Hitomi once more. He remembered the dagger slash as her long hair fell on the tournament field. She had been eight years old. Eight, and full of anger and hatred toward a world that had taken away her only hero. Nothing Yasu did, or could have done, could change her back to the laughing young girl he had known. The days of touching palms were done. A sword filled her hand, and revenge stole her heart. How different it could have been, if the Crab and Dragon had not met for that fateful duel in Bayushi lands.

But they did, and their insult was met. Yasu hardly remembered the reason for the duel—only the outcome. The Dragon resisted the duel until the last moment, when a drunken Hida Yakamo and his men did something disgraceful to Satsu's young bride—some said abduction, some said worse. Sleeping in the child's room, surrounded by shoji screens, Yasu could still hear the low tones of the son of the Mirumoto daimyo and the Dragon Champion speaking late into the night. He could not hear their words, but he understood their tone. Something terrible had occurred, or was occurring. The voices were low, and cold, and dark.

The next morning, the Crab killed Satsu. There were no repercussions from the Dragon.

It was over . . . but not for her.

Yasu swallowed his emotions, trying to force his mind back to his work. He missed her . . . how he missed her. Hitomi was no longer the smiling young girl he remembered but a cold daimyo on her ivory throne. Her laughter came rarely these days, if at all, and her smile was as cold as the mountaintops of his homeland. But under her armor, her heart was still sitting in the center of Satsu's tournament field, weeping blood upon her brother's grave.

Yasu reached another group of fallen samurai and stopped his careful tracking to honor the dead. One body, two—ah, these were Dragon. Kneeling beside one of the corpses, the Kitsuki daimyo lifted the armor plating to reveal the mon. Mirumoto. Careful not to touch the dead flesh of the samurai, Yasu placed the armored scale in his pouch. These men had been in Hitomi's guard. She would not be far now.

A soft moan came.

Yasu reached for his sword before realizing the sound had come from one of the men on the ground. Stepping quickly to its source, he noticed that one of the Mirumoto was still breathing.

"Hai, samurai, can you move?" he hissed, not wanting to attract the attention of either the necromancers or their minions.

The Mirumoto stared up at him with glazed eyes, dried blood marking the man's forehead and neck.

"Mirumoto-san?" Kitsuki Yasu searched the man for other injuries, but aside from a broken arm, there were none.

"Hai, I know you . . . Ki'suki-sama." The voice slurred, hardly recognizable. Teeth were missing. A concussion. Not good signs.

Yasu had some medical training, enough to know that this samurai had likely been struck by a powerful tetsubo to the head and left for dead. Ten hours later, he awoke on the battlefield, lucky no one had stopped to make sure.

"Have you seen your lady? Hitomi-sama? Have you seen her?"

The samurai's face contorted into a scowl, and he tried to pull himself upright. "Dead, by Shinsei, and damn well."

The backhanded strike surprised Yasu as much as it did the other man. The Mirumoto reeled as Yasu drew back his fist again.

"Never speak that way of your daimyo," Yasu said, shaking. The Mirumoto stared up at him in fear, stunned by the sudden assault. "Where is she?"

"There . . . there." The Mirumoto pointed, lying back and reaching to nurse his bruised cheek. "He killed her by that stone."

"Who?" Yasu gritted his teeth.

"Hida Yakamo. She left us . . . to fight 'im. She ran, and he followed, and we were butchered by the Hida infantry. I saw her cut down by his claw. Then they hit me, and . . . it all goes dark. Nothing more, Kitsuki-sama, I swear it. That's all I know."

"Your name?"

"Shiyando. Mirumoto Shiyando."

"Shiyando." Yasu nodded, storing the name in his memory in case he needed it. "Do not worry. You will live to fight for the Mirumoto another day. Can you walk?" When the samurai nodded faintly, Yasu pointed toward the camp. "That way. There is a horse behind that knoll. Take it and return to your daimyo. He will need you."

"Hai, sama."

Yasu stood, walking toward the boulder. A terrible duel had occurred here. Scuffed footprints spoke of a massive assault by a smaller samurai against a man of tremendous size and girth. Here, blood spattered a large boulder. There, fragments of bone—someone had been badly injured. The Kitsuki's analytical mind frantically began to piece together the fight, noting each small piece of information and tucking it away. Footsteps, then a slide and stagger. She had been hurt—a leg injury, Yasu guessed from the soft marks of that foot thereafter.

The Crab's steps were solid and hard, save this one point. They lightened. Perhaps the sign of an injury? Then they began again, as fresh as before despite the blood that trickled along the ground beside them. The blood was thick and dark, the mark of a major vein severed, but there were no bodies beside the boulder, nothing left behind—and here, the blood slowed. There, it stopped completely.

"Shinsei the prophet," Yasu whispered. "What passed here? Wounds do not close, they do not simply vanish. This is not possible. The marks show . . ."

The scrub grass was imprinted, scuffed and bloodied, and fragments of armor littered the hard-packed earth beneath. Hitomi's body was gone, but the signs showed a great amount of blood and shattered armor. Nothing could have lived through such torture. Many bodies were missing from the battlefield, faceless minions of the necromancers and their porcelain masks. Could hers be one of those risen dead, animated by the enchanted clay that clung to their faces and held onto their tormented souls?

Yasu scanned the ground for signs, and saw the marks of another visitor to the battle site. Softer footprints, these, pressed into the ground so lightly that even the adept Kitsuki tracker had missed them for a moment. Someone had come and borne away the body. But to where? For what purpose? The tracks vanished. Yasu cursed, confused. The evidence pointed to her death, but no samurai would steal the body of the dead. It was forbidden. A necromancer might have seized her corpse, but then there would be marks of two pairs of sandaled feet: the sorcerer and the risen corpse. There was only one pair of footprints here, and they vanished into the grass like a snake into water.

Then he saw it, lying on the ground in a dried pool of blood, its silvered blade shining vainly despite the gore on its blade. Cruel marks of striated metal covered its once-elegant surface. Twisted and forgotten, it glittered as if trying to reclaim forgotten glories. Her sword. The sword of the Mirumoto ancestors, honored for a thousand years. Every daimyo had carried it, passed it down to son or daughter with honor and tradition. It was said that the ancestral sword would not break until the Mirumoto had dishonored themselves or the world was about to end.

Shattered, twisted in two, it had been left in the dirt like trash.

"No," Yasu whispered, touching the hilt of the broken blade. "Hitomi . . . it can't be true. You cannot fall."

The sword glimmered a moment in the moonlight, and then the shimmer died. She would never have left her katana behind, and any man who had taken the living daimyo would have carried off the sword as a victory prize—a ruse to further blaspheme the name of the Mirumoto. She must be out there, somewhere within the Crab lines. Another corpse among the servants of Fu Leng. It was the only answer. All the evidence pointed to it, and Yasu's mind was too well trained to ignore what he had found.

Defeated, Yasu knelt beside Hitomi's broken sword and wept.

▲▲▲▲▲▲▲▲

"Broken, my lord, and all the magic of the Agasha cannot restore it." Tamori purred like a cat, unable to contain his smug smile even beneath the protocol of a gathering.

Assembled in the Dragon command tent on top of Beiden Pass's rolling hills, the daimyo and generals of the Dragon murmured in concern at the shugenja's words. The tent was dark, and the night outside seemed to push closer against the thin silk walls, pressing through despite the bright lanterns and the soft firelight.

Daini felt the night pressing closer, capturing him within its iron grasp. His ploy had worked—Yasu had returned with the broken sword—but now everything was falling apart again.

The Kitsuki daimyo did not speak and had hardly moved at all. From his knees, he looked up at the Agasha shugenja and the others, uncaring about or unaware of the Mirumoto samurai that had begun to cluster about them for news of Hitomi. Since delivering the sword to Mirumoto Daini, Yasu had seemed lost in his own thoughts.

"The soul of the sword is broken," Tamori continued quietly, turning his eyes away from Kitsuki Yasu. "It is an omen. The Fortunes have spoken of the dishonor that the children of Shosan have brought to the Mirumoto. The legend of the sword says that it will break only when the Mirumoto line has dishonored themselves or the world is ending. I do not see the end of the world, Daini-san."

Mutters among the Mirumoto troops turned the youth's face red with embarrassment.

"I am sorry, Daini. The spirits speak through this sword's wounds. The line of Shosan is no longer worthy to carry the name of daimyo. A new sword must be forged, a new path chosen," Tamori said easily. "Who is worthy to accept the burden?"

More mutters, and some of the samurai began to speak Yukihera's name.

The golden samurai raised his hands and silenced them. "I am not worthy," he said loudly to the men.

"You tried!" one of the commanders shouted. "You stood for us, Yukihera, and you fought for the Mirumoto! Yukihera-sama!" Hands leapt into the air, waving madly. The murmurs turned to shouts.

With a raised eyebrow, Tamori turned to face Yukihera.

"Are you strong enough, Mirumoto Yukihera, to bear the burden of this duty?" the shugenja asked. He was still holding the broken sword, but now it seemed he would place it at Yukihera's feet.

"What my family demands of me, I must perform. I will send a message to Yokuni-sama, requesting that he place me upon the seat of daimyo of the Mirumoto. With his blessing, I will lead," Yukihera said, a beatific expression shining beneath his golden helm.

Another cheer went up from the men.

"By the fortunes . . . what have I done?" Daini whispered, looking away from the shouting Dragon samurai. He watched as his visions of the future turned to desolate ash. The Mirumoto adored Yukihera, their golden samurai. They would follow him anywhere.

"No," whispered Mitsu, his hand on Daini's shoulder. Mitsu's quiet rebuke kept Daini still, even before his mind could register the thought of leaving the tent. "You cannot turn your back on this, Daini."

Daini looked up into the face of the riddler, expecting more, but nothing came. "I am not daimyo."

"You are not the riddle, Daini. You are an answer. The mountain has many paths to its top. Remember that."

"Yukihera knew that Hitomi would charge—he told me—he kept me from following her." Daini whispered "By Shinsei and the Fortunes. . . ."

"Mirumoto Daini, what do you have to say for your line?" Yukihera said clearly, his voice loud above the cheers of the Mirumoto samurai.

Another samurai might have leapt forward, challenging Yukihera to a duel. Daini was not the warrior that his sister had been. Sixteen, frightened, and played for a fool, Daini knew that to challenge Yukihera would mean his death. Yet to bow to Yukihera meant giving up the position of daimyo and accepting the shame of his family's broken sword.

Either way, Yukihera won. Mitsu was right.

"I . . . await your command, my daimyo," Daini choked, lowering his head.

The gathered samurai broke into cheers.

Mitsu's hand tightened on the youth's shoulders, giving him courage.

As Tamori chanted the ritual blessing of the ascension, Daini looked up into Mitsu's sympathetic eyes.

"We will remember, you and I," the ise zumi spoke softly. "And when the time comes, we will know. Samurai cannot live in shadow forever. One day, they must return to the light."

Daini heard Mitsu's words faintly, through a blur of sound and motion. The Mirumoto clan haori was stripped from him and placed upon Yukihera's broad shoulders as an emblem of his new command. Looking down, Daini saw that his sister's sword—the family sword—had been placed on the ground before him. Shattered. Broken. Like him, it had no saya, no sheath, no home and no purpose. It was Mirumoto still, but of no use at all.

Samurai cannot live in shadow forever.

Wherever this shadow of dishonor would take him, he would follow. "Hitomi, forgive me," Daini whispered, picking up the sword.

8   POISONOUS TRUTHS

Darkness. Shouting. Pain . . .

Agony lanced through her shoulder as if the world were on fire. It ripped Hitomi's flesh.

Jerking awake, she screamed, her voice raw and hoarse. Something was missing. Her hand. Hitomi looked down at the blackened stump that had once been her sword arm, and she screamed again. The burly man held her down, pressing her body back against the futon as the servant once more touched cauterizing fire to the wound.

Shinsei, no! Not my arm, not my hand, no!

Hitomi fought weakly, her strength sapped by countless wounds and endless pain. Her leg was broken. Her skull felt cracked, and blood had dried beneath her tattered gi. The pain abated, numbed, fell away.

The heimin servant removed the flaming brand from the stump of her arm and placed it back in the coals of a nearby brazier.

The room spun crazily, brown wood panels and soft paper screens. Patterns on the screens made no sense to Hitomi's blurring vision. Men. People. Gardens. Colors swirled together, dancing in the light of the brazier's coals.

"The lady will come to speak with you soon," the man hissed into Hitomi's ear. "You will be cleaned first, and given the chance to rest." He nodded, looking back at the servant. The weight lifted, no longer holding her torso flat. The man turned to the servant. "You are done?"

"Hai, Bayushi-sama," the heimin bowed prostrate, touching his forehead to the floor.

Hitomi saw her captor more clearly. A black mask hid his features, but his arms and shoulders were muscular. He wore the burgundy and black of Shoju's men.

This must be a dream, a nightmare. The Scorpion are no more.

She did not realize that she had spoken aloud until he answered. "You are wrong, Lady Mirumoto," the samurai said scornfully, moving back to allow the heimin to pass. He stood, reaching for a pair of swords in their enameled saya that hung carefully by the door. "You will find that you are wrong about a great many things."

Darkness gathered at the corners of Hitomi's eyes, and she raised the stump of her ruined arm. "I want to be wrong about one thing, Scorpion," she gasped faintly, the words an effort. Looking back at him and letting the arm fall, she continued. "That I am alive."

His features remained still beneath his black mask. As he slid the shoji screens open and stepped through, Hitomi glimpsed the hallway and rooms beyond. Suddenly she knew where she had been brought.

Otosan Uchi, home of Emperor Hantei the 39th, the Eternal City of Light.

Just before she lapsed into unconsciousness, she suddenly felt afraid.

▲▲▲▲▲▲▲▲

Wake, Hitomi. The voice was faint but powerful, and it held the ring of immortality.

Her dream changed, shifted, and became the throne room of Mirumoto Palace. The ivory throne stood before her on its high dais, and Togashi Mitsu knelt in his customary place at its feet. The throne was empty.

Wake, child. There is much to discuss, and little time.

A shadow fell onto the throne, and Hitomi saw yellow eyes gleam in the darkness. Mitsu raised his hands with a sorrowful gesture. Blood ran down his bare arms, coating the floor in a crimson stain.

Hitomi.

The sound of her name was stronger now, and Mitsu's kind face turned away. It was not his voice. Welts appeared on the tall ise zumi's back, breaking open as the ise zumi opened his mouth silently to scream. In her dream, the cuts became her own. Intense pain seized her, flooding through her prone body and tearing at her flesh.

Hitomi shuddered and gasped in agony, and her eyes flew open. Panting, she looked about.

A man's shadow knelt in a nearby window and blocked the moon.

Otosan Uchi. The emperor's city. The Scorpion. Was she in the palace? The walls seemed to recede as the terrible dream faded, but the world became no more real. Hitomi raised her hand to touch her forehead, and felt nothing. Staring in shock at the bloody bandages around her empty stump, Hitomi swallowed hard.

Hitomi.

The voice was real; it was everywhere at once, and nowhere at all. The shadow did not move, but perched on the windowsill. The dark form was familiar, but the voice was foreign. The man was thick of body, the muscles in his arms standing out in the moonlight under a thin gi. Gold plating shone faintly beneath swirling hair. The light of the stars glimmered from a metal mempo as wind blew the silk curtains past his face. A mask? A Scorpion.

"Go away, Scorpion," Hitomi said wearily, hatred in her voice. "You shouldn't stare at a captive in this way. It makes you seem like a vulture, waiting for me to die."

I am no Scorpion, and you will not die. The voice echoed strangely in the chamber.

Throwing off the blankets, Hitomi was embraced by the sudden chill of wind sweeping through the window. "A ghost, then?"

Of the future. There is much to discuss.

"I don't talk to ghosts," Hitomi snarled, sitting up to face the window. Now that she had risen, she recognized the golden mask covering the face of the intruder. "You . . . Yokuni?" Stunned to see the Dragon Champion in such a strange place, Hitomi shook her head to clear her thoughts. She scrambled to her feet. "You are here to help me escape," she said.

Escape? No. No one can free you, Hitomi. You must have the strength to free yourself.

I am here only to tell you your destiny.

"Destiny," Hitomi said scornfully, raising the wrapped stump of her right wrist. "There is no future for me, Yokuni. You must know that. Everything I have fought for, everything I am is gone. What use is a samurai who cannot hold a sword? What good am I to my brother, now?"

Yakamo has no hand.

Stung, Hitomi snarled. "No, he has a demon claw. He shares his power with the spawn of the Dark God. Do you suggest that I do the same?" No answer came from the crouching shadow, and Hitomi brushed a shaggy lock of hair from her eyes. Her body ached, pain lancing through her from numerous cuts and bruised bones. Still, somehow, her injuries did not seem as bad as she had remembered—except for her arm. Her hand. "Take me out of here, Yokuni. I do not belong."

No.

Pushing herself to her feet, Hitomi drew a kimono from the table by the bed and put it on, the silk sliding roughly across her naked skin. Clumsily knotting the kimono together, she cursed. "I cannot even tie my own clothing. What sort of daimyo will I be?" Hitomi sank to her knees and pounded her fist against the wooden floor. "My men are dead, my clan has abandoned me, and you will not free me from this place? Yokuni! Am I dead to you?" When he did not answer, something broke in Hitomi's soul, and she let out a high keening cry. Enraged, she shattered the balsa wood shoji screen that had protected the bed from the hallway's faint light, throwing it to the ground in splinters of fury.

I cannot free you. I will not.

"Will not? Do I mean so little, then?" She turned on him, fist clenched.

You mean more than you can know. But I cannot act.

"No? Didn't you act when you sent us to that Fortunes-cursed pass? When you allowed this to happen? Was that because you couldn't act?" Hissing, Hitomi pointed at Yokuni. "This is your doing, Champion. You took my hand, as much as that bastard Crab. You forced us from our mountains. We fought without a leader, without a champion, at the side of a ronin." She spit the word. "Because you refused to act, Mirumoto are dead, and my brother's revenge is lost." Ignoring the tears that streamed down her face, Hitomi glanced about the room, seeking a weapon. "This is your doing, Yokuni. Don't tell me you cannot act. You have already done enough."

I cannot set you free. Your destiny is here.

You must become the riddle.

Hitomi laughed, a sharp cutting cry of despair. "You've come all this way, down from the Iron Mountain, just to tell me that you cannot do anything at all."

He did not answer.

Hitomi lowered her head. Madness hovered over her soul, and she laughed again, glad to embrace it. The laugh echoed through the empty room, and Mirumoto Hitomi sank to her knees. Near her hand lay a shard of the broken mirror, glittering in the starlight. Clutching it tightly and feeling blood ooze from her palm, Hitomi stared suddenly up at the Dragon Champion.

"You will act, Yokuni. You will do something, if I have to force you to make a choice." Leaping suddenly with the shard of mirror in her hand, she sprang toward her champion to drive the glass into his chest.

The trained movements of a bushi, catlike and swift, were invisible to the naked eye. Hitomi's lunge was fluid, astonishingly rapid, with the grace and power of a master of the Dragon sword style. Her attack was lethal, a brutal assault with the speed of a striking snake.

Yokuni did not move, did not seem to blink or hesitate.

The world twisted around him.

A savage jerk, and the sensation of flesh ripping from bone. . . . With shock, the samurai found herself hovering frozen, only a few inches from his still form. Her feet did not touch the ground, nor did her body complete the vicious strike. It stubbornly refused to accept gravity or inertia. Her arms could not move. Her legs had no strength, only the stiffness of muscles tensed for the strike. Only her blood moved, dripping in slow trails down her hand and past the mirror's shard. Hitomi could not breathe. She could not move. She was dying.

Yokuni stared silently into her face. The moment extended, became a century.

Then a terrible force propelled her back from him, hurling her to the ground, a force with the strength of a mountain. The air shot from her lungs, and her flesh was on fire, singed by the speed of her flight, from the motion of the air against her skin. Hitomi felt her body spasm. Every inch of her flesh cried in agony, each muscle cramping from the sudden release of tension. Paralysis seized her, and she was driven to the floor by an invisible stone, pressing against her chest. Unable to breathe, unable to scream, Hitomi stared in awe at her champion's still form. He was doing this, and he hadn't even moved. Dark spots flooded her vision, and sparks flew at the edges of her sight.

Yokuni stared down at her from beneath his impassive golden mempo, watching as the life was nearly crushed from Hitomi's frozen form.

It is too soon.

The force suddenly eased. Hitomi drew a long breath into her aching lungs. Coughing, she scrambled away from the moonlit window, leaving the floor stained by the blood of her torn palm. The mirror shard lay forgotten beneath the sill.

Now you will listen.

Your destiny is greater than your own life, and I will not allow you to cast it aside.

"Will not allow . . . ?" she whispered, gasping as she tried to regain her balance.

When the sun falls on the fifteenth day of the Tiger, the emperor will truly die. Ignoring Hitomi's shock, Yokuni continued in his silent voice. *When he falls, a new power will seize the throne, and only you have the strength to defeat it. The time has come to forget the past and prepare for the future. Fu Leng, the Dark God of the Shadowlands, will return, and you must fight him. He will find you, and you will fight. If you fail, the empire will be destroyed.*

"The empire?" Amazement warred with disbelief, and Hitomi scowled. "What use is Rokugan to me, Yokuni? Look what serving your empire has done!" She raised the stump of her arm, its bandages black with blood. Cold wind rushed over her face, and the white silk curtains began to flutter wildly in the moonlight. "The empire has destroyed us all. It has killed me, it has killed my men . . . and it killed Satsu. Why should I fight for it, when it has never given me anything?"

You still do not understand why your brother died.

She screamed. "He died for no reason! He did not even bloody his sword!"

Bushido demands loyalty to one's lord. Your life is at his command, to live or die as he sees fit. Satsu knew that. He knew where duty stands.

Clutching her hands to her head to drive out Yokuni's voice, Hitomi howled in anguish. "You ordered my brother's death . . . you told him to lose?"

As his champion, it was my right. As a servant of the emperor, it was my duty. Your brother died for the Mirumoto, for the

Dragon. He died because I commanded it, and because it was best for the empire. If he had not, there would have been no one to defend the empire in her time of greatest need. Destiny would have changed. We could not allow that. The time was not right. You were too young.

"I don't understand," Hitomi said bitterly.

You do not have to understand. You are samurai. You only have to obey. For this, and for other reasons, Yakamo was allowed to live. He must continue to live. I will explain no more to you, samurai.

Your brother died for the empire.

"Satsu died for nothing." She whispered, lowering her head and sinking to her knees with her back to him. "Leave me, Yokuni. I will not follow your quest. I will not serve an empire that butchers its sons for 'honor,' and I will not serve you. I am finished with bushido."

From the window, Yokuni looked down at her stoic, kneeling form. The wind swayed the curtains back and forth in its violent breeze, and the first few droplets of rain spattered upon the mahogany floor. Silence descended upon the palace, and only the howling wind spoke.

When Hitomi raised her head, the window was empty of everything but moonlight.

Within moments, thick clouds rose, swallowing even silvery Onnotangu's sky-bound face. Yokuni was gone, his passing as swift and inevitable as the movement of time.

Hitomi stood and walked to the window, pressing her bleeding palm to the cold stone of the sill. The grounds were peaceful, and no sound other than the wind resounded through the palace walls. It was as if Yokuni had never been there. Nothing moved on the ground outside in the gardens. No crickets chirped, and no birds flew through the air. Looking up at the rolling clouds in the silvered night sky, Hitomi watched as the stars in the Celestial Heavens were put out, one by one.

A storm was coming.

9 DEALING WITH DARKNESS

"Fall back!" cried the gunso sergeant as he ordered the withdrawal.

Flags waved, banners swept low to the ground in the familiar pattern of retreat, and the Mirumoto backed away from combat.

"Sergeant," one of the younger men cried, "the Crab are also withdrawing, sir. They've still hold the upper passes, and they've contained our men in the box canyon. I'm sorry sir, to report their death."

The soldier was barely more than a boy, his odd ears sticking out from beneath his father's helmet. Made in the style of an emperor three generations past, the armor had seen very few battles. Each new scuff from a blow, each grassy stain on the golden scale was a tribute to the boy's courage. Still, with the rate at which the Mirumoto and ronin troops were dying, he likely wouldn't live another day. Soon, like his comrades, the young soldier would die on the field. His flesh and armor would rise under the command of the necromancers, and join the Crab lines. While Toturi's armies shrank, the Crab's grew. Each Dragon loss only strengthened the Hida lines.

This place, this war, was a blasphemy.

"Withdraw fully behind Dragon lines to the north," Taki grumbled. "We await the daimyo's command."

The lines of the Dragon were haggard, standing almost indistinguishably beside Toturi's ronin guard. How long could the men stand seeing their own brothers, fathers, sisters, and companions fight against them? The shuffling, rotting hordes of the Crab were eerily familiar. . . . Every man here awoke with nightmares of seeing his own face among them.

In the command tent, Yukihera listened to the sergeant's report. "How many men died in your guard, Taki-san?" he asked.

"Nearly fifty dead, half that wounded."

Yukihera noted the number in precise numerals on the rice paper, totaling men into neat rows. Beside him, a somber Togashi Mitsu stared down at the lists as if imagining blood spread across the page. Each man on that roster was a friend, the brother or cousin of the rest. You did not live for a thousand years in isolation without knowing each member of your own clan. Every death was a blow, every fallen man another personal loss. Yukihera dismissed the soldier. With a curt bow, the weary Mirumoto exited the tent.

"How many?" Mitsu asked.

Totaling the numbers once more, the daimyo answered, "The Crab are ruthless. With this kind of assault, we will fall within only a few weeks—if that. Toturi's tactics are unique, but they are not enough to prevent our eradication. The Crab have reinforcements . . ."

Mitsu's face was grave. "We are their fodder, we are their food. They feast, and we slowly starve."

Glaring at the tattooed man, Yukihera continued, ". . . and we have none." He stroked his chin, feeling the growth of stubble. "But there is a choice."

Togashi Mitsu cocked his head curiously. "There is always a choice, Yukihera-sama. Always."

"You don't like me, do you, Mitsu?"

The tattooed man smiled enigmatically. "Does the stream notice the rock in its path? You guide my actions because you are a daimyo and I am only a monk of Togashi Mountain. That is all."

"Perhaps this will change your mind, ise zumi." Yukihera walked to an ornately carved wooden chest at the end of his low table. Withdrawing a shining key from his obi, he opened the lock. Inside were a number of scrolls, a beautiful ivory tanto, and maps of the pass. "Here. Look at this."

Mitsu stepped forward curiously, peering down into the box.

"We'll make a fool of Kisada, and destroy his troops, as well." Yukihera smiled confidently, reaching into the wooden chest and drawing forth a scroll. Written on strange paper, its edges blackened and torn, the scroll unrolled easily in Yukihera's hand.

"Oh?" said Mitsu jovially. "Tell me, great daimyo, what fool will you make?"

Yukihera glared warily at Mitsu, unsure if the man's comment had been an insult. "I have received a message from Yogo Junzo—a Scorpion, and someone who knows the cost of vengeance. The sorcerer Junzo offers us a force of ten thousand goblins, massive ogres—even the power to use the Crab's own dead against them. Then the Dragon shall see how Kisada likes his own game." Yukihera smiled down at the darkened paper, carrying it to his low writing table and reaching for the brush and ink to formulate a reply.

He did not hear Mitsu rise to his feet, did not see the terror and anger that flushed the tattooed man's skin. Mitsu crossed the room in three great steps, knocking the brush from the Mirumoto daimyo's hands and staring down at Yukihera in rage.

"Mitsu!" Yukihera barked, holding the scroll in one hand and reaching for a tanto at his belt with the other.

"What would you give him?" Mitsu asked, his voice low and threatening. "What does Junzo wish from us?"

"What are you doing?" Yukihera cried angrily. "Your place is not to question me!"

"You are not ise zumi, samurai. You do not see the things I see. What does he want?" Mitsu asked again, catching Yukihera's tanto and twisting it from the daimyo's grasp.

"I am not ise zumi." Yukihera snarled. "No one knows that better than I do, Mitsu. You stand on your high mountain, so sure of yourself. Your pride hides your arrogance. Yokuni would not make me ise zumi because he knew I had the strength to wrest the position of champion from him. He did not let me pass because he was afraid, tattooed man—and so are you. Junzo has asked for only one thing—our aid in helping the Scorpion redeem their name."

Ignoring Yukihera's jibe, the tattooed man threw his head back and laughed, a dark sarcastic sound. "Junzo has no interest in the Scorpion. He has fallen to Fu Leng. The Shadowlands taint has claimed him."

"You do not know that," Yukihera lifted the darkened message scroll once more. "I am daimyo of the Mirumoto, Lord of the Iron Mountain, son of Mirumoto Sukune and descended from the First Mirumoto. Who are you to question me? You are a monk, of no real birthright and no honor. You speak in riddles and ignore the truth. You are nothing, ise zumi," he snarled. "And I am everything."

With a movement swifter than the eye could follow, Mitsu caught Yukihera's wrist and squeezed. Tendons cracked, and Yukihera's eyes widened from the force of the pressure. Without his will, the daimyo's hand suddenly opened. The scroll fell from Yukihera's grasp, tumbling to the floor.

"Now I am the stone, and you are the stream. I will turn you from this course. The Dragon will never make this deal," Mitsu said, his laughing exterior completely gone. "The Shadowlands are our enemy, more even than the Crab."

Pulling his other hand free, Yukihera dealt the ise zumi a sharp blow across the face, knocking Mitsu back. Forced to release Yukihera's hand, Mitsu staggered three steps and fell. From the ground, he looked up at the Mirumoto daimyo and reached to wipe a trickle of blood from his mouth.

"If you touch me again, I will have you put to death," Yukihera said quietly, his eyes burning. "You are a Togashi, but you are not immune to the power of the court and the command of a daimyo of your clan. I have nothing to prove to you; you have no power here. If another thousand Dragon die tomorrow, and another thousand the day after—how long can we stand? There will be no Dragon Clan, Mitsu, no Mirumoto or Agasha or Kitsuki for our champion to command. He did not foresee this."

"What do you see, Yukihera? More butchery? If we invite the servants of the Dark One into our cause, then Fu Leng has won the pass—with or without the Crab. Turn a stone, and beneath it you will see grubs—but the stone is a stone on both sides."

"I am no Crab," Yukihera retorted, stepping into a martial stance. "Do you suggest I sit by and watch as my men are butchered? What allies would you seek, fool? The Crane are crushed, the Lion are spread out through Crane lands like insects in a rice field, and the Phoenix are useless pacifists. There is no one else." He lifted the scroll from the ground and held it out like a weapon. "This is our only hope."

"Then we have no hope at all," Mitsu said slowly, breath hissing out into the tent. "And if you think that this," he pointed to the scroll, "changes that, then you are more a fool than I."

"Then give me an alternative."

For a long moment, the two men stared at each other, tension rising in their stances. At last, Mitsu whispered, "Every choice has two sides. There must be a way."

Yukihera shook his head. "There is no other way."

Resigned, the ise zumi fell to his knees. "I beg you, do not do this thing."

"How sure are you, Togashi?" Yukihera said sadistically. "Certain enough to place your life behind your words?"

Mitsu looked up with concern. "I am certain enough to risk all of our lives."

"Yours will do." Summoning his guards from outside the tent, Yukihera commanded, "Tie him. Take this treacherous ise zumi into the courtyard. Have him build a torii arch on the hillock overlooking the Pass. Then hang him from it by his wrists and feet. He will be lashed one stroke for every Dragon samurai that dies here in the pass. This punishment will continue until he is dead, or we find other reinforcements."

The Mirumoto guards glanced at each other in concern. "My lord daimyo," one said, bowing respectfully. "That will certainly kill him."

"He is strong. He will likely live a few days. He has made his choice, Mirumoto-san." Yukihera glared down at Mitsu and picked up the message scroll from where it had fallen on the floor of the tent. "And when you are dead, Mitsu, if no other reinforcements have been brought, I will contact our ally in the south and agree to his bargain." Yukihera smiled grimly. "There is no other choice."

"A choice will be found, Daimyo-sama." Mitsu said, standing and offering his hands to the guards. "Tie me tightly," he said to them, "that I might not disgrace myself when the whip comes."

"It will be done." The guardsman said quietly, tightening the rope around the ise zumi's thick wrists.

Yukihera watched the ise zumi leave the tent. Mitsu stepped proudly behind the guards despite his bound wrists. It would take a few hours to build the arch, a bit longer to strap the ise zumi to its tall pillars. After that, the guards would report further losses to Yukihera, and he would send the numbers of the dead to the eta responsible for corporal punishments.

He could hardly wait to hear the first screams.

10 AFTERMATH OF OBSIDIAN

Only a whisper of silk betrayed her movements through the palace halls. Silence was a friend to the empress, a gift from the Fortunes, blessing her path. She had lived in the Imperial Palace for more than three years, wife and captive of the boy that commanded from the throne.

Once, these halls were festooned with silk ribbons and brilliant lanterns. Then, they had been covered in blood, and in bodies—the blood of her family and her fallen clan, and the body of her own son.

Shivering beneath her silk kimono, Kachiko threw off the ghosts of the past.

Now, the halls were draped only in darkness. Now there was nothing to consider except the future.

Her guard stood outside the sliding screens of the guest room, a suite far from the main body of the court. This wing was mostly deserted, still haunted by the ghosts of the men who had died in the Scorpion Coup. The eta had not been able to remove all of the blood from between the ebony floorboards, and the emperor did not choose to risk dishonoring his guests by asking them to rest in such unlucky and unclean chambers. So, they were left unused, unguarded, and unwatched.

Perfect for Kachiko's purposes.

"Speak," she whispered, her voice like honey in the warm night air.

"She does not rest," whispered the masked guardsman—her husband's brother, Aramoro. She trusted his loyalty more than that of any man in the empire. "A few hours ago, she woke and screamed in the night. I looked into the room through the peephole, but she was alone—looking out the window at the storm."

"Nightmares," Kachiko smiled. "Good.

"She still lives."

"Excellent. Then she may prove a better candidate than I had thought." Kachiko's smile grew sinister, her eyes narrow. "Open the screen."

Aramoro bowed fluidly and knelt beside the wide shoji doors of the guest suite. With an effortless pull, he slid the heavy wooden screen to the side, shifting it in its path so that it opened only far enough to allow the entrance of his lady, and no more.

Even the dim torchlight of the hallway seemed to be a brilliant sun compared to the darkness within. The samurai-ko knelt by the window, her hand resting on the stone sill. Her other arm, a stump, lay forgotten in her lap. The Mirumoto did not look up when the Mother of Scorpions entered the room, ignoring both the lady and her purposeful bodyguard.

"I see that you live," Kachiko said quietly, her soft voice resonating as she moved in the shadows.

"Do I?" Hitomi asked. "Is this life?"

Kachiko laughed, the tinkling of bells beneath the thunder of the storm. "Your clan might not say so."

"Make no mistake, Lady. My clan will come for me." Hitomi's voice was strident, forcing courage into words she did not believe. "My brother, Daini, and my cousin Yukihera, my friend Mitsu, and the entire Mirumoto house. When they know that I am here . . ."

Kachiko smiled. It would be so easy to break her. "Hitomi-chan," using the familiar, Kachiko stepped closer to the wounded Mirumoto samurai. "I'm afraid not."

"What do you mean?"

The empress forced a bitter smile to her lips, her eyes glistening with false tears. "You must understand. I am certain that they believe you dead. They must have been told—seen you fall. . . ."

"Daini, my brother, saw me fight the Crab. He saw the final strike, and I was able to signal him. He knows I am alive, and will have told the rest of the clan. Even now, they search for me. I do not know what magic you used to bring me here, but they will find you."

"Perhaps you are right." Kachiko agreed, stepping behind Hitomi and looking out at the black night sky. Lightning struck above her, illuminating her perfect features and thin lace mask. The burgundy of her ornate robes stood in sharp contrast to Hitomi's mottled, bloodstained gi. "If your brother knows you are alive, then they must be searching for you. Yukihera, the Mirumoto daimyo, has no reason to believe—"

Hitomi cut her off. "I am the Mirumoto daimyo."

Turning with a gently confused look on her ivory features, Kachiko withdrew a letter from her kimono. "I am sorry, Mirumoto-san, but I do not know how that is possible," she lied easily. "This letter says otherwise."

Unfolding it clumsily with one hand, Hitomi stared down at the neat kanji.

My servant,
    By now you know that the daimyo of the Mirumoto is dead. Her life has been revered with full honor, and her soul is no more. On her death and at

her funeral ceremony, Mirumoto Daini, son of Miru-moto Shosan, abdicated his claim to the throne in favor of my experience and strength.
The Dragon will survive.

Yukihera
Daimyo of the Mirumoto
Lord of the Iron Mountain

Hitomi's face turned pale. "Daini knows I live. He watched . . . watched me . . . fall. . . ."

"He watched you fall and did nothing?"

"No, he . . . no. He is my brother."

Kachiko's caramel eyes looked down in pity at the younger woman. "If he knew, then why did he not tell Mirumoto Yukihera?"

"Yukihera wished for my position as head of the Mirumoto House." Hitomi struggled to put the pieces together. "How long ago—how long was I unconscious?"

"Fewer than two days."

"No. No!" Hitomi crumpled the letter and hurled it toward the wall. "You lie, as all Scorpions lie. Two days is not enough to give up hope. They must still be looking for me."

"Why would they? If you are dead on the battlefield, then the Crab have certainly defiled your body. There would be no remains." Kachiko carefully guided the conversation. "Your troops will have assumed that your flesh was used to feed the goblins that serve the Crab. If it had, you can be sure that there would be nothing left of you."

"Daini knows I live! He knows, and he would have told Yukihera."

"But Yukihera is daimyo, at Daini's request."

"How do I know this letter is truly from my clan?"

The Scorpion empress smiled. "You are still here, are you not? No Mirumoto guards are standing in the corridor, waiting to rescue you. Your clan is master of riddles and enigmas. Do you believe that they know you are here?"

Hitomi's eyes were cold. "They know."

"Yet they have done nothing to free you, or even to contact you. How can you question that they have given you up for dead?"

"Yukihera." Hitomi's eyes narrowed with fury. "He arranged this. He must have given Daini something to convince him to betray me. He has told the clan that I am dead, and now they follow Yukihera. Damn them all."

"You are dead to them," Aramoro whispered from across the room. "I saved your life. By the traditions of our people, that means your life is mine, until your debt to me is paid."

"Debt?" Hitomi snarled. "This . . . life . . . that you give me? This is nothing more than a rotting shell, samurai, and a ghost of what I was. You did not save me. You did not free me. You have only prevented the inevitable." She pointed toward the samurai's swords in his obi. "Give me a sword, samurai, and you will see my gratitude written in blood on your precious palace floor."

"Hitomi . . ." Kachiko's face was a perfect mask of sorrow and friendship. "I know what it is to be forgotten, to have your clan abandon you and to be betrayed by those who should have loved you. I thought that we had saved your life when we took you from that battlefield. Perhaps we should have left you to die. It would have been kinder." Kachiko reached out to the samurai maiden, her scarlet kimono sleeve sweeping delicately against the floor. "But I feel that you are not yet done with this life. You have something undone. Some spirit still haunts you, as the spirit of my clan . . . my son . . . haunts me." Kachiko's soft brown eyes searched Hitomi's black ones. "I can feel your brother . . . willing you to live."

Hitomi turned once more to the window and placed her fist on the stone lip of the wall. She closed her eyes as if in meditation and, with typical Dragon patience, sought something just beyond her grasp. Long minutes went by, but Kachiko only watched the Dragon sort through her anger. Finally, Hitomi opened her eyes. "It is best that I know the traitorous hearts of those I once trusted. I will not be so weak again. A debt . . . my life is yours. How fitting." Her face twisted into a wry half-smile. "It does not belong to the Dragon. No one else came to search for me?"

"My men saw no one. The fields were empty," the empress said. No need to tell her of the Kitsuki—it would only weaken the Scorpion's growing hold over this Mirumoto samurai. Kachiko risked a hidden glance toward a black obsidian box that waited in the corner of the room.

"Yokuni," Hitomi said in sudden revelation. "Why didn't you tell me of their treachery, Yokuni?" she whispered to the night. "You, too, have turned against me."

Hearing the Dragon Champion's name mentioned, Kachiko felt herself grow pale. She raised her fan and whispered. "Yokuni?"

Hitomi nodded, looking out at the storm. "He told me that he could not act to save me. My entire clan has denied me, left for dead in a pit of vipers."

Kachiko allowed the implication to fall unnoticed. "Even Yokuni has turned against you?" she whispered in seeming fear and awe. "I am surprised he did not kill you."

"He has no reason to kill me. I am already dead. What purpose can I serve? Look at me," Hitomi held up the ruined stump. "I am less than nothing. The Mirumoto traitors did not even bother to make certain I was dead. I can be no threat to them—or to anyone."

"We are alike, Hitomi-chan," Kachiko said, moving across the room. Her pale brown eyes locked on the black gaze of the Dragon samurai. "Our clans have abandoned us—mine by ruin and yours by treachery. We were once powerful, but now we are severed from our power. You have lost your hand, and I have lost my power in the court. There are those who have said that I, too, should have died long ago. But I still live. I still fight. You can be strong once more."

"How?" Hitomi asked.

"You serve the Scorpion now, Hitomi-san, with bonds of your own blood. Open that box, and see your future." Her pale arm reached elegantly from the sleeve of the burgundy silk.

Kachiko pointed toward the obsidian box that rested on the far side of the chamber.

Glancing first at Kachiko and then at the box, Hitomi furrowed her brow. "I have no future. I am dead. My clan knows that. Why do you insist that there is more?"

"Because I have seen your spirit, and I know you are worthy. We are twinned in our sorrow—and in our revenge."

"You murdered the emperor. I have spent my life trying to avenge the murder of my brother." Hitomi's face was hard, and her voice was cold. "We are nothing alike."

"For a thousand years," Kachiko murmured, stepping lightly across the mahogany boards of the chamber floor. Her feet made no sound, sliding beneath her kimono effortlessly, "the shugenja of my clan have kept secrets. But no secret was greater than this: the Obsidian Hand, and the Twelve Scrolls of Fu Leng. They were called the Black Scrolls, keepers of the Dark God's magic, and the hand was used to bind them with Shosuro's soul. Eleven of those scrolls still exist. Some were stolen by Yogo Junzo when the Scorpion fell. He is a traitor, even to us." Kachiko's amber eyes were steel, belying her soft movements.

"Eleven?" Hitomi said.

The empress nodded. "The scrolls were said to contain Fu Leng's very soul. For safekeeping, one was hidden long ago—and even the Scorpion do not know where. It is said that when they are opened, the Dark God will be truly free upon Rokugan, and the empire will know his wrath. The Twelfth Black Scroll is forever lost . . . to stop him."

Taking her eyes from Kachiko, Hitomi strode across the room and reached for the box. The lid was strangely cold, almost like hardened ice beneath her fingertips. As she stroked the surface, looking for some latch, hinge or handle, the box began to shift under her hand.

Kachiko and Aramoro exchanged knowing glances as the Mirumoto continued to open the box. Either way, the future would be determined within seconds.

The lid opened, sliding aside with an enchanted click, and soft red velvet peeped from within the obsidian case. For a moment, Hitomi thought that there was a box within the outer shell, but in a moment, she recognized the object.

It was a hand, made of black glass. The fingers, long and thin, creased the aged silk cushion as though they had rested within the box for hundreds of years, yet no stain or dust marred the shining surface of the hand's obsidian sheen. Five black fingers gathered into a curved palm, the stone was carved intricately, with etchings that seemed almost scales upon the obsidian. From the hand, a wrist extended, jutting out of the smooth glass like shards of bone. The stone here was not smooth, but rather jagged and broken, torn from some statue through strength alone. A riddle, surrounded by smooth silks.

"And this?"

Kachiko did not answer Hitomi's quiet question, ignoring the bitterness in the Mirumoto samurai's voice. "Shoju knew that with the last Hantei, the Black Scrolls would begin to open. He attacked the Hantei to prevent that—and failed."

Looking closer at the red cushion beneath the Obsidian Hand, Hitomi thought she could make out stains where blood had touched the pristine fabric. "What is this thing that you offer me, Mother of Lies?" she asked.

"It is the Hand of Shosuro." Reverence touched Kachiko's low tone. "An artifact of the greatest Scorpion that ever lived—our Thunder, who fought against Fu Leng in the first war against the Shadowlands. My clan has held it since Shosuro's death, a thousand years ago. No one has ever been able to wear it. No one was worthy. Those who tried . . ."

"Died." Hitomi looked down at the faint bloodstains on the cushion beneath the obsidian artifact.

"No." Kachiko corrected her. "They did not die, but they often wished that they had. I imagine them even now, their faces trapped within the glass, screaming forever between its black fingers and calling Shosuro's name."

"Why do you show me this?" Hitomi asked, looking down at the dark hand.

"Because I believe that it has chosen you. It is one of the last relics of my fallen clan. For a thousand years, since Shosuro returned from the first war with Fu Leng, the Scorpion have treasured it. It is our greatest relic, our most powerful tool— yet none have ever been able to unlock its mysteries. Shosuro herself once said that the hand was more than her flesh, and less than her soul. It is a mystery to us. The Thunders went into the Shadowlands to fight Fu Leng, and only Shosuro returned. All the other clans' heroes died there, but ours returned. We believe that this hand was the reason why."

"Why offer it to me?"

"Because I can." Kachiko smiled gently and turned away, her hips moving slowly beneath her thin silk kimono. Hitomi caught a glimpse of a scorpion, tattooed upon the empress's shoulder blade.

"This is why Yokuni could not come into the room. Its presence touched him. Perhaps even . . . frightened him?" Hitomi whispered, so low that Kachiko had to strain to pick out the words.

The Bayushi empress's brow furrowed in concern, but Hitomi did not notice.

"The Hand of Shosuro," the Mirumoto pondered. "Will this help me avenge my brother? Restore my place in the Dragon Clan?"

"I cannot say. Its powers are unknown, even to me. But I can promise you that if you choose this path, the Scorpion will aid you in whatever revenge you choose to take. I can give you nothing more powerful."

"Why?" Hitomi stared up at Kachiko as the empress stepped smoothly to her side. "Why would you help me, when my own clan has turned against me? You always have another purpose, Scorpion. What do you gain?"

"Tomorrow, the emperor will announce that he seeks a new Emerald Champion. You will enter the tournament— and you will win. With the power of the Emerald Magistrates, you will be able to crush the Crab, and have the status you need to reclaim your position as head of the Mirumoto House. I will gain control of the Imperial Guard, and all the magistrates of the empire, through you. My purpose is to ensure my own safety from the vipers in this palace, to make certain that though my clan has fallen, I still have power in the court. Your aid can assure that—and this hand can give us both the strength we deserve."

"You swear this, on your life?" Standing with the box in her hand, Hitomi stared into Kachiko's face, and saw what everyone saw there—perfect, impassive beauty, her features accentuated by the delicate lace mask that hid only her true purpose.

Perhaps Hitomi guessed there was more to Kachiko's gift, but she couldn't possibly know what. Perhaps she realized they were a perfect match; a poisonous Scorpion and a fallen Dragon.

"I swear it." Kachiko's eyes were clear, her voice even.

"Then let it be so. If you can give me the means to destroy my enemy and restore my title, then I will be your sword." Drawing the hand from its silk cushion, Hitomi caressed the cracked glass. It was smooth under her fingertips, sharp and solid, and surprisingly warm.

Kachiko took a single step back as the Mirumoto samurai withdrew the artifact from its box, a whisper of breath escaping her slightly parted lips.

Looking down at the Obsidian Hand, Hitomi felt the sharp protrusions that jutted out from its rocky base. They felt like shards of bone, shattered by some immortal blow and torn from its place. "What is this thing?" Hitomi murmured to herself, holding it before her with cautious hands.

At the sound of her voice, or the touch of her breath upon the glass, everything changed.

▲▲▲▲▲▲▲▲

Hitomi stared down into the glass, noting its silk texture and sharp edges. The Obsidian Hand was as smooth and cold as ice. It rested delicately within the box, drinking in the light around it and casting shadows that moved and shifted beneath its fingers. A strange luminescence gleamed within the artifact, sharp and reddish. Around Hitomi, the shadows clustered closer, as if to gain sustenance from the hand. Its jutting stump began to drip a bloody crimson, falling on the floor in splashes of scarlet and black.

The fingers flexed convulsively, gripping at Hitomi's good hand in a vice of iron and stone. The hand squeezed as if alive and held tightly to Hitomi's fingers, piercing her flesh with sharp shards of glass. Below, where the stump of the hand bled, thin tendrils of shadow began to form, writhing like worms against the hard glass surface of the hand.

"Put it on," Kachiko whispered, her voice deadened by the thick shadows that surrounded them.

At her side, Aramoro stepped forward, holding his sword at the ready, staring intently at the artifact.

Kachiko's face was exuberant, her eyes gleaming behind her mask, lips faintly smiling in eagerness and wonder. "Call to Shosuro's spirit within the hand. She will aid you. Let her spirit take its form in you."

It was far too late to let go, too late to change her mind. Hitomi raised her right wrist for one final look at the seared flesh beneath. Then with sudden exhalation, she forced the stump of Shosuro's Hand onto her own.

A scream, a thousand worlds away.

A howl that was not her own.

Become the riddle.

The ancient words flashed through her mind as the hand whispered and roared into life. Hitomi watched in fascination as the shadowy tendrils of Shosuro's Hand clutched her own skin, searing through her flesh with black flames and shadow smoke. They writhed within her own arm, turning the skin to stone and merging with her veins. For a moment, Hitomi could feel the cold black glass against the burning stump of her wrist, but then, a feeling of wonder and awe filled her. The nightmare tentacles crept up her arms, turning the thin veins to black beneath the surface. A sudden wave of heat and power swept through Hitomi.

Shosuro, she thought. Aid me. . . .

Hitomi's back arched with energy, driving her good fist down to the floor and cracking the heavy mahogany boards.

Another scream. This one might have been her own, but Hitomi was too enraptured to notice. The pain was monumental, but the feeling of unbelievable strength and of tendrils racing through her bloodstream was greater. Pain flooded through her, tearing at her mind and pushing her toward the edge of madness.

Hitomi could sense that Kachiko and Aramoro had backed away, the Scorpion samurai ready to protect his mistress in case Hitomi went mad. Even in her torturous pain, Hitomi laughed. If she did go mad, there was nothing he could do. No steel, no armor could stop the strength released in her veins. She felt the agony of shadow rushing into her heart, and then the world exploded again.

Visions flooded Hitomi's mind, visions of times long past and forgotten. Shosuro, Shosuro—the name became a mantra to her. Shosuro, aid me. A vision sharpened, cleared, came forward. She was in a cavern with a man she did not know. He swore his love to her. She turned her back and faded into the shadow. Shosuro and the Scorpion kami, Bayushi.

The world shifted, and another vision opened before her. Suddenly, she was in a great golden palace, on her knees before a lady as radiant as the sun. Something was wrong. These weren't visions . . . they were memories, trapped within the hand. Hitomi fought to keep her own consciousness while she gazed at the golden hall that had surrounded her, aware that the things she was seeing were not real. Yet, as she studied them, Hitomi realized something else. These were not Shosuro's memories.

These were the memories of another being . . . someone far more powerful.

Shosuro, Scorpion Thunder, Hitomi prayed, concentrated on the name, and felt her mind begin to tear.

Another flash. The Shadowlands surrounded her. A white-haired woman with blood smeared across her delicate features howled in pain, slicing through a monster's carapace even as it destroyed her. Shosuro fighting Fu Leng? Other bodies clustered close, and she heard the battle cry of a Matsu warrior maiden. A Crab raised his tremendous axe, and she saw a great pit of bone and blood—Shosuro and the Thunders, fighting in the Shadowlands. Trying to stop Fu Leng before he could destroy the empire. Shosuro again, and Hitomi struggled to keep the vision clear. Her own screams flooded through her, and cold stone gripped her severed wrist. The hand was becoming one with her soul.

A shift, and she stood among the stars again, with the radiant lady at her side. These were the memories of a being far older than mankind, far too ancient and powerful to have ever been mortal. The lady smiled, and her face shone with gleaming light. Yet there was something sinister surrounding her, something tearing apart the sky around them. Hitomi looked down, and in her hands—obsidian hands—a child's empty blanket rested.

Flash, and the world righted itself. She was in Otosan Uchi, looking down at her own blood and knowing it to be false. This was Shosuro, Hitomi was certain of it. Bayushi knelt beside her, whispering into her ear, and Hitomi felt Shosuro's body collapse as if dead. The Obsidian Hand, pressed to her flesh as it now was to Hitomi's, pulsed and burned at her side. Each time she chanted Shosuro's name, Hitomi felt her sanity slip, her mind tearing in agony and the tempest of madness. Something was wrong. The Scorpion were wrong. Kachiko's voice floated through the visions, a memory of Hitomi's past.

Those who tried did not die. I imagine them even now, their faces trapped within the glass, screaming forever between its black fingers . . . calling Shosuro's name.

Shosuro's name.

The memories of Shosuro were in the hand, and yes, Shosuro had once worn it, but its origins were far deeper than the Scorpion had suspected. Another burst of light erupted from the hand, and the starlight was swallowed by flame. Hitomi stared up into infinity. Celestial stars hovered beside her, playthings for her to touch and move as she desired.

These were not the memories of a Thunder.

They contained no mortality at all.

Shosuro did not have power here—though her soul was part of the hand, it was not her own flesh. Calling to Shosuro would only drive Hitomi mad. She had to face the true origin of the Obsidian Hand, or be destroyed. The hand did not belong to Shosuro, the Scorpion Thunder of a thousand years ago. It was much older than that, older even than the kami who had first created the world. In her celestial vision, Hitomi looked down at the face of the newborn world beneath her and recognized the outlines of the land that would once become the empire.

The lady beside her, as radiant as the sun.

The children's blanket. The children were gone, dead by her own obsidian hand. The Moon, who had eaten his children so that they would not challenge his love for his wife . . .

In a flash, Hitomi understood. The hand belonged to Onnotangu, the Moon, ancient god of Rokugan and creator of the Celestial Heavens. Why he had never claimed it, Hitomi did not know; it no longer mattered. Only that the hand was now bonded to her skin, to her soul, and that she was now some part of a greater celestial secret; only that mattered. Shosuro had known this, but had not passed the secret on to her clan.

The Scorpion must have thought that Shosuro's arm had turned to stone, rather than understanding the artifact's true source. In the dream that swelled from the hand's power, Hitomi opened her white eyes and saw eternity. It swirled around her, then began to pull, and Hitomi felt her soul resist. To follow Shosuro was to walk into madness and despair. To allow the hand power over her, to give it uncontrolled rein over her soul, would destroy her as it had destroyed all the other Scorpion that had ever tried to use Shosuro's Hand.

Hitomi smiled. They had all tried to commune with Shosuro, believing the Scorpion Thunder to be the spirit within the hand. Only Hitomi understood its true origins, and could touch its true nature.

She had conquered the hand, and made it her own.

▲▲▲▲▲▲▲▲

In the small guest wing of Otosan Uchi, the shadow around Hitomi began to shine with small bursts of light. The light twisted into rays, arcs, and mists of color.

Kachiko stepped back, placing herself behind Aramoro's protective bulk. She had never been frightened before. Not when the emperor condemned her clan to death, nor when she held her son's dying body in her arms. But this—this strange, uncontrolled magic, the foreign tongue that streamed from the Mirumoto samurai's lips—this was beyond her comprehension.

Lights swirled, and obsidian shards began to form on Hitomi's arm. The stones worked their way toward her elbow in thinning strands of obsidian, like veins on her pale flesh. Shadows clustered closer, bursting into light and then fading away. Soon, the shadows fell emptily to the ground, resuming their former shapes and turning gray and pale. Reality superimposed itself upon Hitomi's agonized visions, and she looked out the window at the sullen light of the moon. The storm had passed.

Hitomi stood slowly, lurched forward, caught herself on a wooden beam. After a moment, she pushed herself upright again, and Kachiko could see the imprint of obsidian fingers in the thick mahogany pillar.

"It is done," Kachiko whispered victoriously. "You are one with Shosuro."

Hitomi's black eyes reflected the light of the moon as she stared into Kachiko's pale orbs. "Yes, Kachiko-san," she smiled darkly. "I am one."

SIGHT BEYOND SILENCE

Toturi looked over the messenger's dispatch, walking briskly through the early morning encampment. The Crab attacks had been light today, still stinging from the heavy Hida losses of the night before. Toturi smiled to himself. Those were losses that the Crab would not recoup into undead—a hundred men, crushed beneath a ton of falling rock and debris.

The Mirumoto sappers had done their job well.

Looking up, Toturi called, "Yukihera-sama!"

The provisional Mirumoto daimyo stood amid his armory, his golden armor making his eyes glow.

"I have good news," Toturi said, smiling and striding eagerly toward him. He stepped past broken pieces of helms and leg plates.

"Any news is good news, Toturi. Nearly fifty Dragon died in the pass yesterday, and more will fall today if the Hida do not retreat farther." Yuki-hera's bright eyes flashed from weapon to weapon. He lifted a naginata from its resting-place in the arms rack and tested its balance. His golden armor gleamed in the sunlight, hardly scratched by enemy attacks.

Beside him, Agasha Tamori bowed to the ronin general, barely reaching a polite depth.

Out of habit, Toturi ignored the shugenja and leapt straight into conversation with the Mirumoto daimyo. "One of my messengers to the south may have found something of use. Look at this." Toturi spread the dispatch across an armor plate, unrolling the edges and pointing at the rough map within. "This is a city within the Shinomen Forest. We've known it existed for some time now, but none have gotten close enough to bring reports of the interior. Recently, though, maps were found among the Scorpion holdings—maps of the Shinomen's borders."

"The Shinomen?" Yukihera asked stridently. "Madness. That's beyond the Crab armies by a full day or more. What could live there? The entire forest is haunted."

"Not haunted, Yukihera. Guarded. Bodies have been found on the edges of the forest groves—bodies speared by arrows, not by ghosts. The Falcon Clan lives here, far to the north. They speak of seeing ronin move through the forest at night."

"Ronin? And?"

"If they are ronin, there is a good chance that many of those men are Akodo. The fallen Akodo will follow me, if I can get a message to them. Enough men, gathered to the south of the Hida and led in a concentrated force against their encampment . . . here." Toturi pulled forth another map and spread it across the first, ignoring the wrinkles caused by the laces of his makeshift table. He pointed at the sketch of the Crab armies. "Here is where their necromancers stay. If they can be stamped out, their zombies will die as well. Once that happens, the Crab armies will be at half strength—and we can destroy them." To-turi grinned, stabbing his finger at the map once more. "With even a small force of ronin from the Shinomen, we can crush them. The maho-users aren't guarded, and few of their retainers are positioned this far south of the main encampment."

"What makes you think we can convince the ronin to help us?" Yukihera asked thoughtfully.

"The men in that forest have escaped detection and capture. They are capable of defending their position, and of creating a ruse suitable to drive out anyone who would do them harm. Those aren't bandits, and they aren't goblins or ghosts. They're organized, established men. They have the capacity to remain hidden and keep themselves fed and their weapons cared for—and they have the advantage of terrain. I'd guess they are Akodo troops that dispersed after the emperor's order." Toturi fought to keep the bitterness out of his voice. "But there is another possibility."

Yukihera nodded. "Scorpion." The Mirumoto daimyo ran his fingers through his thick black hair and squinted golden eyes up at the sun. "If they are Scorpion, Toturi, then they will certainly kill any messenger you send. You killed their daimyo, Shoju, when he tried to seize the emperor's throne. Your family hunted and killed them for their treachery during the coup. They might even ally with the Crab, just for good measure. How can you believe that they will join you now?"

Toturi's keen mind raced through the possibilities, the chances and the options. "There is a way that we can learn the truth."

"Yes?"

"Send a Dragon messenger. Someone not connected to me. If they are Akodo ronin, the messenger can deliver my words. If they are Scorpion, the Dragon have the greatest chance to get their assistance. Your troops at Otosan Uchi during the coup were minimal, and your clan has never warred with the Scorpion."

"You are correct," Yukihera agreed. "That is because we are not prone to flood out of our mountains at the first sign of war." He spoke scathingly, but the irony was lost on Toturi, who was already recalculating the strategies necessary to assault the Crab rearguard.

"Toturi, I advise against it. More ronin troops are not what we need for this battle. We must find allies in the Phoenix or the

Crane, not scattered bullies and bandits." Tamori slid a hand over his smoothly shaved head, distress showing in his eyes.

Toturi smiled at Yukihera and seemed not to recognize Tamori's comment. "Fifty men. If your messenger can return with fifty men, we can take this pass and destroy the necromancers. By the time the Hida have even noticed, our men can escape toward Lake Mizu-umi no Fuko and be gone. If we know when they will attack, we can draw the Crab armies forward here, and here," Toturi pointed at two large buttes near the center of Beiden Pass. "And group archers here, to cover their escape." He smiled again, looking down at the map of the battle with a pleased nod. "Victory."

"You count your victories too soon, ronin," Tamori said scathingly. "Mirumoto Yukihera-sama has not agreed to your plan."

"No, Tamori-sama," Yukihera said thoughtfully. "I think Toturi's idea shows promise. And I have just the messenger for so delicate and dangerous a task. If the ronin in the Shinomen have taken to shooting arrows at those who attempt to communicate with them, then we shall have to send a messenger who cannot be so easily dispatched. My own cousin, Daini, will go."

"Daini . . ." Tamori murmured. Before he could protest, Yukihera turned toward him.

"You would prefer one of your shugenja, Tamori? A thoughtful gesture, but I am certain they would find a horrible death in the Shinomen. You wouldn't want to sentence one of your Agasha to that fate, would you? Or were you suggesting that you go, yourself? Could your magic protect you?" Yukihera's eyes narrowed, and fear flashed over the aged shugenja's weary features. It would be a death sentence.

"No . . . no, of course not. Daini . . ."

"Daini is the obvious choice. With full banners and regalia, so that they know exactly who has come to speak with them. They would not dare assault such an honored samurai." Yukihera's poisonous voice was pleased, filled with smug amusement.

Tamori nodded, obviously unhappily. It was not his place to question the Mirumoto general's decisions, particularly when those decisions concerned only Mirumoto samurai. There was nothing he could do except pray for Daini's fortune. Still, Tamori expression showed that he was puzzling through a riddle, a riddle whose answer was growing all too clear.

"Where is Daini?" Toturi asked, glancing up from his maps.

"At the arch, no doubt, feeding the traitor Mitsu."

"Yes . . . Mitsu." Toturi frowned. "I wish you could find it in your heart to grant the Togashi a reprieve. He seems an honorable man."

Yukihera fingered the tanto in his obi as he replied sternly. "An honorable man who raised his hand against his daimyo is an honorable man who deserves to die. There will be no reprieve." Placing the naginata back on the weapons rack, Yukihera headed for the center of the Dragon encampment.

Tamori followed him, brow furrowed with the riddles in his mind.

▲▲▲▲▲▲▲▲

Daini stood beside the rough wooden arch, lifting chopsticks with rice to the tortured ise zumi's mouth. "Easy, Mitsu-san. There is plenty, and you will only choke yourself if you swallow without chewing." For two days, the ise zumi had hung from the arch, his back bloodied by whip marks and his arms stretched by his own weight.

"Daini," the sharp command came from the side of the clearing. Yukihera and Agasha Tamori approached. They marched up the hillock toward the torii arch, Tamori's yellow robes fluttering in the stiff breeze. Something about the shugenja's walk seemed preoccupied, but Yukihera's strides were certain.

"Hai, Daimyo," Daini fell to his knees, holding the bowl close to his youthful chest. His thin mustache covered the angry curl of his lip as he watched Yukihera approach. The barely conscious Mitsu did not move, but lowered his eyes.

"I have a mission for you. To gain allies from the south." As Yukihera spoke, Mitsu's head craned upward angrily. Yukihera scowled. "No, ise zumi. These are ronin, possibly some few castaway Akodo samurai hiding in the Shinomen. Your ordeal is not yet over, though you may soon wish that it were." Yukihera smiled beneath his golden helm, the ornate horns of his helmet catching the sunlight and casting bright flashes of light. "How many men have died since you were hung upon the arch, Togashi?"

"Seventy, my lord," the tattooed man's voice was hoarse from dehydration, but still strong. "And I have felt each man die." The riddler smiled crookedly, peering at the Mirumoto daimyo through one sweat-filled eye. "Have you?"

Yukihera ignored Mitsu's words and turned again to the kneeling Daini. "You will take the strongest horse and head through the southern trails, over the mountain range. Once past the Crab lines, you will turn west, until you reach the Shinomen Forest. This map," Yukihera held out the crumpled piece of parchment that Toturi had been using as a guide, "will show you where to go."

"Into the Shinomen Forest?" Daini's eyes widened with anger and surprise. "Yuki—My lord, no man has ever entered the Shinomen Forest and lived. The ghosts there feed on the flesh of samurai and make weapons of their bones."

"Yes, I've heard." Yukihera grinned sadistically. "A perfect ending for you, Daini. Broken and fed upon, like your pitiful sister."

Tamori stepped away, turning his face from the conflict. He stared at the nearby mountains as if wishing they were the jagged peaks of his home. Daini's gaze flickered back and forth between the two daimyo, recognizing the silent contention between them. One riddle answered. Tamori was no more Yukihera's ally than Daini . . . but they were both Yukihera's pawns.

With slow determination, Daini rose to his feet. "Do not speak of Hitomi. You are not worthy even to say her name. And neither am I."

"You are still young, Daini, but I will not tolerate such disrespect. I am your daimyo." Malice dripped from each syllable.

"Not until Yokuni has agreed. The decision is his."

Yukihera sneered. "He will have no decision to make. Soon,

I will be the only choice. The Mirumoto line will survive, Daini—through me."

Daini ground his teeth in rage, unable to argue with his commander. Bushido demanded the respect of a soldier to his general; the riddle insisted that one know his place in all things. This was a battleground . . . but not one where Daini could fight.

And still, Tamori looked away.

Daini nodded. "I do not think it will be as simple to destroy me as it was to murder my sister, Yukihera-sama." Daini spat the honorific.

"No, Daini. It will be an even simpler puzzle. Hitomi was the challenge. You are nothing more than the cleaning up." Yukihera smiled. "Now, go. Take a strong horse. You leave tonight, and with luck, you will die tomorrow." Spinning on his heel, the Mirumoto daimyo dismissed his defeated rival.

"I wish you well, Daini," Tamori whispered, his voice nearly lost on the wind. "I can do nothing to aid you. Yukihera has the power of his house, and I must obey him on the battlefield. I have been ordered by Yokuni himself."

"And if Yukihera ordered you to kill me?" Daini asked bitterly.

"Then I would obey. That is my duty. The lines of this maze are clear to me, Daini. There is only one path, and I must follow it."

"Where is my path, old man?" the young samurai cursed. "By Shinsei, tell me where it is, that I can unravel this knot and find the end! If I do not, Yukihera will seize the Dragon, and we will all be destroyed. You can do something, Tamori. You can fight against him. Is there not a way?"

"I am Dragon. We do not interfere." Tamori's face was grave, his skin ashen. "I cannot answer that riddle, samurai."

"Then go, Tamori, and dream of your precious mountains. I hope that you will see them again, you and all your isolationist kin. May they be as you left them—and may the climb up their peaks scrape the blood from your hands.

Silently, Tamori bowed. With a troubled sigh, the master of the Agasha turned and began to make his way down the mountain path.

Daini knelt at Mitsu's feet, his singed flesh burning even in the cool night. "We are lost, Mitsu. The grave has been dug, and now there is nothing left to do but fill it in over our ashes."

"You have made a powerful enemy," a voice said quietly. Daini looked up in surprise. Beside him, Kitsuki Yasu knelt to lift the fallen bowl of rice from the ground. The tracker moved silently, and Daini did not know how much the man had heard. Certainly, neither Tamori nor Yukihera had noticed the Kitsuki's approach, for they continued down the steep hillside without a glance behind them.

"Hai, sama," Daini said quietly. "I know. This is all my fault. I betrayed Hitomi—I allowed Yukihera to seize the throne of the Mirumoto. I deserve to die. It is my place. I have lost my family and my title." Tears streamed down his youthful face. "I am a failure to our clan."

"Yes, Daini, you are." Yasu said uncompromisingly, watching the boy flinch at the words. "But you are still a samurai. You can atone."

"How? Yukihera's mission is suicide. Hitomi is dead. Mitsu will not live another six days." Daini stared up at the older man with anger and remorse. "I should never have been allowed to pass my gempuku. I am no samurai."

"Take my horse," said Yasu. "Do not worry about Mitsu. I will see that he survives. I have enough knowledge of herbs and medicines that I can ease his wounds and help stop the bleeding. So long as Yukihera does not order a frontal assault on the Crab lines, he will live awhile longer. As for the Shinomen . . . I do not know that anything can help you there."

Daini closed his eyes and shivered despite the warm summer night. "Thank you, Yasu-sama."

"If you find allies there, Daini, you will be doing more than saving the Dragon from the Crab. You will be saving Mitsu's life—all of our lives. Yukihera has proposed an alliance with the Shadowlands." As Yasu spoke, the tattooed ise zumi lifted his head. "Yes, friend. I know of Yukihera's plans. It was one of my Kitsuki trackers who brought the message to him from the necromancer. I also know that Yukihera is a man of his word, despite his ambition. He will not send his reply until you are dead.

"But he can make that time come sooner than you think." Yasu's voice lowered to a whisper. "And by sending away Daini, your ally, he will have the space to move. You are his only competition for the position of daimyo, Daini-san. It is in his favor that you die alone and unheralded in the Shinomen. That is why he has sent you on this path."

"He is my daimyo. I cannot refuse him."

"And you will not," Yukihera said flatly. "Travel to the forest, make an attempt in order to satisfy bushido, and then go to Ryoko Owari."

"Ryoko Owari? The Scorpion city?"

"Now filled with more ronin than you can imagine. They may be willing to help you—and any allies, however treacherous, are better than selling the soul of the Mirumoto to Fu Leng. If you are Mirumoto, if you truly have the soul of the Dragon within you, you will stand up, and you will try. You have failed, Daini—but you can still stand. Look to Toturi. He has lost everything; his family, his honor, and his army. Yet he still stands against the Crab, and with his own strength of will, he drives them from the pass. Will you do less?" Yasu watched as Daini stood, brushing the dirt from the knees of his hakima pants. "Will you try, Daini?"

Daini straightened, eyes shining with new hope. "Hai, I will do my best."

"Go then. I'll watch our friend here."

"Hai, Yasu-sama. And . . . thank you." Daini gave Mitsu's weary form a sidelong glance, and then strode from the clearing. He would find a way to make it right again.

Somehow.

⚤ ⚤ ⚤ ⚤ ⚤ ⚤ ⚤ ⚤

Five days later, Daini found himself at the edge of the largest forest in the empire. His horse walked with a limp, its legs strained from the pace he had demanded. Daini wearily lowered himself from its back. It had been nearly two days since he had slept. Tied to the saddle with his obi, he had clung to the horse's neck and prayed to Shinsei that their path was still true.

Even if it had not been, he would have found the forest eventually. It was massive, wrapping like a maiden's belt across the kimono of the empire. The trees themselves stood taller than any building in Otosan Uchi, and three men could not link hands around them. Vines twined and trailed up the sides of the spreading oaks, forming a canopy of leaves some thirty feet above Daini's head. Moss grew thickly on the trunks of the great trees, like a woman's hair, flowing down and pooling on the ground.

The steady whisper of wind through low brush carried with it the scent of jasmine and pine. Even in the fullness of morning light, Daini could see only faint patches of brightness within the forest's gate. The sun peeped through thin holes in the ceiling of green, bursting into brilliance on pools of water. As he walked, the young samurai entered a world of mossy stones and gnarled tree roots as thick as a man's leg.

Stepping lightly into the forest, Mirumoto Daini tugged on his horse's reins to urge it forward behind him. He pushed his way past tangled bushes that clustered at the edge of the groves, cursing under his breath as the vines clung to his wide pant legs. The horse skittered a bit and then pulled back, but under Daini's urging, it followed.

Something like a path twisted beneath the thick brush, and Daini pushed aside green leaves and gnarled vines to find it. Kneeling in surprise, he ran his fingers over the ground. Beneath the dirt lay a thin veneer of broken stone. These were cobblestones, such as the streets in the Forbidden City of Otosan Uchi were said to have. Cobblestones were stepping stones spread across a wide street so that horses' hooves would ring pleasantly. But here? Daini lifted a loose one from the ground. It was old, weathered, covered in a thick layer of dark brown earth.

"Beneath even the simplest stone, secrets can live," Daini whispered, quoting the Tao of Shinsei. "What secrets will I find here, I wonder?" Dropping the stone, he stood and began to push his way through the forest. "Only a little way in, enough to say honestly that I tried, and then we're off to Ryoko Owari.

If we're lucky, we'll find a place to camp between here and there, and get some rest, old boy." Patting the horse's brown neck, Daini rubbed the steaming flesh beneath the stallion's mane. "We could both use it."

The smell struck the steed first, and Daini's horse jerked its head back, nostrils flaring and eyes wide. After only a moment, the wind changed, and the Mirumoto samurai could smell it as well. It was the scent of a battlefield, mixed in with the lush fragrance of pine. Decay and rotting flesh hung on the stiff breeze, tugging foully at Daini's nose. "Easy," he said to the skittish horse. "There, now."

Daini continued forward, pushing against the brush that wrapped lightly around his ankles. Here, deeper inside the Shinomen, the vines and bushes that had covered the ground were gone, unable to grow beneath the darkness of the canopy. Only dead branches and centuries of leaves slowed him now, but still Daini had to move between the great arching roots of the tall trees, stepping over, and sometimes under, their spreading feet.

The smell intensified, and Daini saw a flutter of scarlet around one of the giant oaks ahead. Something moving? No— the flash continued, like clothing swaying in the same breeze that ruffled Daini's hair.

His horse pulled again and whinnied, its frightened voice echoing in the thick wood.

"Easy," Daini repeated, and walked toward the flash of color. Once the tremendous oak was to his side, he could see what caused the flash. "Shinsei," he whispered, and leaned heavily against his nervous steed.

Fifteen men, or more, hung from tall slivers of stone that had been driven into the ground by an unknown hand. The stones were dark gray, their sides covered in thick moss as though they had stood for an aeon. The men, however, were freshly dead, and the smell of decay assaulted the samurai along with the sound of flies.

Many of the men were dressed in Scorpion livery, their intestines hanging scarlet and brown against the crimson and gold of their mon. Torn open by cuts and covered with arrow-holes, their flesh hung skewered upon the tall spike-stones. At least one seemed to have been alive when he was placed, the stone ripping through his belly as his own weight dragged him down farther. His bloody hands still gripped the pedestal, trying in vain to push himself backward up the spike.

Blood trailed in thick pools onto the ground, spreading over broken weapons and shattered armor. Each samurai had a small bundle of items beneath his corpse, as if those who had placed him there cared nothing for his belongings.

These were not the marks of ronin, attacking to keep themselves safe within the forest.

Suddenly, Daini's horse whinnied wildly, It reared and struck at Daini with fearful hooves. Lurching back, Daini released the reins and dropped his hand to his katana. Instead of racing away from the dead bodies, as Daini had expected, the horse launched itself forward between the stones. A few moments of terrified cantering, trotting in circles from stone to stone, the horse finally leapt between two of the spikes and charged into the forest.

The beast hadn't been afraid of the death stench, but of something else. Daini spun, staring out into the dark forest, trying to see what had caused his horse to bolt. His focus leapt from place to place, trying to find some other source.

The horse screamed somewhere outside the grove of stones. Its cantering hooves faltered, and Daini heard the soft thrum of a bow. The samurai skittered toward the stones, hiding behind them and gripping his sword with a tight fist. The horse shrilled another scream—this time cut off. Then came the heavy sound of the horse falling.

The silence was impenetrable. Wind whispered through the high leaves of the giant oaks, but all else was still. The bowman, whoever he was, made no noise at all.

As the echoes of the horse's death faded, Daini closed his eyes and prayed for a swift release.

In this forest, a man with a bow could kill him as easily as a shugenja's spell. The stone pillars were little comfort, covered in blood and spread across the clearing in wide gaps. The edge of the Shinomen was far away, and without his horse he had little hope of outrunning anyone who knew the forest well.

The only hope, Daini thought swiftly, was to let them know his mission. Perhaps words would sway them, where courage could not.

"Samurai!" he shouted, praying that the attacker would pause to listen to his words. "I am Mirumoto Daini, cousin to daimyo Mirumoto Yukihera, and son of Mirumoto Takeshi. I fought at the battle of Woodland Ford against the Lion, and I have fought against the Crab at Beiden Pass. I am an honored samurai, and one who will show you respect. I come to parley, and to seek allies in these woods. I bear you no ill will, no matter what your crime." He paused, forcing courage into his voice. "I wish to speak with your leaders on behalf of the Dragon Clan." They might be Scorpion, he thought quickly. Best not to mention Toturi's name.

No response came from among the trees, and no other sound broke the stillness. The bowman could be anywhere, preparing a perfect shot through the pillars. There was no reason to cower like a goblin when death was so certain.

Daini closed his eyes and remembered his sister's face, unafraid even when Yakamo stood above her. Even when the claw shattered her wrist, she had spit in the Crab's face. He would die like her, and at least, the burden of his shame would be done. Self-pity washed through Daini like a hot breeze, flushing his face as he stepped forward one slow foot at a time.

"I . . . am coming out now." Releasing his sword's handle, Daini walked slowly around the stone pillar. Keeping his hands extended and level with his shoulders, he walked out into the open clearing. "My name is Daini. Mirumoto Daini, of the Dragon. I can aid you. We fight against the Crab and their oni minions, in the name of the emperor."

Something shivered the roots of one of the ancient trees, and Daini froze. They would certainly kill him now. "I am of the Dragon. We have no quarrel with you. I ask that you parley with me, so I can tell you of the dangers that face our land."

For an instant, Daini thought he heard a sibilant hiss. Then, on the far side of the clearing, something shifted. There were more than one of these ronin surrounding him.

Daini tried not to show his fear outwardly, but swallowed hard to clear his dry throat. Shivering, he continued, "I come from the Dragon. My name is Mirumoto Daini. I come to find allies who wish to stop the Crab and their Shadowlands army—the Shadowlands must be stopped. My family has already died at the hands of the Crab and their undead. Will you allow more men to die, and let the Hida spread the taint across the land?"

"No, huu-man," a voice rasped, a strange accent dilating the words. "We will not let the taint spread. And we will begin the cleansing . . . with you."

Daini looked back over his shoulder and saw a man's torso rise above the root of one of the massive trees. An arched bow stretched tautly in the bowman's hands, but Daini barely noticed it.

The archer's skin was as green as the leaves around him, lightly scaled over his wiry muscles. His chest was bare, covered only by the strap of his full quiver, and his head was protected by a helm made of some strange metal-studded flesh. Even those atrocities did not match the archer's true nature.

A massive serpent tail twisted forth from the man's torso, curling around the great tree in a muscular grip. It was longer than two horses and patterned in scales of green and gold diamonds. Opening his mouth to smile at his prey, the archer pulled his bow even farther back, sighting along a jade arrow's length toward Daini's heart. His teeth, fanged like a snake's, shone whitely against his dark green lips. A thick red tongue slid between them, scenting the wind to ensure the perfection of the shot. "Die, huu-man. The Shinomen belongs to us. We will not allow your infection to continue."

Just before the bowman released his deadly missile, another voice stopped him. "No, Balash. Wait. This one is different." The voice was feminine, soft but confident.

The first creature hissed, his tongue flickering in a strange language, one Daini could not possibly understand.

It was sibilant, whispered, half-started, and then continuing in quick lashes of an inhuman tongue.

The bowman backed away reluctantly, anger boiling beneath his olive skin.

The woman stepped out from between two of the trees near Daini and held out a thin wand of jade. "Come here, huu-man," she smiled cautiously. "Take this, and prove to us that you are not one of the Dark Ones. Then, we will parley."

Daini slowly reached toward her, trying to ignore the arrow still pointed at his heart. She was strangely alien, her features human . . . yet foreign. Her eyes were round, lips full and pale, unlike anything Daini had ever seen before. Despite her green-tinged skin and startling amber eyes, her golden hair flowed in long rivulets down past muscular shoulders. Her high cheekbones widened an impish face, and her movements were smooth and flowing. She had no tail, but mortal legs, though Daini nearly blushed to see them bare, uncovered by kimono or hakima. Her own bow lay strapped against her back, and her short toga hung just to her thighs.

Daini touched the jade wand, cautiously at first, and then with confidence, sliding it from her hand. Their fingers met, and Daini felt her scaled skin, cool and smooth beneath his warm flesh. The jade did not shine, nor melt as it would have in the hands of a creature of the Shadowlands, and the woman's face broke into a bright smile. Daini realized that she could not be much older than he, still new to her duties. Perhaps that was why she had spared him.

"He must die," the other archer whispered with hatred. "Mara, you go too far."

"No, Balash. Listen." The two creatures stared at one another for a long moment, heads cocked as if listening to some greater sound.

Another voice from the high branches of the nearby trees called out. "Mara, it is time."

A third man slid from the massive oak, and then a fourth and a fifth, all propelled by a strange tail instead of legs. Their serpentlike appearance startled Daini, and their tails pushed them silently across the ground. They moved in tandem, aware of each other's motions, sliding effortlessly across the dead leaves and vines of the forest floor.

How had he missed them all?

The serpent men wore no gi or haori vests, and their swords were curved almost in half. Golden hilts, not silk-wrapped katana, hung from their strange scabbards. The armor they wore was formed of hardened animal flesh—abhorrent to Rokugani, who would not even touch dead flesh, much less wear it as decoration or protection. He stared openly, forgetting custom and decorum. Jade shone softly from their bracelets and necklaces, and their bows were strung with strange diamond cords, clear and strong. They did not seem to speak any dialect of Rokugani, but uttered strange hisses to each other.

"Come, Mirumoto-daini," the woman smiled and extended her hand to take his. Shocked by her touch, Daini stared in confusion. "Can't you hear?" she asked. "It is time to take you to Siksa, to speak to the Vedic there."

Daini stumbled forward as she pulled, following her with wide eyes. "Siksa?"

"The city of the naga. You will see. Come. You said you wished to parley, did you not?"

"Yes, but . . ."

She smiled again, her strange golden hair moving across her shoulders in a bright wave of sunlight beneath the green trees. "Then come, Mirumoto-daini, and learn."

▲ ▲ ▲ ▲ ▲ ▲ ▲ ▲

From his place in the treetop, Balash slowly lowered his bow, regretting that he did not fire when he had the chance. The infection had been allowed to remain. Akasha had demanded that this huu-man be brought to their city. For what reason, Balash did not know—but even he could not resist the call of the Great Mind.

The huu-man would be allowed to live . . . for now.

12 TOURNAMENT OF THE EMERALD CHAMPION

The empress was radiant. Even if Hitomi had not known her plan, she would have assumed that Kachiko had something ready for the days' events. She moved silkily across the empty throne room floor, making certain that each flower and cushion was carefully arranged for the emperor's audience with the Great Clans. Samurai gathered just outside the doorway, in the gardens of the Hantei, and Hitomi could hear their low talk through the shoji screens of the chamber.

"All is ready, my lady?" she asked softly, keeping her hands folded in her lap.

"Yes, my friend," Kachiko smiled radiantly beneath her lace mask. "And you know your part?"

"As well as I know my name, Empress."

"Then let us not delay the Imperial Court. They deserve their spectacle. After all, it is what they have come to see." A regal smile parted her perfect red lips, and Kachiko locked her honey-gold eyes with the cold black ones of her kneeling Dragon retainer. Then, assured that all was as she had planned, Kachiko swept toward the gardens without another word.

"Yes, Empress," Hitomi lowered her head so that Kachiko would not see her smile.

▲▲▲▲▲▲▲▲

Hitomi listened from the rear of the hall, kneeling behind a carefully placed standing screen. The guests slowly filed in from the gardens, murmuring behind their fans as the emperor's sycophant, Seppun Bake, greeted them. "Samurai, nobles all, the 39th Hantei, Lord of the Seven Hills, Emperor of the Emerald Empire and favored son of the Goddess Amaterasu, awaits inside to hear your council. May the light of the Shining Prince never fail, and may the light of the Celestial Heavens illuminate the empire through his wisdom and his guidance." Bake shriveled into his fine robes, slinking back into the throne chamber.

Through the cracks between the standing screens, Hitomi peered out at the room. Images of tigers and cranes were patterned on the paper of the screen, but through it, Hitomi watched each of the Great Clans bow to the huge Emerald Throne on its mahogany dais. The chamber was splendid, with ornate enamel embellishing the broad beams of the ceiling. A magnificent tapestry depicted the fall of the kami from the Celestial Heavens. On the dais rested the glittering Emerald Throne, symbol of the empire. The throne was similar to Togashi Yokuni's ivory one, but far larger and grander—despite the tremendous rift that cracked its emerald back. The carvings on the throne depicted the sun goddess and her favored son, Hantei. It was wide enough to support two men, and stood taller than any other chair in Rokugan, carved from a single emerald during the first days of the empire.

As the guests bowed their heads to the floor, a palanquin was carried in from the rear of the room. Magnificently jeweled sides sparkled in the light of the afternoon sun that streamed through the open garden doors. Samurai servants, bearing the mon of Crane, Seppun, and Otomo, bowed as the doors of the small palanquin were opened to allow the Shining Prince to ascend his throne.

He moved strangely, not with the strides of a samurai trained to the sword, but with the fragile steps of an old man. His clothing was padded to give an illusion of girth, but his thin limbs seemed barely able to lift the heavy silk robes that pressed upon his frail frame. For anyone in the court to miss the obvious signs of the emperor's failing health would be impossible.

Was this Kachiko's doing? Hitomi would put nothing past her—and if the emperor died without an heir, the resulting wars could destroy the empire.

Kachiko stood gracefully at the edge of the dais. As her husband took three careful steps toward the throne, she smiled at him. Hitomi could not see the young emperor's face, but from his demeanor, he was pleased to see his wife. As he settled himself upon the massive chair, she bowed and stepped to her place behind the young emperor.

Hantei the 39th, lord of all Rokugan, was only a year older than Hitomi. Searching his face, the Dragon samurai recognized the weary lines, the crease in his brow that matched her own. A wave of pity rushed through her. Hitomi was shocked by her emotions, and fought to keep them under control. This was the emperor—the Shining Prince, Lord of Rokugan, Master of Otosan Uchi and the Seven Hills. He was not a man to be pitied.

Stealing another look at his face through the crack in the shoji screen, Hitomi stared at the weariness in the Hantei's pale blue eyes. She clenched her jaw. He was small and dreadfully young. The hollows under his eyes had been powdered and covered with white, but his face still appeared sunken with weariness. Gloves covered his bone-thin hands, and golden slippers covered his feet, barely peeping out from beneath thick green and gold robes.

Courtiers spoke of plague, of the emperor's nightmares about his father's death. . . .

Hitomi shook her head to clear her thoughts. Hantei was the emperor. Sacrosanct. If he dreamed of his father's death, she understood the weariness, the wan appearance, the pale flesh. The dreams of Satsu tore at her nightly, his face echoing before her vision, swimming away with the dawn. Even in the rigid meditations of the Dragon, she could not glimpse the answer to his puzzle. The reasons for Satsu's death were lost to her, yet every night she awakened screaming, feeling him within her grasp . . . only to slip away.

Perhaps this emperor knew the same terrors.

After the court had settled itself, the emperor raised his eyes from his lap, placing one hand on each of the throne's arms. His gaze slid over the court slowly, as if assessing their identities. Occasionally, he nodded as he recognized a favored member of his court, but his gaze never paused, never changed. With a gloved hand, he reached into a golden box held by a kneeling Seppun Bake, pulling forth a carefully written scroll. Though his voice was faint, it still held the unmistakable aura of an eternal lord. Despite his trembling hands, the Hantei was still emperor.

"Noble lords," the emperor began. "For too long, our throne has stood without a protector. It has come to my attention," a pause, a shuddering breath, and a glance at Kachiko, who sat simply and quietly on her cushion at his side, "that with the plague that destroys our land, and the violent incursions of numerous Yabanjin bandit tribes, the position of Emerald Champion has stood too long empty."

The emperor breathed deeply and raised his head to increase the strength of his fading voice. "My lady wife has nobly agreed to carry out the duties of the arbiter of the tournament, and Seppun Bake will be on hand to ensure the faithfulness of those who choose to attend."

Both bowed on either side, respectful of the responsibilities given to them by the Hantei.

"I beg your pardon, samurai-sama," whispered a soft voice, disturbing Hitomi's meditation. "May I sit here?" The girl was a Crane, her white hair swinging in a maiden's foxtail as she knelt with Hitomi behind the dividing screen.

Hitomi recognized the storyteller of the emperor's court, Doji Shizue. No doubt she had come to divine Hitomi's purpose, an intrusion that could not be allowed.

Hitomi snarled faintly, but she could not refuse the Crane's request. If she did, it would draw attention to her location. Enough. The Crane already knew that she was here. It was time to close Kachiko's trap on the rest of the court. "Of course, Doji-sama," Hitomi said coldly. "I was just about to leave."

As the court applauded the emperor's words, Hitomi stepped from behind the screen and bowed to the man on the Emerald Throne.

"Imperial Lord," she said politely, "I stand for the Dragon, in acceptance of your tournament. I need no formal announcement to ask for the chance to serve you, nor any astrologer to tell me that this is my time to step forth." The words were Kachiko's, chosen carefully for their effect on the courtiers, and Hitomi saw that the ruse had worked.

Hitomi knelt in the aisle at the rear of the chamber, her green robe spread around her knees. The Dragon mon shone from her back, and the symbol of the Mirumoto flashed on her sleeve. She raised her head. Black eyes shone in narrow sockets, and her thin nose sliced through her sharp-featured face. Her arms and hands were covered entirely by thick green sleeves.

"My time is now."

The courtiers stared at her, taking in every detail of her clothing, her face, and her attitude. She refused to be cowed by their attention and remained on her knees. As Kachiko had taught her, Hitomi stared directly at the emperor, motionless.

The Hantei nodded, surprised by the woman's forward speech.

Seppun Bake reached for his scroll and brush, swiftly writing down Hitomi's words and her challenge. "The Mirumoto daimyo of the Dragon stands for her clan." Marking elegantly on a roll of blank white paper, the Seppun noted her name and rank.

As Kachiko had predicted, the court fell into silent chaos. If they did not speak now, they would appear weak or unworthy of the position of Emerald Champion—and yet, if their greatest swordsmen were not assembled, those who spoke for the tournament would be poor competitors to the Dragon's blade.

Hitomi glanced swiftly to either side, gauging the opposition. Only one man seemed worthy of her steel—Doji Hoturi, sitting at the front of the court, a strange look of ice and snow about his pale eyes. Hoturi glanced first at the dais, and then at Hitomi as if making a decision.

Come, lord of the Crane, Hitomi thought with malice. Rise. Challenge me, and I will best you, as well.

A Lion stood on the far side of the court. "My name is Kitsu Motso, daimyo of the Kitsu family, son of Kitsu Ariganu, son of the Lion Clan. . . ." He spoke rapidly, and Hitomi ignored his words.

He would be no challenge.

Others rose then: three Lion, two Crab, and a Unicorn. One Phoenix, shivering and confused, was pushed forward by his shugenja master. He seemed barely a boy, and stammered his name.

He would be nothing.

"I, Kakita Toshimoko, master of the Kakita Academy and lord of the twelve provinces of Kunankei, will stand for the Crane."

Hitomi looked up, stunned. The man was a legend, a master of the Kakita style—the one form of iaijutsu in the land that matched the Dragon niten style in precision and speed. She narrowed her eyes, jutting her sharp jaw forward unconsciously as she judged the old man through his movements. He would be a worthy competitor.

But he did not have the Obsidian Hand.

Hitomi's black eyes flashed toward Kachiko, and they smiled as one.

▲▲▲▲▲▲▲▲

The battle at Beiden Pass raged to the south, far away from Otosan Uchi and the emperor's court. The Dragon continued their fight against the Crab, and the Shadowlands continued to raise Dragon bodies and force them into undead servitude. With each hour that passed, Hitomi felt more distant from the battle, farther from her traitorous family and her once-proud duty. Who knew what horrors erupted in the Pass? Mitsu . . . was he still alive?

When she returned to them, would she still recognize the Mirumoto at all? Hitomi looked at her hand, flashing in the sunlight of the tournament field. Would they know her?

The hand had become second nature to Hitomi, and in just a few days, she had learned to recognize its hunger, its urges, as separate from her own. The long fingers curled, and she could feel the day's warm breeze on the stone as if it passed against her own flesh.

Hitomi knelt by the tournament field, her swords in their holder before her, and readied herself for the contest to become Emerald Champion. Around her, the courtiers and other contestants swirled in a blend of bright color. Hitomi, dressed in black silks with only a touch of Dragon gold on her shoulders, ignored them. The wide grassy field echoed with shouts and greetings, but she stared only at her own reflection, encased in black glass.

Six days had passed for Hitomi. Six days since she lost her family, her house, and her name.

An eternity, and the world had changed.

It had been four days since her challenge before the emperor's court, and the field outside the grand palace was filled with the bright silks of banners and courtiers. News of the tournament of the Emerald Champion had spread throughout the city, and entrants from the minor clans had begun to come forward. Each clan was allowed only three entrants, and most sent fewer. To have a great number of samurai entered would imply to the court that the clan's faith was not fully behind their entrants. Fond of appearances, the Imperial Court spent its days discussing the samurai who dared to challenge for the position.

The Emerald Champion was foremost of all the Imperial Magistrates, keeper of Imperial law and title, and the general of the armies of the Hantei. It was a prestigious position, and it was a place of power. Both within the court of the Hantei, and with several standing guard of Seppun, the Emerald Champion's duty to the emperor and to the empire was without question.

On the balcony, the mon of the imperial family waved in a faint breeze. The golden chrysanthemum decorated intricately carved wooden railings that were more for show than for safety. Behind the low rail, two golden cushions had been placed to full effect, commanding a view of the entire battlefield, as well as of each dais below. This was the emperor's own viewing pavilion, high above the rest of the Imperial Court. But one of the pillows was empty—the emperor, too ill to attend the gathering, had sent his blessing . . . and his wife.

One by one, the competitors fell before Hitomi's blade. The hand grew in power with each victory, drawing its strength from their defeat. Each time Hitomi bested her opponent, the voices of the hand sang in her mind, overpowering her own thoughts. It was a constant battle to prevent herself from dealing her opponents a deathblow. At the end of each contest, she grew more and more weary of the fight.

What use was it? They were weak, mortal, useless. What did it matter if they died?

Hitomi growled. It matters, she reminded herself. It matters, because it is my mind and my flesh. If I choose not to kill them, then they will live.

The spirit of the hand fought her, and then retreated deep within her soul. Soon, eight bushi stood on the emperor's tournament field. The last duelists included two Lion, one Unicorn, one Crab, two Dragon, a member of the smaller Fox Clan, and the Crane. Toshimoko still stood.

Hitomi smiled. She would have a chance to test her style against his—and prove niten was superior. Excellent.

The other Dragon, a Kitsuki, walked toward her and bowed with a courtier's grace. "Mistress Hitomi-sama, we are pleased to hear that the rumors of your death are exaggerated."

Lifting him by his throat in the Obsidian Hand's crushing fist, Hitomi glared blackly. "I am dead, Kitsuki. Do not doubt it, or you will join me." Hurling him to the side, she ignored his stunned cry and turned her back on his blade.

The Kitsuki stumbled away, gripping his throat in one hand and muttering apologies. He did not approach her again.

The hand was bitter, hungry for blood and for victory. Hitomi relished its pulse within her own until the call of the tournament master interrupted her reverie.

"Matsu Mori, son of Matsu Agetoki, come forward and hail the Imperial Throne. Mirumoto Hitomi, daimyo of the Mirumoto, come forward and hail the Imperial Throne." The man's voice was as spindly as his raised arms, flapping about in the breeze like winter branches. He snorted in the cold winter air and breathed out a cone of warm mist.

The two samurai stepped onto the tournament field, pausing long enough to bow toward a grand balcony that spread some ten feet above the ground. They turned and bowed once more—far more shallowly—toward each other.

The two samurai took their stances. The Dragon woman crouched low, her hands covered by the long sleeves of her haori vest. Her opponent leaned forward in a typical, aggressive Matsu stance.

The hand growled, and Hitomi heard the noise echoing in her own breath. She felt her opponent's blood pounding in his ears, heard the faint shiver of grass as he adjusted his stance to meet her own. The obsidian around her wrist flexed and tightened on her sword hilt. Hitomi found herself calculating the exact angle her blade should reach as it swung through his neck.

No. This was a contest—not a death match.

The tournament master backed away, raising the white and red flags above his head. When they fell, she would strike—and the Lion would die.

No, Hitomi thought again, struggling for control of the artifact. This fight is not to the death. I will not kill this man. That is not my way.

A shout pierced the still air, and the two opponents drew in a single arching strike.

Seconds froze around the Dragon samurai, and Hitomi felt the world slow to a crawl.

On the far side of her opponent, a tall man in white armor extended his hand to her. Her sword would reach it, if she passed the blade through the Matsu opposing her.

"No," Hitomi snarled. "I know you now, Onnotangu. You will not drive me mad."

Time released, and seconds flew past once more. Her katana sang in the soft breeze. The two duelists' blades chimed against one another. Sliding her blade down his, Hitomi twisted to the right and found herself behind Matsu Mori. Time slowed again.

He is not ready. He is not worthy. He should die, just for challenging us. Hitomi's thoughts shifted violently from control to chaos and back again. The words were her own, the voice hers as well, but the drive came from the ancient artifact on her wrist. She pushed through once more, ignoring the white-stained figure beyond her opponent, and struck clean.

Blades flashed brightly in the winter sunlight, stunningly white on the gray steel of their katana. In another breath, it was finished, and the Lion fell to the ground. Blood began to stain the man's kimono, spreading crimson against the bright orange of the Lion Clan.

Shocked whispers echoed from the field. Hitomi stared down at him, impassively.

He was lucky to be alive. She could see the wound, and it was light. A scratch, cut just below his collarbone. The hand whispered with a thousand voices in her mind, laughing maniacally. This time, the hand had bested her, but not by much. If it had truly won, the Lion would be a dead man.

Hitomi smiled slightly as she bowed to her fallen opponent. She would not be disqualified. Kachiko would see to that. The field was clearing as the Lion's men came to carry him from the ground, and Hitomi walked slowly toward her daisho holder near the Dragon banners. The heimin servants scattered at her approach, afraid to come near Hitomi.

When the tournament master called her forth again, Hitomi rose from her meditation and walked with a measured stride.

The hand laughed expectantly, watching the Fox samurai bow across the field. *Hurt him,* the hand whispered. *Hurt him, kill him, and claim the victory that is already ours.*

"I will control my own actions. I am not your pawn," Hitomi growled, lowering her head so that her opponent would think her words to be a quiet prayer.

The hand continued to struggle, sighing at the taste of blood on her blade.

Pawn, pawn, pawn, the hand whispered in a thousand voices.

"This is madness." Hitomi took her stance, distracted.

The hand shifted to correct for her misplaced angle. *Win, win!* It cried. *Win, blood and win!*

"We will win, but my way." Hitomi felt her stubbornness rising. The same strength of spirit that had demanded she charge against Yokuni in the field of Beiden Pass, that had urged her to attack her own clan champion, looking for death, surged in her veins. For a moment, the hand was silent, as if pacified by her will.

The first strike came as the flags fell from the tournament master's hands. Precise and sharp, it flew toward the Fox samurai's throat with murderous intent. *Tricked!* Hitomi suddenly realized that the strike was a killing blow, and she pulled her arm back with a mighty yank. The strike fell far short, and the Fox's blade passed only inches from her own chest.

The hand, no longer silent, howled with fury inside Hitomi's mind.

Struggling to control the murderous impulses that surged within her, Hitomi twisted and slid her blade against that of the Fox samurai. She was far faster than he, but any release might cause the hand to seize control again—and her opponent would certainly die. "I will control you," Hitomi grunted, pressing her katana's blade against the Fox's and forcing down his guard.

He means nothing. They all mean nothing. Only death, only fury and revenge. You know revenge, Hitomi. It is an old friend, an old ally. Give in to it once more, be our servant and show them our power!

Screaming, Hitomi battered down the Fox samurai's blade and slashed lightly at his chest. Falling to the ground, the Fox dropped his katana and clutched his hand to his bloodied breast. Fear showed for a second in his eyes.

Hitomi backed away, trying to regain her composure. The crowd clapped politely, their uncertainty obvious in the reluctant sound.

The Fox knelt on the ground, bowing his head. Whether he was grateful for his life or only admired her victory, Hitomi could not tell.

The hand's whispers grew ever stronger, drowning out her own inner voice. Swinging her blade to clear it of blood, Hitomi turned to look at Kachiko.

The Scorpion sat now with the Crane Champion. Kachiko's eyes narrowed with laughter.

Damn you, Kachiko, and damn your gift. There must be a way out of this trap, a way to free myself both of the hand's control—and of yours. I thought that accepting Shosuro's Hand would free me, but all it has done is lock your obsidian chains around my wrists.

Hitomi bowed, first to the empress's balcony, and then to her fallen opponent.

Hitomi looked across the field. Only three opponents were left: herself, Kakita Toshimoko, and Kitsu Motso, a powerful Lion General. Motso would have been no competition for her, and she doubted he would prove any for the Crane. The final bout, then, would be Toshimoko and Hitomi—it was only a matter of time.

There must be a way. . . .

Hitomi stared for a fleeting second. Toshimoko. Standing on the field, she raised her sword in salute. The Crane was powerful and wise; the finest iaijutsu master in the empire. He would be difficult to defeat, even with the power of the Obsidian Hand.

Kachiko's words echoed through the hand's cacophony. You will fight—and you will win . . . this hand can give us both the strength we deserve.

I am finished with bushido. . . . Her own voice.

The Hand screamed gleefully, gaining power as its black blood surged through her veins. She had turned her back on the way of the honorable warrior, denied the strength of a samurai's soul. Without bushido, there were no rules, no ties of honor. It was too late to regain what she he had lost. Hitomi was a slave to the bloodlust of the hand and to her Scorpion masters. Through the screams within her soul, she could faintly remember her brother's voice, teaching her swordplay along with the code that ruled a samurai's life. Bushido. Satsu would have been ashamed.

Across the cold and muddied tournament ground, Kakita Toshimoko nodded solemnly, returning Hitomi's salute.

Perhaps there was still a way.

As the other two competitors entered the field for their duel, the Crane courtier Yoshi approached Hitomi.

Ignoring him, Hitomi cleaned her sword with an expert hand. The blood trickled onto the obsidian joint of her thumb, and Hitomi felt an orgasmic chill rush through her at its touch. Maintaining her rigid control, she lifted her gaze to stare angrily at the Crane's pale eyes.

He responded with pleasantries. "Tell me about your sword-style, Mirumoto-sama. It seems . . . different from the standard niten of your clan. Do you find it more effective against the iai-jutsu style than against modern kenjutsu techniques?"

"Lion fights Crane. Don't you think that's more interesting than discussing the Dragon technique?" As she spoke, Hitomi tugged the sleeve of her kimono down over the joint of her thumb. She wiped away the blood before the hand could draw strength from it.

Kakita Yoshi's eyes flickered down, but he seemed not to notice. "Not at all. The Dragon, like the Crab, fight with strength and power. The Crane fight with skill. One sword, one stroke, and no more."

Hitomi grunted savagely, "The Crab fight with cowardice."

"I'm certain Kisada-sama would disagree," Yoshi said cheerfully. The man's hands folded into his sleeves, curling into white-painted claws beneath his serene silks.

The hand screamed for revenge from this frail, pitiful courtier. Hitomi spun toward him. Without a thought, the hand shot out, reaching for Yoshi's tunic. Struggling to control its frenzy, Hitomi exerted her will. The hand stopped only inches from Yoshi's chest. Curling the fingers into an obsidian fist, Hitomi looked at the Crane's powdered face, her black eyes shining with hate and fury. Short hair fell forward into her eyes, sweat trickling down her brow. Inches, mere inches, stood between the Crane and his death, and Hitomi did not know how to keep control. At any moment, chaos could resume, and Hitomi could be lost forever within the hand.

The Kakita never moved, but simply smiled.

"Kisada," she hissed, slowly withdrawing the hand, "can die along with his coward son."

"I don't see how that can happen, Hitomi, if you are here and they are at Beiden Pass."

Almost snarling, she responded, "The Crab will retreat from Beiden Pass. Yakamo's army of Shadowlands filth is not enough to defeat the army of the Dragon. But this," she tore away her sleeve and held out the stone hand. It was grafted to her flesh like a thing alive, creeping over her forearm with long tendrils of black, glossy stone. "This the Crab took from me. But I will take more from them when I see them again."

"Where will you see them, Hitomi-san?" Yoshi whispered.

"When they are done with you, Crane. I will destroy them when they are done with you." Hitomi smiled, allowing the dark blood of the hand to rush through her and show the Crane his own death in her eyes. "Listen to me, Crane, and listen well. You cannot defeat the Crab. No samurai in the empire has that power. Only I can. I saw them at Beiden Pass. I know what they can do." The hand flashed in the sunlight. "They travel with demonic oni, samurai, creatures of fire and acid, with claws of iron and teeth that break katana and Cranes." She cursed. "The very earth moves for their passage. Where will you be, Crane, when they come to slaughter your people?"

Yoshi blanched and drew himself straighter. "I will be where I have always been, Mirumoto Hitomi-san. I know where my first duty lies. From the time we samurai are born, we are taught our first duty, and that lesson remains with us until death, and beyond." Hitomi stared at the little Kakita, listening to his words. "When the world ends and the moon falls, Dragon, I will be with the Crane."

My first duty . . .

Lifting her sword to her obi, she bowed curtly. As Yoshi backed cautiously away, his face even paler than usual, Hitomi stepped onto the field without being called.

"I must not forget my first duty," she said to herself as she turned her back on the Crane courtier. "Satsu. The Crab. I have ignored my true cause for too long. I will kill Hida Yakamo. I have sworn it, and I swear it again, by all the Fortunes. Before I die, the life of Hida Yakamo will end on my blade."

Smiling faintly, she pressed the flesh of her true hand against the silk wrappings of her blade. "Thank you, Crane, for reminding me that I cannot afford to win this battle."

▲▲▲▲▲▲▲▲

The two samurai bowed to one another, turning toward the center of the courtyard as if pulled by a single cord. Their eyes met, the old sensei and the young daimyo. They paused in the center of the motion, respectfully saluting both the samurai and their noble house.

More . . . the hand cried. More . . .

No, Hitomi thought, this time remembering her brother's teachings. She closed her eyes and recalled a day of sunlight, when Satsu had laughed and held her high above the ground. It had been like flying, and the wind in Hitomi's short-chopped hair echoed her memory. There will only be more if you obey me.

I am your master! The hand snarled, tugging at her will. This time, it found no holes in her armor, no escape for its rage.

"You are nothing more than stone." Hitomi whispered, and the peace of truth touched her soul at last.

The courtyard grew silent and still, awaiting the stroke of a single sword, the master's attack of iaijutsu.

Yoshi stood nearby, craning to hear each whisper of silk, each movement of slippered foot and tinkle of ivory charms hanging from carefully tied obi.

Toshimoko was a silent statue, his gray braid moving quietly in the breeze like the tail of some great, chained cat.

Hitomi's hand gleamed in the sunlight, as cold as ice and as devoid of soul.

At last, a bird fluttered between them in a whisper of motion. The samurai moved. Their swords slid free of their sheaths with a ringing whisper, but only one sword struck truly. Twisting free from her stone hand, one half of Hitomi's katana clattered uselessly to the ground. She staggered backward from the force of the Kakita's strike and fell.

Sliding effortlessly down the shattered katana, Toshimoko's blade rang against Hitomi's Obsidian Hand. It leaped from her black glass fingers to point dangerously at the hollow of her throat.

From the ground, Hitomi looked up at Toshimoko's blade, her eyes following the sheen of steel up to his somber gray eyes.

As the Kakita removed his blade from her neck, Hitomi forced a snarl of rage to her features. Her sharp chin jutted out as in anger, and her eyes narrowed. It would be expected—and Kachiko would be watching.

There was no dishonor in losing a match to the greatest iaijutsu master that had ever lived. The Scorpion would have to accept her defeat as genuine. As Hitomi stood to face her opponent, the old Crane stepped back into the shadow of the courtyard and raised the steel katana in salute.

True to the code of bushido, Hitomi bowed low to his blade. It was time to begin again.

13 A SAMURAI'S BURDEN

In a wide valley below stood the strange city of a strange people. Immense stone arches curled among ancient oaks and wrapped themselves like lovers' arms about their impressive trunks. Beyond the strange arched wall, towers covered with centuries of vines and moss rose amid foreign trees, their peaked tops rivaling the uppermost limbs. Vines lifted between them, connecting the ancient towers into a single city, whispering beneath the cover of leaf and bough and trembling in the faint wind.

The Shinomen was thick and deep here, the lush cover turning the woodland sunlight bluish-green. No human had ever journeyed this far into the forest, Daini knew instinctively. Though tales of the cities of the Shinomen were passed among the children of Rokugan, they were never believed.

Not until now.

Following his green-skinned guide, Daini stumbled over roots thicker than his own leg.

His eyes frantically assessed the strange city that clung to tree trunk and forest grove.

Mara stopped a few miles from the city, gazing down with pride at the cluster of buildings. At the break between two twisted trees, a golden arch stood, covered in jewels that were in turn covered in moss. Mara lingered within it for a moment as the other naga slithered past. All of them reverently looked down on the city.

Daini studied the intricate cluster of buildings and looked to the golden hair of his guide.

This was no Rokugani city with sliding paper screens and elegantly curved roofs of mahogany and balsa. These buildings were almost entirely stone, their peaked tops resembling eggs on towering cylinders. The city itself was shaped like a great wheel, spokes radiating out from the central palace and traveling through each area in straight, perfectly measured lines. The central palace was not separated by walls or guards, but open and airy. The pillars around it held aloft a ceiling of vine and shade. Within that cover, a building of gold and ivory rested, its doorways resembling nothing so much as burrow holes, circular and patterned with interlocking figures. Smaller houses clung like clustered mushrooms to the city's arched gates. Stone was everywhere—used in every construction and lining the city's roads like petals of some strange flower. A small river flowed to the north of the city and provided water for the central fountains. Groves of trees to the east hid templelike buildings and carefully tended gardens.

The populace little resembled the folk in the Emerald Empire. Rather than heimin hawking wares and eta shuffling about their tasks, hundreds of naga moved down the wide streets, their long tails coiling behind them. Some wore armor. Others wore robes of green and white fabric that shone like scales and moved like silk. Their skins ranged from dark emerald through olive and to the brightest gold. Some of their thick tails had patterns of diamonds, bands of black and orange, or jeweled brightness. Some of the women had legs, but all the men had snakelike tails that sprouted from their lower torsos. Most were only ten feet long, though others reached a length of thirty feet. Golden hair, unheard of in Rokugan, mingled with black and a strange ruddy brown. Some of the naga were bald, their hair replaced with feathered headbands or painted patterns.

Not a single human moved through the populace, and Daini saw many of the naga near him looking warily down at him from their perches in the high trees. Tremendous bows curved in capable hands, but none drew an arrow from his quiver. It seemed as if they had somehow known he was coming—even knew his business! No one disturbed Mara as she led him to the city's outer gates.

It was a magnificent view, but Daini felt cold chills race down his spine. It was a city of strangeness and danger, unlike any other in Rokugan and hidden less than a day's swift travel within the borders of the empire's largest forest

"Welcome, visitor, to Siksa, city of the mighty Asp." Mara smiled. "You have come at the perfect time, Mirumoto-daini, to see the day's farewell to the Bright Eye." Mara turned to look down at the city, sheltered in a small valley of trees and moss. "I remember when this land was a plain, and the oaks around you were no more than children, struggling for sun. Though others say that the forest has swallowed Siksa, I believe that it has simply become one with the Akasha of the land. One day, it will be great again." The pride in her voice seemed hardly contained, far too eager for a samurai's ears. In Rokugan, a woman would not speak with such . . . raw emotion. "I am so happy to see that the city is awake and alive once more."

Unsure where to start, Daini cleared his throat and pretended he had not heard her open display of emotion. Her words were strange—Akasha? Was that some ceremony the naga performed? "I . . . your pardon, honored guide . . ." Daini began hesitantly, feeling lost in the strangeness that surrounded him.

"Mara, Mirumoto-daini. You shall call me the Mara." Jewels twinkled softly in her earlobes as she smiled, brilliant white against the striking green candor of her skin. "It is my title, and my name."

"Mara. Hai." Looking again at the city within the forest, Daini swallowed hard. "Your people live here?"

She laughed, stepping out from the arch and making her way down the forest path. Her bare feet moved lightly across the ground, pressing against ancient cobblestone and thick roots. "Oh, no, Mirumoto-daini. My people are the Green-snakes. We live to the north, in the city of Nirukti . . . or once we did." The sorrow on her face shocked Daini, and he was horrified to see a tear run from her golden eye. Did these snake-creatures know no manners?

"Nirukti has been destroyed by time, erased as we slept," Mara continued. "We, the Greensnakes who lived through the Great Sleep, now remain here with the Asp. Perhaps one day we will see our city whole again. I do not know." Brushing away the tear gently with the back of one emerald hand, Mara smiled through her sorrow. Then, as suddenly, her face lit with joy. Turning to look to the west, Mara reached to grasp Daini's hand in her own. "Listen! The Bright Eye comes!"

Shocked at her touch, Daini froze. Her hand was strangely cool, her fingers soft and supple.

A faint tension swept through the air, and Daini saw the naga near him move as one, looking toward the west with eager, expectant eyes. All noise within the city hushed as through a great wave of silence brushed against the city's arches. A single guard on the city's high walls raised a strange horn of curved bone to his lips.

The note was soft at first, growing in intensity with the echoes of the forest. As it swelled, Mara's hand squeezed gently. Her eyes grew wide, taking in the radiance . . . and something else that Daini could not hear. Around them both, the single horn sang louder, gaining volume as it spread out among Siksa's frozen populace.

Then, from the west, a sudden ray of sunlight exploded through the open branches of the oaks. Rays of light, white and golden, showered the city in sunset radiance. The horn swelled again, and Daini saw more naga lifting horns to their lips, car-rying the call until it pealed from a thousand instruments. The walls of the city, arched stone that wove through the massive trees, began to glow with gold. Beneath a thousand years of moss, the intricate moldings of precious metal and stones burst into light.

If the walls were clear, Daini thought in shock, the effect would have been nearly blinding. "By the Fortunes . . ." Daini whispered, forgetting Mara's touch. "How did the empire miss this?"

"Siksa, like all the cities of the naga, was hidden by the spell of the Great Sleep. When we awoke, it returned from the mists that had hidden it. Nirukti knew no such fortune. The spell there was incomplete, and many of my people died."

Daini remembered ancient rumors of stones in the Shinomen that would fade and reappear. How many of the old legends were true? Looking at the green-skinned maiden at his side, Daini hesitated to guess. The Shinomen Forest was enchanted. Any samurai knew that. Everyone knew of the ronin and bandits that fled into the forest never to return. The Falcon, keepers of the border of the Shinomen, claimed that ghosts haunted the forest, hiding in stone cities . . . cities such as this one.

"The Great Sleep?" Daini repeated, trying to understand as sunset glowed on the city walls.

"A spell cast by the Cobra jakla, to keep us ready until the Second Burning of the land . . . there is too much to tell, Mirumoto-daini, and I do not have all the words." Mara laughed brightly.

"Yet, you know much of our language. How is this?"

"The Greensnake awoke before the others, and we have been trying to learn the language of your people," she replied. "I am one of the first. You are lucky I was on patrol today, or the others might not have understood your purpose."

"Lucky . . . hai." Daini stammered, remembering how the other naga had seemed unwilling to put down their bows.

The horn tones around them began to fade as the sun moved low in the sky.

Mara tilted her head to the side as if listening. "I see." She said to no one in particular.

"What?" Daini asked, watching the city's transformation. The glow faded slowly, and one by one, the horns ended their siren call. As they did, the stars above the city began to appear, twinkling lightly through the thick cluster of branches and leaves. He looked at the naga maiden beside him. Suddenly, in that instant of peace and tranquility, he realized she was beautiful.

"The Shahadet wishes to see you, Mirumoto-daini. Immediately." Mara's eyes grew troubled. "Follow me, and do not say a word. Your life will depend on your silence." Letting go of his hand, she stepped through the open arch and headed for the city. Not once did she look back to see if he followed her command.

Daini hesitated only for a second. Then, without a word, he followed her into the wide streets of the city of the Asp.

▲▲▲▲▲▲▲▲

Within the city twilight, the boughs and vines of the clustered ceilings took on a snakelike appearance. Daini could almost imagine them twisting above him in scaled masses. Passing beneath them, Mara and Daini reached the palace of the Shahadet. The structure was huge and ornate, hidden beneath the open canopy. A long ramp led down from the mosaic plaza into a massive stone chamber beneath the ground.

A ramp, Daini thought, because creatures with tails cannot use stairs.

At the bottom of the ramp, Mara knelt, pressing her hands together and then touching them to her forehead as she whispered sibilant syllables. Taking her cue, Daini knelt as well and glanced curiously around the tremendous chamber.

At least forty warriors lined the walls of the pit, with arched bows on their backs and strangely curved swords hanging from jeweled belts. Many wore armor of silver and gold, their slitted eyes peering at Daini with a mixture of curiosity and hatred. One opened his mouth in a grinning threat, and Daini saw poison trail in a thin strand down the creature's fangs.

The city of the Asp, indeed, he thought with a shudder.

In the far wall, an alcove had been carved. It contained a tremendous chair fashioned from the stone of the natural earth. The throne sparkled with jewels and ornate figurines, and it had no arms. Behind it, in an elaborate mosaic of patterned tiles, a figure with six arms and a long naga tail danced, its head shaped like a dragon's, with snout and fiery breath. The figure held flaming torches of starlight in eight-fingered hands and dancing on a golden city.

In the center of the room, a young naga hung by his tail, suspended from the high ceiling by feathered vines. He was perhaps fifteen, perhaps a bit younger, by Daini's guess. Below him, a circle of flame lit the room in flickering shadows, and the boy spun gently. As he turned, his hands remained in the white-hot flames, and a pool of boiling water directly beneath his head sent up puffs of strange-smelling smoke.

"That is the water of the River of the Sky," Mara whispered to Daini, noting his stare. She pointed to the blue-black water in the basin beneath the slowly spinning naga youth. "The young Ashamana lingers in his Pah'ra ceremony. Those who drink—or even touch—its water are given a vision of their future. If he succeeds, he will conquer the darkness in his own soul and become one with the great mind of the Akasha. Each of us is given a vision from its power. The river once flowed through my people's city, Nirukti, though the Greensnake ritual of Pah'ra is nothing like this. My own vision on my day of testing spoke of your kind. That is how I came to meet you, Mirumoto-daini. The River of the Sky sent me." She was confident, unafraid, and completely sure of herself.

The other naga surrounding the flames chanted softly, their tongues hissing with fierce pride as the boy's hands blackened in the fire.

"It is his maturity ritual. Your kind have another word for it—gem'puk-hu?" Daini nodded silently, and Mara smiled. "The boy who now tests his Pah'ra hangs above the well. He sees things we do not see and lives within the Akasha in that place of testing. Yet in a way, we are with him there." As she spoke, Mara closed her striking golden eyes and breathed deeply.

Daini looked at the others in the room, afraid to ask his questions lest he break the silence he had been commanded to keep. With him? What did she mean? Of course they were all with him . . . in this room. Or was that not Mara's intent? Did the naga see something that Daini could not see?

"Look at the Asp with the spear," Mara whispered softly.

Daini noticed that one of the warriors slithering around the fire held a spear made of pearl and jade.

"That is the youth's Sehalai," Mara murmured, regarding the Sehalai with narrowed eyes and a cautious tone. "If the Ashamana fails, it is the Sehalai's duty to kill him before the Ashamana's failure taints the Akasha with falsehoods. The Asp rituals are far more bloody than those of my own bloodline." Her voice held scorn, but carefully hidden.

So, these naga were not a single people, then? Bloodline? Was that their word to differentiate their clans? The Sehalai's duty was to kill the one undergoing the ritual. . . . Daini's face turned white. These people murdered their own children? How could they live with themselves? The Ashamana—certainly a title, and not a name, from the way Mara used it—continued to spin, his face dark from paint and the pressure of hanging from his tail. Daini smelled the tinge of flesh burning in the fire, and saw that the boy's hands were blistered and raw.

The tone of the chanting changed, and many of the warriors began to move away from the wall, toward the fire. The Sehalai lowered his spear, shaking it violently as the others parted. His tail shook with a warning rattle. A low thrumming began, rising from the throats of the surrounding warriors, and movement began inside another dark alcove. This one was deeper, perhaps leading into another chamber entirely. The passageway for the creature they called the "Shahadet."

The naga entering the chamber wore no armor, carried no weapon save a single unsheathed blade at his side, curved nearly into a **V** and strangely forged. It hung from a loop around the warlord's chest, the leather thong tightening around massively bunched muscles. Green eyes scornfully swept through the chamber, eyeing Daini and Mara as invaders to this sacred ritual, but he said nothing. The Shahadet raised himself high to oversee the proceedings, standing more than ten feet in the air above another length of green tail. Weaving from side to side, he raised a hand silently, and the Asp parted to allow him to see the spinning Ashamana within the orange and white flames.

"Shahadet," Mara hissed, bowing her head low to the ground. Daini quickly did likewise.

Suddenly all the naga in the room turned as one toward the youth above the fire. Mara gasped, covered her eyes and turned her head into Daini's shoulder.

A scream burst from the Ashamana's throat.

Daini watched in horror as the boy's face blackened, and his hands crumbled to ash, scattering among the flames.

The naga holding the pearl spear hissed loudly, his tail rattling in a frantic chant. Daini looked away, shocked, but he heard the Sehalai strike. There was a scream from the Ashamana. An echoing wail rose from the throats of the other warriors in the room, and a cry of release erupted from the Ashamana's throat. The ceremony had failed.

Around them, the Asp hissed, their sibilant language filled with an almost unspeakable pain and anguish.

"It comes. . . . It comes. . . ." Mara translated in broken words, her voice cracking as the youth swung within the flames.

Daini glanced toward the ritual pool. There hung the Ashamana's body, arched and sparkling with a mystic fire. Blood trailed from his wound as his Sehalai withdrew the spear, and Daini looked away again, overcome by the brutality. Agonized seconds passed as the youth screamed a single echoing note.

Then Daini heard a third stroke from the Sehalai's spear, and the boy's cry ceased.

"The Ashamana . . . has failed." Mara whispered huskily.

Ravaged by wounds and covered in blood and smeared

paint, the youth hung from the high ceiling vines, his white eyes creasing with death. The Ashamana's hands fell, no longer outstretched, and his fingertips brushed the glossy water of the pool beneath his swinging body.

"By the Pale," Mara choked. She pressed her head to Daini's chest as if seeking comfort, and the samurai instinctively reached to touch her golden hair. It was soft, like spider webs and silk, and clung to his fingers gently as he touched her. Mara smelled of sage and the ocean, he thought faintly as his mind sought somewhere to hide that was not filled with blood and pain.

"Huu-man."

Mara moved, her eyes clearing, and she pushed gently away from Daini's arms. "My thanks, samurai," she whispered shakily. "I have never seen a Pah'ra end in Foul. It is . . . horrible."

Daini looked up and saw one of the Asp approach them. The naga's hand lifted as if to motion the samurai to his feet.

Mara stood, pulling Daini up beside her, and faced the Asp. Uncertain what else to do, Daini bowed politely to the warrior and was completely ignored. Mara stepped past the warrior and headed toward the throne alcove. Daini followed her without question.

In the alcove, the massive Shahadet reclined, his tail wrapped about the base of the pillar that served as the seat of his throne. Mara knelt, and Daini did as well The Shahadet stared down at them quietly, allowing the other warriors in the room to assemble once more. Daini noticed that the body of the Ashamana was being attended to by two of the largest Asp. Without hesitation, they reached up to touch the dead body, and Daini's eyes opened wide in revulsion. Warriors—samurai?—touching the flesh of the dead? Revolting.

The Shahadet's heavy-lidded eyes studied the human before him, taking in every detail. The naga had not removed Daini's swords from his side. Etiquette demanded that the prisoner of an Asp be allowed to kill himself in combat rather than starve in a prison. Scornfully, the Shahadet began to speak to Mara, his hissing words punctuated by gestures and the understanding of the Akasha.

·

Mara turned to Daini. "The Shahadet gives you permission to speak. I will translate your words to him, that you may parley."

Daini bowed again, touching his forehead to the ground before the daimyo of the naga. "Please thank the Shahadet for his time."

Mara hissed softly, and Daini continued to talk, trusting her to translate. "My name is Mirumoto Daini of the Dragon." That caused a stir among the naga and with the Shahadet. "I am here to parley with the naga, to ask that their warriors aid us in eliminating our enemies, the Crab."

Mara responded almost as she finished speaking, "Who are the Crab?"

"The Crab are a clan from the south," Daini responded.

"Ah, the south lands," Mara nodded. "The Foul."

The Shahadet's face twisted as his forked tongue slid between perfectly even, white teeth. A pair of snakelike fangs extended just over his lower lip, and as Daini watched, he raised a hand to catch a falling drop of poison. He and Mara conferred for a few moments, and then the maiden turned again to Daini.

"You say that your people fight the Foul?" she asked.

"We fight the Shadowlands and the Crab, who work with them." Daini went on to describe the armies of the Crab that held Beiden Pass, and the terrible oni that fought beside the Hida necromancers. When he was done, the Asp warriors around him were hissing madly, their eyes tinted red with firelight and anger.

The Shahadet had not moved at all from his throne, but his powerful arms had tightened into fists, and his stone face had frozen into a look of hatred. Daini's voice faltered, but Mara prompted him, eager to learn.

The Shahadet spoke once more, and his hissing language echoed from the other Asp. As if they had been provoked, several of them reared above the others, gesturing with their hands and shaking swords in strange leather scabbards.

Mara's face fell, but she raised her hands in a gesture of peace, palms extended toward the Shahadet. Quickly guessing that her gesture was conciliatory, Daini did the same.

The Lord of the Asps stared down with bitter tolerance, and then made a sweeping gesture with his arm.

"What is he saying?" Daini said quietly as the other Asps bared their fangs and raised their weapons. "Will they help me?"

"No," Mara's tone was final. "They refuse to believe you. Right now . . . they're debating what to do with your corpse."

"I can't let them kill me." Daini blanched, his thin mustache shaking as his lips trembled. "If I die . . . all the others of my clan will be destroyed by the Shadowlands.

"There is nothing to be done. The Asp do not believe that you fight the Foul. They say you are working for it, to draw us into your huu-man wars." The serpents surrounding the Shahadet's throne slid backward as their leader lifted his tremendous bulk and reached for a golden spear.

"Let me prove myself."

"How?"

The Mirumoto samurai bowed briefly, startling the naga around him, and stood. Mara leapt to her feet and hissed, clicking her tongue behind her teeth as she calmed them. Walking slowly, Daini stepped toward the empty circle of flame and the large basin of water.

"What are you doing, Mirumoto-daini?" Mara said hesitatingly as the Asps began to close.

"You said the water would give me a vision. Let me show them the future of the empire, if the Shadowlands are allowed to succeed." Terrified, Daini sprinted through the surprised Asps, leaping toward the circle of flames.

"Mirumoto-daini!" Mara threw herself between the samurai and the spears of her people, flinging her arms wide to protect him as she hissed in their strange, snakelike tongue. "No, Daini!" she turned to look at him with terrified eyes. "Not while there is blood in the water!"

Ignoring the raised spears and swiftly strung bows, Daini stared down at the red-tinged waters of the basin, seeing his own face clearly reflected past the flickering flames. Taking several short, deep breaths, he tore the sleeves from his gi and punched through the fire. There was blood in the water, but

Daini did not care. What honor did he have left after he had given away Hitomi's life? The flames bit into his flesh, searing nerve and burning hair, but Daini did not stop until his hands were immersed in the icy water.

How can the water be icy when it boils and flames? The thought lasted a fragment of a second, a fleeting glimpse of what Daini had been, before the visions began.

Fire surged, leaping up only inches from Daini's face, and then fell to darkness. A thin trail of flickering coal laced the edge of the water's basin, lighting the swirling red waters within. Daini felt his burned hands ease, then turn to ice within the water's grasp. It was as if two cold hands clutched his own, refusing to release him from the well.

The water boiled again, but not from heat. Something within the waves moved and writhed. Images began to flicker across the water's surface. Faces that Daini knew swirled in the bloody waters. He saw Yukihera, Mitsu laced to the torii arch in Beiden Pass, the Dragon as they marched down from their high mountains. But these were visions of the past, not the future. Daini reached farther into the pool, sinking his wrists and forearms to strive harder against the water's pull, and felt the visions change again.

Otosan Uchi . . . in flames.

Echoes of madness drifted from the pool's inky bottom, but Daini held fast to the frozen hands. Across the water, false flames reflected—flames of spears and arrows, released against the Dragon. This, then, was the future. Daini saw a tremendous army massed around the Imperial City. Lion killed Lion, and the Crab Champion's face, broken with pain and anguish, screamed soundlessly within the waves—Kisada, fallen.

Again, Daini pulled, and the blood in the water grew clear. Otosan Uchi. The Crab armies and a terrible dark wave of undead stormed from the southern mountains with flesh in their hands and blood on their spears. Laughter swelled up from the water, but it was not the laughter of a man, or of anything Daini recognized. The icy hands suddenly had blades in their fingers, cutting Daini's flesh as he held fast to their watery grasp. The empire lay before him, reflected in the waters of the boiling pool, burned by flame and tainted by the Shadowlands. Armies of zombies and necromancers marched along blackened roads, and Daini saw them setting flame to the Shinomen. In Otosan Uchi, the throne lay on the ground, the crack grown wide. Blood trailed over the gleaming dais, swelling like a river, flowing to the ocean and over the empire.

Something had gone wrong, terribly, horribly wrong, but Daini could not draw back his hands. Visions flickered rapidly across the water, and the incensed hissing of the Asps sounded like a pit of vipers preparing for a meal. Daini kept his eyes fast to the water, pulling the icy hands toward him with all his strength. In the waves, he saw Yukihera, standing beside a rotting corpse that could have once been a Scorpion.

Daini screamed, desperate to free himself, but the hands held fast. The visions came faster, some clear and others blurred, shifting from one face to the next without reason. He saw Mitsu, torn open and hanging; forgotten, on a broken and ruined arch. The ise zumi lifted his rotting head to stare into Daini's wide eyes. Mitsu smiled a festering smile.

Hitomi's face swirled into view, and Daini heard her voice call to him.

Daini . . . my brother . . . how you have failed me. . . .

A black carapace spread across her face, turning her to stone. The obsidian shattered, Yukihera's spear piercing her from behind. Daini felt himself scream again, drawn nearly chest-deep in the boiling waters.

Darkness covered the Crane lands, and the Lion plains were in flames. Was this a vision of the future . . . or of a possible future? Daini screamed again, trying to tear his hands from the water's grip, but the River of the Sky was not yet finished with him. Scarlet spread out across the rippling water of the clear pool, staining his hands the color of blood. Dragon samurai lifted their spears and banners, and Yukihera stood before them in armor made of shining gold. "I have done this for you, brothers!" Yukihera cried. "The Dragon will live. . . ." Yukihera reached up from the waves, his body withering and his features losing flesh. When the white bone shone out from beneath rotting muscle, Yukihera smiled. "Forever."

With a massive burst of strength and terror, Daini drew himself upright, jerking his arms free to the elbows and trying not to listen to the awful, hollow laughter that echoed from the water. As he pulled his hands achingly toward the surface, Daini glimpsed the creature that clutched with knifelike fingers at his wrists. It lasted only a second, and Daini's mind struggled to reject the riddle it portrayed.

The beast had the face of the Emperor Hantei, twisted by madness and rotting with taint.

Flinging himself from the pool, Daini pressed his back against the cool stone of the cave wall. He stared in abject horror at the waters as they slowly grew calm.

Mara knelt beside him, taking his head in her cool hands and searching his eyes for life. "Mirumoto-daini?" she whispered, pressing her face to his.

Around them, Asps rattled their swords fiercely, shouting in guttural tones and hissing, shrieking wails of fury and war.

The Shahadet raised his tremendous bulk, lowering his hands before him, palms down.

As if cowed, the Asp warriors cringed back at his gesture, covering the floor in a writing nest of snakes and weaponry. Their gold armor glinted redly in the bloody firelight, and the lord of the Asp regarded the huu-man with new eyes.

Mara turned back toward the Shahadet, her soft hair brushing Daini's chest as she moved. After only a few sibilant syllables, she nodded and turned back to the Dragon samurai.

"The Shahadet says you have strength and courage. We have never seen such an act from a huu-man."

"I cannot . . ." Daini croaked, realizing that his voice was hoarse from screaming. "I cannot let my family die. Whatever those visions meant, they show me that the future of the empire is in terrible danger. I must go. You cannot understand—the emperor, his family . . . my people . . . they could already be destroyed." Daini felt heat swelling behind his eyes, and he blinked away visions of Yukihera's festering smile.

"No," said Mara, tears forming in her eyes. "I understand. The Foul destroyed my city while the naga slept, Mirumoto-daini. I will not let it destroy another, simply because we choose to sleep again."

"We have to convince them to listen," he began, but she interrupted him.

"They are listening, Mirumoto-daini. Now you must give them a reason to act."

"What can I do?"

The Shahadet raised himself high into the air on his thick tail, towering above the others and holding aloft the pearl and jade spear of the Pah'ra. The massive naga closed his arms, crossing them on his broad, muscular chest and lowering his head over the shaft of the ancient spear. He hissed briefly, click-ing his tongue against his fangs and closing his eyes as if he in-toned some ancient text. The other Asps grew silent, with only a faint hiss of agreement rising from their supine forms. Then, opening his arms once more, he presented the spear to Daini, holding it still with a stoic gesture.

"You will be tested. If you succeed in the Pah'ra, then you will become one of the warriors of the Asp. The naga will not fight for huu-mans. It is not our way. However, if you succeed in the Pah'ra, you will be a warrior of Siksa, a member of the Asp. Then, Mirumoto-daini, you will be one of us, and the naga will fight for you."

"And if I fail?"

"There is no failure, samurai." Daini felt a chill along his spine as Mara continued. "There is only death."

With no other choice, Daini murmured, "Tell him I accept."

Mara stood, grasping the spear by its long pearl shaft and speaking a few quiet words in her native tongue.

The Shahadet's scaled eyebrow raised, but there was no other sign of concern. The mighty Asp released the spear into her hands.

"We have only a short time to ready you for the Pah'ra, to teach you our culture and the words of the rite of passage. At the end of that time, your Sehalai will bring you to the council chamber, and you will undergo the rite. If you succeed, you will gain the favor of the Asp—and the troops you require to save your people. If you fail, both you and your Sehalai will be destroyed." Mara reached to help Daini stand. "Come with me, samurai. We have much to do."

"We?" Daini asked. Though he could walk, he doubted that he would make it very far on his own. His knees shook from exhaustion, and his hands still bled across the cold stone ground.

"Yes, we." Mara said faintly, worry creasing her green skin. "I am your Sehalai."

14 BEFORE THE GREAT DRAGON

The banners of the Dragon armies fluttered in the strong breeze that swept through Beiden Pass, and their shade dappled the faces of wounded, weary men. For a full week, they had fought the Crab. For a week, they had pushed farther and farther into the pass, beating back the constant waves of undead. Toturi's ronin guard continued to grow, though slowly—and between their fresh strength and Dragon training, the northern army managed slowly to turn the tide.

Yukihera knelt at the top of a tall stone cliff, looking over the rise at the windswept valley below. In a series of caves at the far end, where the canyon narrowed to a thin trail, the Crab army camped. Beyond the canyon spread the plains that were once Scorpion territory—the southern end of Beiden Pass.

"If we can beat them out of that encampment," Toturi said, kneeling beside

Yukihera and pointing at the Crab base, "then we can drive them completely out of the pass. With no stone at their backs, the Crab will be forced to turn south and go home to Carpenter Wall."

"If, Toturi. If." Yukihera said cautiously. "The Crab have caves to hide in. They have undead. Three oni still survive, and numerous scattered bands still roam Beiden Pass."

The ronin general harrumphed, clearing his throat in a long growl. "The strongest point is the least guarded." Thoughtfully, Toturi rubbed his stubbled chin. "The Crab are secure in their stone walls. They live behind one, in the far south. Why should they not trust their lives to walls of stone here in Beiden Pass?"

"The caves," agreed Yukihera. "But they don't have to guard them well. Their supplies are secure inside the mountain. We cannot even get to them to burn their food stock, and the underground river provides them all the water they could ever need."

Toturi smiled, rising to his feet. "Don't be so sure, Dragon. Where there is a stream, there is a path." He strode back down the cliff path, leaving the mystified Yukihera to follow, glowering at the ronin's back.

▲▲▲▲▲▲▲▲

"Get up!" The command was sharp, and Toturi slapped the man's feet off the post on which they rested.

The shocked ronin gasped awake, his eyes fluttering and squinting in the broad daylight. His hand vault for his sword.

With a shove, Toturi pushed the man from his resting place, a wide board slung between two hitching posts.

With a thump, the ronin fell to the ground. The man was scruffy, his dirty gi and pants wrinkled from too much sweat and stained by grass and blood. He wore no mon, but only a sword that hung at his side from a long piece of braided cord. Yelping in surprise, he rolled back to his feet as if to repel invaders. Recognizing the general at last, he bowed hastily, slapping his hands to his sides and lowering his shoulders in respect. "To-Toturi-sama." His brown eyes were dark and shadowed, and his burly shoulders were broad with honest work. Unkempt hair spilled around his face, nearly hiding a charming smile.

"Well." Toturi looked at the ronin skeptically, as if measuring the man's girth and size. "Are you awake now?

"Hai." He gave a chagrined nod.

"Good thing I wasn't a Crab." The general half-smiled, and his man nodded in embarrassment.

"This . . . beast . . . will help us?" Yukihera hissed, staring at the ronin in disgust.

"Ookami is no beast. He is a samurai," Toturi said, leaning casually on the post that the ronin had recently vacated. "An old companion of mine, from our school days at Matsu Palace, before I was sent to Shinsei's monastery."

"Ookami. That means 'wolf'." The Dragon scoffed. "Don't you have a real name?"

Slowly turning to level a deadly glance at Yukihera, the man whispered slowly, "I did."

A chill passed suddenly through Yukihera, and he saw for the first time the small tattoo of a lion's head, just below the man's jaw by his right ear. Akodo.

"I need you to do something for me, Ookami," Toturi continued solemnly. "Do you remember when we were children, playing at Matsu Palace, and you found the caves that lead into Beiden Pass?"

"Hai," the man said swiftly, his eyes shifting to Toturi's face.

"Did you ever explore them?"

The ronin's face reddened slightly. "We were forbidden to explore them, Toturi-sama. The sensei threatened to throw us out of the school is we risked our lives so foolishly."

"I know that." The general leaned closer to Ookami, squinting into the man's face. "I also know you never listened to the sensei unless he was giving a lesson. Did you explore the caves?"

A faint pause, and the man nodded.

"Good. Then you still remember the way?"

Ookami shook his head, disbelieving. "Through the river beneath the mountains? In the blind dark? Toturi, that's madness."

"You did it when you were twelve. You can do it again now."

"Send Ginawa. He likes suicide missions," the man said roguishly.

Toturi laughed aloud. "You're going. Take two more with you. And don't forget to bring flint and steel." The ronin general grinned. "You're going to have plenty of kindling to burn when you get to the other side."

▲▲▲▲▲▲▲▲

Screams of "Fire!" echoed from the walls of Beiden Pass. Crab fled the caves, shouting for water and blankets. Behind them issued billowing clouds of black smoke, rising out of the cave mouths and pouring onto the battlefield.

Exactly as Toturi had planned.

Dragon and ronin troops swarmed from the north, taking advantage of the smoke and confusion to pour into the Crab lines. Though the Crab pikemen stood their ground, it was too late to stop the onslaught of the allied forces. They had no shelter in the smoke-filled caves, and no safe ground in the pass. Within a few hours, the Crab had begun to retreat, without supplies and without quite a few samurai—casualties of the unexpected and unorthodox attack.

Now it was only a matter of time. The Crab and their Shadowlands forces could not stand before the united attacks of Dragon, ronin, and Unicorn. In perhaps a day, in perhaps a few hours, the Battle of Beiden Pass would be won, at last.

▲▲▲▲▲▲▲▲

Yukihera's horse pounded up the hillock. He reined the beast in with a strong hand and peered down at the encampment below. The banners of the Dragon were being removed.

Yukihera's tent, lowered to the ground, was being packed by eta and prepared for the long journey back to the mountains of his homeland.

"Home to the Iron Mountain," Yukihera breathed, watching his breath mist in the cold morning air. A smile spread across his classically handsome features, making his golden-brown eyes shine. "To my destiny." The wind blew cold against his face, a reminder that winter, even in these mild southern lands, was not far off.

"Forgive me, my lord," a young guardsman on the hill said, bowing humbly before the Mirumoto general. "The ise zumi have gathered at the torii arch, prepared to take their brother home. May I give them your permission to release Togashi Mitsu?"

"Permission?" Yukihera laughed, a cold, cruel sound. "Togashi Mitsu was to be released from his punishment when the Dragon found more allies. We needed no more allies to win the day, it turns out, but that does not change our bargain. His punishment is fitting for one who disobeyed the daimyo of the Mirumoto, and dared to raise a hand to his superior. Mitsu is a traitor, and he will be treated like one.

"He stays atop that arch, Gunso, until he dies."

With that, Yukihera turned his steed once more, ignoring the animal's pained whinny at the heels dug into its sides. With a caustic smile, the Mirumoto general rode down the hill to collect his men and begin the long journey north.

▲▲▲▲▲▲▲▲

Yukihera knelt in the darkness near the ivory throne of the champion. "Beiden Pass is clear, and the Crab run like whipped dogs, driven back to their wall. Our people are safely returned home." He looked up at the silent figure that rested upon the throne. "I am of the line of Mirumoto's first son. I have won these battles, when the line of Shosan failed." The golden general clenched his hand into a fist. "You must recognize my claim."

"You may lead the Mirumoto for now, Yukihera." The voice whispered like wind through the empty corridors of Mirumoto Palace. It did not come from the man sitting upon the throne, but came from all around, as if Iron Mountain itself spoke. The champion's eyes flashed beneath a golden mask, seeing the future shift and change. "But you will never be their daimyo. . . ."

15 THE AKASHA

His mind lost in turmoil, Mirumoto Daini fell into an exhausted sleep. For a few hours, he was blessed with visions of his homeland—rich earth amid boulders and sharp cliffs, ringed around by high mountain walls. Iron Mountain rose above it all like a beacon, lighting his way home.

He awakened with a start to find Mara bending over him, gently stroking his hair in the soft light of a single candle.

"Is it time?" he murmured sleepily, banishing visions of clouds over jutting mountain peaks.

"Nearly," she replied with a worried glance. "The Asp gather beneath the temple."

Daini sighed. For one month, he had trained. His muscles ached from constant exercise with spear and bow, the naga weapons of choice. His mind ached from trying to absorb as much of their language and culture as possible. The Akasha, he now knew, was a single consciousness that all naga could touch. Like a unified mind, it guided their actions and taught them their past from the gathered memories of their ancestors. If he was to complete the Pah'ra, he would have to touch this great mind, and it must choose to allow him to understand. As with a gempuku, the Pah'ra would make him an adult member of the society.

Any other samurai would have rebelled. A second gempuku? Insulting.

But Daini remembered his sister's words. If you have forgotten so soon . . . then you must begin your training again. Remembering her fallen body, crushed on the field beneath the Crab's iron tetsubo, Daini shivered. In his mind, he turned away once more and saw Yukihera's face beneath his golden helm, laughing. Yukihera, daimyo of the Mirumoto because of Hitomi's arrogance and Daini's pride.

He had forgotten, indeed.

The important thing was to stay alive—at least until he was certain that the naga would return to aid Toturi and the Dragon. After that, it didn't matter anymore.

Poor Mitsu. He must be dead by now—or worse, hanging from his arch in torment, realizing Daini was never going to return.

"Daini, we must go. The Asp are lighting the evening torches." Her green skin was radiant in the candlelight. Her golden hair swayed with each serpentine movement.

He rose from his bed, following her up the dry and dusty stone ramp of the small room he had occupied beneath the city's wall. The naga had allowed him to stay within Siksa, their guards watching every move he made. Even now, as he stepped out into the street, their eyes followed him suspiciously.

"Namaste, honored brother." Daini smiled, imitating the steepled hands and strange half-bow of the naga.

The guard stoically nodded, touching his forefinger to the center of his forehead in greeting.

Just how he was going to defeat the test, Daini did not know. In fact, he wasn't even certain that he understood what was expected of him. The physical exertion, he understood well enough. He would be hung by his legs (bound to serve in imitation of a tail) from the tall stalactite, and he would spin with his hands in the white-hot flames. Then, as the skin dissolved on his palms, he would stare down into the water of the River of the Sky, and . . .

And what?

Visions, like before? Otosan Uchi, destroyed by the Dark God of the Shadowlands?

A shudder shook Daini—one that was not his own. He glanced at Mara, but she was staring at the high parapets of Siksa's arched towers. "Earthquake?" Daini asked.

"They occur rarely, but they are not unheard of. The Vedic considered them portents of great and terrible events coming to pass." The Vedic were naga priests, the largest and most dangerous—and rarest of the five bloodlines.

Once more, Daini followed Mara down beneath the boughs and vines of the clustered ceilings, through the twisted ramps of the Asp temple. The palace of the Shahadet was ornate, gilded with gold and silver, but of all the treasures scattered about the mosaic plaza and its massive stone chamber, only one held the samurai's attention. He looked to the long stalactite hanging from the vaulted ceiling. It was covered with rope and stains of greenish blood.

Mara knelt at the bottom of the ramp, pressing her hands together and then touching them to her forehead. She whispered sibilant syllables. This time Daini knew the words, and as he knelt, he intoned them in a smooth baritone.

"To the Ocean, we are born.
Forest, Lake, Plain, River, and Mountain.
In the Earth, we grow as children.
Greensnake, Asp, Cobra, Constrictor, and Chameleon.
For the Akasha, we must rise.
Warrior, Jakla, Vedic, Scout, and King."

The room was filled with more Asp than the last time, and for a moment, Daini felt a surge of pride that so many had come to see his gempuku. That pride was quickly replace with nervousness when he saw the mocking face of the Balash. The archer lay silent along the wall at the far edge of the pit. He fingered an arrow's sharpened point, ignoring the trickle of blood that seeped from beneath a scaled fingernail. Balash stared hotly at Daini, and his eyes were filled with hate.

The tremendous alcove in the far wall was filled, its chair covered by the impressive bulk of the commander of the Asp and daimyo of the city.

Shahadet, Daini corrected himself.

The throne glittered faintly beneath the massive naga's tremendous tail, and the wall mosaic behind him sparkled with jewels. The starlight from the figure's hands seemed to stretch out across the room, reaching toward infinity. On the ground near the pool lay three objects: a spear of pearl and jade, an unlit torch, and a silver pin as large as a small tanto.

Mara led him to the center of the room, where the River of the Sky bubbled up into the pool of visions. Around it, a white flame burned just at the water's edge. His hands would pass through that flame as he looked down into the waters. Daini shuddered. He would be burned.

Mara stepped through an opening where the fire that had not yet been ignited, sinking to her waist in the pool of silvery water. He followed her silently, pausing just within the edge of the pool. The water reached to his shoulders as he knelt.

"Rise, supplicant," Mara said in the tongue of her people. The sound was sibilant, hissing as much as speech. Though Daini had been taught the words, much of their meaning was still lost to him. He stood as he had been instructed, and also removed his gi and haori vest. Bare-chested, he knelt in the water beneath the long stalactite and crossed his arms over his head.

Taking a handful of earth from outside the circle, Mara brushed dirt across Daini's forehead. "From the earth, you come. To the earth, you will return."

Around them, the Asp hissed, and Daini caught a few scattered words. "Huu-man" was among them. So was "blasphemer."

The Shahadet rested silently in his chair, his eyes dark and shadowed behind firelight.

Brushing her hands across the knob of the cold torch, she touched her soot-covered fingers to each of Daini's shoulders. "Ash is your soul, burned and broken, unawakened by the Akasha." She touched his hands. "Ash is your heart, unknown by your people."

She reached into the pool beneath the stalactite and brushed the water over his hair. "The Akasha cools us, and will protect us even as it releases your soul. As your Sehalai, I choose to stand with you. I accept your visions. I join you in your search for truth." Mara stepped back, lighting the torch in the flames of the circle. With one last look into Daini's eyes, she stepped through the breach in the flame. Lifting the pearl spear in one hand and holding the burning brand in the other, she glanced at the Shahadet.

There was no response. The tremendous Asp did not move, not even to nod acceptance of the ceremony.

Slowly, Mara lit the circle, closing the open space where they had entered and sealing Daini within.

The wide basin of water shifted around Daini's body as the underground river seethed. This pocket of water was icy cold, clear and bright and shimmering with light from the mystic flames that encircled it. The fire itself stood half as tall as a man, boiling the edges of the water, just within reach of someone hanging from the stalactite. As the fires grew around him, Daini felt his face turning red. Sweat broke out across his body. Soon, the heat would become intense.

Another tremor shook the ground. Daini staggered as he rose to his feet. Glaring at the laughing Asps that surrounded the circle, he reached above him to clasp the stalactite. Pulling himself up its wide surface, he swung over the flowing pool of water. Slowly, Daini crawled up the ropes that hung from the pillar of stone. Using the strength of his arms, and blessing the sensei that had forced him to do muscle toning kata five times a day, Daini turned himself upside down onto the ropes that swung from the bottom of the stalactite.

In a moment, he had tied himself below the stone as he had been taught. The world inverted and swayed, and Daini looked through a circle of flame at the gathered naga.

"To the Akasha, I return." Daini said the last of the ritual words in their strange language, the hisses stumbling from his lips. As he had been taught, Daini reached down to take water from the pool into his cupped hands. Slowly, watching the Balash's contorted face as he began the Pah'ra, Daini drank the water of the River of the Sky, and waited.

Nothing happened.

Another tremor shook the earth and Daini began to sway back and forth from the stalactite. His hands outstretched, touching the flames with his palms, he watched as the circle of fire grew closer with each swing.

The naga warriors looked around at the walls of the chamber. Dust filtered down from the ceiling as the ground buckled and rose.

Despite the physical tremors, Daini felt no metaphysical change, no mystic release. No visions swam before his eyes. Blood pooled in his head, and his hands grew hot from the flames.

A shout rose from the Asp by the ramped doorway. Another tremor shook the stone. Daini could not understand the words—they were spoken too fast, were too unfamiliar—but he understood the tone.

An alarm sounded in the city, great pealing bells that echoed eerily through the silent forest. Was there a fire? Daini thought blearily, trying to keep his mind on the Pah'ra ritual. Perhaps the tremors had flooded the river?

One of the Asp near the doorway drew a shining sword from his hip, snarling.

No, it certainly wasn't a simple fire. Someone screamed outside the chamber's opening. One of the Asp charged up the ramp, and others reached for their weapons. Before the first naga could reach the top, a cluster of arrows pierced his belly and tore the sword from his green-scaled hand. The warrior fell, sliding back down from the doorway with a shriek of pain. Others slid rapidly to his aid.

A shadow covered the moonlight that had streamed in from the plaza above.

Men—huu-man warriors—poured down the open ramp. Their shining katana slid through scaled flesh with classic kiop cries. Iaijutsu blows tore apart bone and sinew without pause, and the Asp fell back, confused by this sudden assault on their most sacred temple.

"No!" Daini howled from his spinning vantage.

As the other Asp in the room joined the battle, one of the samurai looked up at the Dragon in the circle of flame. Daini glimpsed a rotted, skeletal face grinning beneath the fine Crab armor.

The Hida had found him. Crab scouts had followed him into the forest, had found the city, had brought their undead troops. Daini struggled against the thick ropes, wishing he had brought his sword into the ritual chamber. Undead carved their way through the naga.

Naga bows and spears were useless in the confines of the spirit chamber. Battered by hordes of lifeless samurai, the Asp fell back around the flames. Only their curved scimitars could turn back the rush of undead.

One of the Asp raised himself above the others, calling to his companions to form a spear line behind a row of flashing swords.

Daini screamed, pulling at the confining cords, but the ropes would not come free.

There was a flash of steel as Balash's sword cut through a samurai's helm. The man fell to his knees before a startled Mara. Clutching the pearl spear, she backed away from the fight. Her face was white, her golden eyes wide and frightened, and she glanced back at Daini through the flames.

"Mara, free me!" Daini called through the fire. "I know how to fight them! The spear!"

Shaking her head, Mara screamed over the sounds of battle, "The Pah'ra . . . !"

"Forget the ritual!" he cried. "Your people need me!"

Rearing up on his massive tail, the Shahadet towered over three of the undead samurai. They charged, but his sweeping spear blows knocked them backward, piercing bone and ruined armor. The Shahadet opened his fanged mouth, roaring in rage. One of the samurai slashed at his tail. The blow was light, but sticky green blood trickled down the naga's scales, turning the green to black.

The Shahadet struck again, his spear slicing through a samurai's half-rotted face. Yellowish blood oozed from the cut, and one eye disappeared in a mass of bleeding jelly.

The samurai did not pause, continuing to attack despite its terrible wound. Its katana swung upward, blocked by the spear—and severed the naga's weapon in two.

Another massive tremor rocked the room, sending Daini spinning crazily above the wide basin. Looking down at the deep waters, he saw the River of the Sky rushing by, deep beneath the small pool, carrying rocks and loose debris far underground. His hands reached out toward the impossibly high flames to either side of the basin. Their nearness burned away the skin on his palms and blackened the hair on his arms. The water rocked and boiled. Daini struggled with the ropes, fighting to free himself.

The Shahadet reared and leapt on a group of zombies, using his massive bulk to crush their bones and tearing their heads from their bodies with his bare hands. Beside him, Mara poked hesitantly with the pearl spear. The Shadowlands troops clustered through the open doorway of the chamber, flooding down the ramp with cries of mad glee. Above, the city overflowed with the sounds of battle.

The chamber rocked once more.

"Mara!" Daini yelled again, but she did not seem to hear.

Shadowlands madmen grunted in satisfaction as they pulled one of the Asp to the ground. Their hands shredded gobbets of flesh from his still-moving arms, ignoring his screams. They pulled away his green-scaled skin.

The Shahadet lifted a katana from a fallen zombie, hacking with it like an axe through wood.

Behind him, Mara raised her hands to her face, covering it and whispering to herself. Her flesh began to twist and change. Her legs merged together, becoming one flesh, sheathed not in leather breeches but in shimmering silver and green scales. While the last remaining Asp warriors fought with all their strength against the horde of undead, Mara's green skin shivered and stretched into a slim naga tail. Her fangs lowered, and the transformation was complete.

Mara lifted the pearl spear, her face furrowed with concentration. Her hands slid down the jeweled length, and she whispered unfamiliar words in their strange tongue. The spear began to glow with the power of jade, driving back the undead with its pure light.

"Free me, Mara!" Daini called desperately, feeling the skin on his palms blacken and blister with the fire's heat.

Only a few of the forty Asp warriors still remained in the pit. The Shahadet stood beside Mara, blood staining his gilded armor. As they fought, overwhelmed by the Shadowlands army, Mara stepped back toward the circle of flame.

"Let me fight! The Pah'ra is not as important as your lives!"

The battle was hard to see beyond the glowing spear and the white-hot circle of fire. Daini could make out only shadowy forms—fighting samurai, spears raised.

"No, Mirumoto-daini," Mara gestured toward the doorway. "We will fight these things without you. You must finish what you have begun. This is your Pah'ra. If I must, I will die for you, that your people will be saved."

A flash of memory blurred his vision.

Daini stood on the field, watching Hitomi die. In his mind, he left her behind, turning away from her tortured screams. She had died for him.

Another memory . . .

Yukihera smiled malevolently. "Give up, Daini. Turn your back. It is what I knew you would do. After all, it is what you do best."

"If I don't walk away from this, he'll kill me too," Daini heard his own voice whisper, and he remembered the words even as he screamed to take them back.

Ten knots held him in place above the wide river pool. Only ten knots, and the Asp were dying.

Nine . . .

One last spinning image . . .

A faintly remembered duel between Crab and Dragon—his elder brother speaking earnestly: "You take care of her, little warrior," Satsu's voice broke through the sounds of steel against steel, whispering among the screams of the dying and the hissing of the Asp. "She will need you," Mirumoto Satsu smiled a crooked, charming smile, and then was gone. A pool of blood spread across the green grass, and a young girl screamed.

At the side of the tournament field, the child-Daini hid his face, placing his back to the duel. Remembering Hitomi's cruel words, Daini screamed again. Do you even remember Satsu's death, Daini? she chided him. It was true. He did not have a memory of Satsu facing the terrible Crab samurai. He could not remember because he was ashamed.

Six . . .

He had not even had the courage to watch his brother die.

"No," his features fell, twisted in agony of flesh and soul. "I have to help them." His fingers fumbled at the cords of the Pah'ra rope, releasing the knots one by one with desperate fingers. He fought against the ropes, seeking freedom to help the naga, yes, but deep in his soul, Daini realized that he was deeply afraid of something else, something awakening within his heart.

One Asp fell, and Daini saw a cluster of samurai surround Mara. The first samurai feinted, his sword whistling only inches past Mara's golden hair. She raised her spear for the counterstrike. The second plunged his blade into her breast, shattering bone and cleaving through her torso with a sickening tear.

Daini closed his eyes, refusing to watch any more. His hands fumbled with the last of the thick rope coils.

Four knots left . . . three . . .

He turned away. Satsu. Yukihera. Mara. Hitomi . . .

He had always turned away before the fight was finished.

"Let me go!" He screamed, tears flooding his vision as the naga bushi spilled their blood from open wounds. Their scales tore like fabric. Sickening noises of bone crunching and last gasps for air scalded Daini's ears.

"Daini . . . no!" Mara cried out as he reached for the last knots. She raised her body from the ground, trying to stand despite the pool of her own blood.

Another naga grabbed the pearl spear. "He has failed." Curling his lip in disgust, the Balash raised the spear to hurl it through Daini's spinning body. The Asp's hate-filled eyes took in his helpless opponent, ignoring the zombie samurai that carved at the flesh of the naga.

Two . . . only one knot stood between him and freedom. . . .

"He will not fail!" Mara screamed. Suddenly she was no longer lying on the floor. Her brutalized body vanished; the pool of blood was gone.

The Balash, his forked tongue hissing in victory, thrust the Sehalai's spear forward to pierce Daini's heart.

Mara materialized between them, staggering with pain and shock as the pearl spear entered her body instead of Daini's heart.

The Balash recoiled in stunned amazement, his hands falling from the spear shaft.

Mara sank to her knees. Her back arched as she slid to the ground.

Daini screamed, stretching his arms out through the flames as if he could reach her.

Suddenly the room spun into focus once more. No dead naga littered the floor. The ground of the chamber was not covered with green blood. The sky through the open doorway was clear and filled with stars, and white flames licked at Daini's hands without burning his flesh.

Daini took a deep shuddering breath and felt his lungs fill with crisp, cool air. Everything looked different. The chamber shone with colors he could not name; his ears heard echoes of sounds too far away to be recognized. The Akasha had touched his mind, but with it came a sense of terrible loss. He had seen the Eternal Mind, but he had not become one with it.

Perhaps no human ever could truly become one with the naga. The Pah'ra had carried him into the Great Mind of the Naga and made him a brother, but it had not remained.

His brush with eternity would stay with him always, but his mind was not one with the Asp. Daini felt as if a great ocean had appeared before him. The Akasha was tremendous; a hundred thousand minds, a million lifetimes all bound together in one collective soul. Perhaps one day he would understand how the naga saw the Akasha, but for now, this small glimpse was enough to change Daini's life forever. He laughed, and he knew that somewhere, his happiness was echoed in thousands of minds all across the Akasha's waves.

At last, Daini understood.

The undead assault had been an illusion, conjured by the River of the Sky and the power of the Akasha. The illusion had tested his faithfulness, determining if he would stand by his word and finish what he had started. Only one knot held Daini aloft above the flickering flames and the bowl of blue water—one knot that meant the difference between success and failure.

Daini grinned in relief, stunned that he had lived through the test. Then, he remembered his savior.

Mara.

She knelt with her hand touching the cool stone of the floor. Emerald blood trickled down one slender arm.

The Balash slid backward with short, choppy movements, his face a mixture of revulsion and horror. His hands left the weapon. Mara reached to take the haft of the pearl and jade spear, her fingers sticky with her own blood. With a tearing pull, she lifted the spearhead from her body, and dropped the ancient weapon to the ground.

"Mara!" The knot would hold him no longer. Daini landed in the water beneath the tremendous stalactite. Throwing off the ropes, he pushed through the mystical white flames, somehow knowing they could not hurt him anymore. He knelt beside her, fingers exploring the wound, emerald blood pouring over his hand as he tried to stanch its flow.

"The Mara has interrupted the Pah'ra," the Shahadet rumbled from his chair.

Suddenly Daini could understand every word. Some small

piece of the Akasha moved within him, realized, teaching him their language.

"No, Shahadet," Daini said gravely in their language. "My Sehalai protected me from the attack of this one." Pointing at the Balash, Daini made a dismissive gesture with his hand.

"This one," the Balash hissed, "saw that the supplicant was attempting to free himself from the Pah'ra and fight the Akasha. This one was performing the duty of the Sehalai, when the Greensnake would have failed and given mercy. This is not a Greensnake ceremony, with their peaceful ways and their weakness. This is the test of the Asp."

The Shahadet closed his eyes, and Daini knew that he was communing with the Akasha. "Let the Daini take her into the River of the Sky. The Akasha will decide her fate. When it is done with her, we will follow you, Mirumoto-daini, our brother, into the war against the Foul. Our place is with you."

Daini lifted Mara's limp body into his arms.

Her tail faded into beautiful, shapely legs, and her amber eyes opened. She lightly placed her arms around his shoulders. "If I am to die, huu-man," she whispered hoarsely into his ear, "I will die in your arms and be content."

The other Asp watched as their new brother carried the little Greensnake through the flames of the Pah'ra, to the basin of the River of the Sky.

The future had been changed forever. The Akasha touched a new mind. Soon, the naga would understand these huu-mans and their war. They would again fight the Foul—but this time, they would not fight alone.

"Mara, you must not love me. It is not to be." Daini stepped through the white flames, his arms tight around her lithe form.

"You are wrong, Daini, for I have known this day would come for a thousand years. When my people slept the sleep of a thousand years, we were not allowed to dream. But I dreamed, samurai. I dreamed of cities that had not been built, and of people that were not yet born." Her eyes dulled with pain, but she watched him serenely, at peace with the world. "I dreamed of you."

Green blood stained his hands as he stepped into the basin. Icy waters closed around his legs. This time, there was nothing in the water to threaten him, no clutching hands trying to drag him under the waves. From the water, he sensed only a great sadness, with a strength and depth he had never known existed.

"You bring us new life, Daini. For a thousand years, we have slept."

Standing on the shore of the Great Mind, he suddenly felt very lost and alone. He could not understand their Akasha. It was beyond him. Yet she was one with a thousand souls in a great ocean.

Another step into the water, and it closed around his torso. "Live, Mara." He inhaled the scent of her hair.

"Your coming was known to us, Daini, and the time of our Great Sleep has ended. Is this why I should live?" Her fingers, weakened by loss of blood, trailed across his chin. "No, not for them. For you. You have awakened me, Mirumoto-daini, beyond anything I could have imagined. I have been your Seha-lai. I have seen your soul, and I am yours."

Two more steps, and he would be in the center of the basin, beneath the great stalactite. The ropes still hung from his perch on the stone, trailing without ripples in the cool blue water.

He whispered, "Your people have given back a part of myself I did not know I had lost." His heart ached for her pain. "You have done so much for me. . . ."

"But you cannot love me?" she asked softly.

"I . . ." Turn your back, Daini, his inner voice whispered. You have done your duty here. Turn your back on her, and return to your people, where you belong. "Live, Mara," he repeated again, the tears stinging his eyes, tears of joy and sorrow.

"Live . . . for what reason? The River of the Sky demands a purpose for its boons. It will not let me go unless I have some strength that is greater than death—some purpose yet to fulfill." Softly, her mouth brushed against the hollow of his neck. "Shall I live for my people, Daini?"

The waves of the Akasha washed over him as he sank into the River of the Sky. Water, cold and clear, swelled around his shoulders and bathed Mara's quiet face.

Turn your back, the inner voice whispered once more, but it was fainter, covered by the distant sound of the Akasha's rolling tide.

Never again.

As the river eased her wounds and her arms grew strong around his shoulders, he stepped forward one final time and felt the waves close above his head. "No, Mara. Live . . . for me." Daini's mind called across the wide Akasha until it found her lips, open and glad. Her kiss was light, gentle and tender.

As he returned the kiss, Daini heard the ocean roar.

16 THE CORNERSTONES OF THE WORLD

The palace was silent. The court of the emperor revolved peacefully. Winds of change blew in gentle, careful gusts, guided by the empress herself. From her place at the side of the empty throne, Kachiko quietly ruled, furthering her own ends.

Soon, the Crab armies would arrive, as she had planned. They would overthrow the weak Hantei and secure the throne in Kisada's name. When that occurred, the Scorpion would come out of hiding, resume their place among the Great Clans, and keep the imperial power for themselves—all beneath the naive gaze of the Great Bear, their ultimate pawn.

Poisoning the emperor had been easy. Keeping him weak was child's play. But replacing him with a more fitting pawn and fulfilling Shoju's prophecy and her own revenge . . . these tasks had been difficult. Soon they would be accomplished.

It had been several months since the travesty at Beiden Pass. The Crab's first failure, thought Kachiko. Their ambition without guidance had nearly cost the clan their lives. Kisada had had to make that mistake before he would take the bait that Kachiko dangled—the Imperial Throne. With that bait, she had proved that even the Great Bear could be tamed.

Months. It had taken months for him to prepare the perfect assault, and only the long cold winter allowed Kisada's plans to be kept secret, even with Kachiko's careful strategies in the court. When the first thaw of spring had arrived, though, they were ready.

The attack would not come from the south, through ice-covered Beiden Pass and snowbound Crane lands. It would come, instead, from the east, just before the spring rains had melted the winter snows and allowed the armies of Rokugan to march again. They could not help the emperor.

The doom of Hantei 39th would come from the sea.

▲▲▲▲▲▲▲▲

Besieging Otosan Uchi was simple. No army had ever attacked the city from the waves of the eastern ocean, not since the gaijin's attack over seven hundred years before. Landing his fleet on undefended shores near the Imperial City, Kisada marched to surround it.

A nearby Lion army arrived in time to repel the attack, but Kachiko bearded the Lion. She sent an imperial decree commanding that the lion leader, Matsu Tsuko, abandon her troops on the field. In the following battle, the Lion were decimated.

Kisada surrounded and took the city. Even as he fought his way past Seppun guards, he sent envoys ahead of him, demanding that Emperor Hantei surrender the throne.

The envoys were refused entrance. For five days, the ailing emperor had forbidden all audience. Even his loyal wife was kept away.

Tearfully, Kachiko wrote out the demands of the envoys. She added to them her own pleas, begging her husband to consider the Crab's demands.

"Leave the city," she wrote. "Gain time for a counterattack. Save your life and the life of the child I promise to bear you."

They were such little lies. Such little tears.

Yet when she sent the note with the emperor's personal guard, an unexpected reply came back. The emperor agreed to meet with Kisada, refusing Kachiko's carefully phrased pleas.

It was the first time he had ever refused her anything.

▲▲▲▲▲▲▲▲

The storm outside the palace increased in fury as the Crab approached. It howled in expectant rage until Kachiko thought it must destroy everything in its path. The winds came from the south, reeking of taint and festering decay.

The people of Otosan Uchi huddled in their small houses, praying to the Fortunes for protection. Lightning shattered the night sky all around the city, carving swaths of smoldering ash in once-green fields. Some bolts struck the wall itself, tearing open great black pits of stone and rubble. Fiery hail fell from the sky, rattling and bouncing along the city's streets. The stones were extinguished only by the pounding rain that followed. Floodwaters swirled ankle-deep through the streets and churned into the swollen river. Market stalls, beasts of burden, and citizens foolish enough to leave their homes were swept away down the waterfall and out to a foaming gray sea. The waters raged against the storm.

"Is the emperor prepared?" Kachiko whispered to Aramoro.

The Scorpion bushi nodded silently. The Crab would enter the throne room of jade and gold and meet with Emperor Hantei. Still, the Hantei had not called off his Seppun guards. He would make Kisada pay to gain the throne.

The sound of tearing shoji screens announced the Crab Champion's approach. One after another, the walls gave way before the Crab daimyo.

At the base of the stairs to the throne room, Kachiko waited for him. Ten Seppun guardsmen gathered around her, each ready to give his life to protect hers. She allowed herself a tiny smile. How little they knew, these Seppun. They guarded the very viper they thought to destroy.

The final screen tore, and a huge, dark samurai burst forth from it. Hida Kisada, the Great Bear, had arrived. His son emerged behind him.

"Invaders!" shouted one of the Seppun.

"Stand aside," Kachiko ordered in a voice as sharp as honed steel. "Your orders are to guard me, and I do not think the Great Bear came all this way to threaten a poor, neglected woman."

Kisada nodded shallowly. At his side, Hida Yakamo stood, his face darkened by somber, brooding thoughts. Father and son warily, gripping their tetsubo and eyeing the contingent of Seppun.

"My lady," Kisada's voice boomed, echoing in the silent halls of the Imperial Palace. "I have arrived to meet with your . . . husband."

"He awaits you, Hida-sama," Kachiko said softly, her voice cultured and gentle. She gestured to the top of the stairs.

Servants opened the jade doors to the imperial throne room. Beyond lay a hallway of gold and mahogany, and at its end stood the Emerald Throne. Upon it sat a young man in gold and green.

As they saw the emperor, sitting alone in his opulent throne room, the Crab soldiers grinned. They already counted their victories . . . despite the warnings that flooded the city and pounded the earth to sod.

On his cracked Emerald Throne, the Hantei awaited them, his body still and quiet. His head was lowered, dark eyes closed.

Striding up the stairs and into the throne room, the Great Bear raised a steel fist. His son stood beside him, though his other men knelt before the dais.

"Imperial Hantei," he said, and his voice echoed like thunder. Yet before Kisada could demand the throne be turned over to the Crab, the Hantei lifted a pale white hand.

Surprised, Kisada said nothing more. The emperor raised

his head, his pale eyes softly sliding from one face to the next. "Kachiko," he whispered, and she moved forward.

"Hai, sama?" she said gently, trying not to let her confusion show. This was not the way he should be acting. He should be cowed, frightened—angered, ranting against Kisada's actions. This cold, composed boy on the throne . . . this was not the emperor that Kachiko had grown accustomed to seeing.

"Remove everyone from my chambers," the Hantei said softly. " I would be alone with Hida-san and his men."

"But . . ." Her protest died before it was voiced. Kachiko lowered her head to the floor. Within seconds, the rest of the courtiers and guards in the room did the same. Rising, Kachiko strode to the rear of the room, followed by bristling Seppun guards and whispering courtiers.

As the grand doors closed softly behind them, Kachiko caught the black-eyed gaze of her companion in the shadows.

Hitomi stood there, silent and unmoving, a statue carved in golden ice—a reminder of their cause.

Kachiko brooded. Something was wrong, terribly wrong. She could feel it in her bones, in the wind that swept through the palace, growing colder with each passing second.

Until now, everything had gone as the Lady of Scorpions had planned, each step perfectly placed, each movement precise. Poisoned, the 39th Hantei needed only Kisada's pressure to surrender the throne. If he was still an honorable samurai beneath his wasted flesh and fragile bones, the announcement of his seppuku would shortly follow.

The empress and her guards waited with the courtiers outside the emperor's throne room, breathlessly waiting for the announcement.

It had come to this. The empire would never be the same. Nothing could change that. The boy on the throne—her husband, for at least a few moments more—could do nothing to stop it.

For a moment, Kachiko's lips curved in a delicate blush of anticipation.

A smile of victory.

▲▲▲▲▲▲▲▲

The palace abruptly trembled at its very foundation.

The walls of the throne room burst into black flame.

A terrible laugh shook halls.

Hitomi glanced back toward the golden doors of the throne room. The floor bounced, and even Kachiko stumbled, clutching Aramoro's swift arm. Hitomi's eyes narrowed. The Scorpion had seemed all too confident, all too eager for this meeting, but now the smile was gone from her pale face.

The laugh continued beyond mortal breath and with a power that reached the Celestial Heavens.

The Moon's Hand clenched into a fist, awakening as it listened to a familiar voice. A terrible anger swept through Hitomi's mind.

Though the laughter held tones of the emperor's smooth tenor, it was rotting with the timbre of evil. The palace trembled once more, shaking on its stone foundations as the very earth heaved. With a shriek of twisting steel and cracking wood, the great doors burst open in a shower of golden splinters. An eerie green light swelled from the throne room, bleeding into the long hallway. Screams came from within the chamber, echoing like the cry of tortured animals.

Something within the throne room glistened, sending out rays of horrible green light. Smoke rolled along the ground, causing the Seppun to choke and stagger, screaming silently as their hands fell from their swords.

Avoiding the noxious vapors, Hitomi leapt back, dragging Kachiko with her. Beside her, Aramoro freed his sword and readied his stance. A few others, wary of the smoke, drew their weapons and peered into the chamber of the Emerald Throne.

The screams continued. Hitomi had heard the calls of the dying on the battlefield, the shouts of agony as a limb was severed from a body. These shrieks were far worse, accompanied by a sound like flesh being peeled from a man's face.

From the throne room, the light scattered over the smoke, illuminating the still-twisting bodies of Seppun guardsmen.

Where it touched a fallen body, the skin pulled back from muscle and bone, ripping it away. Then, as Hitomi watched, the bodies began to rise. Shattered bone healed, twisted flesh knitted into rotting sinew and muscle over grinning skulls. Lifting her gaze from the rising dead, Hitomi stared into the throne room.

Within it, the Hantei stood defiantly before his Emerald Throne. The smoke boiled from his fingertips, tearing the flesh from screaming samurai before him. Hantei held his hands high above his head, his magnificent gold and green robes swirling about him in the storm. On the floor, a great swath of blood stained the rich mahogany. As Hitomi watched, Seppun guards slowly climbed from the floor. The undead bodies in their twisted armor were mockeries of the bold samurai that guarded the emperor. Rictus grins hung from their slack, bloodied faces.

Beyond them, the emperor laughed. He threw his arms open to a shattered roof, the rain and wind sweeping through the throne room and racing in bitter blasts down the palace halls. Shoji screens shredded at its passing, and more green smoke poured through the hallways of the Imperial Palace. Seppun guardsmen clutched at their faces, howling for release as the taint tore through their bodies.

Hitomi's hand moved of its own volition, slicing through the undead samurai that charged toward her. "Kachiko," she growled, "We must go!"

Beside Hitomi, the empress stared down the long corridor of the throne room, into the eyes of the creature standing before the Emerald Throne. "No . . ." she whispered. "It cannot be. . . ."

"There is no time!" Hitomi grabbed Kachiko's fine wrist, pulling the empress down the once-magnificent hallway.

Behind them, Aramoro fought against the tide of undead guards. Zombies shuddered forward, lifting their blades with unholy strength and carving the flesh of servants, guards, and courtiers alike. As each new body fell, the light flickered again, touching their faces and twisting them into leering mockeries. Eyes withered, flesh tore, and black blood spilled from the mouths of each corpse as it struggled to rise from the slick floor.

Screaming courtiers threw themselves at the doors to the outside gardens, only to be cut down by their fellows as more bodies rose from the swirling smoke. The undead legion grew.

Hitomi and the empress came to a stone wall. They were trapped, caught in the sudden press of zombies. There was no escape.

"Here!" Aramoro snarled, his swift blade slicing through another monster.

Hitomi nodded, standing beside him in the stone corridor and driving the creatures back. "We cannot hold them for long."

Aramoro twisted his blade, pushing one of the creatures back with his arm. Beside him, Hitomi slashed the Shadowlands madmen, Seppun and Hida together, their bright kimono smeared with blackish blood.

Kachiko pressed against the stone wall and stared past then all, down the passage to the entrance of the throne room. Her face was chalk-white, her lips as red as blood against her skin. Then Hitomi saw what captured Kachiko's attention.

Through the grand doors of the throne room stepped the Last Hantei, his red eyes glowing with an unholy light. Zombies bowed down before him, offering their broken hands as his soft carpet. He walked upon them carelessly as his skin grew taut over his skull. His eyes sank into his face, leaving only two bright red pinpricks that stared from cavernous darkness. The emperor walked among his minions, caressing each man's bloody head as if the undead samurai were cherished pets.

For a moment, Hitomi remembered a strong man, youthful and noble, in the silks of the Imperial Dynasty. Now the emperor's torn silks were rotted and fouled with the stench of the grave, and he was no longer young. In the growing glow of golden light, the Hantei had become a vision of unimaginable horror. Maggots writhed across his shoulders and down his bare chest. His hands were gloves of skin over bone. A darkness that was almost palpable hovered above the shoulders of the slowly moving figure. What had once been the emperor was now something too terrible to imagine. Something fundamentally evil.

"Kachiko . . . my beloved wife . . ." It spoke, and its whisper was louder than the thunderclaps that tore the sky above the city. "How tenderly you have ministered to me in my time of sickness." The rotten flesh shrank into a smile above gleaming bone and sharpened teeth. Now I repay your kindness . . . with an apt reward." The voice was stone and steel, the tone echoing like cold shadows that haunt the dark of the night. All the things that should have never been spawned, all of Rokugan's dishonor and shame crept along in his fouled robes and dripped like blood from his fingertips. As he reached for her, the undead parted, drawing back from their foul master and cowering behind him.

Kachiko took one hesitant step forward on the bloodied mahogany floor, her feet moved by a power that was not her own. Her face contorted in anger as her legs took each shaking step. Her body arched against the dark god's call. "I know you," she hissed, her honey-colored eyes dark and hateful. "You are not the emperor of this land or any other."

"You are wrong, my dear." It laughed, stepping forward to touch her. The emperor's fingers delicately stroked her ivory cheek, leaving a single bloody smear across her white makeup. "I am the lord of the Shadowlands, the master of all that you fear and despise—and I am the emperor. All that you have is now mine, and all that once was . . . will be no more." Madness rolled in his red eyes, lighting the air around her cheek and spreading like a bloodstain across Kachiko's pale skin. "And you, Bayushi Kachiko . . . you are my wife."

Lightning flashed through the palace, illuminating the writhing bodies of the dead and thundering across the high walls of Otosan Uchi. Whatever Kachiko said was lost to their war cries. The Scorpion empress's eyes narrowed with hatred.

The emperor roared, muscles twitching at his jaw. His hand shot out to grasp her slim ivory neck. He lifted her from the floor. Lightning raced in the sky, flashing in pulses and mad bursts outside the thin paper walls and open windows.

Kachiko's feet kicked lightly, her hands struggling to pull his fingers away from her throat as her face shaded into purple. Unable to escape, she listened to the emperor's sickly whispers, and her eyes narrowed with hatred and fear. As he slowly crushed her throat, the Hantei lifted his other hand to stroke her long dark fall of hair.

Live, or die? Hitomi lifted her sword, preparing to throw herself upon the beast that held Kachiko above the floor. Yet, before she could act, a dark mace raced from her right side. It hurled itself at the possessed Emperor Hantei with a scream of ultimate hatred—a hatred unpossessed by fear or indecision.

Without thought, Bayushi Aramoro plunged his weapon into the creature's back, shouting over the storm, "Go, my lady! Run!"

The emperor staggered forward, losing his hold.

Kachiko fell to the ground at the emperor's feet and gasped for air. Without a thought, Hitomi leapt to her side and reached for her arm, gripping the burgundy silk with one hand and holding aloft her sword with the other.

The Hantei had turned to face Aramoro, and his mad red eyes laughed with fire. "You are doomed, samurai," the emperor chortled, spreading his hands wide in a gesture of indifference. "But your courage is laudable. Will you die with it, or will it leave you before your soul flees the flesh of your body?" He laughed again. "Know this: When I am done, she will be my wife. She will be lovely, indeed, once the skin and blood has been torn from her bones; once the rot and ruin that surrounds her has entered her flesh and made her truly mine."

"Get her out," the Bayushi samurai shouted to Hitomi, raising his ninja-to for another strike. "A life for a life, Hitomi-san. You owe me yours. Take her to safety, and your debt to our clan is repaid."

"Done," the Dragon snarled, holding Kachiko's arm and pulling her away from the emperor. Hitomi's eyes lit at the thought of her freedom, despite the undead that moved down every hall and chamber. They were all that stood between her and her first duty, and surely the hand would be enough to defeat anything she encountered, even in these fouled halls. "A life for a life, Aramoro-san. And may Shinsei have mercy on your spirit."

"Aramoro . . ." Kachiko rasped, her throat sore and bruised. "He will kill you!"

"No time, Bayushi-sama," Hitomi grunted. She carved a path out of the dead end. "We must go now."

"Aramoro!" Kachiko screamed hoarsely as Hitomi half-dragged, half-shoved her away from the blood-covered throne room.

Zombies surged toward them with renewed fury, eager to tear their flesh from their bones.

Looking behind them as they ran, Hitomi saw the Bayushi samurai take a defensive stance. Then the mad god reached for the heavens, and a burst of wild lightning tore through the palace roof, coating them all in debris and rain. She could see no more. Praying to Shinsei for Aramoro's soul, Hitomi hauled the empress through the corridors. The footfalls of the undead dogged them down the halls.

As she raced through the cold stone corridors of the Imperial Palace, Hitomi could hear the bitter laughter of an unrepentant god. It followed them through each twist and turn. Somehow, Fu Leng lived. The dark master of the Shadowlands, fallen god of the south, lord of corruption and decay—he commanded the Emerald Throne, and he held Rokugan's very soul in his filth-encrusted hand.

As she passed each room, Hitomi saw dead men rising at every turn, slaughtering courtier and bushi alike and adding to their fallen number. Each time a samurai fell, he rose only minutes later, animated by the Dark God's will and the presence of evil that now permeated the palace.

"In here," the empress's murmured, pausing their flight. She pointed a finger toward one of the stone pillars that marked the palace's outer wall.

Kachiko touched the wall with caressing fingertips, staring at the stone as if reuniting with an old lover. "Yes, I remember you, old friend. . . ." Kachiko panted breathlessly, lifting her hand to touch a brass lantern-holder. As her fingers pressed against the delicate metal, a panel in the mahogany floor rose to reveal steps below.

The Dragon daimyo stared down into the darkness, listening to the screams of the dead and dying that echoed through the palace around them.

"Ah," Kachiko whispered. "How fitting that we leave the palace this way. Another riddle to mystify you, Dragon. Your champion would be pleased." Gathering her strength, Kachiko took a shaking step down the secret passage, shaking away Hitomi's supporting hand. "Through this passage, it is best that I lead you, Mirumoto."

They descended into darkness, the floor panel closing behind them. Kachiko threaded their way through snaking paths.

"We will enter the gardens soon," Kachiko said in a quivering voice. "The undead soldiers that serve Fu Leng's command cannot find us there. The Imperial Guard does not even know this route exists. Neither will the Dark Lord."

"How do you know where it will lead?"

The empress leveled a scathing glance at her companion. "Because this is how Shoju's armies came in."

▲▲▲▲▲▲▲▲

Beyond the palace, the royal gardens stretched for miles. Rain poured from the heavens, cascading in thick sheets. Lightning danced wildly among the clouds. A high stone wall wandered through the garden hills, surrounding streams and lakes that boiled beneath the downpour.

Fresh earth turned to mud under Kachiko's slippered feet, and her torn kimono flapped wildly in the high winds. Her neck was bruised. Blood stained her white cheek. At her side, a wounded Hitomi marched, oblivious to pain or torment.

Freedom.

"Here," Hitomi said above the storm. "There is a break in the wall. We can rest here before we continue on." A small niche in the stone provided some shelter from the raging storm, but the lighting strikes above the palace continued unceasingly. Hitomi knelt just outside the alcove, watching as the empress sank to her knees within the dirt and vines of the little niche.

"It is over," Kachiko said. Her voice was strangely soft as she looked back at the ruined palace. It had once been magnificent, but had also been Kachiko's prison, where she spent years of tortured existence at the side of the boy-emperor. The Last Hantei had begun his reign by destroying the Scorpion, and would end it be destroying all of Rokugan.

Shoju's prophecy had been fulfilled.

A deep sorrow filled Kachiko's voice as the rain poured bitterly down her ivory cheeks. The blood smear on her face paled and glistened, a trail of scarlet tears against her white skin. "Shoju was right. Our actions brought this prophecy to life. The Last Hantei . . ." Kachiko's voice wavered, but then gained strength. "He has become the Dark Lord's vessel. The palace is now the Dark God's crypt. All my plans . . . all my work, wasted. We have truly become what we most feared." Staring at the palace, Kachiko sank to her knees and stared at the lightning that trailed in gleaming gashes across the black sky. "Shoju . . ." she whispered, "forgive me." The night wind lashed her long black hair across Kachiko's eyes, stinging them shut.

Hitomi watched from within the storm, unwilling to interrupt the puzzle of the Scorpion's words. She could not hear what was said, but only the wild wail of the wind, the steady rhythm of the rain, and the rapid beat of her own frantic heart. Freedom.

A shadow crossed her face. The Dragon samurai looked up. Gripping the hilt of her katana, she peered through the sweeping rain at a familiar shadow that perched atop the garden wall. Lightning burst around them, tearing a swath through the ground and reducing a cherry tree to ash. Its brightness burned Hitomi's eyes, bringing hot tears. In that instant of light, she recognized his form.

"Yokuni."

His voice surrounded her, forming itself from the thunder that resounded about the plains of Otosan Uchi. *I told you it would come to this, Lady.* Deep within the iron mask that always covered his features, Yokuni's voice was etched with sorrow.

Hitomi opened her mouth to respond, but realized his words were not for her.

Kachiko's face was pale and wounded, surprised by the Dragon Champion's appearance. She opened her eyes to stare blindly into the storm. "Yokuni," Kachiko murmured. Her eyes flashed. Hitomi could tell that Kachiko knew his voice, perhaps better than even she did. Quaking, Kachiko pulled her ruined kimono tight about her body.

As lithe as a serpent, Yokuni moved above her, but Kachiko kept her eyes turned away. She did not want him to see her fear.

Hitomi drew away to allow them their space, though she heard every word in her mind.

"T-to hell with you and your prophecy," Kachiko stammered at the voice in the darkness. "Toturi's army is on the march. I will go there and join the fallen Lion. He will have much to gain from what I have learned tonight."

No. The voice was steady and calm. *He knows. Toturi knows his part in destiny . . . as do you.*

She shook her head. "No. No, I cannot. There is nothing left. . . ."

You know what you must do, the voice interrupted. *You must return to the palace. You and your poisons have made the emperor what he now is. You must ensure he becomes what he must become. If you do not, all will be lost.*

"Lost . . ." she whispered. "As Shoju has been lost? As my clan, my family, my very name have been lost?"

Yokuni's hand moved above the stone, crumbling granite to powder. *As the empire will be lost. Each heimin, each peasant and noble—destroyed. The world will become a festering pool of bile. Your family will not be remembered, not by the gods themselves. Each child that runs in the street will be made into fleshly toys for the master's amusement. Every samurai who holds honor dear will be placed on a spike and tortured to death and then to undeath. Lost, Lady, yes. They will all be lost. And more, the very empire that your family once swore to protect will be shattered. Yours will not be the only failure, Scorpion. You will fail in the name of your clan—and in the name of their future.*

You are needed, Lady. And you are wise enough to know not to try to deny destiny. Shoju knew that, even as he faced his death. He taught you, showed you where the path must lie. Do you remember?

She was very still for a long time, but then, slowly, she nodded. "I do."

It is as I told you before. You are to play a greater part in all of this than you know. Perhaps the greatest part. And there are others.

She blinked away the rain in her eyes. "Yes. Six others."

No, the voice said as Yokuni faded into the rain. *Seven. Do not forget that the descendant of Shinsei walks among us as well.*

With that, the voice was gone For a moment, Kachiko knelt in the storm, her eyes turned only toward the green light illuminating the depths of the palace.

"I must," she whispered, her voice barely audible over the wind and thunder. She looked up at the palace one more time, as if remembering some long-forgotten duty.

Hitomi quietly approached.

The empress shuddered but then steadied herself. She rose from the niche and stepped out into the downpour. In muddy slippers, she began the long walk back toward the Imperial Palace.

"Kachiko," Hitomi shouted over the storm. "You cannot go back. Aramoro—"

"Aramoro will understand, little Dragon," the empress smiled bitterly. "He knows the price of duty better even, I think, than I."

"The empire destroyed your clan, and your family, and still you fight for it?

Slowly, Kachiko turned. "Yes, Dragon. The empire destroyed all that I held dear. My own son died at the hands of the empire, when we fought to save it from this," her emphatic gesture swept over the palace and the storm. "And now that destiny has come to pass. I fought against it once, and I will not abandon the battle. It is what my family would wish. Shoju, my husband, taught me that true courage lies in fighting even when you know you have been defeated." Her eyes shone brilliantly in the dancing light of the storm. "I have not yet been defeated, Dragon. As long as I continue to fight, I never will be."

"My duty was to take you to safety," Hitomi was resolute. "I will not fail in it."

The shadow of Yokuni moved along the wall, listening to her every word.

Kachiko's amber eyes searched Hitomi's very soul. "And you have done so. I return of my own choice, Dragon. You do not need to worry about your bargain. You are free." The empress turned away and walked, slowly fading within veils of rain.

Have you gained the strength you sought, child? Yokuni asked from the darkness.

"Have I?" The Dragon daimyo murmured bitterly. "You tell me, Yokuni. I cannot solve this puzzle. Too many of the pieces are broken, the toys of a careless child."

Your time is not done. There is much still to do before the end. The fifteenth day of the Tiger has come, and you have seen the prophecy come to pass. Do you still have doubt?

"And this . . . this is better, Yokuni?"

Even Fu Leng can be defeated.

Prepare yourself for the future. Fu Leng, the Dark God of the Shadowlands, has returned, and Rokugan must fight him. If you fail, the empire will be destroyed.

A flash of insight sang in Hitomi's mind even as lighting crashed once more above the dark palace. "Shinsei's Tao says 'Seven Thunders came from fire and flight, to destroy the Evil One in his lair.' A thousand years ago, they assembled, and they killed Fu Leng. One from each clan. . . ." Her face twisted in anguish. "It is me, isn't it? That's why you can't allow me to die.

That's why you let the Scorpion do this," she held aloft the Obsidian Hand.

"I am one of the Seven Thunders. So is Kachiko, I see. The puzzle is forming, Yokuni, your precious veil is lifting. Seven Thunders must be assembled, to fight Fu Leng, or he will forever rule the empire and destroy the world. Isn't that how the prophecy goes?" Hitomi's voice was bitter and cruel. "Who are the others?"

You will know in the fullness of time.

"Kachiko. Myself. A Crane, I assume, and someone from the Phoenix? 'One Thunder born from each clan,' say the old texts, 'and only together can they defeat the Dark One.'" Hitomi's black eyes narrowed in thought, her face shadowed. "Destroy Fu Leng. Can it be done? We are but mortals, Yokuni. He is a god."

A god who has once before been defeated. Seven Thunders, no more, no less, and it can be done again.

An empty ache gnawed her soul, and a cold hand clenched her heart. "Destiny be damned," she whispered. "Bushido be damned." Yet even as she said the words, she knew that she no longer believed them. Bushido was a part of her, and she could no longer ignore honor or duty—not without giving up everything she had learned.

"Very well, Yokuni, I will serve your purpose once more. But first, I claim my own justice. I do not expect to survive a fight with . . . the emperor." Hitomi's skin crawled as she remembered the mad laughter that rumbled from the Hantei's tortured frame. "I will fulfill Satsu's vengeance before I live my destiny. Hida Yakamo will die." She stared bitterly at the palace, watching the storm crash about its high turrets and sweeping roof arches. "When that is done, I will no longer need my life. I will serve you, and save the empire, no matter what the cost."

No, Hitomi. He is still needed. Put aside your revenge.

"Needed?" She laughed scornfully. "The only reason he is needed is to bleed on my blade—to finally taste his death and see with tortured eyes my vengeance for Satsu. I can do it.

Don't fear for my life, old man. I have been reborn, and Yakamo cannot defeat me this time; his death will be simple. With this," she crushed part of the wall in an easy grip, her Obsidian Hand pulverizing the solid stone into ash. "I can finally be free. Three months in the mountains, and my wounds will heal. The Kitsuki will take me in, their healers will protect me, hide me. . . . In three months, I will be ready to fight again."

If you destroy him, the empire will die.

Her eyes widened in anger and hatred. "Why do you still stand in my way!" she shouted, and the echo was twisted by the storm. She turned to face the shadowy form, and saw the riddle in his eyes.

Suddenly, she understood why Yokuni had always blocked her path, why he had forced her to put aside her vengeance, why he had insisted that Yakamo be allowed to win his duel with Satsu.

Yakamo was a Thunder.

Without thought, Hitomi's black hand found the hilt of her bloodstained katana as if to cleave apart the truth. In agonized fury, she howled, "You cannot rob me of this!"

She peered up at the shadow on the stone wall, but it was gone.

17   THE FALL OF DARKNESS

Chanting filled the twilight, echoing from the broken cliffs of Beiden Pass. The torii arch, scarred and bloodied by its burden, stood against the growing darkness like an oak in the storm, proud and defiant. Even the body that hung from its high crossbeams seemed to hold a silent strength, waiting for the next blow to fall. The first stars of twilight had appeared on the horizon, and it was time to count the day's dead. Even though the Battle of Beiden Pass was long finished, Shadowlands beasts still holed up in mountain crevices. Every day, a few more Dragons died trying to roust them out. Each death was another lash.

Mitsu's breath shuddered in his aching chest, a barely noticeable rise and fall that marked his continued struggle.

Kitsuki Gofumin climbed the hillock with short steps, weary from the day's command. He left his small group of Dragon guards below.

When the war had begun, he had been no more than a gunso. Now, he had become a taisa—captain of a minor unit, second among the Dragon Clan guard stationed in Beiden Pass. His guard was made mostly of Mirumoto soldiers; the two families had combined their armies in these troubled times. Still, the tests Gofumin had endured had not prepared him for this service. Each day, he climbed this brown, grassy hill, and each day, he had wondered whose name he would recognize among the rolls of the dead. There were so few Dragon left in the canyons—and sometimes, Kitsuki Gofumin pondered the riddle of why he and his troops had been left behind. Yukihera had said it was to "aid the Unicorn," but his words rang false against Gofumin's meditations.

Perhaps, thought the captain, Yukihera had left them here to die one by one, to become nothing more than scars that crisscrossed the ise zumi's back. It was possible. The ways of the Dragon Clan were a riddle, and the commands of a daimyo such as Yukihera were the walls of a maze. Dragons were not meant to understand, Gofumin sighed as he reached the top of the windy hillock. They were meant to seek understanding, and nothing more. Anything else would be too much. If you understood the riddle, it was said you would go mad from too much truth.

Five more ise zumi, tattooed men from the Togashi family, sat cross-legged around their brother. Their whispers thrummed in the quiet night, muffling the calls and clangs of the Unicorn encampment. As the darkness grew, the samurai picked his way around the other ise zumi, lumbering toward the arch.

He did not know where the tattooed monks had come from, or how they had known of Mitsu's trials. They had not spoken to anyone in the Dragon armies, nor would they accept food or water when it was brought to them. They had simply appeared among the troops, walking into camp one by one as the days had passed. Each one continued doggedly to the hillock without a word of explanation and took his place in the semicircle that faced the tortured Togashi Mitsu.

When the first chanting had begun, Gofumin came to them to determine its purpose. There was no response from the ise zumi, but Gofumin could tell what they meant to do simply by watching. Their murmurs gave strength to their brother, and their tattoos glowed faintly with a warm golden light as his wounds slowly healed and closed. Magic was at work, keeping Mitsu alive.

I don't understand it, thought Gofumin, but it's better that way. Do your duty and nothing more.

The eta torturer nodded to him as he unrolled the daimyo's scroll. He was prepared to begin the daily scourge.

"By command of Lord Yukihera, leader of the Mirumoto and master of the Iron Mountain, I am instructed to read the names of those Dragon samurai who have given their lives this day." The list was long, and with each name he read, another blow would fall from the eta's whip.

Kitsuki Gofumin gulped, wishing he were not alone with these strangely silent monks and the dark-haired eta.

"Mirumoto Shindo . . ." he began, his eyes filling with tears at the name of his friend. "Dead beneath Tonshu Cliff."

The eta's hand rose. The whip descended with a hissing, high-pitched snarl.

A hand appeared in midair and caught the torturer's wrist. Around the hand formed a white glow—a strange pearl that swelled in the air above Gofumin. He staggered backward. The radiance touched ground and burst open in a bright ray. The hand lengthened into an arm, and the samurai that had reached from beyond the portal stepped fully through.

"My lord Daini-sama," Gofumin gasped. He fell to his knees and shoved his ornate helm off his head. He pressed his face to the ground and hoped that his terror would not show.

"Rise, samurai," Mirumoto Daini commanded, looking out over Beiden Pass.

Below, in the twilight of the battlefield, more portals of light were opening. Strange hooded serpent-men slid through. Their arms rose, glittering with pearl rings and bracelets. They hissed and writhed on the ground as massive tails moved through the portals behind them. The creatures formed legions and rows.

"Where are the Crab?" Daini demanded sharply.

"They—they have been driven from the pass, Daini-sama!" Gofumin struggled to find his voice, not looking up at the monstrosities that had followed the Mirumoto through his strange portal. "The Unicorn . . . the Shinjo and Toturi have driven them back. We fight only the last Shadowlands beasts that linger, holed up in caves. . . . Goblins, undead, oni."

"Oni," Daini said scornfully, his dark eyes hardening. "The oni are in for a terrible surprise. My allies are very good at cleaning out caves."

Serpent men slid one by one through the shining light. Some were as large as four horses. Others were small, lithe and green. All hissed in an unfamiliar tongue; their tails snapped dexterously. They sniffed the air, seeming to sense their prey, and slithered rapidly up the pass, toward nearby caves.

"Cut Mitsu down." Daini released the eta's hand, shoving him roughly toward the torii. "Your services won't be needed anymore. As Yukihera commanded, Mitsu-sama is to be set free when reinforcements arrive. These are the naga, our allies against the Foul, against Fu Leng."

The eta stumbled to obey, dropping his whip and reaching for a small workman's knife. Severing the ropes, he lowered Mitsu's bloodied body to the ground.

"Shinsei . . . told me . . . you would come." Mitsu smiled through parched, bloodied lips. The other ise zumi lowered their chant, their voices whispering into the wind caused by the strange pearl portals.

"Ssh, my old friend." Mirumoto Daini looked down at him in alarm, his eyes filled with compassion and anger. "This ordeal nearly claimed you. Mara, can you help him?"

Behind Daini, a golden-haired, green-skinned woman knelt beside the wounded ise zumi. A pearl glowed faintly in her hand. "I do not know if he will live, beloved," Mara murmured.

"He must."

Gofumin stared in awe at the strange man-beasts, watching as their pearl magic illuminated the battlefield in opalescent streams of white light. He choked faintly, staring at Mara. His eyes took in her emerald skin and strange, scaled hands.

Behind her, another naga slid through the portal, bow arched and arrow nocked.

"I—I should go, my lord," the Kitsuki squeaked, shuffling backward on his knees as a massive green scaled tail flexed near his face. "And, and . . . and tell the Unicorn. . . ."

Three more naga, including what appeared to be a serpent shugenja, eased their way out onto the hillside. They peered down to the caves below and watched with eagerness as Shadowlands creatures were flung, butchered, from the cave mouths. The naga shugenja raised clawed hands above his tremendous hood and chanted in a strange, sibilant tongue. The creature's tongue slid from between his gleaming fangs, his face unlike anything the terrified samurai had ever seen.

Gofumin muttered beneath his breath something he had heard, long ago. "There is no dishonor in fear—only in acting from fear."

"Of course, samurai," Daini said, half-listening. His head cocked, and he hissed something at the shugenja. The snake-man's cobra hood flexed open. Daini asked Gofumin, "Where have the rest of the Dragon units gone?"

"To the north, my lord, to meet with Togashi Yokuni-sama. Yukihera . . . has formally petitioned to become the daimyo of the Mirumoto family after the passing of . . . your sister . . . and . . ." Gofumin's voice broke, but he conquered his terror ". . . your own death."

"Yukihera's announcement of my death has little truth. His riddle has failed him." The Mirumoto considered for a moment. "You say they have gone north, back to the Iron Mountain?"

"Hai, Lord. And then on to Otosan Uchi, if the rumors we have heard from Toturi's men are true."

Daini looked once more at the Shadowlands creatures, butchered at the cave mouths.

One of the naga raised a jade staff, screaming a battle cry as he flushed a demon-beast from one crevice of the Pass. A weary cavalry group of Unicorn pounded past the naga lines to help dispatch the oni.

"Gofumin," Daini said, "let me introduce you to Shashakar, a jakla of the Cobra bloodline—a powerful shugenja among his people."

Gofumin bowed deeply, in respect and not a little fear.

The Cobra nodded his reply, but addressed Daini. He spoke in remarkably fluid Rokugani, perhaps due to a spell. "You would ask about the spell of transportation?" The Cobra's strange, multifaceted eyes whirled in a thousand shades. "I prepared it as you wished, to bring us here. Casting the spell has destroyed the pearls, as is the cost of such powerful magic. It cannot take us farther north. If I were to begin creation of other such travel-pearls, we should have to return to the Shinomen and begin again." The Cobra smiled regretfully, his fangs shining in the faint light of the setting sun. "I am sorry, pale brother. If the armies of the naga are to go north, we must march."

Daini turned to the kneeling Kitsuki captain. "Go find the Shinjo commander. Tell him we are coming to speak with him."

Gofumin bowed again, nearly cracking his head on the ground in his haste, and then scrambled to his feet. It was a ten-minute hike from the hillock to the command tent.

This time, it took him only three.

▲▲▲▲▲▲▲▲

Mara looked carefully at Togashi Mitsu's deep wounds. They festered with sickness from his long ordeal. She reached to bind the worst laceration, placing forest herbs on the sweltering cuts. Mara pressed her lips together in worry. The dragons tattooed on the fallen man's chest and head seemed to writhe under her fingers, coiling about her touch as if gratefully welcoming a friend.

Togashi Mitsu reached to clasp Daini's hand, dragging the samurai closer to his cracked and bloodied lips. "Yukihera..."

"Don't worry, Mitsu. We'll go see Yukihera together and tell him that he has failed."

"No." Mitsu shook his head, gritting his teeth in pain. "The river has gone to the ocean, Daini."

Daini's glance took in the encampment below, scanning the tent banners swiftly. Toturi's wolf mon had been removed, and now a Unicorn banner flew high above the central command tent. A few of the lesser Dragon mon remained, marking the presence of captains and their units—but the flag of the master of the Iron Mountain was gone.

"He's taken the Mirumoto to . . . Otosan Uchi. The emperor . . ."

"The emperor?" Daini felt a rush of heat in his cheeks.

Mitsu smiled through cracked lips. "Shinsei has spoken to me. The city . . . the city is burning. No . . . time." Mitsu's veins stood out in his throat as he struggled to say more. "Shinsei walks with us."

"I know, Mitsu. He always has."

"No . . . he walks with us. . . . Otosan Uchi . . . Fu Leng . . ." Mitsu's voice grew weaker, drowned in agony as his body was rocked by a rigid spasm of pain.

"This human is dying. We have no other choice." Mara's face grew pensive, worry furrowing her brow.

The tattooed men gathered around her, clasping hands in a circle and chanting intently as she reached for a vial of water at her belt.

"Drink this, friend." Lifting the vial to Mitsu's lips, Mara poured a few drops of the River of the Sky into the ise zumi's mouth.

Mitsu's face grew ashen, as gray as a storm. His brown eyes stared at the windswept, twilight sky. He coughed, and bitter liquid flooded his veins. His body spasmed, recoiling in pain. His hands balled into fists at his sides. The chanting of his brother monks grew louder, drowning out Mitsu's sharp scream of agony. His body convulsed once more, steeling itself against death, and then fell limp upon the bloodstained dirt beneath the rough torii arch.

Below the hillock, the naga armies launched a full-scale assault against the scattering Shadowlands forces.

Togashi Mitsu began to laugh. His bellow, a thing of brightness and joy, echoed from the hilltops and danced over the setting sun.

He would not die today.

18 THE FORBIDDEN CITY

The plains of Otosan Uchi were covered in blood. High grasses had been trampled flat by the marching feet of a thousand samurai. Each step over the tortured plains pressed against mud too red to be purely clay.

The traveler's sandals were stained with green and yellow.

On the wide fields around the tortured city, armies camped. Banners of Unicorn purple mixed with the muted colors of the Phoenix, fluttering above sturdy tents in the grass. The Mirumoto standard snapped nearby, and the Hida and Hiruma—but there was no sign of the Crane. The armies of the clans, as proud as they were, were losing. Fu Leng's power was too great. Even the Lion Clan could not assail them. Though the Lion mon flew high above the gathered armies, many Lion had gone to fight for the emperor. They killed their own.

The mon of the emperor flew above a palace whose white walls had been charred black by storm and taint. Here and there, the city burned. In their thousands, undead rose from the fields to march within the high stone walls.

The traveler shouldered her light pack and stared for a moment at the ruined city and the fluttering banners.

Hitomi had traveled for months into the Dragon Mountains and returned, bearing none of the answers she had sought. Still, it was time to strike—now, or not at all. The armies had gathered around the plains of Otosan Uchi, and Fu Leng's power grew. Her wounds had healed, and her arm was as sturdy as it had ever been. Yet while she meditated upon her place in the universe, her soul still cried out to her brother.

Satsu. . . .

His soul had not come to her in the mountains; the riddle had not been answered. Despite her struggle, she could find no peace, no mystic secret, no sudden enlightenment. Something was still missing, and Hitomi had returned to Otosan Uchi to find it. She had come to collect what was rightfully hers, to end the anger that raged in her heart. Only one balm could ease that wound.

Yakamo's death.

Battles had ravaged the field, and Hitomi knelt beside a dying ronin. "Where are the Dragon troops?" she asked him, ignoring his blood, which slowly stained the ground.

"To the north. By Shinsei, I beg you, end my life so I do not dishonor my family . . . my son . . ."

Standing, she loosened her sword in its scabbard. With one swift stroke, she took his head. A year ago she would not have cared. Two years, and she would not have even noticed his plea. Her life had changed.

To the north, a horn sounded the retreat.

The blackened gates of the city swung wide, and a thousand mounted horsemen charged from within the walls. Their steeds were as dark as pitch, their eyes rolling and wild, as red as falling stars. Skeletal samurai rode them, white bone shining in the sunlight. Eerie laughter mixed with the ring of blades.

Hitomi slid her true hand over her smooth pate. She felt lighter now, free of troubles and weights. Empty. Pure. As the hair had come away, shaved from her scalp in the tradition of ise zumi monks, she had chanted. Satsu's name, the names of her ancestors, and the words above the Dragon Throne rang in her mind, purifying her soul. Clean-shaven, she was ready for war.

Become the riddle.

A group of Mirumoto samurai lay crouched in a low gully, shielding themselves from a rain of arrows launched from Otosan Uchi's wall. They needed help, and they huddled to shield their wounded from enemy fire.

Racing toward them, Hitomi slid into the gully as another hail of steel fell down upon them. Barely missing, the arrows lay in the dirt, their steel tips slick with poison and foulness. Beside her, a Mirumoto chui—a lieutenant—bound his arm with silk, using his teeth to tying the bloodstained cloth.

"What's your name, soldier?" she shouted to the wounded man. His troop had followed him into this sparse sanctuary— fifteen men out of the forty that had charged onto the field behind his banner.

"Mirumoto Kuike, Taisa!" He yelled back over the ringing sounds of war. Seeing her golden-scale armor, he had mistaken her for a captain in the Dragon armies.

"What are your orders?"

"Flank the right, seize the hole between those two watchtowers," he pointed with his katana at a breach in Otosan Uchi's wall, "and hold clear entry to the city under my lord's command."

The commands were reasonable, but over a hundred undead guardians, their putrid shrieks echoing from the city walls, held the entry. Kuike's legion had been so badly decimated that the few guards left would never be able to capture the perimeter, much less hold it against a force of that size.

"Are you going to return to the encampment?"

His face turned white. "No, Taisa-sama. I would rather give my life in battle than return to Lord Yukihera with failure."

Hitomi looked at the other samurai in Kuike's command, and saw agreement in their eyes.

"Samurai do not fear to fail, Kuike-san," Hitomi began, but he quickly interrupted her.

"Iie, no, Taisa-sama. It is not failure that I fear. It is Yukihera's vengeance. The last three commanders who did not give their lives in battle for him were torn limb from limb by horses—cut open and left for the necromancers to steal their souls. I would die before I so dishonored my family.

"Given to the necromancers?" Hitomi asked incredulously.

Kuike's voice was strained. "Hai, Taisa, that is what I have seen with my own eyes. It is rumored that Yukihera has . . . an agreement with the Shadowlands. He fights them out of honor, but he offers them tribute in exchange for his own life."

"You would say such things about your own lord?

To her astonishment, Kuike spat upon the ground in anger. "He is lord because of his blood, not because of his honor. I am ashamed to serve him; you should be as well. Better that we all die on this field than return with him to the Iron Mountain with the taint of Fu Leng."

Some distance away, a Unicorn cavalry troop charged a twisted horror with four arms and legs. It dragged down the Battle Maidens, who screamed and chopped with their swords.

Hitomi looked again toward the chui and finally recognized him. "You are Mirumoto Kuike-san, who fought at Beiden Pass beneath Mirumoto Hitomi, are you not?"

"I am. And may her soul forgive us."

"I, too, fought at the pass, Taisa-sama," another samurai said. His voice cracked with fear, his armor was stained with grass and mud. He was a gunso, second to Mirumoto Kuike in command. "And I can say that I would rather have died with Hitomi-sama than seen the Dragon Clan come to this. I was Mirumoto Kenjiro. At the battle of Gusnshu, I had the privilege of fighting beside Mirumoto Shiyando, Togashi Yokuni's own yojimbo. For my valor, I was asked to become Lord Yukihera's personal retainer, his yojimbo. I refused. In my day, I have seen great honor—and Yukihera has none."

"You also accuse him of dealing with the Shadowlands?"

"I can say nothing directly, but he has met with the sorcerer, Yogo Junzo. I have seen them together. I believe, when the war for Otosan Uchi truly begins, the Dragon will be sacrificed for Yukihera's ambition."

"You believe this, and yet you are here?"

The man proudly lifted his chin. "Believe? Yes, I believe this. But I cannot prove it. I have heard him whisper in the night, seen hooded figures moving within his tent—but I cannot stake my honor on something I have not seen. Yukihera is working with the Shadowlands, why, I cannot guess. But I would rather give my life with honor than live to see the day that the Dragon fall. It is bushido. I cannot question my lord, and I will not disobey—but I can still fight."

Hitomi's black eyes turned cold and hard. "No more Mirumoto will die today, Gunso. Look at this." Hitomi sketched upon the ground with a stick, and Kuike's fifteen men gathered close. "This is another way into the city. Go north, to this outcropping, and move the boulder by the bottom of the willow tree. There, you will find a passage into Otosan Uchi. If you take this route, you will arrive in the sewers just beyond that tower." She pointed at the city with the stick, and then drew a route back to the broken wall. "With Shinsei's good will, you will arrive behind the undead and be able to surprise them. That should even the odds. Use this cover," another few quick sketches, "and your bows."

"How do you know this secret passage into the city still exists?" Kuike asked, his eyes widening in astonishment.

"Because," Hitomi said, standing, "that's how I came out." Grinning, Hitomi continued, "Now, go, and keep yourself safe. There's a girl on the slopes of Sekui Mountain who cries for your return. Let us not keep her waiting much longer."

Kuike smiled widely and bowed. With sharp orders, he rallied his men, and they swiftly headed for the outcropping where the sewer opening was concealed outside the city. The battle on the fields of Otosan Uchi continued to rage, and Hitomi tore her thoughts away from the Mirumoto, ready to rejoin the battle.

"Well done, my lady," a quiet voice said.

Hitomi spun, her hand reaching for the hilt of her sword. Behind her stood a single samurai, his brown hood revealing a half-smile. He leaned on a staff with a flute carved into its head.

"Hyoji." She recognized him, though it had been many months since their first meeting in the Agasha maze. The brown-eyed ronin had not changed in all that time. As he smiled at her, Hitomi felt some half-remembered burden in her heart grow light.

"Your humble guide." He bowed, touching his hands to his sides.

"Where did you come from?"

"From the heavens, of course." He smiled easily. "I see you bear the sword of a Scorpion." He pointed at the burgundy saya that rested beside her Mirumoto wakizashi. "Have you given them your fealty?" His voice was calm, but Hitomi recoiled as if she had been struck.

"Fealty? My heart lies with the Dragon, guide. Do not question that."

"I do question it. And I question why you are here." He continued, circling her easily with long strides. "Throw away that Scorpion's sword, and perhaps I will believe that your heart still belongs to the Dragon."

"Throw it away? On a battlefield?"

His smile was enigmatic and clever. "You will not need it. Yakamo is not here . . . yet."

Her face reddened, and she ground her words between clenched teeth. "I will not throw away my sword."

"And what of you, my lady? Where have you been? Have you learned Scorpion loyalty and Scorpion truths?" The guide shrugged. "You have been talking to the Mirumoto, I see? I thought such men were chattel to a samurai such as you. Why did you not throw them to the wolves?"

Wincing, Hitomi remembered her hasty words from the encampment. It seemed a hundred yeas ago that she had said them, and now they rang hollowly in her ears. "You throw my own arrogance in my face."

"I show you lessons. You must choose if you will learn from

them. Tell me, Lady, when these Mirumoto die, will you re-member their names?"

"Kuike. Kenjiro." Hitomi's coal-black eyes narrowed. "Yukihera."

"You remember his name, of course. So do the souls of those he has killed in this 'hidden alliance' with the Shadow-lands. They curse his name—and they curse yours."

"Mine?"

"For leaving them." The guide looked out over the battle-field, watching as Unicorn and Lion samurai screamed, cut down by beasts with fangs like sabers. A Dragon samurai leapt in the way, saving a Lion shugenja from undead blades and sac-rificing his own life. "Leaving them . . . to this." A necromancer on the walls of Otosan Uchi lifted his hand, and the Dragon rose from the ground, his body pulled as if by the jerking strings of a puppeteer.

"Not for long, ronin. Not anymore. The Dragon are my people, my family. I am their rightful daimyo, and I have a duty to protect them." She rose from the gully, striding toward the camps of her people.

"You don't believe in bushido, Lady Hitomi-sama," he chuckled. "Remember?"

She paused at the lip of the gully, looking down at him with a slow, appraising glance. Taking the Scorpion sword from her obi, she tossed it down on the ground before the hooded ronin. "Fu Leng's archers have moved on, ronin," she said sharply. "And so must I. I have a duty to complete. One I have neglected for far too long already."

The Hooded Ronin smiled, watching as Hitomi stalked to-ward the Mirumoto encampment. Looking up at the sky, he tracked the progress of Lady Sun across her heavens and tested the wind for foul air. Sensing a faint tang upon the cold wind, he whispered to his unseen companion. "The day of prophecy draws near. Do you think she is ready?"

The wind tossed mournfully, and the ronin found few answers within the Dragon Champion's silent helm.

She will have to be. . . .

▲▲▲▲▲▲▲▲

The Dragon legions marched with heavy hearts, following Yukihera onto the fields beyond the encampments.

Otosan Uchi stood before them, its stone walls covered in festering mold. The ivy that had once graced its delicate towers had browned and withered. Storm clouds hung over the main gates, and screams of battle echoed from undead throats. Many of the Dragon marched with resignation, knowing that their death awaited them, and that they were unable to do anything to save themselves. Bushido demanded they obey their lord . . . no matter what the cost.

"A thousand Dragon, marching side by side," a voice called to them from before the armies. "A thousand Dragon, ready to die. I think not, Yukihera. Not today."

The wind blew through Hitomi's brown cloak as she stood on the battlefield, her armor scratched with constant wear. She had shaved her hair in tribute to Shinsei's wisdom and her own rebirth. The warrior maiden stared deliberately at the legion commander, daring him with black eyes. Her wakizashi hung in its saya, marked with the mon of the Mirumoto—but her katana, the blade of a samurai, was missing.

Hitomi scanned the faces of her kinsmen, the samurai prepared to fight and die on the fields at Otosan Uchi. If they succeeded, they would save the empire. If they failed, they would doom their own souls. Any samurai would choose to fight against the evil that spread from Otosan Uchi, but these men were too few, too weary to survive the assault. This attack was madness—three legions of Dragon against the gathered forces of Fu Leng. Only Hitomi stood between them and their fatal duty, a duty that the samurai maiden was willing to give her life to prevent.

"Three legions can never make their way through the Matsu and Ikoma guarding that gate. The Lion are confused about their duty, yes, but they aren't stupid."

Yukihera stepped to the front of the command, reaching for the golden sword at his side. "Who dares speak to me in this way?" He hissed. "I am daimyo of the Mirumoto. Have you forgotten your place, samurai?" Yukihera stared at the mon on the short sword in her obi. "You are Mirumoto. If you have forgotten that I rule this family, samurai, I will have to remind you."

"Forgotten . . . and ignored." The words were familiar in their irony.

Yukihera blanched in recognition as she approached.

"My name is Mirumoto Hitomi, daughter of Mirumoto Shosan, master of the Iron Mountain and ruler of the Dragon lands. I fought for the Dragon at Otosan Uchi when Bayushi Shoju tried to overthrow the Hantei line. I battled beside my brothers on the fields of Beiden Pass, and I fell, not to the swords of the Crab, but to the treachery of my own people. You, Yukihera." Her features were a mask of hatred and anger. "You betrayed me. My story does not end there, even if you prayed to Shinsei that it would. I found my way free in the service of the empress, and I bear the burden of the Moon."

Hitomi raised the Obsidian Hand, flexing the stone fingers and watching as sunlight danced from the cold black stone. "I fought the minions of Fu Leng from within the Imperial Palace, and I will fight them again now. But you, Yukihera," Hitomi stepped suddenly forward, grasped the sleeve of his kimono in her stone hand, and tore away the cloth. "You have not fought them at all."

The fine silk shredded beneath the strength of her immortal fingers. It revealed a gray arm, its flesh withered and corrupted by the taint of the Shadowlands.

"You never intended for the Dragon to live through this war," Hitomi said. " You wanted Fu Leng to kill our entire clan, seize their souls, and bring back their rotted bodies under your command. Then you would be the champion of a dead clan. You wanted power over the Dragon, Yukihera, any power. When you could not have it, you vowed to give us all to Fu Leng."

Yukihera ground his teeth in anger. "Your rage has blinded you. You are uncontrolled, useless. You know nothing of true honor, Hitomi, and you never did. I am still daimyo of this clan."

"I may not know honor, Yukihera, but I know everything about duty." Her eyes blazed and her lips curled in a feral smile. The old rage resurfaced, not as an uncontrolled vengeance, but as a blade tempered by loss and sacrifice. "My duty is to kill you."

The Mirumoto stared in awe as the two combatants circled each other, seeking footing in mud churned by war and death. "You have no sword," Yukihera said victoriously. "How can you hope to stand against me?"

Hitomi looked out over the gathered Dragon armies and raised her voice. "I am Mirumoto Hitomi, and I say that this man does not lead you. I know the Dragon's heart. It has been said that the Dragon Clan's place is in the mountains of our home and not on the battlefield. I say that our place is where it has always been: within the empire." She pointed to the great city, now blackened and burned on the horizon. "If you would march against the foulness that would destroy all of Rokugan, I would lead you. But I will not allow you to throw your lives away for one man's ambition. You, the Dragon, are my brothers. You are my family. You are my purpose, and if necessary, I will die for you."

She opened her hand and extended it toward the breathless troops. "All you need do is lend me a sword, and I will clear your path."

Five hundred swords leapt free of their owners' obi, and one by one the Dragon knelt to offer her their allegiance. Hitomi felt hot tears touch her eyes as the Mirumoto knelt in a simple act of devotion and trust, swords held out before them.

"My lady," a gruff old voice spoke. "Take mine."

Hitomi turned, her dark eyes scanning the crowd. Mirumoto Sukune took three steps forward, ignoring his son's venomous gaze. "I took the saya from him, but the blade is my own. I think your father would have been very proud." The words were low but sincere, and Hitomi bowed deeply to give honor to the blade.

"Thank you, Sukune-san," she whispered genuinely, her face a dark mask of regret. Taking the katana in the Obsidian Hand, she straightened and held it out toward Yukihera. "I bear the sword of Mirumoto Sukune, the finest general on the Iron Mountain, and I am not afraid to kill you."

"Then try, little girl," Yukihera laughed bitterly, the taint running like madness in his blood. "This time, I will see that you are truly dead."

Hitomi's pressed Sukune's sword into her obi, and then drew both of her weapons free in a whirling curtain of steel.

With an expert flick of his wrists, Yukihera drew his swords and easily turned away her first blow.

He is strong . . . stronger than I remembered, Hitomi thought. He cut low, and she was forced to step over his katana, nearly impaling herself on his shorter blade. Faster, too. She ducked neatly below his extended katana, raising her own and nearly slicing though his arm.

He staggered back, wrenching himself out of danger with catlike reflexes. His eyes narrowed.

What other gifts has the Dark Lord's favor given him? The taint was a curse, but it could confer powers unlike any other in Rokugan—the reward for selling one's soul. Well enough, Yukihera. You may think that you have the upper hand in this duel. Hitomi smiled, thinking of obsidian and stone. But you are wrong.

She swept in close, black fingers curling around the hilt of her katana. This time, she aimed for Yukihera's neck, but her sword slid from the panels of his elaborate golden helm.

"You have turned your back on us, Yukihera, and so we will turn our backs on you." Hitomi's strikes came faster now, dancing with impatience and anger.

Yukihera, too calm, parried some blows and dodged others.

The power of the Obsidian Hand surged through Hitomi, baring her bone and peeling back her flesh. In her mind, she saw herself, covered entirely by obsidian, seated on an ivory throne among a field of stars.

Revenge, the hand sang in her mind with a thousand voices. *Revenge, revenge and death!*

"Not this time. Not for revenge," she told it with a sharp laugh. She tossed her katana into her left hand, catching it easily and holding both swords. Then, raising the hand to catch Yukihera's sword, she snapped the ancient blade between smooth stone fingers, feeling the metal twist and snap. "This time, I fight not for the past but for the future."

Closing in on Yukihera, she raised her weapons in both hands once more. The golden samurai dropped the hilt of his broken katana, bringing his wakizashi before him to ward away Hitomi. His flesh twisted and boiled, the gray putty of his right arm shifting to cover his neck and face. She slashed at him once, cutting away his enameled breastplate, and saw maggots scurry across Yukihera's bare chest.

She cut again, shearing away his golden helmet and leaving his head bare to the sky. "How does it feel, Yukihera?" she hissed, "to be one of the living dead? I once lived that way," Hitomi regarded him critically, " and I can tell you that there is no easy road back. But since you have condemned me to live among the dead, it seems only right that I let you suffer the same fate. . . ."

"Tamori!" shouted Yukihera. "As general of the Dragon armies, I command you!"

In the crowd, Agasha Tamori moved his hands slowly, whispering arcane words. His fingers moved like lead, unwilling to complete the task—but once commanded, the stoic old shugenja could not refuse.

Hitomi's sight began to blur, a white flame moving across her eyes, stinging like vipers. She screamed with the pain, and felt Yukihera's katana cut into her side. Hitomi twisted as she felt the cold steel, and the wound was light.

She was not dead yet, but the white mist that had been drawn down across her eyes would leave her open to Yukihera's next blow. Her swords trembled, uncertain, and the world became a single white field, echoing with all the brightness of the Sun.

Blood! The hand screamed, and Hitomi sensed power just beyond her grasp. The hand was no longer fighting her, but moving with her will, lending her strength despite the wound beneath her ribcage. *Blood and fury! I will not lose you!* It screamed, parrying Yukihera's next blow on its own. *Hitomi!*

Hitomi felt the hand move, and she trusted her blade to it. Unable to see, she heard and felt the ringing of steel as the hand fought Yukihera with her own anger.

Hitomi blindly leapt forward into a tackle, throwing herself at Yukihera. By the grace of Shinsei, she missed his swords and landed fully against his chest, toppling them both rudely to the ground. Hitomi rolled forward, over her opponent and toward the edge of the battlefield. Keeping her swords in her hands, she crouched and turned.

"Not this way, Yukihera!" she screamed in fury. "Fight me, damn you!"

On the edge of the field, Agasha Tamori flicked his wrists, tightening the spell around Hitomi. It drew the sight from her eyes and crushed the strength from her body. He spoke the final words of the spell, "Eyes cannot see. . . ."

Yukihera paused, watching as Hitomi's swords wove a blind path before her, keeping him at bay. He smiled, taking the time to look out over the Dragon troops. "I am your daimyo!" he howled, raising his bloody sword and swinging it in a wide arc.

"Shinsei, forgive me. . . ." Tamori drew his hands slowly upward, prepared to steal Hitomi's eyes forever.

Suddenly, cold steel touched the old wizard's neck. Freezing his movements, he stared into the cold brown eyes of Mirumoto Daini.

The tanto lay flat against his skin, Daini's breath warm in Tamori's ear. "You cheated my sister of her life once, Tamori, and your cowardice cheated us all of our purpose. You pride yourself on never refusing a command, Tamori, but this is a duty you will find the strength to disobey. I do not wish to kill you. Still, if you make one more move, you will never see your precious mountains again."

The shugenja spoke slowly. "If she wins, we all will die against the Shadowlands. We do not have the troops. We must withdraw back to the Iron Mountain. Yukihera-sama has promised . . ."

"Yukihera has lied to us all." The Mirumoto samurai said.

Slowly, the shugenja lowered his hands and let the spell unravel. "Hai, Daini-san," the old man whispered. "Perhaps he has."

Crouched and feral, Hitomi spun her swords to block incoming blows. Blinking the blindness from her eyes, she peered through a white haze at Yukihera as he lifted himself to one knee. Whatever had robbed her of her vision was gone. As her sight returned, Hitomi grinned and stood. This time, there would be no interference.

Hurt him now, the hand whispered, reaching out toward Yukihera in her mind. *Hurt him, kill him. . . .*

This time, Hitomi smiled. Yes.

Its voice had become her own.

Her sword flashed as it flew through the sky, darkening when it pierced Yukihera's tainted flesh.

The Mirumoto samurai staggered, falling to his knees. He stared at her in shock, still certain that Hitomi was on the ground, blind and beaten.

Hitomi slid the blade deeper into his chest, drawing back her wakizashi. Using the katana to keep Yukihera frozen on the ground before her, Hitomi lifted the shorter blade over her head. "The wakizashi is the soul of bushido," she whispered, staring Yukihera's stunned golden eyes. "My soul belongs to the Dragon Clan. You lost yours, Yukihera, long ago."

Her wakizashi cut through the fallen samurai's neck in a clean, swift stroke, severing his head from his body.

19   BECOME THE RIDDLE

Thunder roared over Otosan Uchi's high walls, ripping open the sky. No rain fell. The bitter, acrid torrents of water had exhausted themselves during the night, turning the ground to mud. Rain had pockmarked rocks and bone and torn open the curtains of the tents. Still, the armies fought, taking no time for rest. The undead behind Otosan Uchi's high gates needed no respite and gave none to the Seven Clans.

Many days had passed, stretching into weeks as the armies threw themselves at Otosan Uchi's walls. One by one across Rokugan, the Black Scrolls were being opened . . . one by one, Fu Leng's powers were returning. His soul was being set free. Was it enough? Would it ever be enough?

Hitomi stared out at the rain beyond the opening of her tent, unable to wish away the dark stone walls of the Imperial City. The fields were covered in blood, autumn rain slowly turning to ice and frost. Still the empire fought.

Hitomi had worked all the while, turning her dedication and courage to the fight. She had become both general and daimyo to her armies, bringing them through battle after battle with the fewest losses of any of the Great Clans. Her name was becoming legend, and her victories became tales of Dragon courage. She had spent her time earning back the respect she had lost, and in doing so, Hitomi had found her home.

The legions of the Dragon readied themselves, sharpening their swords and praying to Shinsei for his wisdom. Hitomi walked among them, greeting the commanders by name and flushing lightly when she saw their earnest bows of respect. Something had changed in the Mirumoto troops—and something had changed in Hitomi.

The commanders had presented her with the ancient Mirumoto katana—the one Yakamo had broken. She had removed the halves of the weapon, wrapped them carefully in her obi, and placed it upon her sleeping mats. Then, Hitomi had reverently sheathed Sukune's sword in its saya. The katana swung easily at her side as she strode through the encampment outside the capital city. The saya clicked against her golden armor like the hoofbeats of an approaching rider.

Time was sliding through her fingers, and there was not much left to spend.

She strode alongside the naga encampment. Daini's strange serpent-men had truly been sent by the Fortunes. Their pearls and healing magic had restored the wounded of the Dragon, doubling their forces overnight. As she walked, the strange, green-skinned people stared at her, their slitted eyes and massive tails setting them apart from every other creature in the empire. Hitomi could not hold their gaze for long. Daini, on the other hand, was comfortable with them. He understood their hissing language, and he translated their strange customs. He had changed. Mirumoto Daini was no longer the prideful, spiteful young boy he had been when he left the Iron Mountain. He had become a man.

"You march through the tents like a boat commander, watching his ship sink around him." Mitsu's teasing voice was like soothing bells, and Hitomi smiled widely. "Do you think you will die today?"

"I may," Hitomi said carefully. "If Shinsei wills it."

"Shinsei wills nothing more than to huddle by the fire and be warm, like the rest of us. I asked him; it is so."

Hitomi rolled her eyes at the ise zumi's words. "If you're speaking to Shinsei now, tell him to get a sword and join us. The battle is about to begin, and we could use another blade." Turning on her heel with a friendly wave, she continued on through the encampment, gathering the Mirumoto for the morning's charge.

Banners fluttered in the dark gray morning, their colors muted by the rain and cold wind. The Unicorn camped nearest to the Dragon armies, and the Crane, who had arrived only last night, had set up their headquarters nearby. The lord of the Crane had been assaulted by an army of Shadowlands madmen within his own provinces, but had driven them back. Well enough. Hitomi wished them all such luck today.

Beyond the Crane snapped Crab banners, their dull gray almost blending with the cold sky. Hitomi turned a cold eye on the fluttering flags, trying to forget what Yokuni had told her. *You cannot kill Yakamo. . . .*

She had no choice. She had sworn to kill him—and if Yokuni's words were true, she might not be returning from the final battle.

"Satsu . . ." Hitomi whispered, asking for answers to riddles yet unsaid. "Guide me. . . ." But in her mind there was nothing but loneliness and the constant whisper of the Obsidian Hand. She looked down at the black glass fingers, curling them into a fist. Today.

Today, she would find her answer, or the empire would fall.

▲▲▲▲▲▲▲▲

"Storm the wall!" Hitomi roared, raising the gold and green flag high above her armies.

On the parapets of Otosan Uchi, undead archers lifted their bows in a long row of sharpened arrows. Steel tips glinted in the faint light of the cold morning. The fields around Otosan Uchi were flat, covered in pockets of raised earth where samurai feet had rushed and fallen, charging toward the city. For months, the high black walls of Otosan Uchi had spurned all their advances. Thousands had fallen on the wide grassy plain of the Imperial City. Thousands more remained to carry the banner of the empire forward once more against Fu Leng's horde.

While Unicorn cavalry rushed past to assault an oni outside the eastern wall, Hitomi led her Dragon infantry toward a breach in the northern wall. Out of it poured undead troops. Dragon footmen and pikemen met them and struck fierce blows. Tamori's shugenja—determined to redeem themselves after their daimyo's loss of face—protected the charging samurai with spells of wind and stone. Huge walls of granite rumbled forth from the ground, springing up to trap the marching undead. Between the high stone walls, the Mirumoto marched toward the breach.

Lightning crashed down from Otosan Uchi's walls, guided by the rotting hands of necromancers. Fu Leng's sorcerers had arrived to turn the tide. White energy crackled into the barricades raised by the Agasha and shattered them. Tremendous chunks of granite hailed down on the Dragon legions.

The Dragon march to the northern wall would not be as simple as Hitomi had hoped.

The Agasha retaliated with driving winds, swirling about the crushed rock and boulders and lifting the fragments into the gray sky. Air spirits, faint outlines against the dark clouds, lifted the stone high into the air. With a fierce breath of wind, the kami hurled their burdens of rock toward Otosan Uchi's protective barriers.

Hitomi led her Dragon armies toward on Otosan Uchi, the high wall of the Imperial City rang from blows of pummeling stone. Earth, rocks, and boulders rose high into the air and plunged in cascade after cascade onto Otosan Uchi's wall. The parapet began to crack. The city's defenses slowly shattered under the assault. At last, with a rumbling roar, a section of the wall crumbled open. The blocks that had held the wall together fell to rubble and loose mortar.

By the time the Mirumoto reached it, crossing the muddied field beneath a rain of arrows, the wall had cracked into a wide breach.

"Into the city!" Hitomi shouted, driving the Mirumoto forward with her own courage.

Beside her, four ise zumi roared, calling on the power of their enchanted tattoos. Fire flickered in torrents from their open mouths, and the dragons on their skin writhed and clawed as if trying to reach their opponents. Another ise zumi leapt through the air. On his wide back, clouds boiling across a tattooed ocean. The leap carried him high above the Dragon armies, to the top of Otosan Uchi's uppermost tower. A third ise zumi screamed aloud, his hands moving too swiftly to be seen. His opponents, five small oni, tumbled aside, stung by the wasps tattooed along the ise zumi's arms.

The Dragon pressed toward the gap, swords glinting in the bright sunlight. They cleft undead skulls like rotten melons.

Ahead, thick voices chanted in unfamiliar tongues. They worked maho, the evil blood-spells cast by necromancers. Red snakes of spidery mist suddenly twisted out through the breach and spread across the fields.

Mirumoto samurai screamed, their lungs shriveling beneath the spell's vicious effect. Every samurai touched by the red mist fell to his knees. The Dragon were outmatched. The horde's dark maho was too powerful.

Hitomi held her breath, determined to reach the bloody gap before the mist could steal her strength, but her knees buckled. The ground raced toward her, and she collapsed among the other Dragon samurai, choking and gasping for breath. Hitomi glanced back to see Tamori standing among his shugenja, gesturing wildly. He cast lightning spells to keep undead soldiers at bay, but it was not enough. The undead poured out through the scarlet mist, unbreathing and unafraid.

Then, from the rear, the chanting of the Agasha changed. A hiss like a thousand serpents filled the air, and fresh wind began to blow. Where Agasha lightning and stone had pounded against the walls and held back zombie bushi, now naga pearl sorcery began to take effect. The breeze turned into a stiff wind, the wind to a gale, and the gale to a full-blown storm.

The force of the blast squeezed the breath from Hitomi's lungs. A thin trail of red mist poured from her nostrils. Other samurai choked, gasping in the clean air. Bloody trails of breath streamed from their mouths.

Near the naga, Daini raised his sword, held it for a shining second, and then dropped it. Fifty arrows, pitifully few for a normal Rokugani contingent of archers, flew from naga bows.

Few, but more than enough. Every arrow struck a necromancer, hiding behind the walls of Otosan Uchi. The shots were nearly impossible, and Hitomi watched in awe as they arced perfectly to their targets. Not a single arrow faltered. Not one missed. Fifty necromancers died.

The naga reloaded their bows, and fired again. When they were done, not a single maho-user remained against the far side of the northern wall.

The Dragon let out a cheer of relief and amazement. Even Hitomi's dark face broke into a smile. She lifted her hand to Daini, thanking him, and he bowed deeply.

The naga jakla continued to chant, lending their strength to the Agasha's spell.

Hitomi rose from the field and once more led the Mirumoto in a charge. Their strength renewed, the samurai of the Dragon crossed blades with the undead, their swords ringing against rusted pikes and ancient axes.

Hitomi climbed over the rubble of Otosan Uchi's wall, shattering two zombies with a single blow. Her katana passed through their breastplates, breaking their rotted bones to splinters. Other Dragon followed her, racing through the breach in the wall.

"For the Mirumoto!" she screamed, fury in her eyes, and heard her shout returned by the samurai.

Another force of undead arrived from deep within the city, bringing with them more necromancers. They lifted their hands to begin casting.

Hitomi raced toward them. "Take the zombies!" she cried to her men. "I will handle the necromancers!"

Her blade descended over one of the sorcerers as he brought his hands together with a resounding clap. The clap sounded with a thunderous roar, and the force of his blow threw back Hitomi's blade. She staggered, holding her sword between them as she fought to clear her ears of the ringing. Her katana cut down once more, this time blocked by a wall of wind that rang like iron.

The maho user chanted swiftly, drawing a thin tanto and slashing at his arm. Blood welled from the shallow cut, and the necromancer lifted a gory finger to draw floating sigils in the air.

Hitomi felt her arm burn and looked down to see an identical cut appearing beneath her armor. The necromancer shrieked with delight, drawing faster as another wound spread across her shoulder, spearing down into her flesh from an unseen blade.

Around her, the Mirumoto threw themselves at the zombie hordes. Their swords flashed, and stalwart kiop screams echoed from burning buildings.

The sorcerer chanted, and flame blazed along the city streets, racing amid the Mirumoto troops and lighting them on fire. Screams of war turned to cries of agony as they burned, lit ablaze by dark magic and blood sorcery. Her men were dying.

Hitomi slashed, but once more the unseen wall blacked her blade. "You can turn my blade, sorcerer," Hitomi snarled, "but you cannot stop this." The Obsidian Hand's fingers flexed, and Hitomi pressed it to the unseen wall.

The fingers curved into a claw, and tore into the invisible barrier. Ripples appeared in the empty air, shimmering blue and white around each of the black stone claws.

The necromancer gasped in shock, slicing again with his blade and frantically drawing more patterns.

Hitomi's leg trembled, bloodied by the sorcerer's spell, and her rib suddenly burned with the cut of an unseen knife, but the Obsidian Hand continued to push through.

"No!" the necromancer screamed, turning to flee as the fingers reached for his throat. "Noooooo—!" The crack of his neck snapping was the last sound he made.

Hitomi looked up, blood trickling down her flesh.

Many Mirumoto bodies burned behind her, but most of her troops had advanced, escaping the sorcerer's wrath. To meet with them, she would have to circumnavigate the city's merchant quarter, now a bloody inferno. Her only choice was to circle east and hope she could reach her men before the city's inner walls.

Racing past zombies and fallen samurai, Hitomi circled the great plaza, determined to reach her clan.

Suddenly, amid the blood, fires, and war of the city's largest marketplace, Hitomi froze.

Before her, the city's western wall crumbled. Siege engines pounded its far side, and cut stones turned to tumbling rubble. A breach opened and widened, spreading like a cancer. Goblin minions of the emperor rushed to stop the army on its far side, but the samurai that pressed through were too powerful and numerous. Among them, a banner flew, proudly proclaiming their clan.

The mon was that of the armies of the Crab. Yakamo's personal sigil.

He stood a head taller than his men, screaming death and rage at the goblins that clustered around him. As his men fell to lesser attacks, Yakamo pounded the ground around him with his tetsubo, turning the small clawed creatures into paste.

"Yakamo no Oni!" Yakamo shouted, and the sound echoed above the crashing roar of battle. "Face me!"

The oni bears his name, Hitomi remembered. He's looking for his oni, but why?

Then, suddenly, she saw it. Larger than she remembered, the Crab oni towered above the undead samurai in its path, crushing them with a sweep of its sinewy hand. It cleared a path with its large steel club, bashing its allies to paste. Its ropy red muscles and gleaming eyes would linger in her memory for years to come.

The earth shook with the oni's approach, each step slaying Crab samurai. It turned with a feral smile toward Yakamo, and Hitomi gasped in surprise. When she had last seen the creature, it had been inhuman. Now it grinned down with a human visage—the face of Hida Yakamo. The huge mouth was covered in the blood of its screaming victims.

Yakamo had kept his fury in check as he advanced on the creature, but when it turned to look at him with his own face and eyes, he could contain himself no longer. His tetsubo swung like a massive club. It struck the creature's head, but shattered on the hard, chitinous skull.

The oni returned the blow.

Yakamo caught the steel club in his hand, crushing it with the might of his fist.

Hitomi gasped. The claw was gone. Yakamo's hand—the hand she had taken from him—had been replaced with a fist of stone. Gleaming green, the jade artifact shone brighter as it touched the oni's flesh. It burned black trails where its glowing fingers carved through carapace and bone.

"Satsu . . ." Hitomi whispered to herself in awe, her black hand gripping the hilt of her katana. "What magic is this?"

Deep within her, the Obsidian Hand ceased its whispering and fell eerily silent. There were no answers to her questions, only more riddles. . . . Riddles she did not have time to answer.

Tearing at the creature with his hands, Yakamo wrapped the oni in his arms and crushed the creature in a massive bear hug. He roared, increasing his grip as the oni's claws ripped at his flesh. Yakamo drew back his jade hand, clenched it into a fist, and plunged it into the oni's chest with a deadly strike.

Instead of screaming in pain, the oni laughed, a terrible half-human sound filled with the popping in sinews. Blood welled up in the wound, spraying out at Hida Yakamo and covering the Crab samurai's face.

Yakamo screamed, releasing the oni to tear at his own eyes. The gore burned into his flesh. Black, seeping holes opened along Yakamo's face, showing bone beneath the pale skin and red strands of muscle.

He stumbled backward to recover.

The oni towered above Yakamo, extending its hands in victory and preparing to slice once more through soft flesh and tissue. It brought is hands down.

Hitomi leapt from behind the rubble of the western wall, her blade cold and relentless. She caught the claws in a single sweep of steel, blocking the blow as well as removing the oni's arm.

The oni turned in surprise, staring down at the small samurai. It screeched an inhuman cry of rage.

Hitomi's sword cut again.

The oni's large hand caught the hilt of her sword to twist it away.

"Sorry, Yakamo," she whispered. "We Dragon are taught to fight with two weapons." She grinned wickedly as she allowed her left hand, the hand bearing her katana, to move with the oni's strength. "You caught the wrong hand," she said quietly, and was rewarded by the gleam of surprise in the oni's almost-human eyes.

The Obsidian Hand grasped the titanic oni's brow. Black fingers of glass squeezed with immortal strength. The chitin shivered. It cracked. Demon brain oozed in gray streams.

The oni screamed with Yakamo's voice. It clawed desperately at her with its remaining arm.

Kill now, kill child, kill Yakamo, the hand purred as acid blood ran over her fist and arm. Her flesh did not pucker, protected by a sheath of obsidian that grew from the hand. *More . . .* it whispered silkily. *More . . .*

Hitomi turned to look down at the fallen samurai, staring into Yakamo's eyes.

The Crab cleared his vision and shook his head, reaching for another samurai's fallen tetsubo.

Hitomi's eyes were strangely cold. The fury and rage that had consumed her soul for so long lay dormant within her heart.

It was as if the world slowed down while the oni fell. Its inhuman face writhed and died. The creature slumped to the ground with a piteous howl of fury, blood seeping from every crack in its skull. Red, scalded flesh twitched beneath the pure light of the sun.

Hitomi stared down at the oni, its blood dripping from her black fingers. She watched the face of Hida Yakamo die. When it was at last dead, the oni lay still, acid blood burning into the ground.

Yakamo stiffly stood. His body seemed to ache with every movement.

Hitomi waited, silent and still. When the oni had ceased moving, its head crushed into a bloody pulp, she looked up slowly from its corpse.

Yakamo shook his head. "I cannot afford the luxury of killing you."

"I thought you were Kisada's son," she whispered, her voice filled with hate. "I suppose he is the coward I always suspected him to be."

Hitomi's taunt was successful. Yakamo charged her, but the fresh Dragon was too quick for the wounded Crab. In a moment, the tetsubo was on the ground, and her blade was at his throat.

It was too easy. Yakamo was wounded badly, his eyes torn by the oni's acid blood, his skin pitted and steaming. The seconds slowed once more, and Hitomi saw each flash of her own blade against his soft throat. The green glow of his jade hand echoed the black gleam of her own, but the voices of Onnotangu and Shosuro were silent.

Below her lay her brother's murderer. One stroke would end her torment. One cut would free Satsu's soul. She raised her sword to finish it.

Within her spoke a voice—one that was not a part of the Obsidian Hand, nor a part of her own riddle. It was a voice

Hitomi had not heard since her childhood, a voice she would have given her life to hear again.

My sister, he said, and she could imagine his softly crooked smile. *Don't you see the truth, after all you have been through? If you kill him, everything I died for is in vain.*

"Satsu?" Hitomi looked up in that frozen moment of time. Her eyes streamed hot tears across her bloodied cheeks.

The world around her did not move. Time did not progress. It was like standing within a child's glass globe, waiting for the snow to fall. The battlefield slowed to a halt, and only one figure moved. He was not dressed in armor or covered in blood, but wore the gi and mon of a Dragon samurai. Surrounded by the frozen butchery of the battlefield, he seemed out of place. Only Hitomi could see him as he smiled his crooked smile.

Satsu.

Yokuni's voice echoed once more in her mind. She became aware of the champion's soul, watching. Had he brought Satsu's soul, at last, to her side?

The time was not right for the emperor to die. You were too young.

Her brother reached toward her, his hand gentle against her cheek. *The death of the last emperor was the key to Fu Leng's return. It was foretold that the Thunders would gather to fight Fu Leng and save the empire. Your soul rings with Thunder, little sister. When the emperor died and the darkness rose, you would be chosen to fight for us all.* Satsu smiled sadly. *You were eight. You could not fight Fu Leng. If I had won the battle against Yakamo, he would have been dead, and Fu Leng would have won. If a Thunder died, if Yakamo died, then the empire, too, would die. I made that choice. You were eight. You could not have fought Fu Leng then.*

Yokuni showed me the future I would create by living. It was a future of darkness and death; both the empire and the Dragon would fall. I could not let you live in that world. Satsu smiled sorrowfully, his crooked mouth sweet and familiar. *My sacrifice was not for the empire, Hitomi-chan . . . it was for you.*

His voice echoed in her mind and brought with it memories she had long ago forgotten. His presence, the nearness of his soul, after so long apart, made Hitomi's heart ache with loss. Her tears flowed freely in slowed time as he continued.

I have always known that Thunder sang in you.

"I must free your soul." Her voice was broken.

Hitomi-chan, my sister, He smiled again, and peace spread across his features. *You already have.*

With a sudden jolt, time started once more. The vision melted like sand through an hourglass. Satsu was gone, or perhaps he had never truly been there, but Hitomi could still feel his soul sheltering hers.

The world had begun again. The puzzle was completed. Hitomi found her sword leveled at Yakamo's throat.

With a shuddering breath, she slid her katana down his enameled breastplate and slowly backed away.

"I won't kill you now, Yakamo," Hitomi whispered, "but you'll always remember that I could have."

20 ON THE STEPS OF MADNESS

It is time," the Hooded Ronin said, stopping before a secret door in a dark passageway beneath the Imperial Palace.

He had come to them in the dark night, gathering the chosen ones to complete destiny's call. The champion of the Dragon and Six Thunders—their number short by one. The Scorpion waited for them just beyond that door.

"I am the last of Shinsei's children," Hyoji continued, "guarded since the beginning of the empire for this day. If you wish for the empire to survive tomorrow's sunset, you must believe me."

No sooner had he finished speaking than the door slid silently open. Beyond it appeared a lithe woman, a softly glowing lamp in her hand. "Follow me, if you would be heroes," Kachiko murmured, her eyes flashing like fire. The Scorpion Mistress led the way, the lamp swaying in her hand with each silken step.

Hitomi followed the others into the Imperial Palace, stepping through the secret door. The light of the palace's interior corridor dimmed as her eyes adjusted from the pitch blackness of the underground passage. Her own footsteps were masked by the tromp of heavy sandals, hidden by the quiet swish of Kachiko's long scarlet kimono.

Yokuni moved up near her, but Hitomi turned away from the Dragon Champion. Yokuni's voice echoed once in the corridor, calling her name softly, but she continued on as if she had not heard.

This was not the time for riddles; it was time for decisions and for death. Nothing more.

"Here," Kachiko said softly, sliding a wooden panel from its place in the wall.

The passage beyond was dark, but a glistening light shone at its end. Kachiko led them down the hall to it. She reached two tall doors. Enameled with polished ivory and shining gold, the side doors to the Imperial Throne room stood closed, awaiting the touch of their master's hand. The Thunders could not have approached through the main doors, for they and the stairs that led to them had been burned away. Kachiko passed her fingers gently over the carvings, feeling the ancient kanji and the heavy steel brackets. Turning, she stood in the shadow of the massive wooden doors. Her perfect silhouette cut the light in two.

"You are certain . . . ?" she whispered.

The Hooded Ronin nodded. "This is how it must be."

A pause, and silence. Kachiko murmured a word known only to the imperial family. The doors swung open silently at her command, moved by magic a thousand years old. Kachiko stood for a moment, readying herself, and then walked into brilliantly lit room beyond, her form lost in the white glare.

The others passed one by one into the palace, leaving the Mirumoto daimyo alone in the darkness.

Hitomi stepped forward, but suddenly a hand touched her from behind. Reaching for her katana, the Dragon turned with catlike dexterity to gaze behind her.

Togashi Yokuni stood in the hallway. He strode around her to stand between Hitomi and the bright passage into the throne room. His cold, gold-tinged eyes seemed almost to glow beneath the dark covering of his helm.

Hitomi stared up at Yokuni for a long moment, impervious to his scrutiny. At last, the unnerving silence won out, and she muttered, "Yokuni . . ."

He said nothing

Hitomi tried to push past him, determined to enter the throne room.

Yokuni's hand moved faster than thought, gripping her chin with the iron force of death.

Again, she stared into those eerie, glowing eyes. Now their light had changed to fields of pure gold, shining brightly beneath the blackness.

You must not fight Fu Leng.

Hitomi started, her hand shaking with sudden rage. "But you brought me—all of us—here to kill him, to save the empire. I have come so far, sacrificed so much. Already you have forced me to give up too much. I will not do it anymore, Yokuni. Not for you, not for the empire, not for anyone." Hitomi drew up her right hand and balled the stone fingers into a fist. Veins of steel through obsidian flesh clenched with immortal fury as her eyes narrowed in hatred. "I have given my flesh, my honor, and my brother's soul. There is nothing left of me for you to take, old man. I am not the child I once was."

Your purpose is not to kill him, but to kill me.

Hitomi felt her heart sink within her chest. To have come so far, fought so much, only to meet with another riddle. . . . Each argument was met with only stoic silence from the face within the golden mask, with the stone of immobile mountains and the resolute gaze of fate. In the future, Hitomi would remember their conversation as if it were a dream, their eyes locked in a struggle of wills. But even in the night, with a thousand stars to comfort and guide her, Hitomi stared into the light of an endless moon and remembered Togashi's eyes. His eerie eyes were all that mattered. They alone had convinced

Hitomi to do his bidding, shining with a glistening golden light that seemed to hold all the warmth once stolen from her world. She could not remember the words.

It did not matter.

"No questions for me to answer, Yokuni? No talk of paths and enigmas, and no more vanishing into the night? No more riddles, Yokuni?" Hitomi said at last, her Obsidian Hand clenched into a fist at her side.

The answer is my death, Hitomi. The riddle is yours to ask.

There was nothing left to say. Nodding, Hitomi turned from Yokuni's grasp, pulling her chin from his fingers and stepping forward behind the others.

"Your strength will not save you. Your courage will not save you. Nothing will save you." The words of the emperor rang in Hitomi's ears as she stepped into the wide audience hall.

Its roof was gone, and the beaming space was open to the starry heavens. The Emerald Throne rested upon its ceremonial dais, raised slightly above the floor by some strange sorcery. On the throne sat the emperor—gaunt, rotten, and shot through with an unholy light.

"Togashi . . ." he whispered, standing from the glowing throne. "At last . . . my brother, I knew that you would come to me. There are too many questions left unanswered. Too many riddles left to solve." The emperor's black tongue licked his cracked lips, and a rotted hand extended claws toward the Dragon Champion.

"No, Fu Leng. I have not come here to listen to your riddles." The voice was clear and strong, shaking the earth with its force. For the first time in recorded history, the Dragon Champion had not whispered, not hidden his thoughts behind murmurs and innuendoes.

Hitomi stared openly at her champion as he reached to remove the straps that held his helm.

Sliding the golden mask from his face, Togashi Yokuni lowered his mempo and cast the discarded helmet aside.

He was human, yes . . . but something more. Golden eyes shone within brown-tinged skin, and black hair cascaded over lightly scaled cheekbones. His eyes gleamed, reptilian in the torchlight, and his voice echoed as if the mountains themselves spoke with him. Lizardlike features moved as Yokuni continued, his voice gaining strength with each word. "For a thousand years, Fu Leng, I have watched over these mortals. I have guided them when they would falter, and I have stood back when they needed to learn their own lessons. I will not see that great work destroyed by your evil corruption. If you wish to destroy the empire, first you must destroy me."

"A thousand years . . . ?" Hitomi murmured in shock.

Standing by his high throne, Fu Leng began to laugh. His laughter was as hollow as Hitomi had remembered it, but now his blackened face shifted with maggots and dripping pus. The lips boiled with each movement, sliding sickly against the dark god's skull. Hitomi felt a wave of nausea sink through her stomach as he floated into the air above the Thunders. "A thousand years, Togashi?" His laughter changed, turning sour and harsh. "A thousand years you watched them destroy all that we once were, my brother—slaughtering our family and destroying the work our father, Onnotangu, began!" Fu Leng's anger shook the throne room. "And for a thousand years, I have been trapped by the sorcery of the Black Scrolls, twisted by their power and enslaved by these mortals you would protect!"

"Brother . . . ?" Hitomi whispered. Her thoughts spun. Yokuni. Yokuni is the first Togashi, the kami of the Dragon Clan. The realization struck her as solidly as a blow, and Hitomi's mind reeled with astonishment. "He has always been the champion of the Dragon. The ise zumi knew; they have always known. This was their secret! They were not discovering the Dragon's Heart . . . they were *protecting* it!"

"And what will you do, Togashi?" Fu Leng asked. "Watch me as I destroy your petty mortals? Ask me riddles as I tear the empire from its foundations and shatter its heart?" The Dark God's contempt was clear, his cheeks bloating in disdain.

"I may have watched for a thousand years, Brother," Togashi said, opening his arms with a gesture of dismissal. "But I am here now, Fu Leng. I am here to show them that you can bleed!"

Togashi looked up at his brother, his golden eyes glowing with the inner light of a god. His face was not that of a man, but rather the features of a dragon cast upon a human mask, slitted pupils of black hiding within his golden orbs. Fire leapt from his mouth, and claws extended from his hands, tearing through the metal mesh of his gauntlets. His body lifted from the ground, limbs elongating into serpentine legs, armor melding into true scales. By the time Togashi reached his brother, he was no longer a man, but a true dragon, master of the Celestial Heavens.

Fu Leng opened his arms, and a cold wind seared through the throne room.

Hitomi looked away, hiding her eyes from the shards of stone and mosaic tile torn from the ground by Fu Leng's laughter. When she looked back toward the battle, there were two dragons, one golden and gleaming, the other black and tainted, its twisted form covered in filth and rotten flesh.

Their fight was swift and bloody. Claws tore wide gaps beneath scale and sinew. Fire roared through the star-filled void, which shattered around them as the two gods fought.

Awestruck, the Seven Thunders watched from the ground as titanic powers battled above them. Hitomi stole a glance toward the son of Shinsei, but no surprise shone on his face—only sorrow, a great abiding sadness that pained her simply to look upon it.

Togashi roared in pain and anguish as Fu Leng twisted his brother's body and snapped his back. He threw the broken body to the floor, laughing as it landed at the feet of the assembled Thunders.

Fu Leng raised himself to his full height and released a pealing roar, celebrating the first of his victories. The sounds was deafening, echoing up through the open ceiling of the throne room.

"Die, Brother," Fu Leng hissed from above them, his form shifting back into that of the last Hantei emperor. "Die, as you once left me to die, in anguish and in fear. And when you do, know that you will forever be, as I was . . . alone."

Hitomi knelt down before Togashi, her Obsidian Hand glowing with a hungry light.

Staring into the strange golden eyes, Hitomi's heart-shaped face twisted with loss and remorse, with all the knowledge she had earned and all the suffering she had borne. "Togashi . . ." she whispered, her voice soft and afraid. "I . . . I cannot . . ."

"To arms!" one of the Thunders cried, drawing his sword and charging before the others into the fray.

They followed, one by one, into the battle that was their destiny.

Fu Leng opened his arms wide, daring them, unafraid.

"You are my champion." Hitomi looked down at the crushed and crumpled form of the Dragon kami, amazed at how small he seemed, lying in dark blood upon the floor of the wide throne room. Her obsidian hand touched his chest, the wounds that scarred his flesh, the spreading blood that stained her kimono. She knelt beside him, pressing his hand against hers, feeling its warmth through her own skin.

You are Dragon. Togashi's whisper was faint, and his fingers brushed against Hitomi's bare forehead as if to comfort a grieving child.

Hitomi looked down at his face, remembering the past, the years at the Iron Mountain—imagining all of the faces that Togashi must have seen come and go during his life. The immortal kami was dying. Within his eyes, Hitomi saw memories, the faces of thousands of samurai flashing by as brightly as stars in the heavens. He remembered every one. And then, as she stared within his golden pupils, she saw something else . . . something that had been lost for a thousand years.

Togashi whispered once more, and his voice was distant and soft. *You must become the riddle.*

Her face a study of desolation, Hitomi lifted her Obsidian Hand above his chest. Then, with a soft whisper, she plunged the hungry black fingers within the flesh of his chest, piercing through armor and bone, breaking open his body and stealing the life within.

Something moved against her fingertips, and she gripped it, crushing Togashi's heart within her iron fist. She drew it out. Hitomi stared in wonder as his heart broke open, revealing an ivory scroll tube, weathered and aged beyond belief. Drawing it forth, Hitomi broke open the seal and gazed upon gold and green kanji that shifted and writhed on thick black parchment,

The Twelfth Black Scroll.

Hitomi lowered her head, grief growing like a cancer in her soul. "Farewell, Togashi-sama," she whispered. "You will never truly leave us."

Then she squeezed his still-beating heart, stealing his strength and feeling the wisdom of ages rush into her body. Hitomi gasped, her spine arching and her mouth dropping open in amazement, touched by power beyond imagining. A thousand memories flooded her mind, and every moment since the world began poured into her soul in a single instant, sharing an aeon of thoughts, of laughter and sorrow—of all the lives and deaths that had ever been.

I shall go mad, she thought, her mind trapped within the scream. She saw the threads of possibility stream out from her, stretching before and behind with the power of the Celestial Heavens. Within their coil, a serpent stretched its sleeping body. Gently, it touched her mind with its own, lending her the strength.

The Dragon Champion's immortal soul twined with hers, offering eternal life. Her mortality vanished in its coils.

Hitomi could hear the other Thunders fighting against Fu Leng, but the battle seemed strangely distant, as though it occurred in another lifetime. Along with their struggle, she heard the echoes of a fight that happened a thousand years ago. One that ended with the creation of twelve Black Scrolls. . . .

. . . She saw all time as it passed; future, present, past . . . all ages . . . *now*.

"Togashi . . ." Hitomi screamed into the Celestial Heavens, and her voice echoed in distant worlds, "I understand. . . ."

His eyes have become my own.

PROLOGUE

Time has turned its back to me, and the end has become the beginning.

The day is bright and filled with sunshine, the Scorpion mountains stark and green against a Crane blue sky. I am alone, standing near the high walls of the Bayushi palace. Every stone is familiar, as though mine was the hand that placed them. I have been here before. I turn, seeing figures gathered about a clear field. The Dragon banner flutters gaily beside the mon of Scorpion, Crane, Lion, and Crab—but I feel no happiness.

I know this day . . . It is my own past.

A small girl dances at her brother's side, grinning eagerly up at the handsome youth. His crooked smile crinkles, and I hear the warmth of his voice. The child laughs, sprinting ahead to bring her brother a wildflower that had bloomed in their path. He accepts it with a solemn bow, and places it in his obi.

I know his heart is heavy.

"Tell me again, Satsu, about Togashi and the kami of the Celestial Heavens?" Her black eyes sparkle with the enthusiasm of an eight-year-old, and her heart-shaped face crinkles with a joyous smile.

"Again?" the older boy says, his frame expanding with a hearty laugh. "No more, little sister. You've heard enough." Reaching the wide tournament ground, Satsu releases his little sister's hand and kneels beside her. I watch as he straightens her kimono, brushes the long hair away from her sweet face. I remember the touch of those fingers, that moment, and I feel his embrace before he stands.

In the throng of people that gather to watch the duel, the young samurai sees his uncle Sukune standing beside a grumpy-faced little boy. "Now, Hitomi-chan, I want you to do what Sukune-sama asks you to do."

"Yes, Satsu," she says, squinting up at him in the bright summer sunlight.

The words are not mine—but the memories are. I remember this, even as it occurs before me. All time is now . . . all places are here.

This is the field where the final days of my destiny began.

"And I want you to remember to study your niten. It is important, and you'll need it when you grow up."

"I won't need it," she said, reaching to squeeze his hand again. "I'll have you to protect me."

He smiles adoringly, rumpling the thick hair that spills from his sister's forehead. He stands then, giving Hitomi's hand to Sukune. The general shares a long gaze with his handsome young nephew, seeing his sister's bright smile in the youth's earnest face. "Take care of her, Uncle."

Sukune opens his mouth as if to speak, then closes it silently. There are no words.

"Satsu!" Hitomi shouts, tugging on her uncle's arm as her older brother steps out onto the green grass of the Scorpion tournament field. "Satsu, Satsu!" she cheers happily, watching him check the balance of his katana in its sheath.

The Crab waits there for him, as he has each day for a thousand years. The Hida's brown skin is dark in the sunlight, and his hand seems to shift for a moment into a titanic metal claw. But, no, that day has not yet come. Gray armor shines dully, and a wicked smile crosses young Yakamo's lips.

I watch as he weighs the tetsubo in his hands, feeling its strength and tremendous iron girth.

"You can't bring that weapon onto the field . . ." the arbiter begins, but a murderous look from Hida Yakamo silences the man. The Crab strides past him without stopping, not pausing until he reaches the center of the tournament ground.

"Come, Dragon!" Yakamo yells, taunting the brave young samurai. "Your lady is a liar, a whore for the men on Carpenter Wall. Remember the words you have said about my father's honor," Yakamo lowers his head like a charging bull, swinging the massive steel tetsubo against the ground in front of him like a warning, "because I am about to make you regret every one of them."

His words echo in the future, spilling from time and space, misplaced by destiny.

"To the death, samurai. May your honor, and Shinsei's blessing, carry you to victory . . . or to eternity." The arbiter's words fall heavily on the crowd, and the gathered samurai watch.

A tiny boy turns fearful eyes from the duel, hiding his face in his uncle's robes. Daini.

The Dragon takes his place at the edge of the tournament field, his hand steady on the hilt of his katana. The Crab crouches, swinging his tetsubo as the field whispers into silence. A pair of red and white flags rise above the arbiter's head. The crowd whispers, staring at the great metal club.

It is forbidden to bring such a weapon onto the field of honorable combat, but I have allowed it.

The arbiter looks at me, and I realize he awaits my command. I raise my hand to the sun.

Satsu's eyes meet mine, and I wonder if he can see the tears beneath my golden mask.

My hand falls.

Had you won, the empire would have lost a Thunder, and we would all be destroyed. I had to sacrifice your life to buy life for all the world.

My own voice rings in my mind as the strike begins. I speak in the future, in a time that has not yet come, in a distant place of shadow and pain.

If he had not fought, the rise of Fu Leng would have destroyed the empire, and there would have been no one to defend against it. Destiny would have changed, and all the world would have been lost.

The tetsubo falls, the sword a split second too slow. His failure is deliberate.

I look into Satsu's eyes when the steel club strikes him, as he feels the pain of his life being stolen away. I see no surprise in his thoughts. There is only agony and honor. The duel is inconsequential. Satsu's lady weeps by the side of the field, watching her husband defend her honor. She will commit seppuku before the sun has set, but her life will be forgotten as history unfolds.

His death changes the world.

Satsu . . . forgive me.

"No!" A scream as Satsu's body falls to the ground at the Crab's feet. The Hida erupt into shouts and cheers of victory, and Satsu's lady lowers her face to the earth, racked by grief. A girl escapes her uncle's hand, charging onto the tournament ground to fall beside her brother's body.

She is eight years old.

I watch as she lifts her brother's sword from his still-warm hand, pointing it up at the titanic Crab warrior. It is huge in her hands, tilted crazily as she tries to see through tears and fury.

Yakamo looks down at the tiny child, surprise warring with arrogance on his features. His kin burst into laughter, seeing their greatest samurai threatened by a stripling girl a third his size.

With a callous gesture, he knocks the sword from her hand, sending the blade spinning into the far ground of the field. "Not today, girl," he says, turning his back on her. "I won't kill you today."

She recoils from his blow, her black eyes haunted and despairing. Hitomi falls to her knees beside her brother's body as the Crab strides from the field. "Satsu . . ." she whispers, staring in horror at the crushed mass of bone and flesh that had once been a crooked smile. Blood stains the grass and covers her fingers as she tries to close his one, staring eye.

"I will avenge you!" she screams, her childish voice breaking with pain. The howl of loss will break her father's heart. She fumbles for the tanto in her brother's obi, knocking aside the wildflower that wilts against his saya. Her hands tremble, her soul stricken with grief.

She lifts his tanto and begins to rend her hair, cutting it away in long, jagged strands. Blood pours from her scalp from the knife's sharp tip, but she does not care. The pain of the cuts is gentler than the agony of her brother's death.

I know the pain. I remember it still.

The girl's face is etched with sorrow, her head covered in ragged tatters of hair and torn skin. The knife falls from her hands, crushing the soft grass beneath her. She extends bloodied hands toward me, reaching to my golden throne, her long brown hair falling from her fingers. The wind is cold, the sky covered in a blue so pale that it hurts the eyes to look upon it.

"Why?" she asks me softly, tears streaming with blood down her flushed cheeks. I cannot answer her. I can see my death in her eyes.

But I also know that one day, we will stand within the Imperial Palace and together we will fight a god. Of all the tortured days from this to that, of all the time that will not pass, and yet does, I can see her soul shining with the flame of Thunder.

I have walked her path. It has been my own.

There is still hope.

We have reached the end together, you and I.
The final days have come.

Glossary

Amaterasu—the Sun Goddess

ashigaru—foot soldier

bokken—wooden practice sword

bu—a coin, money

bushi—warrior

bushido—the code of a warrior

-chan—suffix, young one—an endearing term for a child or lover

chi—the seat of the soul, the power of a samurai

chui—lieutenant

daisho—the katana and wakizashi sword combination worn by samurai

dai-kyu—long bow

die tsuchi—war hammer

doji—castle

domo arigato—thank you very much

domo arigato gozaimasu—thank you very, very much

engawa—roofed veranda

eta—the unclean, the lowest caste who do the dirtiest jobs, such as burying the dead

fundoshi—loincloth

fusuma—an interior paper wall (see *shoji*)
gambatte—fight on
ganbari masu—don't give up
gempuku—coming of age ceremony
gunso—a sergeant in charge of a small troop of bushi
hai—yes
hakima—wide trousers
hanko—"chop mark," signature
haramaki-do—heavy lacquered armor
heimin—the peasant caste
iaijutsu—fast-draw sword technique
iie—no
ishii—a game played with stones on a board
jakla—a naga shugenja
Jigoku—the underworld, the afterlife, or hell
jigokuni ochimuratachi—"the lost," warriors fallen into hell
Kabuki—melodramatic theater
kami—the ancient children of Lady Sun and Lord Moon; also, a
    nature spirit or a god
kanji—characters, letters, runes
katana—the samurai long sword, part of the daisho
kata—a series of exercise or martial arts forms
konbanwa—good evening
kosode—narrow sleeved kimono (undergarment)
-kun—suffix: old friend
kyuden—palace
matte—halt
mempo—armored face mask
maho—dark, blood magic
naga—creatures with human heads and torsos and snake tails
nage-yari—short javelin
naginata—polearm topped by a sword blade
natto—sweet bean paste
nezumi—ratlings, a race of human-sized rats
ninjato—ninja short sword
ninjitsu—the art of ninja
no-dachi—two-handed sword, taller than a samurai

Noh—minimalist theater

obi—a belt of folded silk

on—emblem or symbol

oni—demon

onikage—demon steed

Onnotangu—the moon god, husband of Amaterasu

ono—battle axe

otennoo-sama—great lord, highness, exalted one

ratling—nezumi, a human-sized rat creature indigenous to the Shadowlands

ronin—samurai without a master

sake—rice wine

-sama—suffix: most esteemed, lord, master, highness

-san—suffix: honored, sir

seppuku—ritual suicide

shamisen—guitar played with pick

shiburi—flicking technique used to clean blood from a sword

shiro—castle

shiruken—throwing star

shoji—paper walls, exterior (see *fusuma*)

shugenja—a wielder of magic

shuriken—throwing stars or darts

soba shop—a shop offering food and drink

sochu—strong sake

sumimasen—sorry for causing you trouble

sutra—a meditation or precept

taiko—large drum

taisa—captain of a smaller unit of bushi

tanto—dagger or knife

tatami—mat for sitting upon the floor

torii—wooden archway with two pillars and a crosspiece

tetsubo—wooden clublike staff with iron studs

tono—lord

tsuba—hand guard on a sword

udon—soup with flour noodles

wakizashi—samurai short sword, part of the daisho; the "soul" of the samurai, used in seppuku

yari—a 6-foot-long spear with a straight blade
yojimbo—bodyguard
yosh—"good" an assenting grunt
yumi—a type of bow, fairly short, can be fired by a standing man
zeni—a copper coin
zori—straw sandals

Legends Cycle Clayton Emery

Book I: Johan

Hazezon Tamar, merchant-mayor of the city of Bryce, had plenty of problems before he encountered Jaeger, a mysterious stranger that is half-man and half-tiger. Now Hazezon is caught up in a race against time to decipher the mysterious prophecy of None, One, and Two, while considering the significance of Jaeger's appearance. Only by understanding these elements can he save his people from the tyranny and enslavement of the evil wizard Johan, ruler of the dying city of Tirras.

April 2001

Book II: Jedit

Jedit Ojanen, the son of the legendary cat man Jaeger, sets out on a journey to find his father. Like his father, he collapses in the desert and is left for dead until he is rescued. But rescued by whom? And why? Only the prophecy of None, One, and Two holds the answers.

December 2001

FROM BELOVED AUTHOR
ELAINE CUNNINGHAM ...

FOR THE FIRST TIME TOGETHER AS A SET!
SONGS AND SWORDS

Follow the adventures of bard Danilo Thann and his beautiful half-elf companion Arilyn Moonblade in these attractive new editions from Elaine Cunningham. These two daring Harpers face trials that bring them together and then tear them apart.

Elfsong
Elfshadow
Silver Shadows (JANUARY 2001)
Thornhold (FEBRUARY 2001)
The Dream Spheres

AND DON'T MISS ...
STARLIGHT AND SHADOWS

Daughter of the Drow
In the aftermath of war in Menzoberranzan, free-spirited drow princess Liriel Baenre sets off on a hazardous quest. Pursued by enemies from her homeland, her best hope of an ally is one who may also be her deadliest rival.

Tangled Webs
Continuing on her quest, drow princess Liriel Baenre learns the price of power and must confront her dark drow nature.

Enter the magical world of the
DUNGEONS & DRAGONS®
setting in these novels based on
classic D&D adventures!

The Temple of Elemental Evil
Thomas M. Reid

Years ago, the foul Temple of Elemental Evil was cleansed of the evil that
dwelled there. Or was it? The Temple has brooded in quiet decay as the
seasons passed, but once again, dark forces are stirring in the land. In a
quest to avenge his slain master, a tormented elven wizard must lead
a band of rugged heroes into the very heart of evil itself.

May 2001

Keep on the Borderlands
Ru Emerson

In recent days, the Keep has been increasingly hassled by elusive bandits and
vicious monsters, but the Castellan can't spare any guards to deal with the
problem. An odd mix of heroes-for-hire ventures outside the Keep to deal
with the troubles, but they find more than they bargained for—and maybe
more than any of them can handle—when they venture into the dreaded
Caves of Chaos.

September 2001

Queen of the Demonweb Pits
Paul Kidd

For one man, fighting in the Greyhawk Wars wasn't hell.
It was practice.

When Lolth, Demon Queen of Spiders, seeks revenge against the Justicar and
his companions, it may well be the last mistake she ever makes.

November 2001